D1338494

Part of Comma's 'History-into-Fiction' series

'As the book enters the 20th Century, the chapters become infused with an awareness of the inequalities and discrimination of our age, becoming a call to action. The variety of storytelling ensures that the protests don't feel indistinct or hopeless, yet the injustices described feel depressingly familiar.' - *New Statesman*

'It would be heartening to see more works of historical fiction inspired by Comma Press's approach, serving both to educate and entertain by giving voice once again to people who struggled to make their voices heard in challenging circumstances.' – *Disclaimer Magazine*

'*Protest* is an important collection highlighting the history of dissenting voices in the UK. It teaches rather than preaches and should be required reading for many of our current politicians.' – *Book Oxygen*

'*Protest* is an illuminating and essential read. The perfect inter-generational birthday or Christmas present, it joins up the dots and gives context, which is invariably missing from disdainful, market-led Media narratives, and rote-learning history ordained by successive governments. Buy it and read it!' – *Bookblast*

'A valuable treasury of reminders of earlier struggles and a persuasive call for us to have courage in our current ones with a ruthless class enemy.' – *Morning Star*

RESIST

Stories of Uprising

Edited by
Ra Page

First published in Great Britain in 2019 by Comma Press.
www.commapress.co.uk

A CIP catalogue record of this book is available from the British Library.

ISBN: 1912697076
ISBN-13: 9781912697076

This project has been developed with the support of the
Barry Amiel and Norman Melburn Trust as well as the Lipman-Miliband Trust.

The publisher gratefully acknowledges assistance from Arts Council England.

Printed and bound in England by Clays Ltd, Elcograf S.p.A

Contents

CONTENTS

CONTENTS

'Basically, it is us against them.'

– Howard Zinn

Introduction

'LET'S DO THIS COPPER bastard over.' These are the words my father was accused of saying before his arrest on the anti-Vietnam War protest of 30 March 1968 as it progressed towards Grosvenor Square, then site of the American Embassy. The officer who testified to overhearing him say these words in one of the many court cases that followed – over 200 arrests were made that day – was in fact not the officer who had arrested him. No such words were ever uttered, my dad insisted. In reality, he had instigated an impromptu sit-down in the middle of Regent Street and then complained about the rough handling of his five-month pregnant wife (my mum) by a completely different officer. Come the court appearance, as family legend has it, my dad defended himself and was complimented by the judge, who suggested he re-train as a barrister. Ultimately, though, he was found guilty and fined £15, which his fellow students at Regent Street Polytechnic paid on his behalf when he refused to.

This was the story my dad liked to tell, a wry smile curling the corners of his mouth. The story would end with the recollection of a fellow protester he met in the back of the police van that day, who told him he had been charged with 'kicking a policeman in the groin', even though he was physically incapable of doing so owing to a club foot. 'Don't tell anyone that until the day of the trial,' my dad had suggested. But the man couldn't hold it in that long, and when the police returned to the van, he complained and they simply changed the charge to something else.

What my dad didn't tell us – something my mum only told us recently – was that his arrest that day in March 1968 followed him around for years. On securing a post as a senior lecturer at Chesterfield College five years later, for instance, plain-clothes CID officers visited both his future place of work and the tiny farming village he planned to move into, to warn co-workers and locals about the man about to enter their midst. Indeed it is no surprise that nearly five decades later, my family is still referred to in said village as 'the communists'.

This case is mild, of course, amusing to the point of quaint. For, as many of the stories in this collection will attest, the history of British resistance is littered with much more violent and unlawful crackdowns than a mere creative use of the charge sheet or a spot of minor surveillance. From Boudica's Rising, through Peterloo, to the woodlands around Newbury and beyond, the quashing of unrest is something the British don't do by halves. Every tactic has been tried and, in many cases, perfected: torture, capital punishment (for treason), sabre-wielding cavalry charges, domestic espionage, entrapment, mass shootings, deportation (for the swearing of oaths), the deployment of troops and warships to British ports, plain-clothes snatch squads, Special Patrol Groups, 'kettling', even the use of improvised weaponry. Perhaps the reason why the British haven't witnessed a revolution since the 17th century – and have an international reputation for being mild, moderate, even biddable – is simply that we police resistance 'better' here.

In putting this anthology together, two themes certainly emerged in the protests authors chose to write about: firstly the extraordinary and frankly creative lengths to which British security services have gone to 'manage' resistance; and secondly the growing institutional hostility and wider climate of intolerance that has often coincided with these extreme policing methods. Authors were presented with a long list of historical British protests to choose from, as well as the opportunity to work with a historian specialising in the protest in question, or an eyewitness who'd been there. Unlike in this book's predecessor, *Protest: Stories of Resistance*, where many of the chosen movements seemed to cluster together around wider moments of social progress – what the Welsh language activist Ned Thomas called 'awakenings' – this time many of the authors chose to explore the flip side to that history; times when, instead of moving things forward, people rose up simply to stop them slipping backwards.

Among such rearguard actions explored in this anthology are the Cato Street Conspiracy (which responded to the oppressive Six Acts that followed Peterloo), the Battle of Cable Street (a response by the Jewish community, trade unionists and communists to Mosley's blackshirts mobilising in East London), the Notting Hill Riots (the black community's response to racist attacks by fascist-inspired Teddy Boys), and the Southall Riot (a response to the provocative staging of a National Front meeting in the heart of an Indian community). Whether successful, proportional or legitimate, each protest is open to ongoing reappraisal. But what is worth remembering in any context is what exactly these protests were trying to stop us from sliding into.

Before his death in 2000, the activist Tony Cliff often suggested that 'the period we are living in is like a re-run of the 1930s but with the film running more slowly'.[1] A seemingly intractable, decades-long economic crisis had led to the widespread deployment of racist scapegoating as a deliberate tactic to divide and weaken the working class in order to ensure they, and not the beneficiaries of capitalism, continued to pay for this crisis.

For many, this is too extreme an analogy. But it's interesting to consider the scapegoating Cliff refers to in the current climate. Film-maker Daniel Renwick, in his afterword to Julia Bell's Grenfell Tower story, goes straight to the philosohical core of what we believe underpins society in trying to understand what went wrong: the social contract. One of the differences between democratic socialism and neoliberalism is that the latter implies that the social contract (as originally conceived, between the state and the individual) is not enough. It's not enough that individuals' rights need protecting in return for their law abidance; corporate interests need a voice too. In practice, these interests are always brought into the negotiations by stealth; the market needs to be *free*, so neoliberalism implies, in a way that individuals don't. And the best way to understand corporations, legally and psychologically, is to regard them as 'like people'. Thus corporations enter the social contract not as a third seat at the table, but as part of *our* seat – they become effectively the 'best of us', enjoying all of our rights, but fewer of our restrictions. (How often have the opinions of small-businessmen been granted privileged air time in public debates, over and above mere members of the public?)

Meanwhile, the 'worst of us' slowly get removed from the contract. Rather than being citizens automatically, by virtue of us being human beings, we begin to learn (under neoliberalism) that we have to qualify first – rather like the cadets in Paul Verhoeven's *Starship Troopers* have to earn their citizenship through life-threatening tours of duty. Rights thus transform, in the neoliberal logic, from things that we're born with, to things we might be rewarded with if we deserve them. This removal of the undeserving, the 'worst of us' is something that can be seen historically in multiple contexts, as well as, sadly, the present. Right now it's taking place on many fronts: from the mistreatment of those who simply lack the right paperwork, refugees (who can be detained indefinitely in UK removal centres, and therein enjoy fewer rights than convicted criminals), to the media scapegoating of so-called 'benefit scroungers' (not just undeserving individuals, but undeserving *types* of individuals, somehow congenitally predisposed to 'not pulling their weight'). A third category who have started to be 'othered', in the public imagination at least, is protesters.

This process is perhaps the subtlest. It begins with the emphasis the media places, in its reporting of protest, on very specific details: the strangeness of protesters' clothes, their hairstyles, or other aspects of their lifestyles. Whether this was in relation to the Greenham Common women of the 1980s, the anti-roads protesters of the 1990s (made famous by 'Swampie'), or the Occupy movement of the 2000s, the media's 'othering' of them was a deliberate attempt to create a public perception that these people somehow lived 'outside the law' – as if such a place exists – thus paving the way for them to be treated differently to ordinary citizens. Early examples of how this cultural scapegoating might manifest in legal practice include the increasingly regular prosecution of protesters under counter-terrorism legislation (that special set of legal exceptions put aside for the most 'othered' of all citizens).

In a climate where the 'us' has been dissected, in the public consciousness, into different categories – the deserving, the especially deserving (business elites), and the undeserving ('others') – it's very easy for the scapegoating that Cliff talks about to be institutionalised. Casting an eye over the stories in this book, we realise people working in law enforcement seem surprisingly willing, at these particular moments in history, to treat the 'others' in the fields of protest with an almost complete lack of compassion. Just as people working today in immigration detention, the Home Office, or benefits means testing, have also been regularly accused of callousness.

Institutionalising this 'othering' is a three step-process, it seems. First, you need years of almost daily scapegoating by the popular media (as protests are occasional, saturation hasn't been reached here); secondly, you need a demagogue who publically and privately elevates the status of officers working in enforcement over and above other public sector employees (in Trump's case, his constant fawning over ICE agents); finally, you need a coded signal to those working in enforcement, by said demagogue, implying an unspoken mandate to implement the policy, cutting through the nanny state's red tape, or the 'snowflakes' in the courts or parliament.

Once the first two steps are in place, it doesn't take much of a signal – a mere nod or wink, in fact – to finalise the institutionaliseation of these attitudes. Theresa May's use of the phrase 'hostile environment', as well as other nods, like her promise to axe the European Convention on Human Rights, were all that was needed for the Home Office to institutionalise the tabloid's hatred of refugees. Thatcher's pre-election 'fear of being swamped' was snapped up by the Metropolitan Police Force, who even named their operation 'Swamp 81' in deference to her. The slighter the nod, the subtler the wink, the harder it is for journalists to trace it back to the top. But where journalists fail in this tracing, historians usually succeed.

In *The Origins of Totalitarianism*, Hannah Arendt noted that sufficiently elevating the prestige attached to the law enforcement agencies in your country (stage 2) can lead to police forces in *other* countries taking their cues from your agencies, rather than from their own governments. 'Long before the outbreak of the war,' Arendt writes, 'the police in a number of Western countries, under the pretext of "national security," had on their own initiative established close connections with the Gestapo and the GPU [Russian State security agency], so that one might say there existed an independent foreign policy of the police.' By way of example, she adds: 'If the Nazis put a person in a concentration camp and if he made a successful escape, say, to Holland, the Dutch would put him in an internment camp.'

Could it be that our institutions are not just increasingly hostile to 'othered' groups, but are developing an international consensus with other countries' agencies as to how to treat them, irrespective of each individual government's policies? In as much as these questions of treatment involve logistical challenges (that can be learned from and shared), the answer is understandably yes. But the ethical question – how is the state responsible for them? – is too often informed by a combination of tabloid headline writers, and one particular foreign nation's more televised and media-ready figurehead.

Against pluralism, we see a narrowing down of what constitutes 'us', and the eviction of the 'less deserving' from the social contract, until it only applies to the 'best of us' and those willing to be strapped and bound to a hardening central core – like wooden rods around an axe in a *fasces*. And as Arendt noted, the figurehead at the top of the central shaft doesn't even need to be *our* figurehead.

In case you're wondering what I'm talking about here, I'll spell it out. Fascism.

It's easy to see patterns across different countries' responses to the so-called 'migrant crisis',[2] but less easy to see them in their ethical considerations in security responses to protest. Perhaps this is because we're looking at the wrong figurehead on this issue. For Putin – sixteen years a KGB foreign intelligence officer – there's no such thing as a genuine protester, or an organic protest. For decades during the Cold War, Russian intelligence prided itself on its ability to engineer protests in other countries at the drop of a hat. Recently unsealed KGB files from Yuri Andropov's time as chair (1967–82) show agents claiming to be able to mobilise protests of up to 20,000 people outside the US Embassy in India for a set fee (equating to a quarter-rupee per protester).[3] This is what protest is for Putin: a paid-for foreign intervention. He saw evidence of foreign protest-sponsorship in the Orange and Rose revolutions in Ukraine and Georgia (2003, 2004). He exposed it with his first big hacking success in February 2014, when his agencies released a taped phone call between Victoria Nuland (America's Assistant Secretary of State) and the US ambassador to Ukraine, in which they openly picked their preferred opposition leader to replace President Yanukovych after the anticipated revolution. And he fought fire with fire when he set in place counter-insurgency youth groups such as Nashi[4] and the Young Guard of United Russia,[5] who, when the time came, could simply be paid to meet 'democracy' protests on home turf with counter-protests. (Resemblances between these groups and the Hitler Youth are not entirely accidental).

But why am I talking about Russian intelligence tactics in a book about British protest? Well, until not long ago, the idea of protesters in the West being paid to go out on the streets would have been laughable. But that's exactly what Trump claimed in October 2018 when thousands of women descended on Washington to protest the swearing in of alleged sexual assailant Brett Kavanaugh to the Supreme Court. 'Paid professionals' Trump called them in a tweet that also implied George Soros was the one paying,[6] doubling-down four days later when he claimed the same people were now protesting because they hadn't received the cheques yet.[7]

Putting aside any mental instability on Trump's part, it's interesting to ask: where did he get this idea from? Whether it was from the dark corners of the web, where almost untraceable conspiracy theories can be planted, or whether it's much more directly, from one of his unaccompanied one-to-ones with Putin, it doesn't ultimately matter. In the final analysis, it's an attitude to protest that has its roots in state espionage. Nor do we even need theories Russian hacking or the alleged 'pee-tape' leverage over Trump to see why this attitude towards protest should be shared so easily, between these demagogues: to quote the historian Howard Zinn speaking in 1970, 'Nixon and Brezhnev have much more in common with one another than we have with Nixon [...] That's why we are always surprised when they get together – they smile, they shake hands, they smoke cigars, they really like one another no matter what they say.'[8] Thus we also shouldn't be surprised when one demagogue's Cold War-influenced thinking towards protest hops the pond and becomes another's. And given the way the British government seems to be aping everything the White House does right now, we shouldn't be surprised either when allegations towards protesters, saying they're agents or paid to protest, start flying here.

In short, if protesters aren't 'hippies', living outside the law, they're the post-Cold War equivalent of 'commies', agents of a foreign power, traitors. Either way, they're not 'us'.

Fighting fascism is far from the only battle pre-occupying the protesters in this book. It merely seems to be something 'in the air' at the moment, as bookshops get raided by far-right thugs,[9] parliament is shut down unlawfully for obvious political ends, and nationalists continue to reap the rewards of a referendum result won (in part) by the modern equivalent of tabloid journalism, targeted social media misinformation. The types of protest featured in the following stories actually vary widely, from traditional strikes, marches and demos, through to military sabotage, civil disobedience, even letter-writing campaigns. Some might question how broadly we're defining resistance, here, especially given our decision to include protests that, by accident or design, 'descended' into violence. The reason we took this expansive definition is to avoid the filter of modernity blinkering us from actions that may prove entirely political as time moves on. A riotous event that took place sufficiently long ago, like the Battle of Cable Street, is much easier to file under 'protest' than, say, the anger on Tottenham High Street that sparked the August 2011 riots. Of course, a distinction can be drawn between taking to the streets to call for a change in the law, and taking to the streets to protest the methods by which law is enforced generally. The latter may be historically more prone to morph into a riot, but it's not by any means the only type of protest that does morph into one. To quote Jacob Ross, a riot, or as he prefers, a 'rising' should never be dismissed as a mere act of mass criminality. It is rather a 're-negotiation of the social contract'.[10] What's being negotiated isn't a change in the law, but a change in who those laws are seen to apply to; it's a reminder to the rest of society of whose rights should be protected by the law, who sits at the table. All of us.

Ra Page,
Manchester, September 2019

Notes

1. Grent, Nick & Richardson, Brian, *Blair Peach: Socialist and Anti-Racist* (Socialist Worker).

2. Research is currently being undertaken by the project 'Hostile Environments: Policies, Stories, Responses' to document these commonalities. https://www.thebritishacademy.ac.uk/projects/uk-international-challenges-19/hostile-environments-policies-stories-responses

3. Claire Berlinski, 'Fruits from the Tree of Malice', *City Journal*, Winter 2011.

4. Nashi: https://en.wikipedia.org/wiki/Nashi_(youth_movement)

5. Young Guard of United Russia: https://en.wikipedia.org/wiki/Young_Guard_of_United_Russia

6. 'Trump tweet labels anti-Kavanaugh protesters as "paid professionals"', *The Guardian*, 5 Oct, 2018.

7. 'Trump claims "paid protesters" during Kavanaugh confirmation "haven't gotten their checks"', Politico, 9 Oct, 2018.

8. 'The Problem is Civil Disobedience', speech by Howard Zinn, Johns Hopkins University, Baltimore, Nov, 1970.

9. 'Far-right protesters "ransack socialist bookshop in London"', *The Guardian*, 5 Aug, 2018.

10. The Comma Press Podcast, Series 1, Episode 6: 'The New Cross Fire & Brixton Riots with Jacob Ross and Stephen Reicher'.

Occupied Territory

Bidisha

I WAS FORTY WHEN I got my chance for revenge. I was asleep, having a nightmare that our queen Boudica was dying in childbirth. I smelled blood, I saw flames, I heard her screams pierce the fortifications of the royal household. I went to help, beating on her door, trying to get in.

I awoke with a start in the black chill of the roundhouse. The central fire was out but the sounds were real, hoarse screams ringing the settlement. I heard my friend Cata outside, hammering on my door and shouting for me.

'Rouse yourself! The queen has been outraged, her daughters defiled!'

I stumbled up, dragging my cloak onto my shoulder. I smelled ashes as the trailing edge swept through the dead fire. I thought, *It is happening again.*

I opened the door to Cata and her beloved, Ecen, who leaned in and pulled at me. They looked so much alike they were often taken for siblings, standing shoulder to shoulder, their wiry gold hair bristling.

'What took you so long?' Cata demanded.

'I was having a nightmare,' I mumbled, still clammy from my vision.

'There is one underway. All order is overturned,' said Ecen, biting his lips. He was a bard who had entertained us all our lives, although his guise then was very different from the

1

hunched, rattled man before me now.

'It is betrayal. Mutiny,' said Cata, pulling my wrist so tightly that my hand smarted. 'We must go to her.'

All around us kith and kin came out of their homes and massed fitfully. Some murmured in worry, others shouted 'What is happening?' to the open air, some were excited, as for a solstice feast. We left our cluster of roundhouses and went towards the queen's household, compelled by a dark intimation. Several paces ahead in the dishevelled horde I spotted our friends Tam the woodsman, whose generous form belied his great strength, beside the pale frame of his beloved, Banna the healer. They kept their son Aesu between them, Banna's thin hand on the nape of the drowsy boy's neck. They were accompanied by the weaver, dark Senna, her hair elegantly bound, her clothes so neat she must have been awake, working late by flame light. Someone touched my shoulder and I turned to see Antedios, the apprentice at my workshop, walking with his friends. The young men's eyes were bright; glorious or terrible, they sought incident, adventure.

We collected at the gates of the royal house, which stood open, the chains twisted apart. All the torches of the house were burning. The queen was tied to a post as men who served the Roman occupation – even the slaves of her own house – thronged behind her. Others, leering and laughing, stood at the entrance and pushed us back.

Queen Boudica sagged, kneeling, her wrists bound, her head drooping, her face obscured with blood. Her thick hair dragged on the ground. The Roman raised his hand and the muscles in his shoulder flexed. He brought it down hard and his whip cut through her back. The crowd flinched, writhing in disturbance. Senna and I clutched each other, but there was nothing we could do. We were powerless and humiliated, compelled to watch and wail.

Slaves and junior officers who only days ago had waited on the queen were now ransacking her rooms. A man ran to her and shoved something in her face. It was a gold torc, wound up with other jewellery, whose long chains swung from his fist.

'*This* is your inheritance!' screamed the man. 'Emperor Nero owes nobody anything, others are nothing to Nero!' He raised his head to us. 'All that is yours is ours. All that is ours is ours. For eternity!'

He was so taken by laughter that he threw back his head and his eyes rolled.

'Mad, they're mad,' said Senna, her beautiful face contorting with revulsion. 'Even the lowest Roman slave now feels himself to be the master of our queen.'

'They are *not* mad,' Cata replied. 'To be mad is to be outside yourself. This is who they are. They line up to defile the queen's daughters, back where we cannot see.'

'We need to act,' I interrupted, 'or they will do that to all of us. We must go from here, we can't help like this, dumb and staring. We must join together and decide what to do.'

I drew Senna and Cata away, although Cata glanced back, baring her teeth as if she wanted to tear a chunk from the marauding men's calves. We went to the great hall, the ceremonial place we always gathered to celebrate, to dispute and to share our tales when the winds grew cold. It was the heart of our world, standing for as long as I could remember, its hulking shape visible from every home. When Ecen, Senna, Cata and I got near there were already countless voices reverberating within, easily heard beyond the two ditches and nine fences that protected the tall wooden building.

'It is our king's death that has done this. Now Queen Boudica is a widow, without his protection, the Romans insult her any way they can think of,' Ecen seethed as we crossed the ditch ramps and entered the series of fences, which threw deep shadows over us.

'King Prasutagus was *not* a real king, he was a puppet who was told he was a king by the Romans and believed it,' I said, gaining a few bitter jeers of agreement from those who overheard. 'I despise a man who betrays his own people to invaders in return for a nice life and the title of a king. He did so with Emperor Claudius. He did the same once Nero took Claudius's place.'

Prasutagus's loyalty to Rome was evidently not mutual. His will had left half his estate to Nero, along with the care of his family, assuming Rome would take on the burden and protect them. But people like us would always be barbarians to Rome, easily used and abandoned. Now our 'King' Prasutagus was dead, Emperor Nero laughed and took back his perks. It was as though Queen Boudica and her girls were nothing more than chattels to be broken and discarded.

We passed beneath the high wooden posts of the gateway. Inside the hall, the air was thick. Kinsfolk huddled in small groups, eyes rimmed with darkness, shock buzzing in their voices. Those who subsisted on their farmlands looked particularly haggard as their brief sleep was broken by tonight's violence. Many people acknowledged us: Senna was a renowned weaver and Cata our most prized jeweller, while Ecen's tales and songs had no equal. We moved through the press until we found the woodsman Tam and Banna the healer, who were in a corner deep in conference with Banna's father, Mandubracius. Mandubracius was a plump and wealthy farmer – not that he had plied his own hand to the soil in many a harvest.

'I do my part,' he was saying to the fawning magistrates who clustered around him, all of them old men in cloaks fastened with laughably large enamelled brooches. 'I made my home a stronghold for fighters during the last rebellion against Rome, and they dined and drank from my stores. I asked for nothing in return. My Banna here was only twenty but she tended the wounded night and day.'

I shuddered. What Mandubracius called 'the last rebellion' ruled my nightmares: it was the night my mother died. I forced my attention away and looked around the hall. The torches lining the walls produced just as much smoke as light and as the place grew fuller, foreboding and hysteria mixed in the pithy half-gloom. Lucius the warrior paced, a head and shoulders taller than everyone else. He was worshipped by many here,

4

especially the boys who were too young to have been taken by Rome and co-opted into its armies.

The messenger Saenu slipped between everyone, at once lively and aloof, joining and abandoning conversations and passing news from one group to another. Many men disliked him for some reason, but I had worked with him many times. He was an expert trader, able to persuade anyone of anything.

'What say you, Saenu?' I called when he flitted past. 'What have you heard?'

'Lady, it is *grotesque*,' he said.

'And yet you smile,' snapped Ecen, for even now Saenu's eyes were bright, his thin lips curling at the edges.

'It is not a joke. We must fight back, before the centurions come and take everything,' said Lucius, pushing between us with his sweaty bulk. 'The Romans fear an uprising, and so they should. I remember when they dared to disarm us.'

'But they did not, in the end,' remarked Saenu.

Lucius looked down at him, his neck reddening in rage.

'Well they *tried*. I have had *that* insult sticking in my throat for thirteen years. We are not to be trampled on by invaders in hobnailed boots, who keep us in poverty and fear, taking our belongings and taxing what we keep, making us farm for them like beasts of burden, paying a tribute just to exist –'

Lucius stopped short and turned away. He had spotted something over the heads of his tribesmen.

'She is here! Queen Boudica is here!' he exclaimed, his eyes shining.

He went directly to her, the crowd peeling open before him. Saenu scampered in his wake. The rest of us shoved and strained in the sweltering confusion. Suddenly we saw our queen blazing above us, pacing and gesticulating on the dais. Lucius stood guard close by. The queen's voice was inaudible, although she was addressing us with all her force. We lowed in rage for her and her daughters. A woman cried out, 'Those innocent girls!' The queen's shoulders were braced and she took small, crooked steps. Her hair stuck to her back, which was

5

soaked black with blood. Her brow, however, was fierce, her scowl fixed, the light emanating from her as intense as that of Andraste, the goddess we invoked lustily now, the goddess of war. Indeed, in that moment, she *was* her. I saw Queen Boudica raise her fist and bring it down sharply, and so the war began – the war of the wronged women.

It took weeks to prepare. Nearly every person in the settlement visited my tool-making workshop wanting some new weapon made or an existing cudgel, pick, mace or blade perfected. My apprentice Antedios and I worked every day, smelting new spears from first light until the moon was high. As we worked, we beat time and sang of great warriors, as once we were.

The farmer Mandubracius tested his strongest and fastest horses. He was enviably rich in them. His daughter Banna made the salves and poultices that would heal wounds, grant vigour and ease pain, testing how best to preserve them through long days' travel. Land workers readied the fields and reaped what they could, making offerings to Epona the mother-goddess to bless our war with her bounty. The chariot-makers' workshops were constantly at labour crafting fast, hardy chariots for battle and larger wagons to carry our possessions and transport our families. The warrior Lucius barked orders to all who sought instruction in combat and many times I watched Ecen and Tam train with him, far from the stage and the woods they loved so much. Senna followed along, weaving warm but light cloaks, blankets and bedding, patterning bright colours in chequered squares of wool and flax, her hands perpetually stained with dye. We buried our wealth hoards – what little we had. Queen Boudica and her daughters were sequestered with their advisors. I imagined the queen getting ready for war, promising her children revenge, justice and vindication. I felt a cutting sadness to have no kin of my own, to make such a pledge. I had not been able to protect my mother; she had not been able to protect me.

The night before we left, Antedios came to help me gather my belongings. We cleared the largest pottery pieces from the long knee-high shelf that ran around the room, folded my clothes into dense bundles and collected my light ornaments together.

'We can settle anywhere once we've won,' he said, gazing over at me, his hand resting on the last of my things. My home was now stripped of all colour and decoration, save for the dappled hides that would warm me through my final night.

'Of course. You can do anything. You're young,' I said lightly, like any workshop owner to their apprentice.

Antedios was barely twenty, younger than I had been the night the soldiers came for my mother and me. Roman soldiers had killed my father when they invaded our land when I was 23. Roman soldiers killed my mother when our tribe rebelled against the occupation four years later. And after they killed her, Roman soldiers did to me… what soldiers do. When both my parents were dead, I inherited the workshop, making farmers' tools. And the time since then had passed, as time does. And now I was 40.

Every spring since my mother died, I took a brooch crafted for me by Cata, placed it in the stream at new moon, and mourned. Then I joined my friends in the woods. Me, Cata, Ecen, Banna, Tam, Senna, the messenger Saenu and others. We drank, we danced, we lamented what we had lost. After this rite, my dreams would always be violent. I'd sweat under the skins, remembering the sound of soldiers' armour and the smell of their flesh. They had pounded on our door with their shields, then set the thatch alight.

The night the Romans killed my father, they killed Antedios's parents too. He was only a small boy and he never spoke about them, even though my family knew them well. I had known him since he was a baby. I sometimes thought he cleaved to me because of that. This time Antedios would have the chance to fight and win, not lose like I did.

I awoke when dawn pried through the tiny gaps in the woven circle of my roundhouse. Its curving wall of interlocking branches had been my haven for many years.

We left for the city of Camulodunum, a beacon the Romans regarded as their capital in our conquered lands. We were a vast, slow moving train, singing and full of zeal. I rode with Senna and Cata by my side. The men, Ecen and Tam, followed behind. Little Aesu rode the same horse as his father, leaning back into Tam's comforting frame. Saenu cantered up and down the caravan, alert as a hound. The morning was cool and grey, and we crossed ragged heath, easy rivers, low scrubland and sparse, airy woods. It was only when we came onto flatter, more open territory that we felt wary, for we knew the Romans had been here, imposing their order.

'They imprint our land with their pale roads, like lash marks,' said Cata as our horses picked across the tightly packed earth, 'and watch us from their little forts as if *we* are the intruders.'

'Other foreign things come down these routes too,' commented Saenu, jangling beside us on his threadbare mount. 'They transport the things they can't live without. Oil, pottery, herbs, ornaments. Gifts to bribe our puppet kings.'

'And now we sacrifice ourselves to avenge his queen,' said Senna with a battle-timid sigh. As comely as always, no part of her looked like it was girded for the ugliness of war.

I felt Cata stiffen up but before she could speak, I answered Senna myself.

'Yes – we ride to avenge Queen Boudica. As we should. But we also ride to avenge *ourselves*. We have borne the insult of their presence too long. We should be ashamed.'

'But to fight in revenge, with no planning?' said Senna, pulling her cloak over her front.

'Revenge is justice when violation goes unpunished,' I said. I had comforted myself with these words many times as I smouldered for vengeance over the years.

'But what power do we have?' Senna pressed. 'They have their strategies, their experience, their armoury. We are... metalworkers and farmhands, not soldiers.'

Cata couldn't contain herself any longer. Leaning right

across me, she flashed her eyes and hissed to Senna:

'We are fighters. We have cause, we have pride, we have honour. We have fine weapons made in workshops like *hers*, the best in the land.'

'Those are farmers' tools, not weapons,' retorted Senna. 'I know we have cause, Cata. I know they do wrong. I am loyal, I would never say otherwise. But I am not ashamed to say what you all refuse to: I am afraid.'

I remember our three victories all in one piece, even though they spanned the seasons. It was deliriously hot, the unstinting heat of a forge, a scorching, unforgiving rage, a slash of pain that left me spent and washed me clean. First, we took the city of Camulodunum, then a tiny upstart town called Londinium, and finally Verulamium. And then came the battle.

'*Look* at it!' whooped Lucius ahead of us, pointing his stubby finger as Camulodunum came into view.

I saw a grand settlement so utterly unlike our own dwellings that it resembled a vision in a confounding dream. We gaped, some of us bunching and tangling together, others slipping to the side and straying from the track. We rode in – such was the Romans' arrogance, the place was defended by neither ditch nor wall. We saw Roman roads paved hard and set out unnaturally straight instead of following the land or spreading from the centre like a spider's web. Our horses grew nervous at the unfamiliar surroundings. The buildings around us were straight sided, topped with the bright regularity of hard red tiles instead of dark thatch. They were all of indomitable width and smooth immensity, plastered the same deathly white and glowing as they reflected the sun.

We saw nobody on the streets. There only a bated, heavy absence.

'They call this place the *Colonia Victricensis*, colony of the victorious,' said Saenu, riding as easily as if he saw this every day. 'Until ten years ago this was their military base, for the twentieth legion. Now they are satisfied we'll give no more trouble, the top infantry are gone. Only retirees now.'

'You mean this is where their old soldiers feast and fart their way through their final years, waiting for death in luxury, like pigs,' snarled Cata.

Saenu was unperturbed. Everything in life was interesting to him, even the settlements of those who hated and occupied us.

'The local senate meets there,' he said, pointing at a particularly imposing structure, 'and over there is a forum and theatre, for three thousand people.'

'Let them enjoy them in their own lands. This is not to be their little piece of Rome,' I said.

'The old military buildings are for the people now,' he said mildly.

'What people? Occupied people? Or settlers?' I demanded.

'Most here are not Roman citizens, except the legionnaires and administrators.'

'Then they are collaborators! They have no dignity,' I said, raising my voice as our drums and battle cries called us to attention.

Saenu refused to fight with me or feed my anger.

'The people here did what they had to, to survive,' he said as we rejoined the main procession. 'The settlers drove our brother tribe the Trinovantes from their homes, stole their land and made them prisoners and slaves. We are lucky that was not done to us.'

A steady drumbeat took up, accompanied by the martial cry of our people. Our convoy cohered and rode as one, our hooves striking, our chariot wheels crunching on the gravelled streets. In the heart of the town I finally saw strangers for the first time. They were wearing Roman costumes. Those with wits had fled or barricaded themselves indoors but the unlucky remainder stared up from the streets, their faces drained of sense, wiped clean with dread. With a slanting slash of his long sword, a man four horses ahead of me axed a lad in the throat, only half severing his head. A cheer went up as he circled back to hack again, until the neck was chopped in two.

We melted the city into fire until there was no thing left intact, as was only right for a place named for Camulos, our old god of war. Cata, Ecen and Tam stayed by my side, Cata and Ecen holding hands at times and bursting into cackling laughter. Tam broke into a building, his burly strength shattering the barricaded doors. I ran in after him and found a family cowering there, a man and his two children, the wife missing, the little ones crouched tight with their arms over their faces. Tam rushed to them with his scythe raised, then halted like a stuck horse. I understood his hesitation: he looked at the family and saw himself and Banna and little Aesu staring back. But I had no family. I saw only weak and traitorous collaborators who knuckled under while first my father and then my mother had been killed for having the honour to fight back. I struck upon the family with my long knife and as they huddled ever tighter their screams rang through me with peculiar familiarity. I too had once screamed like that, and received no mercy.

Tam and I ransacked the next rooms until all around us lay the oozing, shattered remnants of wine amphorae, flagons, glass and pottery, great two-handed jars shaped like teardrops broken and leaking at our feet, swimming into the flames.

I smashed through these Roman indulgences, thinking of how we starved in winter while their kitchens held sacks of grain and soft fruit, baskets of beans and herbs to be ground at the mortar and cooked on a gridiron over the fire or in the hearth. Yet the real valuables had all been taken, for we found nothing truly sumptuous. An old mattress lay abandoned, its woollen stuffing bursting from a gash in the side. On a counter, someone had forgotten a glass locket showing a sea nymph. I picked it up, imagining an idle young wife wearing it. I put it down in disgust.

'All that's left are the last signs of their vapid frolic-making,' I said to Tam, toying with a bronze dice shaker next to a board game I did not recognise.

'We must get out of here,' said Tam who was backing away, coughing, his eyes streaming. 'The building is collapsing.'

11

We ran out just as the edifice sank into itself. Someone pushed past me. It was Senna, her cloak bunched up on her shoulders, her arms laden with stolen armour. A delicate silver drinking cup glinted at the top of her pile. When she saw me, she gave a sheepish laugh, half frightened and half exhilarated, like a naughty child.

The building we had fled was now no more than a smouldering pile of black and red detritus, although its blaze did not spread. The roof tiles had failed to ignite and the daub from the walls was changing form in the flames, softening and bending but not catching on fire.

I said to the men behind me, 'Keep the buildings lit, one by one. Feed the fire as tenderly as you would an ailing babe. The Romans should know the *colonia* they planted in this soil will not take.'

It was too hot to stand still so I ran along the street where all was aflame and twisted bodies lay burning at the sides. I heard a yelp behind me: Senna stood with her arms empty, her loot scattered at her feet. A local woman was gripping her shoulders, shaking her and babbling.

'They said you would come,' gabbled the woman, her hair plastered to her face. 'They said it. We heard chanting a-nights, harbingers of devastation. There were yells and voices in the senate and laughter in the theatre. The statue of Victory toppled overnight – and it fell,' she peered around warily, 'looking yonder, as if it wanted to flee. They said that Roman soldiers would be misled by those loyal to *you*, the queens of vengeance. And now you are here!' The woman stroked Senna's face and Senna squirmed to get away. 'But we did not know you would be so beautiful. We pleaded with Catus Decianus to help us but the procurator has been as silent as a worm. I beg you, spare our lives!'

I got between them and Senna wrenched away, her shoulders bowed.

'To Claudius's temple!' a wild-eyed tribesman boomed, running past. I followed, pulling Senna with me, although she kept swerving away to stare at the colossal statues everywhere, gleaming gold. They were so oversized that it was as if Claudius and Nero had been transported here from the realm of the greats, armed, proud, mounted, their locks shorn like animals in summer, their gazes fixed above our heads, always seeking the next place to conquer.

The warrior Lucius swaggered on the temple steps, surrounded by his men.

'Destroy this place!' he shouted, brandishing his cudgel. 'They made us build it and the cost was borne – by ourselves. Our taxes have paid for our murderers' monuments!'

Behind us the town blistered and burned. The buildings were finally coming apart, the timber cracking and the red and black clay of the daub bubbling as the fire reduced it to a paste. In other places everything had melted into a thick black layer, too hot to approach, in which fragments of broken buildings had been swallowed up: chunks of painted plaster from the rooms, shots of roof tile and pottery, even door keys. All were submerged in the scalding murk.

My hands were sticky with blood, my clothing black and reeking. I felt a hand on my shoulder and spun round with my fist raised, but met only Antedios's quizzical look. I lowered my fist. I saw his arms were empty.

'You do not take anything?' I asked.

He shrugged and squinted at the ground.

'You find no satisfaction in fighting?' I pressed.

He shook his head and his face took on a closed, stubborn aspect I knew well from our work days.

'I will not fight women and children or frail old men. The able have fled,' he said. 'There is a river nearby that passes through marshland into clear water. Those who can, have gone. What is there to fight for here?'

'We fight for a purpose – to expel the settlers and end the occupation. Keep your thoughts on that,' I urged, impatient to join Lucius.

'But we are not fighting settlers or soldiers here – or even retired soldiers. We are fighting... ourselves. Our own kind. These wretches aren't even fighting back.'

I replied, biting my words, 'I have not waited so long only to spare those who live alongside our parents' killers, and dress and speak like them. We punish them for their treachery, their disloyalty, their weakness and their acquiescence. Come, Antedios, raise your weapon. We have sparred together many times, testing our wares. Treat it like that.'

'Our grudge is with the Romans. We are not fighting Romans,' he said.

'Romans, he wants Romans!' yelled Lucius, stalking a few paces away from us. He turned to beat on the temple doors. 'They are in here! Hiding. Two hundred of them — ill-armed at that. Join us!'

His men gathered to storm the building, readying themselves to scale its walls. Ropes tumbled thickly from the roof and they grasped them, tested their hold and began to climb. Antedios went with them, conscious that I was watching.

I heard crazed laughter and familiar voices shouting back and forth. Following the sound around the corner, I found Ecen and Tam braced high up on a statue of Claudius, the giant bronze face reflecting the fires all around. The immense statue exuded a gloating vanity, as if Claudius bestrode the world. Except now, Ecen and Tam were sawing back and forth at his enormous head.

'Didn't I say your woodsman skills would come in useful?' roared Ecen as Tam sweated and strained, his blade stuck fast in the former Emperor's bronze throat.

Finally the head tore off, its sawn edge ugly and jagged, and the men slithered down and landed hard, clutching it, unable to speak with glee.

'A fine trophy,' choked Ecen, rolling on the ground with the head pinning him down, his arms stretched wide around it.

'It's a tribute to the queen and booty from our victory,' panted Tam. The men lay together, smug and sated as if after a long lovemaking, Claudius's head gleaming beside them with its big nose and ears catching the light.

Black midnight rose and a stinking heat hung in the air. Lucius and his men took up their positions around the temple roof and the base, where I lingered, seething in the sticky dark.

For two days I stayed on the steps of the temple. The sky was black with smoke and dark motes of destructed matter. We waited out the soldiers within, listening as their cries and threats grew weaker. It gratified me. To hear your enemy scream in terror and plead for their life, as you once did. To hear their pleas come to nothing, just like yours.

On the third night, as the moon rose, it was time. The Romans' cries had become groans, their pleas mere sighs.

'We can wait no more or they'll all be dead. This makes a mockery of us. We are no cowards! We want to fight our enemy, not starve them or suffocate them or freeze them to death,' said one of Lucius's men, a sinewy sort with a hungry face.

Lucius nodded and gave the sign. More fighters climbed up the sides of the temple, the ropes creaking. The men on the roof began in unison to strike at the tiles, which made a clattering sound like falling bones. Before long the men dropped through, and we heard the screams and bellows of the trapped garrison through the night. The temple doors thudded with the ferocity of the slaughter within. When it was over, Lucius's men burst out covered in gore, their teeth bared, howling at their first taste of true punishment.

Then they stiffened up. Through the smouldering gloom we saw the glint of armour approaching. The infantry had come, the ones so familiar from my nightmares, and I would confront them at last. All fatigue left me.

'It is the ninth division. It seems Decianus does want a fight after all. Ready yourselves,' said Lucius, and unlike his usual bluster his words were low, cautious, like a beast gathering his pack, not wanting his voice to carry. Joining him on the steps, I smelt my attackers once more, the memory unchanged since the day it happened. I had a sudden certainty – *the men who attacked me are here* – but those men would be generals by now, not young infantry soldiers like these. The men approaching were merely the same age as those who had attacked me.

We made a half circle around Lucius, drawing together as the soldiers approached. They were just as wary, taking small steps. Their hands were on the pommels of their short swords, high up on their left hip. I did not see any Roman's face clearly, only their armour-stacked shoulders and the tops of their helmets above curved red shields that concealed nearly their entire bodies.

It was only then that I realised I had no weapon. I picked up the nearest thing I could see: a long metal spike from the door fastening of a plundered building. Then they were upon us, running swiftly up the steps. We fought pressed up against the temple walls, in the very lap of Emperor Claudius. A soldier's shield butted into me and I slipped to the side and sank the length of the spike into the exposed space just beneath the Roman's ear. It went in with a slick lack of resistance and protruded from his cheek, dripping with matter. The Roman gurgled loudly and a pop of blood burst from his mouth and spattered my lips, but his face was an empty stage mask. His shield and sword fell from him as his arms went slack. I felt a blaze of triumph and almost immediately after, shame and revulsion. I let go of the spike and kicked the dead soldier down the steps. I picked up his sword and tried to hoist his shield as well, but it was too heavy. I threw it down upon him.

After that first kill it was easy, for a death-lust was upon me. We beat their paltry band, who perished in a mist of blood. Next to me Antedios and a Roman soldier had abandoned their weapons and were trading blows with their fists, staggering and spitting out teeth like drunken, feuding clansmen. They grappled two paces forward, two back, grunting and pummelling each other's ribs. I thrust my sword into the Roman's thigh, close to the knee, and he didn't even notice, so involved was he in hurling Antedios down the blood-flooded steps. Eventually his movements grew slower and he collapsed. Even so, Antedios didn't finish him, but left him to die alone.

When there was nothing left, we moved west to Londinium, battle woken and ready, the queen at our head, flanked by nimble war chariots bounding lightly on the road. We were dark with sun and fire, red with spilt blood. We did not cover great ground, but made steady pace along the tracks.

Of course, Saenu the messenger noticed my zeal. He cantered beside me, his thin fingers pinching his horse's mane. I wondered what kind of fighter he made. A sneaky assassin, no doubt, when the occasion called.

'You are quite the woman-at-arms, now,' he teased. 'Like fierce Cartimandua of the Brigantes. Her people liken her to Minerva.'

'Nobody here is like Cartimandua,' I snapped. 'Cartimandua is another of ours who collaborated with Rome – that is why her people compare her to the *Roman* war goddess. *She* should have married King Prasutagus. They could have been traitors together.'

Saenu smiled as if my rage was but dawn dew evaporating pleasantly on his skin, and in truth it was impossible to stay angry when the joy of war lifted us up. My friends and I rode together, looking about. The way to Londinium was neither natural and rough like the roads in our lands, nor bare and ordered like the Romans' implacable paths. It was lined with little shops and we grew lively as we came upon them, for there were countless signs of life and interest.

'But do you notice the silence?' said Senna the weaver. She had no battle scars, but her knapsacks were certainly fuller than before with all her plunder. She nodded towards a bare, gravelled area. 'The market is empty.'

She was right. Londinium was clearly a bustling place, normally.

'Word of our conquest has spread,' I said, satisfied. 'Messengers can pass down these paths far quicker than we can. It is good that people fear us.'

The road was fronted with tall, straight settlers' buildings of earth and timber. The settlement on one bank of the river was strict, either facing the water or standing stiffly side-on. But the streets were empty and I felt that many of the houses were, too.

'The people must have gone south by road, or rowed out on the river. We would be in unwelcome territory if we followed them. Roman-loving Togidubnus of the Regni rules southwards,' said Saenu the messenger. 'We must be careful. There's rumour of Governor Suetonius and his soldiers on the march. But they are not in view.'

'That is good, is it not? If they have seen us and turned back?' Senna asked him hopefully.

'Not necessarily. He may sacrifice this encounter and hold back for some later onslaught.'

We rode deeper into the silence, occupying the entire span of the road, which was easily two carts' wide.

'They laid good foundations. Sand, or clay, or silt,' said Tam, with a sigh for his former life. 'And see these timber drains. They know how to keep the place clean. What labour went into it.'

'Our labour. Slave labour,' seethed Cata. 'The labour of anyone who dared resist.'

All that day we incinerated Londinium, until the heat grew too great even for us. I recoiled from the blaze. The blistering miasma pushed me back down the side streets and I ran desperately, my blade loose in my hand, trying to find some air that was not gritty with embers. The buildings were now collapsed black sticks emitting bitter smoke like a last breath.

I ended up bent double and gulping for air on the bank of the river, my innards rattling as I coughed. The river was wide and slow, the ruined town blazing so hot that the water oozed with steam. When I had cleared my gullet at last, I raised myself up.

The bank descended steeply and I saw, far below me, a woman somewhat older than I. She was robed in black, huddled close to the ground, scrabbling at it. At first I thought she was burying a child, for the bundle she pressed into the mud was large and round. I drew closer and saw the bundle glinting with coins. She was burying her hoard, scraping out a hollow with two flat stones.

I could have struck her down there and then, but she sensed me, turning her head without fear. Her glance was so ordinary, as if we were meeting at one of Mandubracius's solstice revels, that my war-spirit fled like milk from a cracked pot. I poked my muddy weapon towards the hoard and said,

'The tides will submerge it or carry it away.'

'You are not from here, you know nothing about the tide,' the woman cut me off.

She stood to face me, dropping her digging stones which I saw were actually curved pieces of broken pottery. There was something about her that made me feel small, as if I had been caught by my mother doing a shameful thing.

'Do you know,' she said with cool presumption, 'we have envisioned it all in these waters. Our seers dreamt of the flow running red with blood, a spectral town floating in ruins, bodies washed up on the tide. We understand your grudge: it is the same as ours. This land is occupied territory. But why punish us? We are the victims too.'

'You are rich, that is obvious, you could leave,' I retorted, the weapon shaking dumbly in my hand as I gesticulated.

The woman's lips thinned to a single line and she crossed her arms.

'Why should I give up the life I built and run away from my own home? You know nothing about me or what I've survived.'

'We are here to purge a sickness called Rome,' I rang out, although I felt a furtive, gormless expression forming on my face and my voice died away.

'You are replacing one sickness with another,' she replied.

She stared me down, unimpressed. Time slowed and I seemed trapped there, stuck fast in the mud. Then she blinked, opened her arms, tipped back her head and parted her jaws so wide I could see all her teeth and the back of her throat. In a frightened flash I thought, *She is a Druid sorceress!* as she raised her outspread hands over me and began the hex, 'I curse you, warrior of the Iceni —' and I turned tail and ran up the bank, frightened, her mocking laughter lashing my back.

We rode northwest to Verulamium. By now our carts were heavy with plunder and the sour stink of burning permeated everything we carried. I told no one about my encounter with the mystic by the river at Londinium. Perhaps I had not just been foolish but actually bewitched. Perhaps the spirit of my own rage had taken form and met me on the riverbank. Or worse, the Romans had sent their gods to play trickster with us. I wondered if all of us had met similar apparitions, who spat curses into our faces and scuttled through our darker dreams.

Outwardly, however, a breathless zeal connected us. We were a convoy of kin as well as warriors: Banna was prized as the great healer of the rebellion and led a troupe of girls and boys who followed her teachings, including her own son Aesu. We had been travelling for so long that babies were being born safely under Banna's care even as whole towns compacted into flames.

We had gained many allies on our procession, fierce tribesmen like the Trinovantes, who were willing to lay down old disputes, at least for a time, against a common enemy. I had no idea how many we slew together. My nights were filled with images of burnt and piled bodies and I awoke with a sensation of scalding and suffocation. I gained a new nightmare to add to my torments: I was back on the steps outside Claudius's temple, stepping out of the way of the soldier's shield and stabbing him in the neck. In the nightmare, he looked up at me as he died and I recognised him as one of the men who had attacked me after killing my mother. Only he was not defeated in death. Instead, he jeered at me. I was gripped like a perpetual victim in a curse, a jinx destined to repeat with inexorable, fated regularity. I awoke trembling, humiliated, knowing that no matter how many Romans I killed, I would never avenge that first assault. I would always have his stain on me.

In Verulamium I saw a long, timber building with a tower at one end, already set alight. I dismounted and followed Cata, both of us laughing, and we hurtled inside, under its colonnade. It was like a fiery cave, its earthen floors warmed by the flames overhead, great chunks of flaming thatch falling about our shoulders, the walls warping around us.

Black smoke poured in. The heat was so fierce that we crouched under its weight. We broke into a strange white dream of a bathhouse, its tiled rooms filled with milky steam as our fires created a mist of heat. Moisture dripped down walls painted with images of leaves and vines entwined with musical instruments. Cata and I skidded on the slippery floor, unable to see as far as the corners of the rooms through the smoke. We found two young boys barely Aesu's age sheltering in the farthest corner of a half empty pool. I descended, my hands outspread, my clothes trailing in the water, leaking red blood and black dirt in spectral swirls. The boys could only gibber and call for their mothers, who were surely slain by now. As we trod closer, they shrank back. Cata and I were not mothers ourselves and perhaps Banna or Tam would have dealt with them differently, or Senna with her timid heart. But Banna and Tam and Senna were not there.

There was a slow crash behind us and the roof came down, blocking the way we had come.

'The tower,' choked Cata, grabbing one of the boys by the arm, 'there's a tower at the end of the row.'

I snatched the other boy. Both were so afraid that they went limp and weightless in our grip, slippery from water and from their clammy fear. We pulled them out of the baths. All was now ablaze, a furnace of red and gold roaring so loud that I couldn't hear my own voice. At the end of the building the timber tower had not yet been reached by the blaze.

'Go up there,' I shouted at the boys. Cata and I forced them up the first few steps and up they ran, trusting, as children are.

Cata and I fled from the parade. The colonnade was completely collapsed, the workshops and baths flattened into

21

bubbling, blistering red. The fire entered, spiralled up the tower and chased its way to the top.

Finally, when there was nothing more to destroy, we left the smoking ruins of Verulamium. Every instinct told me of the fight to come and of the closing circle of our destiny. All of us felt it.

Nobody slept the night before the last battle. Instead, we drank and sang and performed our war rites, trapping hares in the woods and making our last blood-offerings, unfastening our tunics to reveal our limbs to the moon as we pled for succour. Cata and I robed ourselves in Senna's brightest cloth, worked lime into our hair and let the white mixture stiffen our locks into serpentine coils.

I opened the armoury well before dawn. The warrior Lucius came to join me. He was excited and the anticipation made us light and easy with each other.

'No more torching little traitor brats or sticking dead heads on spikes. Fair combat at last! And in the open air, with a willing enemy!' he said, looking lustily at the weapons I'd set out before us. 'I've had nearly a year of this. I was promised war, not arson.'

'It seems we have enough weapons for ten lifetimes,' I said, walking down the table and adjusting the handles like a mother neatening her children.

'Well – they are coming. Two of their legions, the fourteenth and the twentieth, led by Suetonius Paullinus himself. Ten thousand men come with him, armed and trained. Even their horses are armoured.'

'Even them,' I said, trying to sound sardonic.

'But we still outnumber them,' said Lucius hastily. He flexed his hands and the muscles in his forearms rippled. 'And when we've won, we can hie to the groves and eat and sing and carouse like the savages they say we are.'

By the time we were ready to move, with everything loaded onto the wagons, the sky was lightening. I rode with Ecen and Cata on one side and Tam on the other. Tam was alone, for

Banna and her father Mandubracius rode up ahead with the queen, and Aesu was back with the other children, away from danger. The care of our family carts was given over to Senna who had, as I expected, abstained from combat.

The queen rode at the front and I was awed to see her, although she was a tiny figure at such a distance. She stood upright in her chariot, her hair loose and rippling, thick metal glinting at her wrists and throat, a large brooch fastening her cloak and robe which were dyed deeply – Cata's and Senna's work, I knew, for nobody was better than them. I admired the queen for refusing to hide her face, for refusing to be shamed by what had been done to her, for pulling rage out of her pain. She had risen to war the night she was dishonoured; I had waited thirteen years for the same courage. Our anger lay in the long scar-red burning we scored across the land, a slash of fury that scorched so hot it was impossible to approach: the Boudica line. We left our mark, a slice of wounded rage layered through the territory the Romans stole from us and defiled with their touch.

We towed slowly uphill as the sun rose and the air thawed, until we were on the plain of a valley that tilted up to meet a wood. I heard heavy hooves come up alongside us. It was one of Lucius's men, riding a colossal iron-grey horse. He shouted in a constant peal, 'They are here! They are here! They are here!'

Our convoy split up. The queen and her aides rode to meet the enemy head-on. Banna and her apprentices branched off to set up a camp for the wounded. The family groups diverted to sheltered land lower down the valley.

We warriors streamed behind the queen on foot and on horseback, screaming and beating our weapons. We held aloft our spears and knives, our long swords and stolen broadswords, our fieldworkers' scythes, even jagged stones, while others fisted their bright oval shields proudly. My friends and I gathered pace and in that wild gallop I found all the hate-words I'd stored up spew from my mouth in a revolting flood. My voice was

23

unrecognisable to myself. It was rough, and bitter as poison.

We raced up the slope and crammed together so tightly that my horse became frightened and reared up on its back legs, twisting in panic. I lost my seat and fell, the horse thudding down beside me. It scrambled up and bolted, slowing only when it was near the family carts, where it paced, tossing its head and trembling. I righted myself and ran with all the others, pounding towards the wood. We drew closer, crushing in together. I saw the Roman army standing above us, the shadowy wood at their back. At last, we were to fight our occupiers and rid them from our land. So the battle began.

It is happening, I tell myself, my heart beating louder than any drum. *War is here.* We mass and stir on the plain, singing, swaggering, brandishing our weapons. I lose sight of my friends, becoming separated in the forward-thrusting throng. A man nearby holds up a horn shaped like a boar's head, with bulging enamel eyes. When he blows through the horn, the boar's wooden tongue clacks like a clapper, the noise ripping out crudely. The Romans stand at a distance, silent, close together. They do not react.

More of us gather, but there is no outlet for our numbers, only a wall of Romans in red cloth, brown leather and silvery iron armour. Our family carts border us to the rear, a curve of heaped possessions and pillage. Looking back, I see the small round heads of children and their mothers' unbound tresses as they shift restlessly, watching. No woman could pick out her man in this shoving, baying, ornamented crowd, no matter how in love she might be. The sun pounds on our heads. I see our queen on her chariot, her hair a river of fiery bronze. She calls to us, exhorting us to fight, but I am too far away to hear her words. Squeezed in together, we gaze up and the light she emits is that of the sun. I know we will win. The queen's name, after all, means Victory.

Light falls on the Romans, hitting their slanted lances and the points of their javelins. Their wealth glitters and clinks together: the segmented armour and mail draped over man and horse, the sleek daggers and short double-edged swords, the shaped helmets, the poles of the banners and pennants they hold aloft. It is an armoury complete, covering hearts we will never reach.

Without warning they charge, pulling forward from the centre of their line. They surge down the slope, horsemen first, lances low. We push forward ourselves, striving uphill, only to be smashed back and thrust out to the sides as they come into the body of us. I am carried almost off my feet as they shove us aside, the breath squashed from our lungs.

There's a thick whistling noise over us and a burning heat passes into me in a quick hard volt. A javelin has sliced my shoulder, leaving a bloody groove. It tears through the neck of the man behind me and he falls, twitching. Then the Roman soldiers are among us. They are protected, the bulbous metal boss in the centre of each shield crushing our ribs when they ram them into us. Then out lashes their wide sword to pierce the body with its pointed edge.

A huge, gauntleted forearm swings towards my face, with the rest of the soldier hidden behind his shield. He knocks me off my feet and smashes the bottom edge of the shield onto me, just missing my stomach as I twist to avoid it. I get up, dizzy and clutching myself, my vision whirling, and see the Roman archers notching their bows in the distance, raising them as one. The arrows sweep through us in finely curved lines. Far away, but distinct, I see my apprentice Antedios shot through the heart. His gaze catches mine as he falls, his hand reaching for me. An arrow rips my thigh with a quick snatch of pain, its barbed tip tearing the muscle open. Panic rises as I keel to the side and bright blood washes down my leg. I raise myself, fighting on through a deadly rain of arrows and slender spears that penetrate our bodies easily but snap like twigs when they hit anything hard.

The Romans splinter into our ranks, their swords pulled clean from their scabbards, their horsemen hacking at ours.

Looking into a Roman's eyes, exactly as I did that night so many years ago, I see once again that I am nothing to them, I have no soul and no name. The Roman squaring up to me laughs as if he will relish what is to come. I can smell the man who attacked me thirteen years ago. I remember the sound of his voice and the texture of his skin. I am knocked about by the fighting around me but I sway weightlessly like a spectre. Nothing can touch me. I am far away.

The Roman whips his sword in front of me so fast that all I see is a streak of silver light. I don't move to avoid it, I just follow it with my eyes. The tip flashes towards my throat but only catches a lock of my hair. I watch the shorn hair separate and drift away slowly. I am holding a bulbous mace in one hand, propped forgotten against my shoulder, and down by my side in the other hand I have a short slim knife. I turn slowly towards my attacker but in front of me stands Queen Boudica herself, surrounded by flames. She is tall, and so beautiful that my eyes are almost burnt. Her arms are raised, her hair is red as fire, her eyes are glittering green. They fix on me with great love and trust, as my mother's once did – as, indeed, my own eyes did, before all trust was stolen from me – and I think, *My queen is younger than I am*. She leans in, shakes me by the shoulder and speaks my name. The warmth of her touch flows through me like honey. She says, 'Fight. *Fight*. Rise up and fight! You will not survive unless you fight!' The queen's tendrils of fire reach out and cloak me in her regal embrace. They scald me to the ends of my nerves but there is no pain, only power and the thrill of her voice. Her words shock me awake.

When the fire withdraws, I swallow dryly and blink. My flesh is chill where the sweat has cooled. I open my mouth. I am about to speak, to address my queen, but she has disappeared and in her place is the Roman again. He advances, his sword pulled right back, his eyes on my mace, but I do not freeze this time, I slip in and plunge my knife up under his chin, spearing his tongue. He jerks in shock. I pull it out and he staggers, gripping his jaw, his teeth clenched, his eyes wide and watering, blood pooling between his fingers. I smash down my mace and lodge it in his brain.

Now I am wrestling with a man whose hands are around my throat. My vision starts to thicken and fade. I remember my legs and kick him, but I hit armour. His fingers lock together and everything goes black for a moment. He convulses, struck across the back by my friend Tam, his solid woodsman's bulk blocking the sun. Then I am knocked to the side by a blow to the temple. I am crouching on the ground clutching my head when I hear a warning cry and then the dark trundling of wheels. Our own chariots have run inwards to join the fight. They are upon us and the Roman who throttled me is crushed under its wheels.

The chariots careen past, their paired riders planted lightly on the woven platform between the wheels. They rise, dip and bump, standing with ease, balancing and stepping on the central shaft as playfully as acrobats, hammering left and right. I hear a familiar cry and see Cata raging as she stands over the body of her fallen lover, Ecen.

I stagger up again, head pounding, deaf but for a ringing noise, and something strikes me bluntly in the jaw, wrenching it out of place. I crack it back in and grab a fallen soldier's sword half-submerged in the mud. I see a stocky Roman running alongside one of our chariots, his sword steady in both hands. He chops into the back of the charioteer's knees. The charioteer collapses, the reins go slack and the horses divide, running away from each other. The chariot twists over and throws out the injured man. The panicking horses trample the fighters, tribal and Roman alike. We try to scatter but we can't move, we're blocked by our own wagons. My sword is knocked out of my hand and I search for it and find myself face to chest with a silent, swordless Roman in smeared armour. He punches me in the face.

When I come round, I'm lying at the edge of a pile of corpses, but the war is still raging. I see the messenger Saenu slinking down towards Banna's camp, done with fighting, his skinny form nearly naked, marked with weals and bruises. I don't know how much time has passed, but the sun is low and veiled in cloud. The corrupted-meat taste of death is in my throat. Across the valley, bodies lie in bulbous heaps, the flesh grey under blue paint and red blood. My legs are weak, my clothes twisted tight around me, my hair in cracked ropes matted with mud and lime and body matter. My face is too split and swollen to touch. My gashed shoulder and torn thigh throb with pain and the raw flesh surrounding the wounds is inflamed. My head spins, my stomach turns, my vision tilts queasily. I force a sword out of the stiff grip of a dead Roman and run back towards the fight.

Afterword: The Once Friendly Queen

Prof Richard Hingley
University of Durham

THE REVOLT OF BOUDICA in AD 60 or 61 took place around seventeen years after the initial Roman conquest of south-eastern Britain under the emperor Claudius. Claudius's military forces had quickly conquered southern Britain – a territory already divided into a large number of distinct peoples with important centres (or 'oppida') such as Calulodunum (Colchester) and Verulamium (St Albans). These were significant meeting places, religious centres and places where Iron Age kings were buried. There was relatively little unified resistance to the advancing Roman military, although we know that some battles were fought in the early stages of the conquest. As Roman campaigning advanced into Wales during the late AD 40s and 50s, the scale of armed local opposition increased.

The Roman governor, Aulus Plautius, would make peaceful alliances with local leaders in Britain wherever possible and at least one 'friendly kingdom' was set up in AD 43 under a leader called Togidubnus (or Cogidubnus) who ruled the Regni (meaning 'people of the kingdom') in southern Britain, around Chichester. We know from an inscription found in Chichester in West Sussex during the early eighteenth century that Togidubnus was made a Roman citizen by the emperor Claudius. As an older man he may have lived in the very elaborate Roman villa at Fishbourne near to Chichester. Cartimandua, ruler of the Brigantes of central Britain, who features in Bidisha's story, was another ruler friendly to the Romans.

Tacitus tells us that Prasutagus was Boudica's husband and it is probable that he would have been made a 'friendly king' around this time. Prasutagus ruled over a people called the Iceni who lived in present-day northern East Anglia. Togidubnus, Cartimandua and Prasutagus were all pro-Roman rulers who retained power over their lands and peoples in exchange for the payment of taxes and the contribution of men to be trained to serve the Roman army.

By the time of the uprising in AD 60, much of southern and central Britain had already been occupied by the Roman military. The south and east had been pacified and the Roman army had moved on to campaign against the resistant peoples of central Britain and Wales. The emperor Claudius had died in AD 54 and been succeeded by his step son, Nero, who was viewed by many classical authors as a corrupt tyrant.

The events of Boudica's uprising were described by two classical writers who possessed relatively little information about Britain or its inhabitants. Gaius Cornelius Tacitus, who had grown up in southern Gaul (present-day France), wrote about Boudica on two occasions, several decades after her death. Cassius Dio, living in the eastern Roman empire, wrote a contrasting account of the events surrounding Boudica, over a century later. Both these authors conveyed strong views on the roles of women. Although Tacitus made allowances to some extent for Boudica's actions, the idea of female rule was condemned in imperial Rome.

Tacitus and Dio may have had access to some contemporary records of the uprising, but they inevitably projected the views of the dominant Roman culture that had subsumed southern Britain into its empire in the aftermath of Claudius's invasion. These are the only accounts left to us by classical writers when we consider the events of the uprising. Dio and Tacitus both wrote of Boudica's speech to her armed followers prior to her last battle against Rome which they entirely invented to entertain their patrician readers.

Tacitus tells us that the Roman commander Suetonius Paullinus was attacking the island of Anglesey in northwest Wales at the time of Boudica's uprising, remarking that the death of Prasutagus (probably of old age) was the trigger for all that followed. Tacitus tells us that Prasutagus had made the emperor Nero his joint heir along with his own daughters. He thought that this would protect his kingdom and family, although this was to backfire and his kingdom was plundered by Roman officials as if the Iceni had been conquered. Dio tells us that another cause of the uprising was that some loans to British kings were being called in and this may have caused other wealthy individuals to support Boudica's campaign against the Romans. This seems to have been a classic case of inefficient management on the part of the Roman occupying forces. The governor, Paullinus, was away campaigning in Wales and his subordinates behaved in a highly inappropriate way in abusing Boudica and apparently raping the royal daughters of Prasutagus. Boudica subsequently rallied her people who, with the assistance of the Trinovantes, rose against the Roman occupying forces.

Tacitus tells us that the Britons advanced on the 'colonia' (colony) at Camulodunum and burned it to the ground. The oppidum at Colchester had been the main focus for the Roman invasion of AD 43 and the emperor Claudius had received the surrender of a number of British kings there. The Roman military had constructed a legionary fortress at this important Iron Age centre after the invasion and, by AD 60, a Roman colony had become established, populated by the soldiers retired from the four legions stationed in Britain. In addition to destroying Camulodunum, Boudica's forces defeated the Ninth Legion which had been sent to defend the town, a humiliating defeat for the Romans.

The Britons then went on to sack and burn the newly developing town of Londinium (London), a trading settlement of several thousand people, before destroying another town at Verulamium (near St Albans, Hertfordshire).Verulamium was an urban settlement of a pro-Roman community and appears to have been granted the status of a 'municipium', an important Roman town at this time.

Archaeologists have found widespread traces of the destruction of these three towns in the form of a thick layer of burned material from buildings that contains some of the possessions of the people who lived there. Tacitus states that 70,000 Romans and their allies (pro-Roman Britons) died. Although human remains have rarely been found during excavations of the destruction layers of these three towns, this may not have been an exaggeration.

Tacitus describes a final battle between Boudica's followers and the Romans and, despite his detailed description of the topography, the location of the site has yet to be identified. He states that the 10,000 Roman soldiers commanded by Suetonius Paullinus were substantially outnumbered by the combined forces of the Britons. Tacitus writes how Roman order and determination prevailed and that 80,000 Britons died with the death of around 400 Roman soldiers with a number also wounded. The Romans then set out to restore order in their province of Britannia and were to maintain their rule over much of Britain for another three and a half centuries.

Bidisha's story incorporates much of this information in her tale of Boudica, exploring an account of Roman Britain that gives a voice to the oppressed. There has been a long tradition of portraying Boudica as oppressed, relatively powerless, and deeply resistant to Rome.This image of the wronged woman of a colonised people has attracted many poets, novelists and cartoonists to Boudica, even today. By suggesting that Boudica was instinctually anti-Roman, such accounts have ignored the evidence for Boudica's membership of the aristocracy of her people, and also the evidence for Prasutagus's support for the Roman occupation. It appears more likely that, as the wife of a king friendly to the Romans, Boudica was able to read and write in Latin and that she lived in some luxury prior to the events of AD 60. She was evidently pushed into fighting by the outrageous way that the Romans treated her family and people.

The Victorians were rather more enthusiastic about Boudica's supposed royal associations, as the statue 'Boadicea and her Daughters' on Westminster Bridge in London illustrates.[1] Erected in 1902, just after the death of Queen Victoria, this statue served to celebrate British ancestral resistance to foreign domination. Boudica has always provided a problematic example for British nationalists and regionalists. After all, is she an ancestor for people who want to claim English ancestry, or is she more relevant to the Welsh and Cornish (whose ancestry is perhaps less mingled with the blood of Romans, Angles, Saxons, Jutes, Frisians, Vikings Normans and other later peoples that came to settle in Britain)?

The Suffragists of the early twentieth century used the image of Boudica in their campaign for voting rights in the context of the intolerance of the established male elite. The Boudica in Bidisha's tale provides just such a figure of valiant resistance against the imposition of aggressive power. Indeed, we need just such alternative readings of the past to combat the insistent nationalism that allows the myth of Boudica (like the image of the goddess Britannia) to be wrongly appropriated by supporters of such causes as Brexit.

Notes

1. Boadicea was the name formerly given to the historical character that we call Boudica.

Black Showers

SJ Bradley

'Steer, Bartholomew; Bradshaw, James; and Bradshaw, the same's brother.'

Edward Coke stood in the gaol entryway, a near-blue hand protruding from his cloak. Marble fingers too numb to flex, clutched a leather bag.

Rain hammered the cobbles of the inner courtyard of the prison, the same as it did on the cascading streets outside. 'See the gaoler inside,' the guard said. 'He's the man to help you.'

A key the size of a child's hand plunged into a door so sturdy it could have stayed a cannon.

'Gaoler!' he called. 'Here comes Mr Coke, the Attorney General.'

Inner prison walls: bars hammered and clacked, echoes rattling their way through each terrace and corridor of misery.

The wailing inside almost cloaked the sound of the door. Dark settled around Edward Coke as a horde around a gibbet. 'There shall be a charge of treason,' he muttered. He was not yet at the cells: he waited in the gaol entryway.

Voices. Hundreds howling wolflike, donkey-like, a menagerie from human mouths. A thousand animals caged and baying for release.

'Quiet, you dogs!'

Edward looked towards the voice. The gaoler was a broad

man, tall as an apple tree, thick as an oak. A single tallow candle fluttered on his desk. 'They call themselves men,' he said, 'but how can that be, when they roar the same as beasts of the field?'

The gaoler clapped a hand against the bars. Thick hands that could stop a man's breath in his mouth. 'The man you sent ahead has arrived,' he said. 'He's working on the prisoner now.'

Edward followed the gaoler down in the darkness. 'I sent no man ahead,' he said.

The ceiling of the stairwell they climbed down seemed to drip with tar, and the candle from the gaoler's hand revealed little. It was a corridor of pleas they walked through, hands reaching out in an undergrowth of supplication.

'Please, sir –' a woman's arms, red with scabs, skin clinging to bone, 'may you help –'

She looked thin, her eyes weaselly, darting as though looking for an opportunity.

'Back,' snarled the gaoler. 'That one's a thief and a whore. Hands filthy as a privy. Don't let her touch you. Back!'

The corridor's end: stone steps down, twelve below ground, a narrow turn. The chill of interment. 'We kept the three men separate,' the gaoler announced. 'This is the one you want first. Bartholomew Steer.'

There were two men in the room. One in black washing steel implements by the light of two candles, another was hanging against the wall, dripping. Black lines inched down his torso so slowly it was as if the blood were already exhausted from the task of seeping through the skin.

'Sir?' Edward said.

'You arrived late, Mr Coke,' the man at the table said. 'Most of the work is already done.'

Steer hung from hay-thin arms against a wall that was wet as the outside of the prison. There was hardly anything left of him. They were windowless and underground here, the damp seeping in as though the gutters outside were emptying into this very room.

'Who sent you?' Edward said.

Smith opened a bag. The low light glinted on sharp ends. Inside was a hawthorn of implements. 'The crown wanted the truth,' he said, 'and he has bolted forth with the truth today. He has confessed all.' He turned fully, and Edward recognised his type: the slippery confidence of a skilled servant protected by a lord's favour.

Steer moaned on the wall, eyes lolling. 'I burnt no grass, I dried no springs or lakes,' he said. No, there was not much to be done. The man was already more than three-quarters finished. Edward looked at him, skin drooping off bones, eyes deep in the skull. A man could not lose so much of himself from a couple of weeks in gaol, he thought. Possibly he had been whip-thin already at the time the messengers had seized him.

'"There will be a great rising of the people,"' Smith quoted, reading from a paper on his desk, '"to pull down the enclosures. They shall pull the corn out of the rich men's barns, and from there they shall go to Vincent Barry's manor, to spoil him, and cut off his head." That's his confession, and that he incited other men to meet him on Enslow Hill, to pull down the enclosures and rise up against Vincent Barry and other Lords, with violence and threats."'

Edward looked at the gaunt body on the wall. The prisoner's head hung loose, an overripe blackberry left too long on the bramble.

'"Before the year went about, there would be much threshing out of Lords, and cutting of throats,"' Smith continued. 'Those were some more of his words. Will you have me send this confession to your offices, Mr Coke?'

A wheezing sound came from the prisoner, the sound of air being pushed through broken bellows. 'We starve,' he said, 'we starve.'

★

'What news?' Miller had his hands in his pouch. What grain he had was a sorry sight. The ears had been thin and the grain empty, like flecks of dried wood.

January was a thin time at market. Hampton Gay's stalls were a lingering drought, a long message sent from three years of poor harvest.

'This market is not what it was,' Martin Tanner said. Bearded, grey-flecked, his face and hands telling a story of forty years spent in the saddlery. 'There's nothing to buy and nothing to sell, and most of our young men are gone. Taken on for work in London, or the other thing.'

'They say six young men were taken from Hampton Gay, Enslow, and Harrington by Norris and his messengers.' Miller looked around the square. In Midwinter this market was abandoned. The ground was grey-black, and the trees dark and empty as night. Cobbles shone with recent rain. 'They say these young men had meant to rise in Enslow, and tear down the enclosures.'

'Six men?' Tanner almost laughed. 'I heard that only four went to Enslow Hill with the aim of rising. I heard that there weren't enough of them even to open a gate, never mind pull down an enclosure.'

'No young men from our village went.' Miller rocked back on damp boots. 'There aren't enough of them left to go. I tell you there are hardly enough of them left even to come to this market. The march of the enclosures have seen them off. The Lords turn people out of their cottages, and then let them again a few months later at a higher lease, but without the land. That's if they let them again at all. There's nowhere for people to live and no land for them to work. We haven't half the number of ploughs in our village.'

The tanner waved a leather-beaten hand around the square. Its back was pocked with light patches and scars from the instruments he used. 'What they say was a riot,' he said, 'was no riot at all, and let me say this. The Lords keep closing off land for their own pleasure, and the likes of you and me be damned. Not much longer may we tramp in Woodstock Forest, because Henry Lee shortly will enclose it. They say he wants it to graze his sheep – of which he has two thousand.'

The square echoed with the sound of clipping hooves, and the two men fell silent for a minute. A coach and horses rich in livery passed the lane that led from the market to the main road: black horses driven by a coachman in red.

'Two thousand,' Miller said, shaking his head. 'I heard it was closer to three.'

'I wouldn't discount that,' said the tanner. 'What's worse,' he said, 'is they don't toil like the rest of us. Lord Norris didn't earn his own estate. It was inherited from his father.'

'A handful of grain.' A filthy sack of a man approached. 'I beg of you, or a piece of bread, any thing.'

The two men watched as the beggar walked on, hand outstretched. 'Get you gone,' the stallholder said. The beggar paused by them a moment, and then moved on.

'That poor devil,' Tanner said, 'starves more than any of us, and yet don't you wonder how there came to be only four men on Enslow Hill. I wonder there were not more.'

Miller dashed his hands of the corn dust and stared out into the empty square. ''Tis a shame,' he said. 'Yes, 'tis a crying shame. What is to become of Bartholomew Steer?'

★

In the dock at Oxford Special Court sat three men, shivering like wet dogs on a cold day. The courtroom shone with beeswax, its wood glowing.

To one side sat a row of fine men, groomed and polished, in shirts and jackets. Lord Norris and Vincent Barry, who was the Lord of Hampton Gay, and Henry Lee, his sharp blue eyes on the accused.

Edward Coke stood and bowed to the judge. 'Your honour, here are the charged, Burton, Bompass, and Bradshaw. The charge shall be treason.'

'What of this other man I hear of,' the judge said, 'Bartholomew Steer?'

The judge, all puffed and powdered, squinted over the desk.

He wore a velvety cloak. 'Am I to understand that he refused to leave his cell?'

'Dead, your honour,' Edward Coke replied. 'He died in custody.'

'Then read me his confession,' the judge said. 'Such as it may lend to this trial.'

'It says, your honour, that Bartholomew was the one who did incite others to meet on Enslow Hill, from whence they would go to knock down enclosures, and knock down certain people: Mr Frere, Lord Norris, Mr Peers, Mr Vincent Barry, Mr Whitton, Mr Lee, and Mr William Spencer, some of whom are in this room today. From there, they would go to London, where they would join the uprising of the apprentices there.'

'And these three were to join?' the judge swept a glance over the three men. Then, for a moment, he caught the gaze of Vincent Barry. 'Well, there can be little question, it seems to me, as to what the course of this court must be.'

Richard Bradshaw's face sank. The two men beside him, Bompass and Burton, moved their fingers as though knitting a fine scarf. They stared at the ground as though it could hold the method for their escape.

'One man may have incited others,' the judge said, 'but these three still acted of their own will, did they not?'

'That is not a fact in dispute, your honour,' Coke replied.

'Your honour, if I may.' One of the fine men of the jury stood: Vincent Barry, the sun landing on his soft woollen suit. 'Should this outrage not be justly punished, it will give rise to other boldness. Inferior multitudes would gather in large groups to cause chaos and disorder. Gentlemen would be afraid in their own homes.'

Another of the men stood. 'There have been many riots in Kent and Essex, your honour. No doubt you will have heard that there was an uprising in London, where the rabble went to the gaol and broke the prisoners out.'

A murmur amongst the jury.

The judge nodded. 'Your comments are noted, Mr Rathbone.

The charge is treason?'

'It can be nothing else, your honour,' Edward Coke said.

'Is there evidence that these men gathered?' the judge said. 'That their intention was to join with the uprising?'

Again, Edward Coke nodded. 'Yes, these men joined with the group that met on Enslow Hill.'

The judge shook his head. 'This court will maintain order, in of itself, and in respect to these men. We cannot allow threats and a gathering of multitudes by the lower sort. They are guilty and they shall be sentenced. What have you to say for yourselves?'

Bradshaw stood, sleeves filthy, his hair matted with oil. Had he lived a month in a ditch he could not have gathered more dirt. 'Your honour, sir, I beg for mercy. Ours was a small gathering, of four men only, and look at our weight now. Bompass here, after three years of poor harvest, he couldn't lift an ax. Look at my arms, sir. I was once a miller, a job needing strength, and now look.' He showed an arm with nothing to it, a peapod slug-eaten from the inside. 'Every day I ground corn and none of it was mine to eat. I was the finest miller you could have known. I watched the grain slide through those stones and come out fine, the best milling you have ever seen, and I handed that flour to a rich man who has never known hunger and never will, a man who has enclosed the common land that was once used by men like me, to use it for himself, to graze sheep or make a park for his own pleasure. Sir, I was a good worker, I worked hard, but no amount of work could save my family from three bad harvests in succession. I went hungry, as did my wife, as did my children, and many others like us. Your honour, we have had a thin time –'

'That's enough,' said the judge. 'You may not give this court the excuse that you were hungry. Many others were hungry and did not go to Enslow Hill, so what do you say to that?' He went on: 'The sentence shall be that the prisoners shall be hung, drawn and quartered. No other punishment for this crime.'

The fine men of the jury sighed in unison, their shoulders releasing a half-inch or so.

The judge struck the desk. The sound of the gavel echoed around the room. 'Take them down.'

The grass around Enslow Hill was more crowded than the Mop Fair. Miller and Tanner joined them, two amongst a crowd of a hundred. 'What news?' Tanner asked.

'The crows will have a good feed at least.' Miller, an old man of forty four, glanced across the shining sky. Pupils the size of poppy seeds, and just as black.

It was an early summers' day. Fine, the sky cornflower blue stretching over the low rolling hills. The grass was pale with drought. On the hill, the hangman's gibbet towered like a burnt-out cottage.

'I'm glad now that I didn't go,' Tanner said.

Two men were stretched out on that dread stage, Bradshaw and Burton. Wooden platforms had been brought and hammered together on the hill for the purposes of the execution. The crowd stood gathered around it, stretching back almost into the surrounding forest.

It had already started. Both men were being quartered by the hangman, working away at their insides with a long saw. Bradshaw screamed, his belly splashing blood into the air.

'Go where?'

'I would not have gone anywhere,' Tanner said. 'At least I wouldn't have come here to this hill that night even had I known about it.'

'You would have been a fool to,' Miller answered, 'and what's more, should you have planned to go to it, you would be a fool to tell anyone afterwards.'

An old woman passed through the crowd, carrying a basket of berries. 'Fine fruit, sirs,' she said. 'Ha'penny a bag?'

A groan ran through the crowd. The hangman had moved across the platform, to the other prisoner. Sweating, wearing a mask, his arms tanned with the sun. Above the gibbet, black birds cawed and circled in the trees. Everybody now could see the insides of both men, breaking through carved splits in their bellies. The man on the left writhed as though he thought he could save himself.

'Miss, we've a penny,' said a girl's voice. The old woman moved towards her, lowering her basket.

Tanner waited until she had gone, then said: 'They're saying Mr Steer told everything. The plan, the men, who else was there, everything.'

'Do they say so?' Miller glanced over at the gibbet.

'They say those were his last words. They were wrote down and brought to the court. A man called Mr Coke took note of them. There was not one part kept secret, and now,' the tanner went on, 'the Government has banned plays, to stop the gathering of people. You cannot see a play in London, nor at the Spring Fair, nor anywhere else.'

'Well then how are we to know anything?' Miller said. A scream broke from the stage, such as one might hear from a man fallen beneath a plough. Both convicted men were being dragged upright, and moved towards the gibbet. Their eyes were blank, unseeing. 'Or be entertained, either?'

One of the men fell, guts spilling out of him. The hangman kicked him and dragged him to his feet. His arms pulsed and strained with the effort of dragging dead weight.

Tanner shrugged. 'Another thing they say is that grain will become cheaper now. There will be more of it. It will be brought in without taxes.'

'Who said that?' Miller shook his red-furred head. 'I do not believe it.'

'A coachman who works for Lord Frere heard it. It was discussed at breaks in the journey, when they went from here to London. He overheard the Lords talking, and has been repeating it to everybody.'

'Oh!'

Cries broke out in the crowd as bodies were hoisted to the gibbet. Bradshaw's head lolled loose. A chatter started in one place, then another. 'Knock down the enclosures,' they said. 'Knock them down. Knock them down. Knock them down.'

'Here's another thing they say,' Tanner said. 'The law is to change. A man called Francis Bacon is after changing it. It will say that the Lords will no longer be able to enclose the towns and villages, nor let a cottage without land.'

'Knock them down,' the crowd muttered. 'Knock them down. Knock them down.'

'That law will never come in,' Miller said. 'No Lord will let it.'

Bradshaw and Bompass were moved from one place to another. They wobbled and fell, spilling on the stage. The hangman pulled them to the gibbet as though they were two sacks of flour.

'This Francis Bacon says it will,' Tanner insisted, 'and Lord Frere cannot do a thing about it. The coachman told me he awakes cursing Mr Bacon's name in the morning, and continues it into evening time. They all meet to try and stop it. William Frere, Henry Lee, George Whitton, Vincent Barry, Henry Morris, William Spencer.'

'Knock them down,' the crowd chanted. 'Knock them down. Knock them down.'

'Maybe on this day in one year,' Tanner said, 'we will gather on this hill to see William Frere and George Whitton on the gibbet.'

His words were lost in the murmur of the crowd.

*

'I am come to see William Frere,' Edward Coke said.

The manor house in Water Eaton was broader-fronted than three coaches standing together. It had mullioned windows and a thick wooden door.

'Mr Frere is not home, sir,' the porter said. He was ruddy-faced and wore a black jacket: 'but if you say your name, I can tell him who called.'

Edward Coke said: 'He knows I am here. Go inside, and tell him it is better for him to come and see me.'

'I'm very sorry, sir,' the servant said, and he spoke with

genuine regret, as though breaking bad news, 'but Mr Frere was called away on important business this morning.'

Edward ran a hand over his bag. Almost square, soft leather, a document bag stuffed with folded paper and maps. Sketches of how the town of Water Eaton had once been, and how it was now. How much of the town had been closed in, stopping roads, and fencing away land that had once belonged to the cottages. 'I have come a long way,' he said.

He was already closing the door. Two inches of his face framed between door and jamb. 'I am so sorry, sir,' he said. 'As I said, Mr Frere was called away.'

★

The Attorney General's office was all hard wood and soft sunlight. Edward Coke stood by the window, and at the table sat his secretary, a young man with pen in hand.

'This letter is to go with writ, Jeremiah,' Edward said. 'For the Sheriff. Write it as follows: M'most worthy sirs, the Queen has set forth a law to stopd the level of enclosure, where enclosure meant highwayes are stopd, or villages and houses destroyed and dispeopled, or tillage greatly decayed. In parts of North Oxfordshire various villages and houses are indeed destroyed and tillage greatly decayed contrary to these new Acts, the Maintenance of Husbandry and Tillage and the act Against the Decaying of Towns and Houses of Husbandry.

'I have gathered evidence to prosecute various Enclosers who have greatly decayed tillage in these villages. Their names include Francis Power and William Frere and five others. See the writ also sent with this letter.

'The evidence is henceforth: various maps shewing the extent of enclosure, and accounts shewing dispeopling of said villages. It can be shown that each of these above named have broken these two laws. I do entreat you to table the prosecution at earliest moment, and fail this not at your peril.'

It was a whitish-grey morning, clouds the colour of slush. What light there was came shyly into the room.

'Tis ready for signing, sir,' the boy said. 'Shall I call the errand lad to run it?'

Around the room, on the desks and chairs, were Edward Coke's bags. The square leather document bag, containing papers and maps. A stuffed leather bag, like something a doctor might carry, a bag that had seen the inside of a dozen prisons in London alone.

'Yes, Jeremiah,' Edward said, he sitting down at the table to sign and seal the letter. 'O arrogance exceeding all belief!' he murmured. 'That under brightest smiles hideth black showers.'[1]

'Do you require a carriage, sir,' Jeremiah asked, 'to take you to a gaol or anywhere else?'

'Not this morning,' Coke said. His eyes rested first on one bag, then the other. 'How things change, Jeremiah.'

'Pardon, sir?' The boy stood uncertainly by the door, the letter in his hand. The weak sunlight landed across him.

'You'll hardly remember, boy. You would still have been playing whip-top. Not long ago, I prosecuted six men who wanted to knock enclosures down in the villages around North Oxford. I did indeed prosecute them with treason, and they received the highest sentence for that crime.'

The boy had grown up in London, and had never seen Oxford. All the same, his work had brought him into contact with tales from the law. Stories of statute from court cases recent and long gone. He nodded. 'Yes, sir,' he said.

'Some years on, and the law has changed, and I shall use that new law to prosecute those Lords and men who built the enclosures the first set of men wished to knock down.'

'Yes, sir,' the boy said, again.

Often times Mr Coke and other men of the court talked to him this way. It was a kind of conversation that required little in the way of an answer, he had discovered. All they wanted was to say their thoughts aloud, as if they were speaking to a coat stand or a livery peg in the stables, or any other object that could not repeat their words elsewhere.

'Well then,' Edward Coke said.

Now the Attorney General came to, shaking himself, his eye resting on Jeremiah true and alive, as though seeing him for the first time. 'This is a matter of grave importance. Why do you wait?'

Note

1. Lines from the play *Summer's Last Will and Testament* by Thomas Nashe, from *Thomas Nashe: Selected Works* (Routledge Revivals), edited by Stanley Wells (Routledge, 2015), p107.

THE OXFORDSHIRE RISING, 1596

Afterword: Enslow Hill

Prof John Walter

University of Essex

In 1596 ENGLAND WAS facing a third consecutive year of harvest failure. On the eve of the harvest a correspondent confided to Burghley, Elizabeth I's leading minister, 'I greatly fear that this year will be the hardest year for the poor people, that hath happened in any man's memory.'[1] Reports of outbreaks of disorder seemed to give substance to these fears. Food rioters in Somerset were reported to have sworn, 'that they were as good be slain in the market place as starve in their own houses'.[2] Such episodes hinted at the darker nightmare of rebellion by the people, 'the many-headed monster'. This was the fear that gnawed at government and gentry in 1596.

England in the 1590s faced a series of challenges that has led historians to label the decade 'the crisis of the 1590s'. Economically, renewed and rapid population growth had seen both rising inflation, especially in the price of food, and a significant growth in landlessness, land-poverty and unemployment. Socially, the consequences were divisive. While economic change brought a significant increase in the numbers of the landless poor, those with land and capital benefitted from the same forces. By the late sixteenth century, perhaps some 40% of the population depended to a greater or lesser extent on the market for food and work. When the harvest – the 'heartbeat' of a pre-industrialised economy – failed, as it did regularly, both prices and unemployment increased sharply. Without any form of organised social security, tensions rose in a society where subsistence crises and regional famine threatened the lives of the poor and harvest-sensitive.

In a society that lacked an effective bureaucracy and therefore hard economic or population data, the causes of the growth of poverty were poorly understood. Both government and people adopted traditional explanations for inflation and landlessness within what E.P. Thompson has called the 'moral economy'. Poverty, this held, was a direct consequence of the moral failings of individuals (though this might come to encompass a class) who sought to manipulate markets by hoarding and to appropriate land through enclosure, hedging in land and turning arable land to pasture.

Enclosure and dearth were the immediate context for the attempted rising in Oxfordshire. Enclosure, highly visible in the countryside, exacerbated the problems of landlessness for a growing population. The rural poor found themselves in the midst of a crisis for which enclosure was a shared explanation of both government and people. In Oxfordshire, the poor had considerable local experience of enclosure, and their mental map of it was coloured by recent examples, pushed through by unpopular landowners little concerned with popular expectations of the relationship supposed to exist between (the good) landlord and (the dutiful) tenant, and too willing to sacrifice men for sheep. Beyond the world of experience lay the world of rumour. Both government and people thought enclosure to be gathering pace. Like their betters in a statistically innocent age, the poor found it difficult to distinguish rumour from reality. That 'sheep and sheep-masters doeth cause scarcity of corn' was proverbial knowledge. This was echoed by those caught up in the Oxfordshire rising among whom it was reportedly often said: 'Corn would not be better Cheap until some of the hedges were thrown down.'[3]

★

In 1598, the vicar of a small Oxfordshire parish confided to his parish register, 'that in the years of our Lord God 1597 and 1596 wheat was sold for 11s, barley for 7s, and beans for 6s 8d. This was a sorrowful time for the poor of the land. God grant that such a dearth and famine may never be seen again'.[4] Fear of famine was at the centre of the poor's consciousness in what one termed 'this hard year'. Examined after the attempted rising, one man told his inquisitors, that 'commonly as ... [he] went to Markets, he heard poor people say, that they were ready to famish for want of corn, and that they thought they should be enforced for hunger to take it out of men's houses.' Another recounted meeting a man on the road and, on being informed that grain was selling at famine prices in the region's market, posed the question central to the poor's fate in 1596: 'then what shall poor men do?' 'Rather then they would be starved, they would rise', came back the reply. Dearth was the immediate cause of the rising.[5]

The earliest evidence of the rising to throw down enclosures comes as the dregs of the disappointing harvest were being gathered in. The idea seems to have been first canvassed at a meeting of what were to become two of the main propagandists, James Bradshaw, a miller, and Bartholomew Steer, a carpenter, in the summer of 1596. According to Bradshaw, it was Steer who first moved the idea of a rising and offered to be its leader. By mid-November his plans had matured. The emphasis was now on cutting down gentlemen rather than their hedges. Steer detailed the bloody route they should take among the local enclosing landlords:

> after their rising they would go to Mr Power's, and knock at the gate, and keep him fast that opened the door, and suddenly thrust in, And... he with his falchion [sword] would cut of[f] their heads... And then they would go to Mr Berries and spoil him and cut of[f] his head, and his

daughters' heads, And from thence they would have gone to Rabon's house a yeoman & spoiled him likewise, and from thence to Mr George Whitton and spoil him, And then to Sir Henry Lea and spoil him likewise, and then to Sir William Spencer & spoil him, And so to Mr Frere, and so to my Lord Norris'.[6]

There they would find armour for a hundred men, horse and artillery. Thus armed, they were to go 'with all speed towards London', where they knew discontent was rife among the apprentices, angry at the savage punishment of some of their number in protests over dearth in the previous year.

A less obvious but just as important reason for the potential discontents of this group was their age and status. Most, like Steer, were young and unmarried. This is not perhaps surprising. The early modern agrarian crowd was often a youthful crowd, reflecting the tactical freedom from ties of dependent family and confirming contemporary fears of the licence of liminal youth. But where it is possible to recover the precise age of individuals involved in 1596, this argument can be taken a stage further. They were angry, but ageing young men. In their twenties, they stood on the threshold of social adulthood, but their lack of land, low status and enforced unmarried state left them in limbo. Then, as now, it was the young who were among those hardest hit by economic crisis. For a group with such experiences and disappointed expectations, enclosure offered a potent symbol for their frustrations. Their failure to gain or retain a toehold on the land and their increasing dependence on an uncertain market for food and employment could all be attributed to enclosure, of which they had local, recent and vivid experience.

Steer was young, but he was a good student of the tradition of early modern disorder. Lacking the authority of age, wealth or office, he drew on rumour, myth and magic to promote the rising, among other promises telling of 'a mason that could make balls of wild fire... which he would fire houses as occasion should serve'.[7] He also drew on a plebeian tradition of riot – local, national and even international – to beat down a fatalistic acceptance of the status quo among his audience. Enslow Hill itself was chosen as the place from which to launch the rising because it had been the site of an earlier rising. Interwoven with specific allusions to past riots were rumours of popular successes. 'The poor did once rise in Spain and cut down the gentlemen and since that time they have lived merrily there', Steer claimed.[8] To the poor, he preached the politics of Cockayne.[9] Meeting a fellow carpenter, he asked, 'how he did this hard year'? When told 'that he wrought hard to find his wife and children, having seven sons, bread and water, and scarcely could doe that', Steer replied, 'Work? Care not for work, for we shall have a merrier world shortly… I will work one day and play another.'[10]

At local fairs and markets, Steer and his companions sought to recruit those 'that would rise & knock down the gentlemen & rich men that take in the commons, and made corn so dear'. But he was still scrabbling to gather support on the eve of the rising. (The shift in Steer's plans from an attack on enclosures to the assassination of enclosers may have lost him support since it ran against the grain of a tradition of protest in early modern England in which violence – if not threats – was usually directed against property and not persons.) Disappointed of promised support, Steer angrily declaimed what was to become his own epitaph: 'If all men were of [that] mind they might live like slaves… But for himself happ what would, for he could die but once… he would not always live like a slave'; 'if there were but three more which did go, he would be one of them'. His words were sadly prophetic. Accompanied by a handful of others, Steer waited several hours at Enslow Hill before disbanding.

But informed against, the conspirators began to be rounded up. Frightened, the government ordered the ringleaders to be brought to London under strong guard and the personal supervision of the sheriff, 'their hands pinioned and their legs bound under the horse['s] bellies and so looked unto as they may not have conference one with the other in the way hither'. Lodged in separate prisons, their examination was entrusted to a small but powerful committee, headed by the attorney-general Sir Edward Coke, which was empowered to employ torture – 'for the better bolting forth of the truth'.[11] Coke took the threat posed by the rising very seriously and he seems to have prosecuted the conspirators with the rigour which earned him comment in later and less obscure trials. He recommended that the rising be prosecuted as treason for compassing to levy war against the queen. Coke's constructive use of the law of treason to prosecute the conspirators as rebels, which caused anxiety even for some of the judges, is striking testimony of the alarm with which the government greeted their discovery. Three leaders were subsequently indicted at the Oxfordshire assizes on 24 February before a jury of local gentlemen whose deliberations were doubtless made easier by the inclusion of some of the rising's intended victims on the panel. The surprising absence of Steer and James Bradshaw suggests they were already dead, victims of their interrogation or the short life expectancy of the incarcerated.

Of those tried, Richard Bradshaw and Robert Burton were condemned to the barbaric sentence of being hung, drawn and quartered. By an irony that must have afforded considerable satisfaction to the local gentry, they were executed at Enslow Hill within sight of the enclosures that had led them to that fate. Their miserable end was doubtless made to serve as a macabre example of the fate accorded those who had the temerity to challenge the landed classes' hegemony by a justice, which numbered among its servants as jurymen named victims of the proposed rising.

Neither obelisk nor blue plaque marks such humble executions. But the rising won for itself a more positive memorial. Reprisal was not, nor could it be, the only response of the government that lacked either a standing army or professional police force. With limited forces of repression, early modern governments needed to be attentive to the complaints of even their poorest subjects, especially in years of crisis. While the government took measures to preserve public order, it also publicly renewed measures to combat scarcity. In the crisis of the 1590s, the threat uncovered by the rising nudged the government into a more general inquiry into enclosure. This led to the prosecution of leading enclosers by Attorney General Coke in the Star Chamber – at their head two of the intended victims of the rising.

Steer's dreams were the landed classes' nightmares made flesh. His spectre went on to haunt the parliament of 1597. The attempted rising served warning that the economic returns of unregulated enclosure might be over-shadowed by its social and political costs. It was perhaps more than coincidence that those who zealously tortured and prosecuted the conspirators were to become the leading protagonists and promoters of the famous anti-enclosure legislation passed in the 1597 parliament. Though the weight to be attributed to the rising – one of a number of factors impelling the government to take action – must remain conjectural, as an encapsulation of a latent threat, known in detail to key individuals in government and parliament, it probably played a role out of all proportion to its scale. If so, Bradshaw and Burton (and the others) won for themselves a very different memorial.

The Oxfordshire rising, though stillborn, had (and has) important consequences for the history of early modern England and for how historians interpret that history. An administrative drive to curb enclosures and police the grain market and renewed legislation against enclosure (part of a remarkable bundle of bills proposed or passed in the 1597 parliament to deal with popular grievances) all followed, some directly, from discovery of the rising. The response Steer's plans invoked from government provides valuable evidence about the fragile relationship between rulers and ruled and the obligation this forced on the government to enter into a dialogue with the people. The subordination of the poor within the 'dialectics of deference', while born of growing dependence, had to be actively maintained. Early modern elites knew better than to believe that the seeming passivity of the rural poor meant an absence of tensions or discontent. The poor had to be continually won over. The Oxfordshire Rising was then more than just a story of might-have-beens. It had important consequences, not least for how we write our history.

★

'Riot' and 'rebellion' provide a privileged point of access to popular politics, providing as they do a moment when the opaque surface of the past is punctured, allowing subordinate groups, rendered otherwise silent by inequalities in power, literacy, access to print and to the preserved record, to testify to their attitudes and beliefs. In the case of the Oxfordshire Rising, the government's pursuit and prosecution of the conspirators provides valuable evidence from opposite ends of the political and social spectrum of contemporaries' perception of the crisis. In particular, the detailed interrogations make it possible to examine how the poor perceived, interpreted and sought to respond to change in their society. In the 1980s, and writing both in the developing school of what has come to called micro-history and what was then hailed as the revival of the narrative, I tried to use these records to tell a story that restored agency and identity to Bartholomew Steer and his companions.[12]

Following my original article, Batholomew Steer and his companions have since enjoyed an intriguing afterlife. Steer's biography now appears in the august *Dictionary of National Biography*, and the Oxfordshire Rising has provided the subject of an interval talk on Radio 3 and an intellectual inspiration in the work of the renowned artist and film-maker Patrick Keiller.[13] Now comes SJ Bradley's short story. When I wrote my account of the rising, I did so within the discipline and constraints of an academic article, history grounded in the archive and surviving empirical record. I did so in part to correct previous passing references to the Rising which wrongly spoke of hundreds being involved, estimates owing more to the exaggerated fears of a frightened government, and to explain why the rising failed to mobilise the rural poor. SJ Bradley's vivid retelling of the story, grounded also in the historical record through our conversations, offers a powerful reminder that in the historical past it was authority (often an avenging, and censoring one) that gave the poor their voice. Her story-telling emphasises the challenges and the threats of savage reprisal that help to immobilise an otherwise angry poor. Where the historical record fails to record the emotional timbre of the story (though their anger comes through clearly in the examinations of the would-be rebels), the fiction writer's imagination can remind us of their fear — and of their bravery.

Notes

1. British. Lib., Lansdowne MS. 81, fo. 152v.

2. British. Lib., Lansdowne MS. 83, fo. 49.

3. *Certaine Causes Gathered Together, Wherein is Shewed the Decaye of England,* in *Four Supplications, 1529-1553 A.D.,* ed. J. Furnivall and J. Meadows Cowper (Early Eng. Text Soc., extra ser., xiii, London, 1871), pp. 93-102.

4. Bodleian Lib., Oxford, MSS. D. D. Par. Wendlebury d. 1, fo. 43.

5. TNA, SP 12/261/10.ii (exam. Rog. Ibill); 12/262/4 (exam. Rog. Symonds); 12/261/l5.iv (exam. Rich. Heath).

6. TNA, SP 12/262/4 (exam. Rog. Symonds).

7. TNA, SP 12/261/10.ii; 12/262/4 (exams. Rog. Symonds and Barth. Steer). On the importance of fire in the popular *mentalité,* see Keith Thomas, *Religion and the Decline of Magic: Studies in Popular Beliefs in Sixteenth and Seventeenth Century England* (Harmondsworth, 1973), pp. 17-20.

8. Steer's reference here to the largest sixteenth-century Spanish rising, the Revolt of the Comuneros (1521) or later smaller revolt, offers an

important reminder that the poor were not cut off from the circulation of news and ideas in early modern Europe.

9. Cockayne was an imaginary place in medieval myth of ease and excess (especially of food) whose pleasures contrasted with the harsh realities of the poor's life: Piero Camporesi, *Bread of Dreams: Food and Fantasy in Early Modern Europe* (Oxford, 1989).

10. TNA, S.P. 12/262/4 (exam. Rog. Symonds).

11. Acts of the Privy Council, 1596-7, pp. 373-4.

12. John Walter, 'A rising of the people'? The Oxfordshire rising of 1596', *Past and Present*, 107 (1985), 90–143, reprinted in Walter, *Crowds and Popular Politics in Early Modern England* (Manchester, 2006), 73–123.

13. John Walter, 'Steer, Bartholomew (bap. 1568, d. 1597?), *Oxford Dictionary of National Biography* (2004); 'The Tudor World', BBC Radio 3; Patrick Keiller, *The Possibility of Life's Survival on the Planet* (Tate Publishing, 2012); *Robinson in Ruins* (UK, 2010; DVD British Film Institute, 2011).

The Cap of Liberty

Martin Edwards

'IT WAS MURDER.'

The old man was mumbling. The young woman bending over his rough bed could barely make out his words.

Even on a September afternoon, the cellar room was gloomy and smelled of damp. The solitary window was broken. Someone had mended it with a large oilskin, blotting out most of the light from the city street above. A candle, unsteady on the top of an old tin trunk in the corner, cast a flickering yellow glow.

'Hush, Mr Kidd, don't upset yourself.'

A kindly concern widened Elizabeth's blue-grey eyes. She was the wife of a minister at Cross Street Chapel, and sympathy came naturally to her; this was as well, since in hard times, plenty of Manchester folk were in need of a sympathetic ear. She glanced up at the man's daughter as he fell back on the pillow, exhausted.

'Your father's feverish,' she murmured. Old Jeremiah's eyes were shut again, his breathing uneven and discordant. 'He doesn't know what he's saying.'

Agnes Cheetham was a skinny, anxious woman of 35. Once upon a time, she must have been pretty, with those high cheekbones and delicate features, but the cares of life had stooped her shoulders. Her brow was wrinkled, her complexion sallow. She might have passed for fifty or more.

'He keeps muttering. As if he's having the same nightmare over and over again.'

'The fever is talking,' Elizabeth said. 'The mind is strange, it roams everywhere. Please don't worry yourself.'

'But I do worry,' Agnes said. 'He seems terrified.'

★

That evening, with the children asleep, at least for the moment, Elizabeth sewed at the circular mahogany table until her husband emerged from his study to join her. As was their custom, they told each other about their day.

Elizabeth had been brought up in a peaceful Cheshire market town, and on moving with her husband to Dover Street on the edge of the city, she had been determined to countrify their home. A watercolour of the Llanberis Pass hung on the wall, a reminder of pleasant days travelling through north Wales. The house was kept warm and fragrant. She prided herself on choosing flowers that could survive the smoke from Manchester's factories, or at least those that remained open during this time of economic depression. This city was called the chimney of the world, but even the smoke swirled uncertainly these days. White roses bloomed in the decorated Rockingham garniture on the mantelpiece. The scent of scarlet honeysuckle drifted in through the open window from the tiny, well-kept garden. It was hard to conceive that the damp cellar lurked barely a mile from where the couple sat.

Elizabeth told William about the old man. 'Life has brought him low. Agnes told me that he was a tallow chandler. But he's not enjoyed good fortune for many a year. His late wife was an invalid for years, and when he became consumptive his business failed.'

William nodded. A tall, angular man, not yet forty, he had a shock of hair that was already turning grey. He liked to say that it was because his playful young wife led him such a dance.

'I recall meeting Jeremiah Kidd, a long time ago.' William had a good voice for a preacher, rich and sonorous. 'Kidd struck me as a decent fellow, but kept himself to himself. Certainly he was respectable. I believe he was once a Special Constable.'

'Really?' Even Elizabeth's restless imagination struggled to picture that frail old fellow as a guardian of law and order. 'Not that Special Constables have always behaved respectably.'

'He was present at Peterloo. I gather that the massacre so sickened him that he resigned his post.'

'As it sickened every decent person.'

'His grief was personal.' William considered. 'If I recall correctly, a friend of his was killed. Someone told me that Jeremiah was never the same man again.'

'I can understand,' she said. 'So many human tragedies – and for what? We keep listening to fine speeches about the lessons learned. Yet here we are, twenty years on, and how much has changed?'

William frowned. 'Oh, I don't know. Look at the progress we have made. Your relief work, the Domestic Home Mission...'

'Oh yes, it's all well and good, and you and I do whatever we can. But the larger question remains.' She sighed. 'The Chartists and the Leaguers are at each other's throats. For all the high hopes of our young Queen, are things so different from when the Prince Regent ruled the roost? So many folk walk a tightrope between work and want. But now...'

'Work is hard to come by?' he suggested.

'Exactly. No wonder voices are raised in protest. One family of twelve I visited this afternoon lives on nothing but oatmeal, water and milk. Another has sold every stick of furniture in order to buy food. Agnes Kidd and her husband have five children under ten, all crammed into a ruin of a cottage. As well as a sick grandfather in a cellar so musty that it will be a miracle if he survives another week.'

★

The following afternoon, Elizabeth returned to the cellar on Meal Street. Agnes said that her father had been delirious

61

during the night. She'd sat with him for hours, and then had to cope with a querulous, teething baby and a five-year-old who had gashed his knee. Her shoulders were slumped, her eyelids drooping. She was so exhausted that she could hardly speak.

'Let me sit with him while you get a little rest,' Elizabeth said. 'No argument, please. Shoo!'

Once she and the old man were alone, she listened to him snoring for a little while before he began to come round. When he forced his eyes open, she reminded him who she was. The minister's wife, here to keep him company.

'Murder,' he said. 'You've come about the murder.'

'I don't know about the murder,' she said softly. 'You'll have to tell me.'

For a long time, Jeremiah Kidd was silent. To Elizabeth, it seemed as if he were gathering his strength. Eventually, he said, 'Peterloo.'

'It was a dreadful business, wasn't it?' she said. 'So many innocent people caught up in the violence. So many wounded, so many killed.'

'Innocent,' he repeated.

A questioning look came into his bloodshot eyes. Of course, she thought, he was a Special Constable. He must have played a part in putting down the riot. Did he feel a sense of shame, exacerbated by the loss of someone he cared for?

'It was twenty years ago.' She patted his hand. 'We need to get you better. Don't think about it.

*

Yes, it was a long time ago, he thought drowsily. A long, long time.

In those days, he was a different man. Forty-seven years old, with a wife and daughter and his own small candle-making workshop in a courtyard off Piccadilly. His wasn't an easy trade, and he could never escape the stench of sheep fat. Three of their children had died in infancy, but even so, the Kidd family was better off than many in Manchester. The city hadn't prospered since the defeat of the French. Winning the war was all well and good, but the government seemed incapable of making the best of the peace.

Lancashire's spinners and weavers suffered more than most. With wages cut to next to nothing, it was all they could do to put bread on the table. The cotton workers had gathered in St Peter's Fields, determined to seek reform. They intended to march to London, carrying woollen blankets to sleep under. But their protest had alarmed the authorities, and when they reached Stockport, the Riot Act was read. One man died, and only a few dozen Blanketeers made it as far as Derbyshire.

Their outrage was easy for Jeremiah to comprehend. In their shoes – or under their blankets – he would have wanted to march. The danger was that protesters were easy prey for folk bent on sedition. The Ardwick Bridge conspiracy confirmed his worst fears. The plotters planned to burn down mills; or so it was said. He had little patience with the millocracy, those hard-nosed businessmen who earned fortunes while the workers who made them rich got poorer year after year. But he dreaded the prospect of revolution. In France it had brought twenty long years of death and destruction until Boney received his final, humiliating come-uppance on the fields of Waterloo.

Lately, Jeremiah had begun drinking at The Thatched Tavern. He'd become friendly with Caleb Stiles, the landlord, after their daughters got to know each other. The inn's name, redolent of rural England, was a misnomer; its roof was made of slate, and it was tucked away down a dingy alleyway in the city's most disreputable corner. Most of the customers were raucous veterans of Waterloo. Stout, jovial Caleb was the life and soul of any party, and Jeremiah enjoyed his company.

Caleb was a forthright fellow with strong opinions which he was never afraid to air. The radicals only cared about whipping up anger. As a husband and father, he could not stand by and see the country brought to its knees by so-called reformers. They were nothing better than ragamuffins, flaunting their ridiculous red caps. Decent people needed to stand up for what they believed in. That was why he'd become a Special Constable.

'You should do the same as me,' he insisted to Jeremiah. 'Don't just stand by. Nobody should mither about the threat to hearth and home if they aren't willing to take their turn to protect property and the public. Think about your family. Peggy, and that lovely daughter of yours. Don't you owe it to them?'

Caleb was persuasive. What he said made sense. If there were to be a better tomorrow for Agnes and others of her age, England must not go the way of France. It must be saved from the threat of destruction. Jeremiah became a constable for the St Peter's district. If trouble flared in Manchester, he was ready to do his duty and stand up for law and order.

He prayed that it would not be necessary. His friend saw things differently. Caleb hated the radicals. He was spoiling for a fight.

★

'Caleb.'

'What was that, Mr Kidd?'

Elizabeth had drifted into a reverie. She liked to write little sketches about people, and she'd published items of verse and prose in collaboration with her husband, an accomplished poet himself. In her dreams, she pictured herself publishing a story that was entirely her own work. At present, she was content to make up tales in her head, simply to amuse herself.

'Caleb,' he said again. 'Caleb Stiles.'

'What about him?' she asked. 'I'm afraid I don't know the name.'

'Caleb,' he murmured. 'Murder.'

★

'Caleb Stiles?' William thought for a moment. 'Yes, my dear, I recall the name.'

'Who is he?' Elizabeth asked.

'I heard about him when I arrived in Manchester. He was one of those who died at Peterloo.'

'Ah.' So Jeremiah's maunderings about murder possessed some meaning, even if only to him. 'What happened to Stiles?'

'He was an innkeeper who became a Special Constable. Like poor old Kidd.'

'And he was the friend of Kidd's, the man who died?'

William Gaskell gave a brisk nod. 'And now, my dear, if you will forgive me, I really must finish writing this sermon before I go to bed.'

★

The two families, the Kidds and the Stiles, spent an increasing amount of time in each other's company. Madge Stiles, as outgoing and gregarious as her husband, always made Jeremiah's wife Peggy and their daughter welcome at the inn. Peggy helped out in the bar, and Madge insisted on paying her for her efforts. Every penny helped, she said, and she never wanted to presume on the kindness of others.

Madge's girl, Cissie, had taken Agnes, who was twelve months younger, under her wing. A crowd of young women was always to be found at the Thatch, and Agnes, a quiet and naturally solitary lass, had the chance of being with pals of her own age. Jeremiah only wished his daughter could be a little more cheerful. If anything, she'd withdrawn even more into herself. But what could a father do?

Thanks to the hospitality of the Stiles clan, Peggy and Agnes were never left on their own, and that was something to be thankful for. Jeremiah was increasingly preoccupied, and although he tried not to alarm Peggy by confiding his worries about money, he was sure she'd guessed something of their difficulties. Business was becoming brutally competitive. Pressure on prices meant that he was earning less, and needing to work longer in a desperate attempt to make up the difference. Things weren't quite as bad for chandlers as they were for weavers, slaving sixteen hours a day for a wage of ten shillings a week, but that was small consolation. At least being a Special Constable did not take up much time, but he was beginning to fear that he'd be pressed into active service if the radicals continued to foment discord.

Henry Hunt, the orator, was due to return to Manchester to address a demonstration calling for parliamentary reform. Caleb regarded him as a rabble rouser, and was convinced that his supporters were plotting insurrection. He told Jeremiah that he'd heard the magistrates possessed secret information about the agitators' plans.

'There will be trouble,' he predicted. 'You mark my words.'

For once Jeremiah argued with his friend. 'Reason will prevail.'

This was his belief. In the end, rational thought was what separated man from the beasts.

'You're fooling yourself.'

'Hunt has sworn that he and his friends are men of peace.' Jeremiah was determined to hope for the best. 'He's instructed his disciples not to bring weapons.'

'He's pulling the wool over your eyes,' Caleb jeered. 'Don't be fooled by his soapy sentiments. Hunt is a traitor.'

'You think that we will be called upon to keep the peace?'

'It's a racing certainty.' Caleb laughed. 'Make sure your truncheon's polished!'

*

'Agnes tells me that you seem a little stronger,' Elizabeth said on returning to Jeremiah Kidd's bedside.

His eyes were open, and he'd taken a little nourishment. 'I'm dying.'

Elizabeth blinked. The old fellow was still a ghastly colour. He might be proved right, but her task was to imbue him with confidence in the possibility of survival. If he lost the will to live, the end would come very soon.

'It's about the murder,' he said.

'Now don't go upsetting yourself,' she said, suppressing pangs of curiosity. 'A good rest, that's what you need.'

'Peterloo,' he said, levering himself up in his bed.

Elizabeth sighed. 'That terrible day. This city will never forget.'

'I haven't forgotten,' he said, but the effort of speaking made him groggy, and he slumped back on to the ragged sheets.

★

Of course he hadn't forgotten.

Colour and sound. St Peter's Fields bursting with humanity. Flags and banners held aloft. Conical caps of liberty, flashes of red in the melee, perched on the poles. Cheering, shouting, Henry Hunt struggling to make himself heard. At first the demonstration had the character of a party. The reformers were happy and excited. Men and women who believed their time had come, that now their voices must be heard.

And then the response. Confusion culminating in catastrophe. When was the Riot Act read? Jeremiah never even heard it. Voices of reason were drowned by the noise and the wildness, the beating of hooves, the screams and moans of the injured and the dying. The shriek of the trumpets and the roars of 'Front!' and 'Forward!' as the Hussars made their charge.

Men and women trampled under the hooves, crushed by wagons, ripped by swords that glittered in the summer sunshine. Bodies piled on top of one another. Blood everywhere. People weeping and wailing in hurt and horror. If this was a mob, it was a mob of souls tormented by grief.

Soldiers racing up and down, flailing around with their swords, furious as a pack of rabid hounds in search of a hare. Reformers with flagpoles transformed into makeshift cudgels, fighting to stay alive. A tattered banner in the dirt on the ground. Jeremiah read the slogan. *Liberty or Death*.

Many of the images in his mind were blurred, as if by the clouds of dust billowing around St Peter's Fields. His memories were obscured by disbelief at human stupidity and casual wickedness as well as by the chaos of the massacre. Did he really watch a cavalryman, with a single slice of his sabre, cut off the right hand of a woman sheltering in a doorway? Was it true that he'd witnessed a burly Special Constable from the St Clement's district slashed across the face by a demented horseman of the 15th Dragoons? Even amid such mayhem and terror, how was it possible for a constable with a baton to be mistaken for a reformer wielding a pistol?

He'd blundered around on that hateful afternoon, armed with his truncheon, but determined only to use it to defend himself. When he wept, for all the tragic sights surrounding him, he wept for something he could not even see.

Lost innocence.

★

'Jeremiah Kidd is failing,' Elizabeth reported that evening. 'For a few minutes it seemed as though he might be on the mend, but by the time I left, he was in a bad way, and his poor daughter was deeply distressed. He will not stop raving about innocence and murder.'

'Memories of Peterloo,' her husband said. 'The slaughter of the innocents.'

'I suppose he was caught up in the frenzy.'

'So many people were. Some constables tended to the wounded, even though they were implicated in the violence that had taken place. As if they had recovered their senses after succumbing to a fleeting madness, and yearned to expiate their sins.'

She bowed her head, and William put his arm around her. 'I can see how distressed you are. You don't have to go back to the cellar tomorrow,' he said. 'You cannot do everything.'

'Tomorrow might be my last chance to see him.'

'Even so, my dear. The relief work you do is invaluable, but...'

'No buts.' She lifted her chin. 'I shall return to the cellar.'

★

'How is he today?'

Agnes shook her head. 'Very poorly, miss.'

'Is he still going over the same old...'

'Yes, miss, it's awful.' The woman's face was wan. It was as if she were talking to herself. 'Even after all this time, it is so very hard to bear.'

*

He had stumbled on the truth by accident. A couple of minutes after leaving home to do his duty as Special Constable, and join the ranks of the militia at St Peter's Fields, he'd caught sight of his daughter in the distance. She was staggering down an alleyway. He caught up with her within moments, and realised she was blinded by tears. Her breath smelled of gin.

'Agnes! What's the matter?'

At first she wouldn't tell him. He led her home, but it took time to persuade her to talk to him, and even longer to discover the truth. The reason why Stiles and his wife had been so welcoming, so keen to have a young girl around the Thatched Tavern.

The Stiles had pressed their upstairs rooms into service as a makeshift bawdy house. Madge kept Peggy occupied while Cissie schooled Agnes in what was required. Nothing to be ashamed of, the older girl said. You simply learned to shut your mind off when you were in company with the men. Pouring gin down your throat helped to ease the pain. They liked young flesh best, and a roll around with a slip of a thing like Agnes was a regular tonic for an old soldier.

It was a way of making ends meet, Cissie giggled.

*

'She was innocent,' Jeremiah muttered.

'Who was?' Elizabeth asked.

'My little girl.'

'Agnes?' Elizabeth smiled. 'Well, of course. She's done nothing wrong. All she wants is to take care of her father. Make sure you are comfortable.'

'It was wrong.'

'What was wrong, Jeremiah?'

He stared into her blue-grey eyes.

'Murder.'

★

Was there such a thing as a fate worse than death? Was what Agnes had suffered so terrible, when other innocents were being pierced by bayonets, and crushed by horses' hooves? Jeremiah never doubted he was right. Saving her was not enough.

Because he'd been talking to the girl, and then making sure she was safe and sound in her room at home, he was late coming to St Peter's Fields. Ranks were being broken, the charge was about to start, the sweaty reek of death and disaster began to fill the air.

As the massacre unfolded, only one thing filled his mind. He must hunt down Caleb Stiles. Keeping the peace meant nothing to him now. The sickening scenes of wretchedness and cruelty all about him were a macabre peep-show. The savagery appalled him, yet he knew that at heart he was a savage too. Before the day was out, he would prove it.

He searched high and low, dodging countless indiscriminate swipes of staves and sabres as anarchy reigned in the streets of Manchester. At last he chanced upon Caleb Stiles. He was in a small courtyard off Dickenson Street, standing astride a man's body. In his right hand, he held a bloodied truncheon. In his left was a conical cap of liberty.

'Well, Jeremiah!' Stiles's grin was broad. He was breathless, but jubilant. 'I didn't see you in the Fields!'

'I was detained.'

'Not spoiling for a fight like the rest of us, eh?' Stiles peered. 'What is this man? Shame on you, your truncheon's still a virgin! I don't see so much as a smear of blood.'

'I didn't want it to be defiled too soon.'

Caleb Stiles gave an animal's throaty growl. 'Ha! You're just like...'

'Like who?' he demanded.

'Never mind,' Stiles said roughly. 'See my trophy?'

He flourished the cap. 'So much for liberty! This fellow can join his fraternity in Hades. They are all equal there, the scum. Let them protest as much as they please. See if Satan takes heed.'

Jeremiah looked at the motionless body on the cobbles. It belonged to a man in his middle years. He was still clutching a segment of a broken flagpole.

Stiles kicked the corpse. 'Winded me with his stave, the bastard, but I had the better of him. Look!'

Waving his truncheon like the conductor of an orchestra, he gestured to Jeremiah to approach the body.

'Come here, and see the look of wonder in his eyes?' Stiles threw back his head and laughed. 'As if he doubted that I'd do for him, the rascal!'

Stiles was right. The dead man's features were twisted in astonishment. Just like Jeremiah, he'd under-estimated man's capacity for evil.

Without a word, Jeremiah lifted his truncheon and gave Stiles a fearful crack on the forehead. The innkeeper fell to the ground with a squeal of pain. His truncheon slipped from his grasp, and so did the cap of liberty.

'That was for me,' Jeremiah said, and swung the truncheon again. 'And this is for Peggy.'

Stiles groaned. Blood poured from the wounds on his scalp and forehead.

'What...'

'I'm protesting, can't you see?' Jeremiah lifted the truncheon again. 'And this is for Agnes, and all the other girls you ruined.'

He brought the weapon down with as much force as he could muster.

★

'The trunk,' the old man whispered.

Elizabeth frowned. 'You want me to open the trunk?'
'Yes.'

She lifted up the candle and fiddled with the trunk's clasp.

It was old and rusty and there was no lock. She lifted the lid.

'Is there something you wanted?'

'The cap,' he breathed.

She rooted around in the jumble. There was a wooden truncheon, covered in dark stains. And underneath some old papers, a conical Phrygian cap in faded red. She pulled it out and showed it to him.

'Is this what you mean?'

'Yes.' He coughed. 'Put it on me.'

Elizabeth raised her eyebrows. He was very sick. What fancy had taken hold of him?

'You want to wear the cap?'

He nodded. It seemed absurd, but she was not minded to argue, or question his sanity.

Almost reverently, she placed the cap of liberty on his head. He closed his eyes.

His breathing became noisy and disturbed.

Elizabeth ran to the door. 'Agnes! You'd better come.'

★

'It was for the best, I suppose,' his daughter said afterwards.

The tears were drying on her cheeks. The undertaker had removed Jeremiah's body. The funeral arrangements would need to be made, but all in good time. There was little more that Elizabeth could do.

'It was strange, about the cap,' she said. 'All his talk about innocence and murder. I suppose he was remembering Peterloo.'

'Yes,' Agnes said in a strained voice. 'I'm sure he was.'

'A man he knew was killed, wasn't he?' Elizabeth shook her head. 'Caleb Stiles.'

'Stiles was good for nothing.' Agnes's voice was suddenly harsh. 'I knew his daughter, and she was just the same. We had nothing to do with them, afterwards.'

Elizabeth was startled. 'I heard they were friends.'

'Yes,' Agnes said in a muffled voice. 'That's what a lot of people thought. Father never put them right.'

'Ah well.' Elizabeth didn't know what else to say. 'I suppose his memory failed. I thought there was some particular tale he was trying to tell.'

'You did?'

'Stories fascinate me.'

'Sometimes,' Agnes said, 'it's less painful to forget the past.'

Elizabeth's brow creased. 'But Peterloo won't be forgotten.'

'No.' Agnes was crying. 'Never.'

Afterword: The English Uprising

Prof Robert Poole
University of Central Lancashire

THE PETERLOO MASSACRE WAS the bloodiest political event of the nineteenth century on English soil. On Monday 16 August 1819 troops under the authority of the Lancashire and Cheshire magistrates attacked and dispersed a rally of some 50,000 pro-democracy reformers on St Peter's Field, Manchester. Twenty minutes later hundreds of people had been injured, many by sabres, many of them women, and some children. Eighteen people would eventually die from injuries received that day. Dozens of independent witnesses were horrified, for there had not been any disturbance to provoke such an attack. The authorities, however, insisted that a rebellion had been averted. Waterloo, the final victory of the European allies over the Emperor Napoleon, had been four years earlier; now, at 'Peterloo', British troops were turned against their own people.

These losses were deeply symbolic, for working people also felt that their interests had been sacrificed in the peace that followed twenty gruelling years of European war. On top of a severe post-war economic slump, hundreds of thousands of demobilised troops came home looking for work. To compound matters, in 1816-17 and again in 1819, there were two sharp cyclical slumps in the dangerously over-stretched cotton industry whose capital was Manchester.

In these post-war years, the gap between rich and poor was at its historical extreme. The sources of this inequality were political as much as economic. In 1815, the landed classes and farmers had their 'peace dividend' in the form of the corn laws, which kept corn prices high by preventing imports of grain. The middle classes were rewarded by the ending of the wartime income tax. Working people however continued to pay taxes on essential items like malt, soap, candles and paper, as well as record prices for food.

Any struggle for economic survival had first to become a struggle for political rights, for during the war years the regulations protecting trades had been entirely abolished, and trade unions and political organisations banned – all by acts of parliament. Only just over a tenth of the adult male population had the vote, a figure which had halved over the previous century. Manchester itself, like most northern and midland industrial towns, had no MP at all. Radical reformers like Henry Hunt, the speaker at the Peterloo meeting, insisted that the solution was to give control of parliament to the people through universal suffrage (understood as adult male suffrage). This required breaking the power of the 'boroughmongers' who had used the war to strengthen their grip on political power and milk the system. This was a time when the rhetoric of 'the people' against parliament, so sinister in our own more democratic age, really did seem to promise liberation.

A mass petitioning campaign for parliamentary reform in 1816-17 had mustered at least three quarters of a million signatures on seven hundred local petitions. These were brusquely rejected by parliament, the majority of them rejected as illegitimate either for 'insulting language' (complaining that the Commons did not represent the people) or simply because they were printed instead of written by hand. Among those rejected was the biggest petition of all, one of thirty thousand signatures from Manchester. The result was the attempted march of the Manchester 'blanketeers' towards London in March 1817 to present their petitions for reform in person. This was intercepted by troops on its way through Cheshire and the north Midlands. Dozens of reformers were arrested and imprisoned without charge for months under emergency powers which suspended 'habeas corpus', the right to a fair trial. Three weeks later there were further arrests as the desperate 'Ardwick conspiracy' was foiled by the Manchester police and magistrates who claimed they had detected a plan by radicals to attack Manchester. The affair was clearly a matter of desperation for the few radicals who took part, but there is good reason to believe that spies and informers cooked up the entire affair.

In 1819 reformers moved away from secrecy and conspiracy in favour of a mass, peaceful, constitutionalist movement which sought to assert itself forcefully, yet peacefully, in what historians have dubbed the 'mass platform movement', or the 'English uprising'. The meeting in Manchester on 16 August 1819 was part of a national movement, centred on the industrial north but extending to Birmingham and London, designed to overwhelm government by sheer weight of numbers and force democratic elections, rather as the pro-democracy movements of 1989 would overthrow communist rule in much of central Europe.

Manchester was at the centre of a great network of industrious towns and villages extending for fifteen miles in all directions well into the Pennines, whose domestic handloom weavers turned the thread spun by Manchester's cotton factories into finished cloth. Processions of weavers and their families, dressed in their Sunday best, carrying hand-woven flags and banners with messages of hope, flooded into Manchester. The most impressive, led by the weaver Samuel Bamford and accompanied by a band of music, came from Rochdale, Heywood and Middleton. Its men had practiced orderly marching in the countryside around Tandle Hill and White Moss, proudly drilled by old soldiers, wartime veterans and volunteers; there were also several female reform societies present whose members dressed in white and marched together bearing flags and the eponymous caps of liberty referred to in Martin Edward's story, some of which they planned to present to Henry Hunt.

The cap of liberty, although most recently associated with the French revolutionaries, was in origin the Phrygian cap, the

Roman symbol of the freed slave. Until the war with France broke out in 1793 it had been carried by Britannia on pennies still in circulation. By displaying it radicals were not only baiting the authorities but laying claim to an older strain of patriotism which had mobilised against the threat of invasion by Napoleon only for its hopes of national reform to be dashed after Waterloo.

Manchester in 1819 was perhaps the most socially and politically divided town in Regency England. It might have been economically modern but it was governed through an archaic jumble of parish and manorial institutions, a bench of magistrates, and a police commission, all controlled by a High Tory elite who circulated between them through an obscure network of revolving doors. Although they waved the flag and commanded troops of volunteers during the war, they had no sense that the lower orders could ever qualify as citizens. In Manchester, troops were deployed vigorously during the wars against food rioters, striking weavers, and Luddites opposed to the experimental powerlooms. The town's police force consisted of a handful of paid constables and watchmen, headed by the deputy constable Joseph Nadin, a former thieftaker who relied on a network of private agents and informants motivated by a mixture of blackmail and reward. Political spies and informers fitted in easily to this network.

Publicans were important links in the loyalist network of control, for they depended upon the magistrates for their licences. They were in return expected to deny their meeting spaces to reformers and to co-operate with police operations, while a blind eye was turned to their own infringements (unless they were rivals to Nadin himself, who owned several pubs of his own). There were many publicans among the three hundred or so special constables sworn in to provide additional support at St Peter's Field, and fourteen more among the hundred members of the Manchester and Salford Yeomanry who caused so much of the carnage. Visiting loyalist journalists and others were issued with special constables' staves to show to the troops for protection.

Ironically one of the accidental victims of Peterloo was Thomas Ashworth, accidentally run down and killed in the cavalry advance. Ashworth was landlord of the Bulls Head Inn, a loyalist headquarters in the Market Place, next to the Royal Exchange, an embarrassment about which as little was said as possible. Special constables then joined the Yeomanry in the attack upon the hustings. A number of them were seen kicking and truncheoning an Oldham cotton spinner, John Lees; when he died three weeks later it turned out that they had murdered a Waterloo veteran. Special constables were reviled by reformers, although many of them did also assist the wounded. On the morning of 17 August one of their number, Robert Campbell, was subjected to a revenge attack. Seeking to escape from crowds besieging his house in Ancoats, he was chased, beaten and stoned to death in public on the false rumour that he had killed a child the previous day. Both the fictional Caleb Styles and his enemy Jeremiah Kidd fit well into this half-lit loyalist underworld.

Martin Edwards's story is set in the Manchester of 1839, which had finally emerged from high Tory domination after gaining two MPs in 1832 (and one for Salford) and a borough council in 1838. Manchester's free-market liberals were now in control of local affairs, while the former opposition Whig party was in government in Westminster with the approval of the young Queen Victoria. Engels had yet to visit Manchester to make his famous report on *The Condition of the Working Class in England,* but social investigators were already at work exposing the shocking state of housing, health, and education. Concerned middle-class men and women visited the homes of the poor to offer practical charity and spiritual consolation.

Prominent among Manchester's social visitors were members of the unitarian Cross Street Chapel, including its minister William Gaskell and his young wife Elizabeth, the protagonist in Martin's fictional account. Brought up in the Cheshire market town of Knutsford, her uncle Peter Holland was medical officer both to the paternalist Styal Mill and to the Cheshire

Yeomanry who were in action at Peterloo. She would later portray industrial Manchester in all its harshness and class alienation in her novel *Mary Barton* (1848), and the two worlds of town and countryside in *North and South* (1855). She was committed to seeking to heal the social divisions which she found, but for her this had to begin with the middle classes understanding the suffering and bitterness of the poor.

The memory of Peterloo would have still been vivid in the half-reformed Manchester of the 1830s. In 1835 the French visitor Alexis de Tocqueville found in Manchester's politics 'the very rich on one side, the working classes on the other' and was struck by 'the people's fear of soldiers'. Hugh Hornby Birley, the Yeomanry captain who had attempted to arrest Henry Hunt at the point of a sabre, had gone over to the Liberals. The new regime, both locally and nationally, was in turn challenged by the Chartists, the political heirs of the radicals of 1819. When they rallied in their tens of thousands on Manchester's Kersal Moor in September 1838 they re-used banners from 1819. Several pubs in the area still had signs with portraits of Henry Hunt and other radical leaders, and Wigan's chartists acclaimed Feargus O'Connor, the Chartist leader as Hunt's successor. In offering words of comfort about Peterloo to the aged Jeremiah Kidd – 'Now don't go upsetting yourself . . . This city will never forget' – Elizabeth Gaskell might also been concerned not to re-open harsh political memories.

Manchester's social and political divisions would prove enduring, though perhaps they were never quite so sharp-edged as in 1819. Manchester school free-market Liberalism was succeeded towards the end of the nineteenth century by a social reforming liberalism and then in the twentieth century by Labourism while Toryism developed its own social and imperial agenda. Whatever their positions on other issues however, no political party in Manchester has ever been able to hold power unless it was business-friendly. On 16 August 2019, Manchester acquired a fine Peterloo memorial at long last, but it shares the former St Peter's Field with upmarket hotels and a conference centre while the approaching thickets of skyscrapers darken the land nearby. Meanwhile, the economically struggling boroughs of Oldham and Rochdale face the loss of much of their green belt to sprawling development as the battle of Kinder Scout, so much part of Manchester's radical heritage, is renewed closer to home. The green lanes and landscapes around Tandle Hill country park where Samuel Bamford and the other heroes of Peterloo rallied, marched, and renewed their weary souls, are threatened with obliteration by sprawling development. Let this not be Greater Manchester's memorial to the heroes of Peterloo.

Savage

Kamila Shamsie

UNLESS YOU KNEW WHAT you were looking for, you would never see it in him. Even I, in full possession of the facts, had to observe him very closely that New Year's Day evening of 1820 when he arrived at Upper Seymour Street before I noticed something in the hair and lips and that slight tinge to his skin. In all other respects he was my brother's son – a slightly younger, taller version of Robert as he had been when he came to see me on the docks as one of the ships was about to set sail and said he would like to be apprenticed to the ship's physician, and was prepared to leave right away. That was the last time I saw him – more than twenty years ago.

England didn't please him, the boy, my nephew, Charles; that was evident immediately. But England pleased no one that winter, all frost and snow and discontent. I made clear to him that first evening the terms under which he was to live with me: he was my heir, but not my son. I had never sought a family of my own, and though I recognised my responsibilities to my late brother's only child I wished to be allowed to live my life with as little disruption as possible. He was welcome to my library, and to join me for supper, but beyond that he would have to find ways of occupying himself for the next few months until he turned sixteen, when I would purchase a military commission for him. He agreed readily, thanked me with perfect manners, and asked if he might pull up a chair closer to the fire. Winters were never like this in Jamaica, he said, and I told him winters were never like this in England, either.

'How so, sir?' he said, and I saw he understood I didn't only mean the weather.

I could have explained to him then the strange mood that had the country in its grip, for which the best explanation I had heard was that the sick, mad king in Windsor had infected the entire realm. Not for much longer, if the stories were to be believed, and perhaps then this mood of restlessness, of something near revolution – though not that, please God not that – would pass. But it was late, and the fire was burning down, so I said it had never before been so cold for so long, and showed him up to his room.

In the weeks that passed, he became a welcome presence. In the mornings we sat together by the fire, slowly picking our way through *The Times* and the *Morning Chronicles,* and he read the Tory and Whig view of events in England, and heard his uncle's commentary on both. There would be a period of reading in the library after that – he had a particular taste for my books of history – and at some point, earlier or later, he would bundle himself into all his layers of clothes – he had seemed so genuinely surprised when I sent for my tailor that I wondered if he expected me to allow him to go through an English winter with only his father's old coat to keep him warm – and disappear until supper. I never asked him where he went. I did not like him to know how much I had started to wonder about him, and his life.

What I wondered most was if he knew who – what – he really was. My brother had mentioned it only once, in an anguished letter which was followed speedily by another asking me never to mention it, never even to remember it if forgetting such a thing were possible. 'The matter is settled. He is to be raised as Charlotte and my son. We are going from here to a place where no one need know that there is anything else to the story. Charlotte says it is a mark of God's wishes for the boy that he looks entirely my child and no one else's.'

It's possible, I expect, that I suggested we go to the theatre together to watch Mr. Kean in *Othello* despite the bitter cold because my curiosity wondered if his response might reveal something. He agreed readily enough, and sat beside me through the play, responding in his gasps and his applause just as any Englishman would. But when we left the theatre he said, 'Othello was not as I imagined him when I read the play.'

'In what way?' Mr Kean played a lighter-skinned Othello than any that had been seen before, and I assumed this was what he meant.

'Less intelligent. There was nothing to him but passion, and savagery.'

I knew then that he knew who he was, and I was filled with shame for what I had done. 'He could hardly play him as an English gentleman.' I touched his shoulder as I said it, to let him know that I considered him an English gentleman. He smiled in agreement, and I was surprised by the extent of my relief.

The weeks passed. The temperature rose above freezing. The mad king died. I waited for the world to right itself. But instead a group of radicals, including one William Davidson – a black man from Jamaica – were arrested at Cato Street for their part in a ridiculous and grotesque conspiracy to behead the members of the cabinet. By now, I was so accustomed to seeing Charles simply as Robert's son that I didn't think he would have any specific interest in this Davidson, a man of unmistakable blackness who showed no sign in his countenance of his English father. Charles certainly did not mention him particularly when we read about the events and I expressed satisfaction that the ringleader, Thistlewood, had been captured after initially making his escape.

He did ask me why I thought the men wanted to do something so violent and extreme as beheading all the members of the cabinet and I told him there were always men who stood ready to commit acts of violence against their betters, and we must be grateful for those who remain vigilant against such radicals and save us from them. He seemed satisfied by this response at the time, but later, over supper he said, 'Do Peterloo and the Six Acts have nothing to do with this?'

I knew by now that some of his wanderings took him to coffee houses where there were conversations and newspapers such as would not be found in Upper Seymour Street. It came as no surprise that in these places such views would be aired, and I was pleased that he had come home to me to set his thoughts straight.

I said I had never defended what happened at Peterloo. No doubt it was true that the intentions of the speakers at that public event was to ferment disorder but even so, the Cavalry should not have responded so over-zealously, and without reprimand. The deaths of those English men and women should not have gone unpunished. But it was necessary to understand how perilous a state we were in. Radicals – such as Thistlewood – were everywhere, seeking to exploit the unhappiness of the poor, and they would have used Peterloo to stoke many fires if the government had not responded with the Six Acts, limiting the Radicals' power to hold meetings and publish fiery tracts. 'It is stability that matters, Charles, do you understand?'

He nodded very seriously. 'I do, uncle,' he said, fervently.

More time elapsed. Spring came and as the days thawed and lengthened my boy was out more and more hours than before, often coming home with the stink of the public house attached to him. But we always supped together, and he was always courteous and sweet-natured. I had begun to wish I had never offered to buy that military commission – all those years ago, I thought I was helping his father to propel himself forward into the world, but I only propelled Richard away from me. He took to the life of a physician, but not to one at sea, and when my ship anchored in Jamaica he chose to stay there, away from any influence I could have brought to bear on his life. Perhaps, I said one evening to Charles, as though it were a minor matter, perhaps given his taste for reading he would prefer university to the military. A man of letters, why not?

He smiled his perfect courteous smile, thanked me for the offer, and said he would consider the matter.

This was, if I'm remembering correctly, just a few days before the conspirators of Cato Street were sentenced to be hanged, drawn and quartered. We read the news together on an April morning, with the birds singing in the trees outside.

'Of course they must die,' I said. 'But it seems unnecessary to bring back such a medieval way of doing it. An axe would do the job just as well, and with less savagery.'

'Because Englishmen aren't savage.' He said it so mildly I didn't even look up, and only made a noise of assent. I was barely aware of him leaving the room, or of the sound of his footsteps climbing up the stairs and then striding across his bedroom which was directly above where I was sitting. When he returned he sat down again, and leaned forward, his elbows on his knees, and waited for me to look up at him before he started to speak.

'When the Cavalry massacred Englishmen and women gathered peaceably in a field to hear a speech, that wasn't savagery. When the government said they had done nothing wrong, even though they didn't read the Riot Act first, that wasn't savagery. When the rich live in gilded palaces and the poor die of starvation, that isn't savagery. When Parliament is corrupt and resists reform, that isn't savagery. When laws are passed to prevent Englishmen from gathering together to speak their mind, or to publish their thoughts, that isn't savagery. But when all that repression and injustice leaves men with no recourse but to take drastic measures to throw off the chains that bind us – then, Uncle, what then? Is that savagery?

All this in a quiet tone, without any emotion, and the last question asked in that familiar tone from every morning when we read the newspapers together – the tone of one who wants to learn from his uncle. Only now did I see the mockery in it.

'It is savagery. And to defend such acts is savagery too. I don't know what company you've been keeping, my boy, but I must ask you to quit it.'

'Do you think Davidson, the man of colour, was more savage than the others?'

'I have never said such a thing.'

'There is so much you don't say, uncle. So much you don't ask.'

'You are a child. What should I ask of a child?'

'Ask me on what terms my father's wife agreed to raise me as her son.'

He stood and walked towards the window, and opened it though the early morning was cold. 'Even those who are sympathetic, who think the Cato Street conspirators had cause, even they never stop to think that perhaps Davidson had more cause than others. Perhaps he knew who you are better than you do.'

'Close the window, and stop this nonsense.'

He turned to face me, and the trees threw their shadows on his face, darkening it. He held out his hand, and I saw it had a piece of paper in it.

'What is that?'

He hesitated. It was almost as if he thought I would get up from my chair and walk over to him. Then, in a few steps he was beside me, pressing the square of newsprint into my hands. I read.

TAKE NOTICE, That on Monday the 16th day of July, I will put up to Public Sale, at the City-Tavern, in Kingston, between the hours of 10 and 12 of the clock in the forenoon, a Negro Woman Slave, named SARAH, a House-Servant.

'My father kept this' he said, still in that tone without emotion. 'I found it when he died. It was his wife's condition for raising me. The night after the funeral of the woman I called 'mother' my father spoke to me of the other one – of Sarah. He was not without feeling for her, it seemed. But as you once said, it is stability that matters. All English gentlemen, and those who aspire to be them, know that. Look at the date.' He tapped his thin tapered fingers – not Richard's fingers – on the paper in my hand. 'I was born on the 12th of July. I wonder a great deal about those four days before my father sold my mother. Do you think they allowed her to spend any part of those days with me?'

I bowed my head. I could not look at him. He returned to his usual chair and picked up the newspaper that he had earlier discarded. 'What do you think will happen with the matter of the king's divorce?' he said, amiably.

'You are in my house, sir!' I said. 'I feed you, I clothe you, I have offered you any future you want. I give you all my affection. Why do you treat me so poorly? I had no part in the decision made by your father. I never knew of it until now.'

'Do you think my father would confess all this to me, and not confess the basis of his brother's fortune?'

It was almost a relief to have it out between us. I stretched out a hand to him. 'I supported the Abolitionists. I sold my ships almost fifteen years ago...' Soon after I had news of your birth, I almost said, before I stopped myself. He knew his own age.

'When you had wealth enough to last a lifetime, and the abolition of the slave trade was a looming inevitability.'

'When I saw the wickedness of the practice. When I was convinced of it by those who wanted reform – and who used the words of morality and godliness and enlightenment to convince. That is how reform comes about. Not by butchering the Cabinet and placing their heads on pikes and displaying them on the street as these foul men of Cato Street planned to do.'

'The same men whose butchering will be a public display by the orders of the government. And meanwhile, slavery carries on unchecked in the colonies, and England profits from it.'

'That will end, too. The Abolitionists are tireless. I support their cause. Financially, you understand. I am not unaware of my... responsibilities.'

'A few conspiracies to behead slave-owners might be more effective in speeding up reform than the tirelessness of the Abolitionists, or your attempts to buy your way into heaven with the wealth you mined in hell.'

I could not read his expression. I knew nothing of his character, or of what he might be capable. I had thought he would be my salvation, but I understood, then, that if my wealth had come from the mines of hell, so had he. And like Prospero at the end of the *The Tempest* there was nothing to do about my Caliban but say, *This thing of darkness I acknowledge mine.*

I rose from my chair. 'Enough talk. Mr. Milton awaits me in the library. And who awaits you? Mr Gibbon?'

'I am finished with him,' he said, standing up. 'Today will be something new.'

He followed me into the library, his tread soft, almost soundless.

THE CATO STREET CONSPIRACY, 1820

Afterword: Arming Ourselves As They Did

Prof Malcolm Chase
University of Leeds

THE MURDEROUS CONSPIRACY EXPOSED on 23 February 1820 fits awkwardly into the usual narratives of the English way of 'doing politics'. Half a mile to the north of what we know as Marble Arch, Cato Street (a mews off the Edgware Road) still looks an unpromising site for revolution. The conspirators had not met there regularly: the Cato Street loft had been selected as a rendezvous because of its proximity to Lord Harrowby's home in Grosvenor Square. Harrowby was a Cabinet member, and supposedly all his Cabinet colleagues were to be entertained at dinner by him that night. Thistlewood and his colleagues planned to murder them all. Their decapitated heads would then be publicly displayed and armed supporters mobilised across the capital. The overall aim was to destabilise politics and usher in a 'provisional government' more sympathetic to radical reform.

Close to the heart of this conspiracy, however, was an informer in the pay of the Home Office, George Edwards. He was not the *agent provocateur* that many sympathetic to the conspirators claimed; but he had worked diligently to force the pace of the plot and ensure that the core group were apprehended in the most compromising circumstances possible. Tragically one of the arresting party, Robert Smithers, a Bow Street police officer, was fatally stabbed by Thistlewood. Most of those in the loft – including Thistlewood – escaped, although four conspirators were discovered hiding beneath a heap of straw. A detachment of guardsmen captured another five. Arthur Thistlewood was arrested the following day.

Found guilty of treason and murder at trials in late April, Thistlewood and four other conspirators were hanged and then beheaded on May Day. The dismemberment of their corpses (the gruesome final stage of the death sentence for treason) was remitted. Five other conspirators were transported for life to Australia. Under a pseudonym, Edwards was given safe passage to Cape Town. These eleven men, however, were very far from the total number of those involved in the Cato Street conspiracy.

The plot was rooted in one of the most innovative intellectual strands of the English radical tradition, that associated with Thomas Spence. A gentle Geordie of diminutive stature, Spence had moved from Newcastle to London in 1787. He was one of the first political thinkers to develop a coherent case against private ownership of land: the earth and its fruits are essential to human survival, and to deprive any person of access to them is therefore tantamount to murder. Spence's impassioned refusal to accept that the passing of time conferred innocence upon the private ownership of what had once been enjoyed by humankind in common had a radical corollary: all 'are equal by nature and before the law.'

After Spence died in 1814, his followers were consistently at the heart of ultra-radicalism in London. It was they who organised a massive rally at Spa Fields, Islington, on 2 December 1816, intended as the signal for a general uprising. Expectations for the Spa Fields meeting ran high in both capital and provinces. The meeting dissolved into rioting and the intended rising was aborted; but, as Home Office intelligence sources reported from Lancashire, all radical reformers 'agree in expressing the fullest determination to have mustered and armed immediately, in case the disturbance in London had been attended with Success.'[1]

The events of December 1816 were pivotal to the evolution

of Cato Street. The 'Spencean conservative committee', in which Arthur Thistlewood and another conspirator, shoemaker Thomas Preston, were prominent, concluded that a mass meeting, however large, would not alone generate the momentum necessary to destabilise the capital, and that the authorities would always be prepared for unrest. Thereafter the Spenceans favoured covert tactics. Plans were devised for a *coup d'état* in February 1817 and again the following August, during Smithfield's annual Bartholomew fair. Preparations were called off at the last moment when the conspirators were confronted by hastily assembled official precautions. An informer reported that Preston, who had earlier taken final leave of his family, 'declared he was so disappointed, that if he had had a Pistol by him, he thinks he should have blown his brains out'. The plot was serious enough for the Home Secretary to compare it to an earlier failed *coup d'etat*, the Despard Conspiracy of 1802. (One of those executed after Cato Street, Richard Tidd, was rumoured to have been involved in that too.)

Peterloo – the tumultuous dispersal of a peaceful political rally in Manchester on 16 August 1819 – galvanised the Spenceans. At least eighteen were killed (including four women) and over 700 injured. 'I compare the present time to the crisis of the French Revolution,' declared Spence's biographer Allen Davenport, 'we must arm ourselves as they did'.[2] 'High treason was committed against the people at Manchester,' Thistlewood defiantly told the judge a few minutes before he was sentenced. In mid-October 1819 he had toured the north while other Spenceans worked beershops and taprooms in London's poorest districts. They contemplated using a rally on Clerkenwell Green on 1 November as the signal for an armed rising, but the subdued popular mood reinforced their conviction that only clandestine action could succeed. Then, in December, 'the Six Acts' (severely restricting freedom of assembly and political reporting) were pushed through parliament. George Cruikshank, the most celebrated cartoonist of the age, immediately responded with a satirical depiction of John Bull, 'the Freeborn Englishman', deprived of his senses by the Six Acts, blindfolded, his ears stopped, his mouth padlocked shut and his hands locked in a vice.

Shortly afterwards James Watson, the Spencean leader most committed to legal and constitutional agitation, was imprisoned for debt. Without his restraining influence, conspiratorial plans accelerated. The death of King George III on 13 January led to a general election (required by law at this time). There was also widespread speculation that George IV might cause further political turmoil by insisting that he be allowed to divorce his estranged wife, Caroline. One of the worst winters in living memory was biting hard. Temperatures as low as minus 23 centigrade were reported; but the atmosphere in the pubs and clubs that the Spenceans frequented was febrile. A hoax newspaper announcement, planted by the Home Office on 22 February that Cabinet members would dine together the following evening proved irresistible. One conspirator, James Ings (an unemployed butcher), laboriously wrote out by hand placards for display the following day: 'Your tyrants are destroyed – the Friends of Liberty are called upon to come forward – the Provisional Government is now sitting'.[3]

At his trial Ings described himself as 'a man of no education and very humble abilities,' yet he had been successful in business and a property owner in Portsmouth. The conspirators were not the desperate poor recruited off the London streets. The reason why George Edwards gained the conspirators' trust was because his brother William, a *bona fide* Spencean, introduced him to them. And William was a City of London police officer. Thistlewood, a Lincolnshire stock breeder's son, had trained as a land surveyor and twice held commissions in the militia. William Davidson's English father had been a prosperous lawyer in Jamaica; before he trained as a cabinet maker Davidson had pursued studies in both law and mathematics in Scotland.

Nor was Davidson the sole member of the Spencean circle with connexions to the West Indies. An earlier member of the Thistlewood family had been a wealthy slave owner in Jamaica. Thomas Preston had visited the Caribbean as storekeeper aboard a merchant ship. Robert Wedderburn, perhaps the fiercest intellect among the Spenceans, was the son of a Jamaican plantation owner and Rosanna, an African-born house slave. Rosanna had been sold back to her original owners by Robert's father when she was five months pregnant.

Service in the Royal Navy brought Robert to London, where he encountered Thomas Spence. It was an almost epiphanic moment. Spence recognised 'that the earth was given to the children of men, making no difference for colour or character', Wedderburn wrote in his outspoken periodical *An Axe Laid to the Root*.[4] A licensed dissenting preacher, Wedderburn's chapel in Soho was a centre for insurrectionary activity. Thistlewood depended 'more on Wedderburn's division for being armed than all the Rest',[5] one spy reported. Just four weeks after Peterloo, another informer quoted him predicting that 'before Six Months were over there would be Slaughter in England for their Liberty'. Wedderburn, however, avoided being embroiled in Cato Street as he was arrested for blasphemy in January 1820.

The government was primarily concerned to secure swift and exemplary verdicts upon those in the loft on 23 February, without compromising its intelligence network. So even Thomas Preston avoided prosecution, though he was the designated leader of a raiding party on a military arsenal in the city. Official policy therefore obscured the extent of the lesser figures whom we might characterise as orbiting the core conspiracy. Organised London tradesmen such as the shoemakers, coachmakers, tailors and typefounders were apparently poised to give support if the conspiracy succeeded.

In May 1829 the *Vermont American* newspaper reported the death of George Sparrow, one of three or four otherwise unknown conspirators who had fled to North America immediately after the raid on Cato Street. Over the decades that followed several more surfaced independently of each other, each revealing substantial knowledge of the conspiracy. One had worked alongside two of those executed (Tidd and Brunt). On his deathbed in an Essex workhouse in the 1860s, he confessed he had been on his way to Cato Street when Smithers and the arresting party arrived, so he dived into a pub. He was subsequently arrested and questioned but to his relief released. Spencean tailor Charles Neesom, an early advocate of vegetarianism, admitted in his unpublished autobiography that he was 'very nearly implicated' in Cato Street.[6] Almost certainly the longest surviving conspirator was a master shoemaker who, aged 81 and still insisting on anonymity, detailed his involvement in an account published in the *Boot and Shoemaker* trade journal in 1879.

There is, then, nothing implausible about the figure at the centre of Kamila Shamsie's 'Savage'. Historians, constrained by a responsibility not to over-interpret their sources, are concerned most with the 'real', tangible and cautious about matters of psychology and emotion. Only a fictional account can take us close to the deeper-felt realities of lived experience. As winter at last yielded to spring in 1820, there must have been many, like Kamila Shamsie's anonymous narrator: men and women who anxiously reviewed, at times with a suspicion bordering on panic, the actions and opinions of those closest to them.

Notes

1. The National Archives [TNA], Home Office Papers [HO]40/4/1(2), fol 42, Chippendale to Fletcher, 3 December 1816.
2. TNA, HO 42/197, report of constables Plush and Matthews, 18 October 1819.
3. Malcolm Chase, 1820: *Disorder and Stability in the United Kingdom* (Manchester UP, 2013), p.78.
4. Malcolm Chase, *The People's Farm: English Radical Agrarianism, 1775-1840* (Oxford UP, 1988), pp. 82-3.
5. TNA, HO42/197 (18 October, 1819).
6. 'Memoir of Mr. C. H. Nesom, compiled from an autobiography left by himself...', quoted in *National Reformer* 2/63 (30 July, 1861), p. 6.

THE MERTHYR RISING, 1831

Before Dawn

Anna Lewis

JUST AS THEY ROUNDED the pass, the cloud began to break. Through the gaps fell one beam of light then another, so straight and pure that Tomos pulled up his horse. The Jenkin boys stopped too. If William had said that the light was an omen, God showing them the way or somesuch, they'd all have felt comfort, but glancing at them over his shoulder he only laughed.

'Close your mouths, why don't you? It'll take more than conjuring tricks to get this done.'

It was, of course, why William was the one they listened to. Tomos tapped his heel against his horse's flank, and they moved off.

The first time he'd seen Merthyr, from that same position on a spring evening five months before, it had looked otherworldly: a mass of chimneys and blazing furnaces, the sky above it impenetrable with smoke. The grass at the roadside was grey with dust, the noise as he imagined a storm at sea might sound. Now as they descended towards the town, half the works were silent. Bars of late sunlight played over the stacks and towers.

The streets themselves were already in shadow. Picking through slop and muddy pools, nothing was familiar: only the long arm of the mountain on the valley's far side, red where in May it had been green. The lanes narrowed, a plume of starlings twisted across the sky. Then a woman's voice called from a doorway, and Tomos realised where they were. The Miners Arms. In a moment the windows were crammed with faces, two lads were leading away the horses, and on the cobbles their party was at the centre of a small swarm. After the quiet in which they had ridden, lulled by the thick clip of hooves on earth, the jostling voices were briefly incomprehensible, but through his exhaustion Tomos picked out one then another and began to translate.

Beth allwch chi ei wneud? Sut allwch chi helpu? What could William do, how could he help them? Would he come and speak at their chapel, their club? Would he speak to the ironmasters, the magistrates? Some men started to address Tomos directly, while others behaved as though his words had sprung from the air and spoke on earnestly to William. This he remembered from the last time they were here, but the questions were more urgent now.

William would have stayed as long as the crowd remained, but dusk was gaining and the air was cool. The Jenkin brothers had slipped inside. Tomos touched William on the arm, and raised his voice to the crowd. 'Mae eisiau bwyd arno,' he said, 'But come back tomorrow. We're staying here, come as soon as you like.'

In the spring, when the National Association for the Protection of Labour first sent William down from Lancashire to Merthyr, the workers had paid him close attention. As a union man he understood power and how to grasp it; as a man of God he understood righteousness and that it was already theirs. That rebellion had met with disaster, but in Merthyr the men held firm with their demands, and back in Bolton it was agreed that William should return.

At Guest's Dowlais works, as well as at the Plymouth works, the men had been told to give up their unions or face dismissal. At both they'd gone out in September, blowing the furnaces. Elsewhere the men kept working to support those on strike, but a month had passed and supplies were running thin. The morning after their arrival, Tomos and the Jenkin brothers had barely left their room before men and women began to appear from unlit corners of the inn and ask: had they brought the relief from the north.

It was the same all over town. 'Have you brought it, ydy e'n dod? Is it coming?'

It was a promise that no one would admit to having made; no one seemed to know where it came from. The little band in the Miners Arms had only the funds they'd raised for their own mission, on the journey down, and that went on their board and lodging. Every time Tomos stepped onto the street he was thronged by beggars. Occasionally at the edge of the scrum he saw men being shoved away, and heard the hissed accusation: 'Special!' So even those tradesmen who had turned soldiers in the spring were going hungry: well, they had no customers.

In the Miners Arms, Tomos shared a room with the Jenkin boys, while William slept alone. He ate alone, too, if he ate at all. Each night after the three had finished their meal, William called them into his room, poured out gin and passed around the cups. They drank in silence until William was ready to speak. There were lines on his face that had not been there in May, and in the silence Tomos thought of something the elder Jenkin boy had said to him, on that first long ride down: 'He changes. I'd hardly know him for the man I saw in Bolton, and he could be queer then.'

'You didn't know him well there?'

'I heard him speak. That's the reason I agreed when the union said they were looking for men to show him into Wales. And then, when I met him the night before we left, I thought – well, I didn't know if I'd been mistaken. But I was ready to go, and as it turned out, there was no mistake.'

Surely there wasn't. Once you got past that strange girlishness William could have – the expectancy in his gaze, the slightly too expressive face – it was obvious to Tomos that you couldn't put your faith in a better man. During the first journey in May, William had preached in every town and village along the road, sometimes three or four times in one day. They visited the same places on the second journey down, and in each town a crowd was waiting.

When William spoke about strength, about love, about friendship, Tomos felt his words shine back from the bodies before them. 'For you are all children of the light, children of the day. We are not of the night, nor of darkness.' Standing beside him, Tomos thought of the workmates he had left behind in Denbighshire, hacking and scraping deep inside the mountains. He understood. He wanted everyone who heard to understand.

Back in Merthyr they roamed the pubs and clubs where the unions met. Men huddled there for hours, as much to keep warm as for the company: a heavy frost had begun to fall each morning. In clubs and on street corners William repeated the words he had uttered on the Waun in May, and Tomos stood at his side, translating and amplifying him. 'Don't let your brothers in work keep you. Each time one of you eats a mouthful of bread from your brothers, bread stays on the table of the rich. That table is groaning! Insist on poor relief from the parish. The parish will demand it from the rate-payers, who cannot afford to pay. Then the whole system will groan – let it!'

People listened, as they had listened on the Waun.

William started to organise the men into groups with their families, and to billet them in their home parishes outside the town. Returned to the villages and hamlets of their birth, they lodged on floors and in doorways, in out-houses with the animals. The men demanded poor relief from their parishes; the parish officers begged the magistrates for guidance, the magistrates implored the Home Office. Merthyr, which for so long had drawn in all the life around it, was beginning to exhale.

Among the workers there were women, stackers and cinder girls, stooped from bending on the surface of the tips. They were sunburnt as the men were pale, some with piteous children clutched around them. On an evening late in October, when Tomos was trudging alone back to the Miners Arms, a woman stepped out from the mouth of an alley and stumbled clumsily on the rubble. Tomos stopped. She righted herself, smoothing down her skirt with a show of fussiness, then looked up sharply.

'You're one of William Twiss's men,' she said. 'How is it you're all from up north?'

Her boldness caught Tomos off guard, so he hesitated before answering. 'Mr Twiss is from Bolton, in England, he preaches for the colliers up there. The union sent him into Wales.' He paused. 'To Wrexham first. That's where I met him.'

She nodded, then broke into English. 'Do you want me to help you? You northerners do have trouble with the language. I'll come now, if you like.'

Hers wasn't the first offer they'd had: their retinue had attracted a stream of local interpreters, but when they realised they wouldn't be paid, they tended to fall away. Tomos said as much, then added: 'You don't want to come to our lodgings, anyway. It's full of unwashed men, up to the ceiling. And lice. You'd do better getting home.'

She laughed. Tomos lifted his cap and turned. After a second, there was a scuffling on the cobbles behind him and she caught hold of his elbow. In surprise he shook her off, but she kept hurrying at his side. He slowed down. Catching her breath she started to talk, and didn't stop until they reached the inn.

Her name was Mari. She had no reason to get home, no children to get back to: she'd had a daughter, but lost her to the cholera. Her husband had been a Dowlais man, and was half-crushed in an accident the year their daughter died. Although still alive he was bound to his bed. His mother had moved herself into the room they shared and tended to him all day long, never letting Mari near him. If she wanted a moment with her husband, she had to wake him in the middle of the night while the old woman lay snoring on the floor, and interrupt the little peace he had. There was no hope of a word or caress from him, but they could look at each other.

All the time she spoke, her breath streamed into the air in front of her. Tomos kept his eyes on the white vapours while he listened. Already the edge of winter was pressing near, in the thinning trees on the hillside and the violent red skies that claimed the end of each afternoon. At the door of the Miners Arms he stopped, and looked at her fully. He meant to tell her to be patient, be brave, to go home to her husband and wait. Her hand was already on the door when she turned to look back at him. Hunched and shrunken, she was scarcely bigger than a schoolgirl, but held his gaze level. He saw then: when she had offered to help them, that was exactly what she had meant.

It looked to Tomos that William was growing thin. He seemed never to eat. Once or twice he staggered in the street: it could have been his empty stomach, or it could have been the gin. The landlady in the Miners Arms brought a bottle upstairs every evening, handing it to Tomos without a word when William failed to answer her knock. Tomos ate, and the Jenkin boys ate; it wasn't that there was no food in Merthyr, it was that none of those on strike could buy it. The bread tasted to Tomos like cloth, the cheese like clay; he took gulps of gin to force it down. In the inn he sat with his elbows on the table, his hands softly clasped before his lips to shield the small ripples of indigestion. The Jenkin brothers took no such caution, belching and poking their tongues around their teeth. Tomos saw the way the room watched them.

Walking around the town, Tomos was forced again and again to remember what had happened in the spring. It had started with something near glory on that hot, dry day at the very end of May, when he'd stood on top of the Waun and watched the fields disappear beneath the crowd. How many thousands were there was impossible to tell; the whole hillside was moving. There were banners and bursts of song. A hundred yards back the Waun Fair was underway: horses huffed in the pens, and harnesses flashed. When it was William's turn to speak, Tomos stood with him. They spoke of how the cuts to wages turned good men into debtors, about the Court of Requests and the cruelty of its bailiffs. 'You have been petitioning Parliament for years,' cried William, 'and no notice is taken. Bring the matter to a short conclusion. I advise each one of you to refrain from working any longer…' Through the quiet, a horse's whinny carried over from the Fair.

Three days after the muster on the Waun, in Riverside and Ynysgau men broke open the houses of bailiffs, pawn-brokers and loan-sharks. From his lodgings, Tomos had heard the roar as men surged from one part of town to the next, accompanied everywhere by the crash of breaking wood and glass. All day that went on, then all night shouting, and the endless agitation of a horn.

The next morning he had lingered in the crowd outside the Castle Inn, where the ironmasters had joined the hapless magistrates. He stared up at the soldiers and Specials in the windows pointing their muskets, and glimpsed Guest, wild-eyed. The sun was relentless, thunder beginning to roll around the hills to the north. A man slumped in front of him, falling onto the shoulder of his neighbour. Some in the crowd had been marching for more than 24 hours. Tomos started to push backwards between them, calling for William, and when they first swept forward he had to fight against the tide. He struggled away, and was in a distant street when he heard the soldiers open fire.

When they first returned to the town, William had preached for a while about those days in May and June. His voice had reached a road's length in every direction. 'Anyone who wants to come with me must forget himself, take up his cross each day, and follow me. For whoever wants to save his own life will lose it, but whoever loses his life will save it… For the greatest love a man can have is to lay down his life for his friends.'

But everywhere in Merthyr, wherever William spoke, the ghosts of June gathered. Tomos could almost see them between the shoulders of the living: men, women and children, leaning forward as though to hear more clearly. He thought that William saw them too. Lifting silent faces they listened, and listened, until autumn was all but burnt out, and William's voice was a leaf falling on grass. 'As the Scriptures say: There is no one who is righteous, no one who is wise. All have turned away from God; they have all gone wrong; no one does what is right, not even one…'

Hallowe'en came. When they had travelled down the border in May, the orchards of Herefordshire were cloudy with pink blossom; when they had passed through in early autumn the trees were studded with young red apples, as though hundreds of tiny fires burned among their branches. Entering his lodgings in the late afternoon, sun already past the top of the mountain, Tomos found a group of farmhands from Carmarthenshire gathered over a bowl in which half a dozen apples floated. One leant down with his hands behind his back, snapping at the apples with his teeth, while the others cheered. The Jenkin brothers stood looking on and laughing. Tomos could smell the gin.

He stepped back into the hall. William was in his own room, and Tomos liked less and less to disturb him. He turned back to the stairs, and out into the bitter air.

He started westward, away from the town and towards the last of the light. As the road started to pull upwards he grew warmer, and strode more vigorously into the mountain's shadow. On the sides of the road thorn bushes gave way to bare, ragged fields. Slowly he became aware of the silence at his back: the works empty, the furnaces out. Sheep bleated in a distant field. Further down the valley a chapel bell, slightly fast, chimed five.

He marched until hunger overtook him, then turned around. The town had fallen wholly into darkness, the western edge of sky blocked by the mountain above. Across the valley was the way they had once taken to the Waun: bright streams of people had swelled over the hillside from every direction, crossing and mingling with their own. Now, as he stared through the gloom, he saw small lights ranged on the distant scarp, and more in the fields below where he stood. The Hallowe'en fires were built.

At the far edge of the field immediately beside him, red sparks spurted towards the sky. There was a crack of dry wood splintering, and a girl's loud laugh. Somewhere below was William, wordless in his room, and a thought returned to Tomos: He changes. That, though, was unfair. William's truth and his inconstancy both lay in the same place: he was a mirror, deep and clear. People saw their hearts reflected in him.

His legs urged him back down the mountain. In the town, outside one house then another, men were carving out turnip-heads, their children giggling with excitement. Finished heads were balanced on doorsteps and windowsills, lit from within by the stubs of fatty candles. The image came to Tomos of a child he had never seen: Mari's daughter, hollowed by cholera, gazing into darkness with bright, glowing eyes.

He burst into his room, which was empty, and smelled of apples and sweat. There was nothing to be heard behind William's door.

The Jenkin brothers came stumbling in together early on All Hallows morning, the younger one with a bloody nose and both of them blazing drunk. Tomos did not see the Carmarthenshire boys again; no one came to the inn to ask for William, or to beg for relief. Ahead of Guy Fawkes Night, the magistrates armed and mobilised two hundred Specials, and two days later the cavalry rode down from Abergavenny. The magistrates had lost their nerve, but the men had been too hungry for too long. There was a pall over the town like ash. Tomos stood at William's shoulder as the crowds reduced, Mari at the preacher's other hand. News came that the Dowlais men had given up the union, and a week after Guy Fawkes Night the Plymouth men resolved to go back to work.

Some mornings later Tomos woke before dawn, and sat up shivering at the window. A quiet rain was falling. A door banged in the street. He looked down, and saw a lantern move fleetingly along the wall of the inn; it passed under the window and out of view. Some minutes later came the careful sound of hooves on the cobbles. A horse emerged from the side of the street. The shape on its back was William's.

Tomos had known it already. He had known for days. The horse moved slowly, conscious of its unsteady load. Tomos felt a low pang, close not so much to hunger as to the memory of food. Over the roofs to the east a red gleam appeared in the sky. It might have been the sun rising, or the first flames of the furnace.

Afterword: A Red Flag Raised

Dr Richard C. Allen
Newcastle University

ANY STUDY OF INDUSTRIAL south Wales in the first half of the nineteenth century would naturally expose the friction between industrial entrepreneurs and their employees. In this period one event has loomed large in Welsh industrial and political history – the Merthyr rising of June 1831. This nevertheless ignores the wave of strikes and industrial conflict before and after the summer of 1831, particularly the growth of Chartism and the Newport uprising in 1839. These were heady times when early attempts at early trade unionism to advocate workers' rights were visualised by the authorities, regionally and nationally, as the outpourings of radicals who were hell-bent on raising the red flag of revolution. The reality is somewhat different.

As a backdrop to what happened in Merthyr in the summer of 1831, it is important to remember that popular protest had long been associated with Wales. From the end of the eighteenth century onwards there were frequent riots in both rural and urban Wales against the prevailing political, social and economic conditions. Violent outbursts were common with disturbances occurring in the industrial south, the rural west and in the northern reaches of the country and, in many cases, order was restored only after the reading of the Riot Act and the deployment of troops. Between 1809 and 1812 strikes were used as a means by the employees at the Dowlais and Cyfarthfa ironworks to redress their social and economic grievances. The workers were rarely successful in achieving their aims, especially as the Combination Acts (1799 and 1800) meant that strikes were illegal and those involved in such activity could face imprisonment for three months or hard labour for two months. After 1815 and the end of the Napoleonic wars, the situation worsened. There was a widespread economic depression and with a rapidly increasing population, coupled with increases in the cost of grain and rents, the enclosure of common land as well as a general lack of employment, resentment was growing.[1] The great ironworkers strike of 1816 in Merthyr was a result of an impending wage reduction of 40%, the prospect of further unemployment, and the use of the hated truck or company shop where workers were forced to buy their supplies.[2] Throughout the industrial belt, which stretched between Glamorgan and Monmouthshire, hundreds of miners and ironworkers sought to rectify the injustices, as they perceived them, of the employers. Such orchestrated activity led to violent outbursts and many industrialists, including the Crawshays and the Guests, quickly acted to preserve their property and their lives by calling on locally-based soldiers and cavalry to protect them.

Increasingly other tactics were employed by the workers. From 1815 onwards the Scotch Cattle, a clandestine movement, prevailed in their Black Domain in Monmouthshire and southern Breconshire, and intimidated employers, landlords, bailiffs, and strike-breakers ('doggies') with warning notes, midnight visits and violence.[3] In conjunction with such actions, calls for parliamentary reform, especially an expansion of the electorate and an end to bribery and corruption, had been voiced from the last quarter of the eighteenth century onwards. There was a desire to see the end of rigged elections where gentry families would either intimidate voters or simply buy their allegiance in the days before the secret ballot existed.[4] Nineteenth-century radicals provided new reform momentum in Wales and progressive literature from England began to be disseminated in Wales and even translated into Welsh. In the period before the uprising in Merthyr, reform meetings were held across the country and petitions for reform were presented. Although the demand was for electoral reform, it was assumed that such a measure would lead to the amelioration of the worsening social and economic conditions in the industrial heartlands. The Tory governments of the 1820s nevertheless rejected demands for reform including Lord John Russell's bill of February 1830. The defeat of Lord Wellington's Tory administration in 1830 was accompanied by a pledge by Lord Grey's Whig government (in November that year) to preside over a measure of parliamentary reform. The limited scope of this proposed electoral change was quickly exposed, however, and another general election was held in March 1831 with only one central topic – a Second Reform Bill.

Welsh elections were often accompanied with violence and 1831 was no exception. There were riots in Carmarthen in late April and special constables were employed to disperse the angry protesters (none of whom had the right to vote it should be added) with a further request by the magistrates for soldiers to be permanently stationed in the town to quell any unrest. In Merthyr there was also history of popular protest with riots taking place in 1800, 1810, 1813 and notably in 1816 when thousands marched against the ironmasters. And yet the riot that began on Friday 3 June 1831 turned into a massacre with 24 fatalities – even more than had been experienced at Peterloo, in Manchester, twelve years earlier. Although there were 800 soldiers in the vicinity the labourers held the town for nearly four days.[5]

Naturally, the lack of parliamentary reform had provoked one level of resentment, but other causes played their part. The Scotch Cattle clearly had a presence in the town, while the decision by William Crawshay Jnr to reduce the wages of the ironstone miners in March 1831 at Cyfarthfa and Hirwaun motivated the workers to seek redress of their grievances. The situation worsened on 24 May with Crawshay's decision to dismiss 84 puddlers (or ironworkers). The increasing combination of workers in friendly societies, notably in London, Manchester and in north-west Wales, was replicated in the industrial south of the country. Certainly, political-union clubs existed in Merthyr and Aberdare, and members agitated for reform, but the decisions made by Crawshay dominated the social, economic and political landscape of Merthyr and the surrounding area. There was a long tradition of political activism with agitators offering advice before riots or promoting the cause of liberty during such events. The London Corresponding Society alongside clandestine groups held meetings on the hillsides, read from the works of noted political philosophers such as Voltaire, Tom Paine and Henry Hunt, and promoted an end to harsh living and working conditions, including the truck shop system and the recovery of small debts in the Court of Requests. There was certainly growing resentment at this form of exploitation and a widespread sense of social and economic injustice directed against Crawshay and other industrialists or political figures, such as the Breconshire MP, Colonel Wood. These sentiments were echoed by political agitators and union preachers, including William Twiss, the key historical figure in Anna's story. Twiss was a Lancashire representative of the National Association of the Protection of Labour (NAPL or more commonly known as 'the Union'). Although a shadowy figure, Twiss's role as a fundraiser and significantly as an orator was pivotal, having visited the town in the spring of 1831, before returning again in the autumn, where Anna's story begins. These demagogues advocated democratic rights, called for better living and working conditions, fair wages and an end to the truck system. Indeed, Twiss is referred to in the authorised account of the Secretary of State for the Home Department the following autumn.

Historical accounts and modern analyses of the uprising in Merthyr have triggered different responses. Historians have argued that the events at Merthyr were simply bread riots or the precursor to Chartism, while more pertinently they have been described as a massacre of 24 protesters. So, how should the sequence of actions taken in early June 1831 be assessed? Reform meetings were regularly held and on Wednesday 1 June, Richard Fothergill, the ironmaster of Aberdare, was threatened by an angry crowd at his home at Abernant House who demanded that he withdraw the claim that the workers were overpaid. In an atmosphere of increasing violence, Crawshay's labourers thereafter burned effigies of parliamentarians or those who had sought compensation from the Court of Requests and confronted civic dignitaries who opposed parliamentary reform or were perceived to be oppressive. Local and regional newspapers, such as *The Cambrian*, were quick to condemn 'the daring and atrocious proceedings' of the rioters and their alleged organisers.[6] The authorities condemned the lawless aggression while others went as far as to suggest that the rioters were revolutionaries or Jacobins.

The next day (Thursday 2 June), Lewis Lewis (*Lewsyn yr Heliwr*), along with other representatives, gathered outside the home of Thomas Lewis, a shopkeeper who was known for his exploitation of workers. Confronted by special constables, and in the presence of magistrates, the Riot Act was read to them, but it proved to be a hollow statement as the workers ransacked Lewis's premises and other shops whose owners did not support union activity. Unsurprisingly, the shopkeepers and other traders requested the magistrates seek military assistance. The situation quickly escalated with an attack on the home of William Coffin, the clerk of the Court of Requests, and the mob, contrary to popular opinion, comprised young workers, boys and women. Many other labourers were still at work and in this sense the action was representative of many bread riots which had occurred in previous decades.

Influenced by those who sought parliamentary reform and unionism, notably Twiss, as well as a desire to end the economic exploitation of workers, a larger gathering of miners met at Merthyr on 3 June to present their demands to the ironmasters at the Castle Inn. Carrying banners and other radical symbols, including a red flag,[7] and demanding cheap bread, this was not a peaceful demonstration, but rather the use of physical force to correct both political and economic injustices. The demonstrators cordoned off the streets and again the Riot Act was read. Crawshay and his fellow ironmaster Josiah Guest called for the rioters to disperse and insisted that they would only listen to the demands of the workers via a delegation a few days later. The 93rd Highlanders, who were now providing protection for the ironmasters in the Castle Inn, were increasingly threatened by the large crowd outside. Who gave the order to fire has never been determined, but most likely it was a reaction to the attempt to seize a soldier's weapon. Repeatedly the soldiers fired on the mob before they retreated. The dead and injured were then carried away with several dying of their wounds later that night or days afterwards. Those who died included an elderly woman who was simply a bystander and a twelve-year-old boy. Although the crowd was unsuccessful on this occasion, they had regrouped and Lewis Lewis urged them to repeat their attack on the Castle Inn.

Urgent requests from the Merthyr authorities led to the dispatching of the Glamorgan militia from Cardiff as well as the yeomanry. In response, the rioters blockaded roads in and around Merthyr, and ambushed military supply routes. Nevertheless, there were divisions among the rioters – some were willing to negotiate with the ironmasters concerning wages, while others sought further demands and were increasingly threatening. Further waves of unrest were apparent in the industrial centres of Glamorgan and Monmouthshire but, unlike the 1816 strike, workmen from these areas did not march on Merthyr. On Sunday 5 June, over 400 soldiers were dispatched to Dowlais to counter any further insurrectionary activity. The Riot Act was read once more and the soldiers with fixed bayonets were able to disperse the crowd. Further divisions among the rioters became increasingly apparent, but historians have debated whether the deal reached by the workers with Guest amounted to a great betrayal.[8] Although there were attempts by the rioters to secure Merthyr, by the following

Tuesday (7 June), at least 18 rioters had been arrested and Lewis Lewis had also been captured. Effectively the siege of Merthyr was over and many of the men had returned to work after receiving a promise by Crawshay not to reduce wages.

More arrests occurred in the following days and on 11 July the prisoners were brought before the Glamorgan Assizes. Several were acquitted, others were transported for life to the penal colonies in Australia, but Lewis Lewis and Richard Lewis (*Dic Penderyn*) faced treason charges and were sentenced to death. Lewis Lewis was charged with being the ringleader of the rioters and causing the initial bloodshed, while Dic Penderyn was found guilty of wounding a soldier at the Castle Inn. The former was later reprieved but on 13 August Dic was hanged at Cardiff gaol. This was in spite of popular support for clemency and the attempts by Joseph Tregelles Price, the ironmaster of Neath, to get the Home Secretary to overturn the decision. An unlikely folk hero, Dic was a 23-year-old miner who, after being unjustly condemned, became Wales's first working-class martyr. The evidence against him was certainly flimsy at best and it is now generally believed that he was innocent of the crime that he was alleged to have committed. In contrast, Lewis Lewis certainly played a leading role in the rising. His reprieve has nevertheless led to suggestions that he had a close relationship with the squirearchy or even acted as a spy for the authorities.

The rising at Merthyr was primarily orchestrated to return goods taken by the Court of Requests to their 'rightful' owners, to force the ironmasters to rescind their decision to reduce wages, and to end the truck system, and not as sometimes assumed to recognise workers' rights or their unions. Historian David Jones certainly implied that unionism developed independently of the riots.[9] Indeed, it can be pointed out that while the rioters carried the red flag of reform, they did not use the symbolic union oath as a distinguishing feature of the protest. Despite the early presence of William Twiss in Merthyr and the production of associated union literature as well as the activity of the NAPL in North Wales, union activity was clearly in its infancy in South Wales. A large meeting had been arranged on the Waun on 30 May and this was attended by Twiss. This led to the creation of lodges of the Friendly Society of Coalmining in Merthyr and elsewhere in coalmining districts lodges were established with the intention of instilling solidarity among the workers.[10]

Significantly, as Anna's story shows, the protest movement certainly did not end in June. In the autumn and winter of 1831 further unrest occurred. As noted, Twiss and other English union delegates had already been present in the district earlier in the year, while the September disturbances, including lockouts at the Dowlais and Plymouth ironworks, were distinctive from the summer events in that the workers were not armed. So, what impact did Twiss, the 'Union Agitator', have on the workers and how was this activity recorded in official papers and newspaper reports? Clearly, his reputation and union clubs more generally were deliberately targeted. The *Carmarthen Journal and South Wales Weekly Advertiser*, a supporter of the Tories, was certainly quick to denounce these associations and Twiss in particular. It reported on 25 November 1831 that William Thompson, MP, the former Lord Mayor of London and a proprietor of the Penydarren ironworks, had met his workforce at Merthyr. He was deeply critical of the union leaders and believed that the swearing of 'secret and illegal oaths' was 'detrimental' to any cordial relationship between master and workmen. He offered the men an 'entire amnesty from the past', observing that if they returned peacefully to their work everything that had occurred would be 'forgiven and buried in oblivion'. Attention was then turned to Twiss and how the workmen had been duped into believing him.[11] The following month, the same newspaper reported that the majority of the workmen at Merthyr had gone back to work and, in a stinging attack on Twiss, a correspondent noted that the workers were now 'convinced of their folly in listening to that deceiver' and his 'nefarious practices'. A further report in the same edition throws some more light on the events and Twiss's involvement.

He had left the Merthyr Arms on 15 November, but the newspaper noted the influence of union preachers on workers at Cyfarthfa and Nant-y-Glo who continued their protest for better rights and wages unlike the workers at Dowlais and Plymouth who had 'wisely renounced the Union'. In what might appear to be a smear campaign, the newspaper alleged that Twiss had squandered union funds on alcohol and tobacco, while stating that he cared little about 'his poor misguided victims... [their] wants and sufferings... as long as he could get his gin and tobacco'.[12] What was the reality of the situation? Historians have differed. Gwyn Alf Williams considered these later developments as possibilities but not the misappropriation of the funds, while Eric Evans and more recently Joe England have certainly drawn attention to the alleged activities of union representatives, especially Twiss.[13]

The events of the autumn and winter 1831 were clearly different to those experienced in the summer months. The informal combination of colliers and ironworkers was an important development in the history of trade unionism in Wales and gave the workers confidence to seek address of their long-held grievances. Despite some natural reservations about the Repeal of the Combination Acts in the mid-1820s, even William Crawshay I accepted the legitimacy of the unions, but not all were in favour. Josiah Guest, among other industrialists in South Wales, was vehemently opposed and any worker who had union membership was informed that they would be dismissed at Dowlais and Plymouth ironworks.[14] Approximately 3-4,000 men were locked out at Dowlais and Plymouth from September to the early weeks of November. Their peaceful protest eventually came to an end as they were resigned to return to work irrespective of the legitimacy of their actions. As Joe England has observed 'the legality of their action after what had occurred in June was of huge emotional and psychological importance. This was not treason, it was not violent, it was lawful'.[15] The unions and the activity of union preachers nevertheless posed a considerable threat to the establishment, and discussions were held at the highest levels concerning the legality of unions and membership of such societies. Fudge and prevarication on behalf of the authorities nevertheless denied the workmen the right to poor relief which went against the opinion of the Home Office that union members, if their organisation was deemed legal, had the right to relief payments.[16]

But what of William Twiss? Did his unionism pose a credible threat that had to be contained and was he maligned as a result? He clearly left a mark as union membership increased, but the issue concerning the misappropriation of the union funds remains. Gwyn Alf Williams and Eric Evans certainly refer to this in their work but there has been some ambiguity concerning Twiss's departure.[17] Joe England nevertheless contends that Twiss's 'betrayal' of the workers left a bitter taste behind, which might give greater credence to the tale of his departure with the funds in his pockets (or indeed his belly). Indeed, England refers to the longevity of this popular account of treachery and Twiss's dishonesty, and cites the view of a rollerman of Merthyr who, in 1869, 38 years after the Merthyr riot was asked about union membership. His response was terse that they did have a union once, but 'the young man run away with the money'.[18] Was this a reference to Twiss? Possibly. Did he purloin the funds? Again, this is possible, but was he collecting the funds to be taken elsewhere? This is unproven but what is clear is that post-1831 union activity continued to be as relevant and indeed prevalent in and around Merthyr as it had been in the heady days of June and in the autumn of 1831. Gwyn Alf Williams emphasised the effectiveness of the union and their programme in the South Wales valleys: to prepare selective strikes, to manipulate the poor law, and to use boycotts, persuasion and intimidation if and where necessary. Moreover, cemented by the solemn oath and profound secrecy, its discipline was ferociously effective'.[19] This Twiss had encouraged and if the view of William Howell, a filler at Dowlais, is taken into consideration it shows how such views had penetrated the workers' psyche. Howell was brought before the parish vestry on 15 October 1831 and, according to the *Cambrian*, showed defiance in his belief that the union oath he had taken was 'as binding' as any other. Moreover, when questioned about his skills and trade 'secrets' with non-unionists, Howell vehemently protested they should not 'knows what all this means from the beginning; it is some of the *bloody* turncoats who say that' and that the Union was 'important and necessary', so much so that he would 'rather live on sixpence per week than give it up'.[20] As such, unionism posed such a serious threat that the authorities and industrialists, including Crawshay, sought to brutally crush membership and it potentially gives credence to the view that the characters of union officials and preachers, like Twiss, were deliberately tarnished.

A meeting of the workers 'on the hills' was called for on 17 October and this was to be attended by Twiss, the 'Great Agitator' as Colonel Love of the 11th Foot called him, but the meeting did not take place as the momentum for direct action seemed to be waning. Neverthless, the crisis in the South Wales industrial belt was heightened with rioting in Bristol at the end of October with the expectation of further violence in Merthyr and throughout Carmarthenshire, Glamorgan and Monmouthshire. The events of June and the death of the 24 had not been forgotten and a meeting of union activists was planned for 7 November, while, in contrast, the authorities ensured that the military were kept on alert. Union funds were running low, but still there was a desire to propagate the view that the workers would prevail and there was talk of revolution in the air. Twiss, in what seems to be typical of his rhetoric, read from *Isaiah 24:21*: 'And it shall come to pass in that day that the Lord shall punish the host of the high ones that are on high and the kings of the earth upon the earth. And they shall be gathered together as prisoners are gathered in the pit and shall be shut up in the prison.'[21] Tensions were clearly running high and the deployment of troops to quell any unrest was uncertain as requests were coming in throughout the country, but the resolve of the workers quickly broke and the union began to witness a steady withdrawal of members as they returned to work on 14 November. It is at this juncture that Twiss left Merthyr. The *Cambrian* reported that he 'made his escape' and the corruption allegations began.[22] Although these latter developments cast a dark shadow on the wider events of 1831, the riots in Merthyr throughout 1831 clearly showed that popular protest in Wales was far from over while the momentum for political, social and economic reform would gather pace in the Chartist movement throughout the remainder of the decade and beyond.[23] Twiss may have left the area but the activism of union officials and preachers as well as the determination of the workers and their personal sacrifices, despite the many bitter disappointments of 1831, were not forgotten.

Notes

1. For details see David J.V. Jones, *Before Rebecca: Popular Protests in Wales, 1793-1835* (Allen Lane, 1973).

2. This is discussed in Joe England, *Merthyr: The Crucible of Modern Wales, 1760-1912* (Parthian, 2017), pp. 64-100.

3. Initially this was a clandestine organisation of Monmouthshire ironworkers, but later involved other industrial workers. It existed from 1822 until the mid-1830s in the heartlands of industrial development in South Wales (the 'Black Domain'), but it was also a feature of later periods up to the late 1850s. Its mythical leader was 'Ned', 'Lolly' or 'the Bull'. See David J. V. Jones, 'The Scotch Cattle and their Black Domain', *Welsh History Review*, 5, 3 (June 1971), pp. 220-49, and his later study 'Scotch Cattle and Chartism', in Trevor Herbert and Gareth E. Jones (eds), *People and Protest: Wales, 1815-1880* (University of Wales Press, 1988), pp. 139-64; Rhian E. Jones, 'Symbol, Ritual and Popular Protest in Early Nineteenth-Century Wales: The Scotch Cattle Rebranded', *Welsh History Review*, 26, 1 (June 2012), pp. 34-57. Also, compare with

general insights of radical movements in D. T. Wright, *Popular Radicalism: The Working Class Experience, 1780-1880* (Longman, 1988), pp. 64-74.

4. For further details see John Belchem, *'Orator' Hunt: Henry Hunt and English Working Class Radicalism* (Clarendon, 1985); Nancy D. LoPatin, *Political Unions, Popular Politics and the Great Reform Act of 1832* (Macmillan, 1999); John E. Archer, *Social Unrest and Popular Protest in England, 1780-1840* (Cambridge University Press, 2000); Rachel Eckersley, 'Of Radical Design: John Cartwright and the Redesign of the Reform Campaign, c.1800-1811', *History*, 89, 296 (October 2004), pp. 560-80; Katrina Navickas, *Protest and the Politics of Space and Place, 1789-1848* (Manchester University Press, 2015).

5. See Gwyn A. Williams, *The Merthyr Rising* (Croom Helm, 1978); England, *Merthyr*, pp. 101-13.

6. *Cambrian*, 11 June 1831, p. 3.

7. This was symbolic of the call for reform and the first time such a potent expression of radicalism had been raised on British soil.

8. Jones, *Before Rebecca*, p. 149.

9. Jones, *Before Rebecca*, pp. 157-8.

10. Williams, *Merthyr Rising*, pp. 110-12; England, *Merthyr*, pp. 114-15.

11. *Carmarthen Journal and South Wales Weekly Advertiser*, 25 November 1831, p. 3. His involvement and activity in Merthyr in the autumn and winter months of 1831 is similarly discussed in the *Monmouthshire Merlin*, 12 November 1831, p. 3.

12. *Carmarthen Journal and South Wales Weekly Advertiser*, 9 December 1831, p. 3.

13. Williams, *Merthyr Rising*, pp. 208-23; Eric W. Evans, *The Miners of South Wales* (University of Wales Press, 1961), p. 47; England, *Merthyr*, pp. 114-19.

14. England, *Merthyr*, pp. 115-16.

15. England, *Merthyr*, p. 116.

16. Gwyn A. Williams, 'Merthyr 1831: Lord Melbourne and the Trade Unions', *Llafur: The Journal of Welsh Labour History*, 1, 1 (May 1972), pp. 3-15.

17. Williams, *Merthyr Rising*, p. 220; Evans, *Miners of South Wales*, p. 47.

18. 'The Merthyr Iron Worker', in Norman Macleod (ed.), *Good Words* (Strahan & Co., 1869), pp. 35-44 (statement on p. 42), 1 January 1869, and cited in England, *Merthyr*, p. 119.

19. Williams, *Merthyr Rising*, p. 209.

20. *Cambrian*, 15 October 1831, p. 3; Williams, *Merthyr Rising*, pp. 214-15.

21. Williams, *Merthyr Rising*, pp. 217-19; *Monmouthshire Merlin*, 12 November 1831, p. 3 although the *Merlin* suggested that this was 26:21.

22. *Cambrian*, 19 November 1831, p. 3; 26 November 1831, p. 3.

23. For details of Welsh Chartism see *Llafur*,10, 3 (2010).

We Will, We Will, We Will

Kim Squirrell

'WE WILL WALK THE whole eight miles,' said Aunt Betsy.

'We will,' said Molly.

So they set off first thing, Molly, Betsy and the other women. The ice cracking under their feet and the wind fingering its way through the hedges and into their bones. When sunlight jewelled the beads of dew on the blackthorn Molly's tears came, such beauty seemed to mock their solemn march. If her uncle George were here he would find something to cheer them. As though she heard her thoughts, Betsy linked her arm and pulled her in, stepping up the pace. Molly was glad to be back. She first came to stay when her aunt was ill, and now she was needed again, only this time it was Betsy's heart that was sick, with her husband wrongfully arrested and brothers and friends besides, six men in all with their families at breaking point with fear and worry.

They were making good headway when they came to the top of the rise so they rested a while and watched the last of the morning mist sweep across the fields towards Dorchester, grand and glittering in the cold sunlight. Heartened now their destination was in sight, they walked on and had just reached the outskirts of the town when the sound of cartwheels clattered behind them and a voice rang out.

'Hey there!'

Molly turned to see Charlie Legge, driving his brother's cart.

'If you will, Mrs Loveless,' Charlie said and addressed each of them in turn. 'Allow me to take you the rest of the way.'

The women, blue and bitten by the March wind, gladly accepted his offer, but for Betsy who walked on until Molly ran after her and persuaded her to climb up and be helped.

Was it only last summer Molly was striding down to the chapel with Betsy's baby on her hip? With the apples fattening on the orchard trees and the stream full and singing? That day she found the chapel door thrown open and drifts of dirt blown in? She put the baby down and started to sweep, the dust spooling into the air so much she had to wave it away to keep from choking.

'You're just moving that dirt around, maid,' came a voice from behind.

Molly swept harder. The baby waddled over and sat in the pile of dust, clouds billowed up anew. Molly started a fit of coughing and a tall swarthy boy strode in and lifted the little one up, who straight away started to cry.

'I've swept more floors than you,' said Molly taking the baby out of his arms, 'and you're holding him like he's made of glass.'

The boy offered her his hand.

'What?' asked Molly.

'Let's see them,' he said. 'These working hands.'

Molly moved her arm behind her back.

'Ahh so you *are* afraid of me,' said the boy, grinning.

She narrowed her eyes and held out her hand.

He turned it palm up. 'Well,' he said, pulling on her fingers, 'these are fine enough for a lady's maid at the very least.'

Molly snatched her hand back. 'Just because you work for the big house doesn't mean you know anything about anything, Charles Legge.'

'Who would want to know anything?' said Charlie, walking away backwards. 'I'd rather know something.'

Back at the cottage Molly handed the baby over to Betsy to be fed and set about making the supper. She looked in the meat safe; their meagre ration of bacon was all gone, so she had to be content to scrub the potatoes and put them on to boil with an extra pinch of salt.

After supper George invited her to sit with him and Betsy at the table.

'I have something for you to do, Molly', said George. 'If you're willing to put your talent to good use.'

'My talent?' asked Molly.

George turned to Betsy who smiled and said, 'We've seen your drawings Molly.'

Molly flushed and looked from one to the other, 'I thought you wouldn't approve. Mother says the devil makes work for idle hands.'

'I don't consider it idleness,' said her uncle, but a God given gift, that sketch you made of the baby, the sheep shearers at work, you captured the life in them and that is what we need.'

He placed a set of illustrations in front of her. The first was an engraving of a standing man with his skin stripped away, in the next he was all sinews and tendons, and in the third he had the pit holes of the skull and all his bones exposed.

'They are from a book of anatomy,' explained her uncle.

Molly felt uneasy at seeing a body in pieces. But the more she looked the more she wanted to look.

'I need a likeness of this,' said George tapping the skeleton, 'with an hourglass in the right hand. And another figure is needed which I have no likeness for, so it is for you to imagine. And that one should represent Death.'

'George!' said Betsy, 'start more gently... isn't this first task enough for now? Had you not better explain more of it?'

'Is it for your sermons, Uncle?' asked Molly.

'No... but a good cause all the same. We are to start what is called a Friendly Society, a way for those of us who work the land, to help ourselves and each other to a better life. It has been done by weavers and tailors in Exeter. Your uncle John in Bridport has joined with other flax-dressers. They are planning great things... they are doing great things to aid working people in their hardship. Is this something you might help with, Molly? What do you think?'

Molly's first attempts were poor, she had the proportions all wrong; the legs too long, the head too small. Her uncle had asked for it to be much larger, so she had to scale it up with no idea how to do it. If her mother could see how much paper she was using, she would crack a switch across her knuckles.

'You're trying too hard,' her aunt said. 'Walk out... find something else to draw and come back to it.'

Molly walked up to the churchyard where the yew fanned across the path. She stood in its shadow, looked up through the curving branches and got out her paper and pencil. She caught a movement out in the light and kept perfectly still. Charlie Legge came into view. He stopped at a grave. She thought to call to him, but standing as he was – his black livery sharp against the white wall of the cottages – she started to draw him instead: head bowed, feet slightly apart, arms at his side. She recalled his warm fingers tracing the skin of her palm. She continued to draw him as he moved away, quick, urgent strokes with her eyes still on him until he was out of sight. She walked over to read the headstone. 'William Legge, departed this life October 10th 1818', almost fifteen years ago, only a month before her own father.

As soon as she was back in the cottage, Molly set to. The skeleton came easy now she saw it as a body not a pattern or a model to be copied. She captured it so well, a broad grin spread over her uncle's face when he saw it.

'Now, one more figure from you Molly, if you please, and they both must be made into banners and you shall come with me, to Dorchester.'

It was market day in Dorchester, cattle and sheep hurdled in pens, fowl screeching in their crates and game hanging from the butcher's hooks. George stopped to examine sacks of grain. The woman next to him had two small girls, whose pale fists were fastened tight to her skirt. They looked to be about three and four but a glimpse of their faces revealed they were older.

'How is anyone to afford it?' the woman said to the trader, who acted as though she wasn't there and trained his full attention on George.

'Will you not answer, sir?' asked George.

The man looked the woman up and down. 'I have to live too, Missus.'

'You have more meat on you than my little ones,' she said and scooped up the smallest and held her out to him. He did not meet her eye; he could see the child was all bones. He looked at George and reached under his table, pulled out a bag, filled it, and pressed it into her hands. She tried to give him a coin but he refused, she went to take his hand, a pained expression bloomed fleetingly in his eyes. He waved her on.

'I'll thank you to stare at me no more,' said the trader. 'Or I will make no profit today.'

'Bless you, sir,' said George and they moved on.

Though the market place itself seemed busy the stalls soon petered out.

'It's not so big as I remember,' said Molly as they came to the last of them.

'It is not unusual when the harvest has been poor, but some will be selling what there is elsewhere for more profit… which only serves to make the hardship greater here.'

'Grandma told Charlie and me about the common land where people could graze their geese and sell eggs at the market and everyone had a strip of a field they tilled and planted together. There used to be woodland too, she said, for firewood and nuts and berries and game.'

'Ahh, your grandmother tells a fine tale,' said George. 'That's not to say there's no truth in it Molly, no indeed, it is true that having common land allowed people to do more for themselves. Some still mourn the loss of it.'

'But Charlie told us how enclosure improved the land and we ought not stand in the way of progress,' Molly added.

'Improved it may have been, my father saw the last of the common land divided into farms and turned to arable and pasture, but were the people's lives improved alongside it? Not at all, for they were locked even further into dependency, having to pay for what was once freely theirs to use.'

'Surely it is for the benefit of everyone to make improvement,' insisted Molly.

'It may, but think on it; the land was taken away from those who had little and given to those who already had more than they need. I'd say it is our duty to "stand in the way" of such "progress".'

'There are lots of things Charlie thinks we shouldn't stand in the way of.'

'You bring that boy along one day,' said George. 'Betsy and I should get to know him.'

They came at last to the shop, the sign reading: 'James Whetham Painter'. In the window, portraits, cartoons and scenic paintings were so closely displayed it was hard to know where to look. The woman behind the counter wore a fixed smile. She greeted George with stiff enthusiasm.

'Mr Loveless isn't it? And what brings you to our door? Some lettering perhaps?'

'I am needing two banners,' said George as he laid out the drawings.

The woman lifted her glasses and peered at them. 'And what size would they need to be?'

'They should each be six feet and with dark backgrounds.'

'It's for your ministry is it Mr Loveless? Fire and brimstone coming to Tolpuddle is it?'

George didn't answer and she looked over the drawings again.

'I imagine Mr Whetham can make sense of them,' she said closing them in a drawer. 'You will have to call back in a week or two.'

'I shall be back home by then, Uncle,' complained Molly as they left the shop.

'Nevertheless you must come to see it done. They are your designs, unless you don't want to own them.'

Molly was not embarrassed by them, even though the second figure was strange. She had worried at first, over how it was to be done, then recalled the churchyard and William Legge's headstone. She walked the boundary until she found the grave but the headstone had nothing unusual on it. Where had she seen it? She crossed to the yew tree and took up the position she had the day she saw Charlie. She walked slowly towards the grave, looking to the right and to left, looking down... and there it was, embedded in the ground. She scraped away the soil and moss and sketched it, as best she could. She ran all the way home and drew and drew until she had it right, a skull face with wings outstretched either side. Above it she copied out the words her uncle had given her.

'Remember Thine End.'

She held it up and appraised her handiwork. Had she done it? Was this enough? Her uncle had asked her to think about those words. 'How are we to be truly God-fearing without the contemplation of our own mortality,' he'd said. Yes, she had done it. The rightful fear of God was in it and she had put it there.

The following Tuesday, when Molly and George arrived at the Whetham's shop, there were no banners. The painter threw Molly's drawings on the counter.

'What's this, Mr Loveless?' demanded the painter, his thin lips drawn in a hard line. 'What could you possibly want with such images?'

'It is for a society, Mr Whetham, you know the kind of thing.'

'I'm a devout man, Mr Loveless. I don't hold with this.'

'It's not for my ministry, but a Friendly Society of our own making'

125

'It is one and the same I should say, and it is a wonder that business at your so-called chapel did not make it clear to you what God-fearing people think of these, "things of your own making!"'

'I see,' said George carefully. 'If you cannot oblige me I shall go elsewhere.'

'You are welcome to,' said the painter. 'Good day.'

They walked a while in silence, until Molly asked what the painter meant, what was the business he spoke of.

'I won't speak of it Molly, but to say that it proved how much the powers that be hate a man who can read his own Bible and think his own thoughts…It shouldn't be wondered at … Aren't Church and master hand in glove and only concerned with their own gain… not content to pass judgement themselves, they persuade working folk to believe dissent is witchcraft and not simply standing up for what is right!'

Molly had heard her uncle speak plain and bold many times, though this time there was heaviness in his voice. She remembered Betsy telling her of the weeks before Molly's father died. It was the first time they worshipped at the chapel. A mob, a hundred strong, gathered outside and would not let them pass. They abused and tormented the congregation, some were wounded, women among them. It so grieved her father, already sickening, that he scarce lasted the month. Her uncle would have been a young man then and it seemed even now he couldn't turn the hurt about. Even though he could always do that for them. When they had little to eat or not enough wood for the fire Uncle George would warm them with a story or find a scripture to feed their souls. Because he shared whatever he had, good things seemed to come to them. Though hungry, they were never in despair. Wasn't there always a way?

'I will do it, Uncle,' said Molly. 'I will paint them.'

George looked closely at her. 'Do you really think you can Molly? It is a thing of importance and must be executed well… you have never painted before.'

Molly met his gaze. 'I believe I can, Uncle, if you will trust me to.'

George offered her his arm. 'We can purchase paint and brushes. You can work in Thomas's upstairs room. 'And,' said George, 'I have just the thing to inspire you.'

They dived down a narrow alley and came to a modest building which, when they opened the door, revealed itself to be quite grand. Shelves stretched along the walls and over and around the doorways. There were all kinds of objects used as bookends: stuffed animals, carved figures, a cabinet full of sparkling rocks and tiny skulls. Molly explored the books, running her fingers along the spines as she read: *The Red Gauntlet* by Walter Scott; Spenser's *The Fairie Queen*. She lifted out a large volume of renaissance paintings. Most of the pictures were black and white but one or two were coloured. She recognised the Bible scenes: the serpent in the garden, the annunciation, the last supper. Then she came to an angel, black-winged and beautiful. Her Death figure has wings. Could she make them like these? A dark woman, dressed in black, appeared from the back of the shop. Molly quickly slid the book back onto the shelf.

'How can I help you today, Mr Loveless?' asked the woman.

'I wonder if you might extend your kindness to my niece here Mrs Harp,' said her uncle, 'and show her the book. She is a gifted young artist.'

'Indeed?' said the woman. 'If she is half as accomplished as you are with words Mr Loveless, I shall be interested to see her work.'

Mrs Harp led them through to the back of the shop. The room was small and sparsely furnished; a couch, a desk, two elegant fireside chairs. Light flooded in from a tightly curved bay window. The pale green walls were freshly painted and the large rug, although worn and faded, was richly patterned. Mrs Harp fed the fire and jiggled the logs until the flames leapt up. She opened the draw of her desk and took out a slim volume.

127

'And you can read, Molly?' asked Mrs Harp, with a note in her voice that betrayed her doubt.

'My uncle has taught me,' answered Molly.

'Very good, very good,' she said, her dark eyes bright with pleasure. 'Now may I see your hands?'

Molly gave them up for inspection. Mrs Harp looked them over, touching the groove in her finger where her pencil had made its mark. When she was satisfied, Molly was allowed to sit in the fireside chair with the *Songs of Innocence and Experience*.

As they returned to the shop her uncle asked Mrs Harp what news she had of her brother.

'He now has the vote, Mr Loveless,' she said. 'Which is a start...'

Molly opened the book and heard nothing more. She turned the pages carefully, taking her time over the illustrations, each one aglow with washes of colour and line. Just as slowly she was drawn into the strangeness of them, a feeling on the edge of excitement that tingled at the nape of her neck. Soon her hands trembled and itched for the chance to trace on the page the arc of her own imagination. Then a manual on oil painting was brought and she made a list of pigments and seed oils. Her uncle said they may not be able to fulfill her wishes entirely, but they might go to the plasterer who was bound to know of something. Then she asked to see the book with the black-winged angel and George had to tell her three times before she heard him, that it was time to go.

When Molly finally brought Charlie to the house, they found Betsy struggling with the boys who had brought in the neighbour's hens. George and young Sam Wright had just come in from the fields, wet and muddy and deep in conversation, standing by the fire, refusing to sit. Molly heard a rise in Sam's voice a shade below anger, for he was quick to it. She got the boys to bed and Betsy got the men to the table.

'You must remember that we are all created equal and in

the likeness of God,' said George. 'It was only action that separated Cain and Abel, not being shepherd or farmer, first born or second but action and so it ought to be now, if a man works hard and fair then he should thrive whatever his station and that is what we work towards.'

'All well and good, George, but how are we to change this present state of things? You met with them and made agreements that have all now been dishonoured. Our wages...? Cut again. Take what's ours. Isn't that what we need? Not more talk!'

'Volume,' said George.

'Shouting won't get us anywhere.'

'By volume I mean numbers,' answered George, 'The masters are of one mind and they have the ear of the great and powerful of a similar mind, but we have these.' And George laid his hands on the table, the skin cracked and brown with the ploughing and harvest of twenty years that no amount of washing had ever moved. 'These,' he said, 'are our voice and our power, our hands and the work of our hands are the loudest voice we have. If we deny them our labour it hits them where they can hear it.' And he tapped his pocket as though it were full of coin.

'And that's what you mean to do?' asked Sam.

'It is all there is in our power to do... better that, than break machines... or heads.' said George.

Charlie was staring at George's hands with a look of disdain.

'These offend you, boy?' asked George. ''And what of the masters' hands, clean and sweet with rosewater? Yet are they red with our blood. Though these hands be black they are something to be proud of, hands that make and break and mend.'

'It's not your hands, Mr Loveless.' Charlie replied. 'It's just that our master has been good to us. My father and grandfather and his. When my father died he gave me a chance. They have the greater responsibility. What do we know of it?'

'Nonsense,' said Sam.

'We know how we might live better if we had what was rightfully ours,' said George

Charlie was about to speak but instead cast his eyes down.

'Come with me when I next go to preach, Charles. See how people live!'

Charlie shifted uncomfortably in his chair. He looked over at Molly and nodded. 'Perhaps I will, Mr Loveless,' he said.

Charlie did not go with George. Nor did he ever come to visit her again. Yet here he was, on the Dorchester Road, come to help them and would he sit with them in that place full of clean hands and not be ashamed?

The streets of Dorchester were abuzz with expectation. The Assizes were a great draw and people came from miles around. Inns and shops, keen for the trade, had bolstered their wares and hiked their prices.

'They're all here for the spectacle,' said Molly as she climbed out of the cart.

'Let them look,' said Betsy.

When they got to High West Street a throng of people came into view stretching all the way to the courthouse steps. Charlie went up to the head of the line and held out his arms and shouted.

'Loveless coming through.'

Everyone moved aside to let them ahead so that the women were first to enter the towering doors and climb the stairs to the gallery. Long-legged Molly in front leading her aunt by the hand. Hobnails clattered on the stone steps, skirts lifted, the walls rising high on either side, with no rail to steady them. A light above, that when they reached the top was cold and cheerless. Before them, a steep rank of benches, with no way down except to step on them, one after another. Molly was so busy looking at her feet, she didn't see the people already there in that great room, taller than a church. When Aunt Betsy was hesitant to go all the way down – 'For it is too steep!' – Molly squeezed her hand and pulled on it like Betsy used to when Molly was a child. Her aunt half smiled, as though she remembered, and nodded herself into resolve. They clambered all the way down to sit at the front rail. Behind them other members of the families, the Stanfields, the Hammetts and Brines and more besides, unknown to them. Molly dulled her ears to their remarks and mutterings afraid of what she might hear. Before them the empty chair where the judge would sit and ranked either side in boxes, stern faces, amused faces, all better dressed and better fed than their company, a jury of farmers and masters and others with property. To the right, the place where the witnesses would stand, and before them where Uncle George and the others would come up from the cells. There was an echo to this place beyond hearing that lent a weight to every word spoken. In the crowd someone had already got out a parcel of sweet buns and a flagon of small beer and started handing it round. From somewhere the sound of a chain and the smell of woodsmoke. The jostle and fidget of bodies impatient to see what spectacle would play out before them. The only stillness was a solitary figure dressed in black standing below, a model of patience and preparation.

The man in black called them to order and the judge entered with others following all grave and terrible. Sickness stirred in Molly's belly and the air grew heavy and impenetrable. A bell rang and the men came up to stand in the dock. George coughing and leaning on his brother James. Betsy grabbed Molly's arm and Molly covered her hand with hers. A robed man stood up and quoted the law, how it is illegal for any society to administer an oath. A dread of something yet worse filled Molly up. First to give testimony against them was John Lock who recounted how he had been blindfolded and taken to an upstairs room where he'd been asked to kneel and swear the oath. He was told to look at a skeleton and think on his life's end. Then Edward Legge was called and Molly shifted and looked at Charlie who nodded and set his jaw. And Legge told how he had been made to kiss the book and was charged to swear, being reminded his soul would be plunged into eternity if he did not keep the secret. He too recalled there was a picture of Death in the room. Molly flushed hot and cast about the faces, all eyes trained on the men accused. She could not hear another word as in her ears the pounding of her own heart made her ashamed, as if she too stood accused. For wasn't it her imagination that struck fear into men's minds? Those oaths they were made to swear, for which they now stood in peril, were they not prompted by her hand? She could not shake it. She sat, stripped and naked before all eyes.

The painter was called and made himself seem honourable and the constable told how he'd found a book with the names of those who had taken the illegal oath. Others were called to testify to the good conduct of the men and, in their defence, reasonable and earnest words were said. But the judge turned all speech into his own poisonous words of condemnation and the six were taken down.

That night Molly lay tormented in her narrow cot. She had been quiet on the way home, listening to Sarah's raging and tears – Sarah, with a child on the way and her husband condemned to who knows what punishment.

'It's all been arranged too neatly,' Charlie contested. 'The cautions posted in the village were put there only weeks before and all to frame their guilt. And did you see how the judge did not read out George's words, but mumbled them to the jury. Well he might! For wouldn't anyone hearing George Loveless be moved.'

There in the cart, Molly looked at him anew. He who once was hers, who cleaved to the Church and the masters and believed in bettering himself through deference and knowing his place. 'Will you come to chapel then, Charlie?' she asked. He only smiled in reply.

Despite this warmth in her heart, Molly could not rest nor sleep. For the sound of the oath still rang in her ears that the men had testified to and that she had such a part in. But who could she confide in, who would understand?

In the morning her mood had turned to sickness and she could not get up. Betsy sat by her bed and coaxed her with chamomile tea. She slipped in and out of a fitful half sleep and fought the oblivion of dreams where she might speak and confess. But she did dream. She dreamt of the upper room, golden with candlelight, of how her heart leapt at the forms that grew there under the sweep of brush and paint. And she saw again the pages of books alive with angels, saints and demons that loosened themselves and followed her, sat with her at the table and lay beside her at night as she crafted her figures into life. And Blake's swirls and swags of colour, that shaped movement and form, made men and women seem to move. Those lines and tones of his she copied into the face and the great dark wings of her own creature. And she would lurch awake, hot and heavy-headed to Betsy calling her name, only to fall again into her tormented sleep. Until, after three days, the nurse was sent for.

'She has no illness I can find.' she told Betsy, 'Perhaps she is sick of soul.'

Her aunt sent for a preacher. The only one who could come was from Weymouth – the three preachers of their own village being locked up in Dorchester gaol. He sat with her and prayed, asked what ailed her: was she sick with the love of someone, or was it the fate of her uncle and brethren that brought her so low? But all Molly could see in her mind's eye were the paintings hanging in the upstairs room of Thomas Stanfield's house and the men brought before them and in her imaginings it was she looking down on them through those cavernous eyes. She could not speak of it. So at last they brought Charlie who sat beside her and told her she must get up and take him to chapel. At this, Molly managed a smile.

'Is it me, Molly?' he said. 'I have tried too hard to steer you from what you believe. That day in the orchard when you asked, did I think all men equal, and I said not, and I sneered at you and called you a malcontent and all those other cruel words.'

Molly raised herself up. 'It's not any of the things you have done.' she said. 'Not anything anyone has done, but all my own doing and I can tell no one.'

Molly began to cry. Charlie sat on the bed and took her by the hand, 'Tell me Molly. Tell me, that loves you.' And it all came spilling out of her in harsh whispers, the books, the paintings, the oaths and the treason.

'But Molly.' said Charlie. 'There is nothing new in these oaths. This is the point on which everything turns. Your uncle has done no wrong. There is nothing wicked in the swearing of an oath. It is how these things are done and everyone allows it. Their society is not illegal, not treason, not any of it. People are already coming forward and saying so.'

Molly searched his face. 'Is that really true, Charlie?'

'It's all true and that's what matters, Molly. Not the law or the masters but what we know to be true.'

'You sound like Uncle George, Charlie.'

'I could do no better. But it is your aunt, Betsy, who has schooled me in all this, Molly. It is her you should confide in as she can ease your conscience better than I.'

At that Betsy came in carrying broth and tea, having all the while been waiting to be called. Charlie kissed Molly's cheek as he left.

It was easy now to talk to Betsy. The small quiet woman, who Molly thought she knew so well, proved that her heart, though sore, was not broken but strong and unwavering.

'What will happen now, my sweet girl, is that we will suffer. This is the beginning of it. The masters have not finished with us yet. They will try and break us. Without our men we seem an easy target, so we must steel ourselves.'

Molly heard the same weight in her aunt's words, the same certainty she loved so dearly in her uncle's.

'I must tell you now Molly... that George and the others are sentenced...'

Betsy's mouth could scarcely let it out. 'Seven years... transportation.' Molly held her and the two wept together.

'I have something,' said Betsy, pulling a scrap of paper from her pocket, 'George has sent us these lines.'

Molly read them out:

God is our guide! from field, from wave,
From plough, from anvil, and from loom;
We come, our country's rights to save,
And speak a tyrant faction's doom
We raise the watch-word liberty;
We will, we will, we will be free!

'Now,' said Betsy, 'we won't have George's clever words, or Thomas's thunder. We won't have James's storytelling. But we do have you Molly...What will you find to hold us together and give us heart?'

Molly knew what she would find and this time she wouldn't need to look in a book. When she next took up her brushes, she would fashion a new banner, one that would stretch clear across the wall of the upper room, five women marching, arm in arm.

Afterword: To Swear an Oath

Dr Marcus Morris

Manchester Metropolitan University

GEORGE LOVELESS, HIS YOUNGER brother James Loveless, Thomas Standfield, his son, John Standfield, James Hammett, and James Brine were arrested on the morning of 24 February 1834. They were charged with being present at Thomas Standfield's cottage and swearing an illegal oath during an initiation ceremony for the Friendly Society of Agricultural Labourers (formed by George in Tolpuddle in 1833). The society, essentially an agricultural trade union, was formed with the intention of resisting wage cuts and bargaining for better working conditions with local landowners. Local landowner and magistrate, James Frampton, initiated the prosecution of the six men by contacting the Home Secretary, Lord Melbourne, to complain about their activities. He provided evidence collected by a spy who had attended meetings at the cottage. The six were held in Dorchester gaol until their trial on 17 March 1834 at the county court in the town. The jury, made up of local landowners, found them guilty after being instructed to do so by the judge and the men were sentenced to transportation to Australia for seven years. Once in Australia, they were assigned as convict labourers to various employers, George Loveless in Van Diemen's Land (Tasmania) and the rest in New South Wales. In their absence, the London Dorchester Committee raised funds to support their families.

Agitation against the convictions and sentences began even before they had left the country, with a public outcry over the injustice and support from high-profile radicals including Fergus O'Connor and William Cobbett. Within a month, they had been ascribed the epithet 'martyrs' in some quarters (although they were more widely referred to as the Dorchester Labourers until the twentieth century), and a campaign was launched to overturn the injustice these martyrs had suffered and to assert the rights of labour and working class radicals. An 800,000-signature petition demanding the Labourers' freedom was presented to the House of Commons. Demonstrations were also arranged, including one on 21 April 1834 where up to 100,000 would march through London to Parliament in protest. Such pressure forced the home secretary, Lord John Russell, to grant conditional pardons in June 1835 and full pardons in March 1836. George returned first, in 1837, his brother, James Brine and the two Standfields in 1838 and James Hammett in August 1839. They were all greeted as heroes on their return, attending processions, meetings and dinners in their honour, while the Dorchester Committee obtained the leasehold on two farms in Essex for the martyrs and their families. George Loveless would also publish his account of the trial, *The Victims of Whiggery*, to much acclaim and success, with the pamphlet becoming a mainstay at future Chartists meetings. Indeed, they were to act as a continued inspiration, their experiences acquiring an important place in the mythology of the history of trade unions, radical protest and the labour movement, both in Britain and internationally.

This place in mythology means that aspects of their story are relatively well known, with George Loveless invariably seen as the leading man and the other martyrs his supporting cast. Of course, there was a wider, directly affected supporting cast. These men came from interconnected families (Diana Standfield was Thomas's wife, John's mother and the sister of George and James Loveless), most with wives and children to support. It is thus particularly illuminating that this story is from a female and familial perspective. Molly's story may be in part conjecture; there is no evidence to suggest that she would have painted the oath banner, for instance. Indeed, as alluded to in the story, that she could read at all would have been unusual, with only around 40% of women literate in the period. In many ways, though, the Loveless and Standfield families could be regarded as unusual. George Loveless in particular has been described as a 'remarkable farm labourer',[1] as the driving force behind the society. Their families clearly supported these men directly and indirectly in their actions and shared their views. Four of the martyrs and their families were also connected by their faith. As Methodist lay preachers, nonconformist and outside local church society (as we see at the painter's shop), George Loveless felt that they had been victimised as much for their faith as for being trade unionists. He certainly was an open and staunch critic of Anglicanism and the idea of a state church in general, and therefore a potential target.

Though Loveless suggested the martyrs' religion played a part, most historians have centred their explanations for the authorities' actions on the local labour and political context, wider economic issues and their fears of a growing trade union movement. Trade union activities had been repressed in Britain in the late eighteenth and early nineteenth centuries, especially through the Combination Acts that had outlawed any form of combination or meeting that might lead to combination. In the wake of the French Revolution, the British elite were fearful that such revolutionary fervour might cross the Channel. However, despite such attempts at repression, political radicalism was on the increase, as were associated demonstrations, rebellions, anti-government publications and workplace militancy such as that practiced by the Luddites. Partly in response to this, the Combination Acts were repealed in 1824, though a further Combination Act limited unions' activities in 1825 (indeed, they were not fully legalised until the 1871 Trade Union Act). After the 1824 repeal, unions developed rapidly, especially in the textile industries. There were also attempts to establish general unions, including Robert Owen's Grand National Consolidated Trades Union in 1834, which would support the Tolpuddle men. In this context, trade unionism spread to Dorset and, with Loveless's union, began to take in agricultural labourers. It had thus been portrayed as part of the wider development of the trade union movement and reflective of changing social relations, which many in the elite saw as a threat to their political, economic and social positions. It is no coincidence that the First Reform Act was passed in 1832 as an act of political appeasement, even if its effects were very limited.

Unionisation in Dorset was a conscious attempt to displace older forms of protest and negotiation and to establish new forms of organisation.[2] By extension, local landowners and farmers saw it as an attempt to displace those who benefitted from older traditions and practices. They were clearly fearful of what these developments meant for their social, political and economic standing. It was seen as an attack on the very fabric of rural society. Such concerns were exacerbated by recent events and prevailing economic conditions. The nineteenth century with its agricultural and industrial revolutions may have been a time of rapid economic growth, which in itself stimulated the growth of unions, but it also saw significant moments of economic recession. The early 1830s was one of those moments. There had been a series of bad harvests, which meant both a scarcity of goods and an increase in prices as seen at Dorchester market in the story. Undoubtedly, for agricultural labourers like Loveless these were hungry years. The cost and availability of goods was compounded by the levels of unemployment and reduced wages. For landowners and farmers, these conditions and such agitation raised fears that recent tensions and disturbances, especially the Swing Riots of 1830, would reoccur; they were therefore keen to crush the Dorchester Labourers before it got to that stage.

The Swing Riots in 1830 had been an uprising of agricultural workers across southern and eastern England (the name came from Captain Swing, a fictitious character who became a mythical figurehead for the movement), which resulted from anger at the tithe system,[3] the Poor Law system[4] and tenant farmers who had been progressively lowering agricultural labourers' wages. There was also anger at the enclosure of common land, as referenced in the story by Molly, George and Betsy. The riots had been localised and fragmentary, but had seen strikes, violence and machine-breaking. Local farmers and landowners were reluctantly forced to increase wages and provide more generous relief – a reluctance made clear by these increases being rescinded in the following years. Indeed, James Frampton, who brought the charges against the Tolpuddle men, had criticised such concessions at the time, arguing 'that it was only encouraging the people to rise'.[5] Moreover, Frampton and his property had been physically threatened during the riots, which might explain the zealousness with which he tried to bring down the martyrs. This rescinding of the wage increases and relief was partly responsible for George Loveless forming his union; their explicit aim was to see agricultural labourers paid ten shillings a week. He certainly saw his society as a direct continuation of Swing and as being part of 'a general movement of the working class',[6] while Frampton had accused Loveless of being part of the riots in his letters to the Home Secretary demonstrating his concern about what the society's action might result in.[7] Frampton and other landowners thus saw this, and other unions, as a direct threat to their long-held social and political positions, and perhaps more importantly, their wealth. The unionisation of agricultural labourers, moreover, was a new development and a particular threat to an area that relied on agriculture as the main source of income.

This context, alongside the particular motivations of James Frampton, help explain why the Dorchester Labourers were targeted when others were not. However, attacking the society presented a number of legal challenges. Simply put, they were doing nothing that was illegal. It is for this reason that the Home Secretary recommended Frampton charge the men under the obscure Unlawful Oaths Act of 1797. Clearly, the use of an obscure law – passed after Royal Navy mutinies during the war with post-revolutionary France, it prohibited the swearing of secret oaths[8] – was a political act intended to intimidate agricultural labourers and workers. The Unlawful Societies Act of 1799, which superseded the 1797 act, could have been used but was deemed less severe. Even so, it took a carefully selected jury and a judge who was hostile to trade unionism and intent on securing a conviction for the Tolpuddle men to be found guilty. In part, this was because it was not clear what represented an illegal oath, even when advice was sought from the Attorney-General and the Solicitor-General. As Charlie notes in the story, 'there is nothing new in these oaths' and 'your uncle [George Loveless] has done no wrong.'

That the taking of oaths and initiation ceremonies was a common occurrence with unions and friendly societies complicated the case against the Dorchester Labourers. Oaths had definite purposes: to maintain internal discipline; to instil a sense of unity and cohesion; to prevent plans leaking; and to intimidate potential defaulters in a period when unions and societies had no legal recourse. To emphasise these purposes particular artefacts and images were used as part of these ceremonies and they were reinforced by religious sanction. It is for this reason that we see Molly being asked to paint a skeleton in the story. A symbol intended to demonstrate that betrayal merits death. There was one further complication with oaths for the authorities and that was their centrality to the ritual culture of the elite. In particular, we can see this with elite and influential societies such as the Freemasons. It seemed that what was fine for the upper classes was not for the working classes. For these reasons, the public outcry against the conviction and sentence in 1834 centred on the perceived injustice and is in part why the Dorchester Labourers became martyrs, acquiring a totemic place in the mythology of the British labour movement.

The Tolpuddle Martyrs have retained a significant place in labour's collective memory even into the twenty-first century. In many ways, this legacy is out of proportion to their contemporary impact, to the local nature of their struggle and especially to their demands of earning ten shillings a week. They did have a contemporary political impact, as we saw in the immediate response and in moments such as George Loveless being elected as a delegate to the first Chartist Convention in 1839. However, in reality, the martyrs' union had only a limited direct impact, was located in an unimportant area for the history of trade unionism and in a trade (agriculture) of diminishing importance. It was the massive growth in trade unionism and the formation of the Labour Party at the start of the twentieth century that renewed the martyrs' legacy, as they sought heroes and causes from the movement's past to legitimise their struggle and which the current crop of activists could emulate. Through their influence, a number of commemorative schemes were established and extended in the 1930s. Several memorials have been erected in Tolpuddle, there is the Tolpuddle Martyrs' Museum which sits on the 'Tolpuddle trail', while the 'Martyrs' Tree' (an ancient sycamore tree that is seen as a symbol of trade unionism) is maintained by the National Trust. In 1934, moreover, to celebrate the hundredth anniversary of the martyrs, the Trades Union Congress organised a major commemoration in the village (in many ways writing the story of the martyrs we are familiar with now). This carries on to this day in the form of the annual Tolpuddle Martyrs' Festival when around 10,000 people descend on the village every third week in July. So many still celebrate the martyrs because their story matters and has as much relevance now as then, acting as an inspiration to many. Injustices still abound, legislation is still pursued to limit the power of the unions (for example, the Trade Union Act of 2017), wages still stagnate and conditions are still poor for many workers. The symbolism of these past heroes is just as important to contemporary trade unions, as the symbolism of the oath banner was to the martyrs themselves.

Notes

1. This was a common contemporary description of Loveless, as discussed by W.H. Oliver in 'Tolpuddle Martyrs and Trade Union Oaths', *Labour History*, 10 (1966), p.7.

2. These older forms of protest were often localised, more or less spontaneous, and confrontational in nature, taking the form of machine-breaking, rioting and the causing of disturbances. These protests were met with an equally direct and confrontational response from Britain's elite.

3. Originally granted to English churches in 855 AD, tithes were a tax that required one tenth (or one 'tithe') of all agricultural produce to be paid annually to support the local church and clergy. Often this was paid in kind, with produce given directly to the church. After the Reformation in the sixteenth century, a large proportion of church-owned land and associated tithes passed into lay ownership and monetary payments became more common. By the nineteenth century, it was felt to be an out-of-date and unpopular practice in an age of industrialisation, religious dissent and agricultural depression. The Tithe Commutation Act of 1836 ended payment in kind, and over the course of the nineteenth century tithes were gradually reduced. They were finally abolished in the 1977 Finance Act.

4. The Poor Law was a system of relief traced back to Tudor England. The Old Poor Law, codified in the late sixteenth century, was administered haphazardly at a local parish level (with around 15,000 parishes) and paid for by local rate payers. It provided relief to those too ill or old to work. However, this was highly stigmatised and deliberately kept to barely subsistence level. 'Outdoor relief' was provided in the form of payments, food and clothing, while

'indoor relief' was most commonly provided through workhouses. Conditions in the latter were consciously poor and uninviting, so that nobody would choose to be admitted to the workhouse. By the nineteenth century, the system was considered to be woefully inadequate and would be replaced in 1834 by the New Poor Law.

5. James Frampton, *Account of the Queen's Own Dorset Yeomanry* quoted in Tom Scriven, 'The Dorchester Labourers and Swing's Aftermath in Dorset', *History Workshop Journal*, 82 (2016), p.5.

6. George Loveless, *The Victims of Whiggery: a Statement of the Persecutions Experienced by the Dorchester Labourers* (London, 1837), quoted in Scriven, 'Dorchester', p.3.

7. Letter from Frampton to Melbourne, 29 March 1834, quoted in Scriven, 'Dorchester', p.7.

8. In April and May 1797, the crews of two Royal Navy ships – the Spithead and the Nore – mutinied independently of each other. The Spithead's crew were essentially striking over pay and conditions. On the Nore, however, not only did the crew share these economic grievances, but were motivated by political radicalism. The mutinies were extremely concerning for the British government as the country was at war with France, hence legislation that prohibited clandestine political associations and ad hoc agreements such as those that bound the mutineers.

To Plot, Plan, Redress

Eley Williams

SOME MIGHT SAY THAT we pulled on our toughest boots and our cleanest petticoats, ran combs through our beards and stepped out into an owl-hot, hoot-shot night. The very moment that we crossed the threshold of our homes, some might say that we felt the mud of the road pull at our bootsoles: imagine if this was true and that the sound was something like that of smacking lips as if the road was learning our language or tasting mischief on the air. It might be said that it was not a cold night but there was a wind. A breeze pulled at the horsehair on our chins so that some of it grew too close to the lamps in our hands: it hissed and popped and frizzled, let's say, until we drew back and shushed each other. Let's say some of us frowned and some of us giggled and some of us adjusted unfamiliarities of cloth around our hips. Let's say we walked on.

Some say we had toasted corks on forks at our hearths that evening, rolling them and dipping them above the flames as our babies slept and as our wives and daughters rolled their eyes at the ribbons in our laps. There is no end of eye-rolling these days. Our horses roll their eyes in something like a fever, the magistrate rolls his eyes when we pull at our pockets to show their emptiness. We roll our eyes at the coarseness of our thumbs against the grain of the ribbon in our laps. *We'll hardly be wearing your Sunday best*, we might have said to our eye-rolling daughters. *Everything you have in this world is just borrowed for a short time*, we might have also told them, attempts at reassurance, and they might have sing-sang this wisdom back in chiding tones as they laid our dinnerplates down before us. Less cheese than we would like and the bread is hard. Some might say that a number of our wives and daughters pulled beards up to their chins and asked whether it was a style that suited. We nodded, and whole households became sisters of a sort as the sun rolled its eye and headed for bed. Some say that on such evenings we learned just how many things can fit within a pocket and not impede one's stride.

It might be said that the fields that night were grey with moonlight and each stalk seemed furred with silver, appeared somehow heavier like the edge of a moth's wing. Say we 'stole' through the night or 'marched' through the night or 'hallooed' or 'trumpeted' or 'shrieked'. *Gweiddi. Canu.*[1] Say that we set our broadening shoulders against the moonlight, picked up our skirts and took to the road two abreast.

Maybe it will be told in time that we came from folktales or folklore. Some might say that something like folklore ran in our blood or rose in our gall that evening. People might say that say we were freed-from-swaddling crimbil children[2] who grew up raiding their parents' laundries and mangles for fresh linens and took to the streets. Some of our faces had changed for the night. One of us had a jaw daubed red with ochre and a forehead inked and sooted. Her eyes were not wild but steady, stepping with purpose. Our elbows touched one another, the rims of our bonnets sometimes soft-clashed together. Some might say that we met others on the road and fell into step with their tread.

There are words like 'trust' and there are words like 'trusts'. There are nouns like 'extract' and there are verbs like 'extract'. Some might say that we have had hushed meetings by candlelight, and that we swapped the words 'lye' and 'lime' with 'lie' and 'layman', 'tithe' with 'tooth and nail' until the air was strained through our lapping. We exchanged idioms and anecdotes: 'taking its toll', 'reaping what you sow', 'silk handkerchief from a sow's ear'. We learned new shorthands and taught the younger attendants how to use a percussion cap. We taught ourselves how to sign notes with new names. Some might say that we mimed practice swings of arms in the looking glasses at home, privately, hefted sledgehammers to our shoulders to check that our smashing would not be checked by the small, creased matter of tight cloth across our chests.

Here's an extract for laymen, pulled from the pulpit and the desire-lines of bibles' concordances:

And they blessed Rebekah and said unto her: Thou art our sister, be thou the mother of thousands of millions, and let thy seed possess the gate of those which hate them.[3]

Some might say that there was a lad in town who once boasted he could count to a million. Some might say that we filliped his ears and pulled his bonnet down further over his eyes. It should be said that we were in good spirits, quite few of us, made gladmouthed with hope, but we cannot control the tale. We can control the saw's teeth against the wood and whether we keep a good lookout, and we can make sure to count the tread of foot after foot along the roads we know so well.

Here's a call-and-response that's fit for any psalmistry or folktale. Say there's the shape of a woman, bent against the moonlight with her wide hands held above her eyes. Her voice is strong and seems, perhaps, unnaturally high. She might say,

What is this my children? There is something in my way. I cannot go on... and her daughters might form a ring around her, smoothing their beards and wringing their hands:

What is it, mother Rebecca? some might say they cry. *Nothing should stand in your way.*

And she, aggrieved: *I do not know, my children. I am old and cannot see well.*

And we, in chorus: *Shall we come and move it out of your way mother Rebecca?*

And she: *Wait! It feels like a big gate put across the road to stop your old mother.*

And we: *We will break it down, mother. Nothing stands in your way.*

And she, kicking a boot against the timber: *Oh my dear children, it is locked and bolted. What can be done?*

And we, readying our hammers and our saws, feeling for our firecrackers and raising our voices, our ranks seeming to swell as the words bloom in our throats: *It must be taken down, mother. You and your children must be able to pass.*

And she, stepping back: *Off with it then, my children.*

And then there might, some say, be a surging forward and an earnest full-blooded delight, and the sparks of our lamps and the stars might be like spittle and the fizz of splinters might be all a-jumping in the sky.

Here's another extract, said aloud so often:

A woman shall not wear a man's garment, nor shall a man put on a woman's cloak, for whoever does these things is an abomination to the Lord your God.

Here's another extract, fresh from our hammers to your ringing ears:

Dyfal donc a dyr y garreg.[4]

Some might mutter into their teacups and brocaded cuffs that the people are too good-natured and law-abiding to wreak such havoc. Some say the same wigmaker who fashioned some of our beards is the same man employed to furnish the magistrates' clappable pates. Some others say that there's a book in a top drawer which lists the quick and the dead, while some say it records the names of those who had refused to pay obscene charges. We charged the gate, unseemly but newly comely. Some say there are kerchieves beneath our chins, and that merrymaking and grins might be exchanged as window frames come loose in our hands and as daughters flex their power and their right to the road. Some say we spoilt our skirts or dropped our petticoats in the scrums. Some say that the name *Rebecca* means to 'tie firmly'. Some say many of our number were apprehended and our faces washed with bitter soap, and that the name *Rebecca* means 'snare' or 'noose'. I believe the scholar who says the name's etymology shares roots with 'soil, earth'. I have rebecca beneath my cap and in my hair and under the nails of my fingers. That's for all to see, but not for me to say.

Some might say that there is a real Rebecca who stands as the tallest woman in the village. Versions of this story imply that we had to borrow her petticoats and dresses, her smocks and all her linens, because they were the only ones that would fit over our heads and about our waists. We could not possibly comment but we might make a quip about clothes horses and whinny you away from our table.

Some might say that daughters gabble and shriek, that we were shrill in the street and disported ourselves. They might use the word *déshabillé* and think that either we do not know what this means, or that such a term might better make their roads impassable or their gates impossible to rend asunder. Some might say all manner of things with all manner of words. Some say our name derives from 'clods of earth', but we will drown them out with our tin horns and the sound of breaking glass. Some might say that they saw Charlotte for Twm and Nelly for Alun and Miss Cromwell for Owain. *Sticks and stones*, we might say in answer, our ribboned caps flung high. Our horses carve smiles into the mud with their footfalls, our coats are turned inside-out but our hearts are on our sleeves and our glory shall be in hearing the hinges of a gate say, quite precisely, *feu-de-joie*, à la *dérobée*,[5] as queerly clad and caddish lads make it crystal clear that this clodded path is ours to tread.

Daughterly and unmistakeably, some will say what some will say and what we shall do will shake your rafters. Come, then – let me tie this here about your waist and beneath your chin.

Anticipate our hems at your gateposts, we say, and our rites of passage. Make sure you mark our words.

Notes

1. Wailed. Sung.
2. In Welsh myth, 'crimbils' were changelings left in the place of fair-haired children kidnapped by fairies (or Tylwyth Teg).
3. Genesis 24:60.
4. Welsh proverb: *Persistent blows shatter the stone.*
5. Bonfire, stealthily.

Afterword: Rebeccaism

Rhian E. Jones

ALTHOUGH RELATIVELY LITTLE-KNOWN in broader history, the Rebecca riots hold a place in Welsh history and folk-memory as a vivid and compelling story, as well as a relatively unusual example of successful direct action by ordinary people. The Rebecca riots were a series of disturbances which began in 1839 in Carmarthenshire, and arose again in 1842-4 when they spread across south-west Wales and beyond. They are most widely remembered as a protest against the imposition of toll-charges on privatised roads, beginning with the first attack on a tollgate at Efailwen in May 1839, and ending with the British government's Commission of Inquiry into the causes of the riots in March 1844, which recommended changes to the tollgate system. A significant feature of these attacks was the use made by participants of spectacular costumes, notably male rioters wearing female dress including bonnets and petticoats. The story of the riots is usually told through striking and colourful imagery, with rioters destroying tollgates under cover of darkness, often on horseback, while led by the iconic and anonymous figure of 'Rebecca'. Rebecca was not a real person but a character; 'she' could be played by anyone, and when taking part in protest 'her' followers called themselves 'Rebecca's daughters'. This idea of a symbolic figurehead was common in protest at the time – the Luddites had their leadership figure known as General Ludd; the Swing

Rioters had Captain Swing, and the Rebeccaites had Rebecca.

These protesters were not opposed only to the imposition of tollgates, even though this remains their best-known target. Rather than simply 'riots', the events constituted a wide-ranging popular movement, deserving of the alternative term 'Rebeccaism'. The movement was generated by the social and economic changes of the 1840s in Wales, exacerbated by dissatisfaction with a remote and neglectful political establishment. Nineteenth-century Carmarthenshire, the part of Wales where Rebeccaism first arose, was still overwhelmingly rural, with most people working on farms as agricultural labourers, and to a smaller extent in coalmining or craft. Above the labouring population was a very small middle class, and above them, at the top of a very shallow social pyramid, were the landed gentry, a handful of family dynasties who not only owned land and had inherited wealth but also monopolised local and parliamentary politics. Welsh MPs at this time were often absent or took no part in parliamentary debate, and there were barely any democratic or constitutional outlets for ordinary people to address the political and economic changes that were materially affecting their lives.

'Rebeccaism' arose in a context of growing impoverishment and economic depression among the tenant farmers and labourers of Carmarthenshire, caused by bad harvests, the financial demands of high rents, Church tithes, poor rates and other taxes, and increasing privatisation of common land. These widespread grievances were expressed at large public meetings, which often took place under cover of darkness on isolated hillsides to avoid the attention of authorities. Once their protests got underway as a movement, 'Rebeccaites' not only took direct action to remove and destroy tollgates, but also opposed the New Poor Law and its workhouses, resisted the enclosure and privatisation of local land and rivers, fought with landlords, bailiffs and local gentry, and demanded financial support for unmarried mothers and their children, who had lost their right to child support under the New Poor Law. The discontent of participants with social and economic issues beyond the imposition of tollgates helps to explain why the unrest continued after 1844 – most notably, similar protests took place in 1860s and 1870s Radnorshire against enclosure, evictions, and the privatisation of the River Wye. The movement's iconography has continued to appear in instances of popular discontent up to and including the present century, often used in ways far removed from its original function.

In nineteenth-century Wales, as across the wider world, the onset of industrialisation generated social unrest and resistance by ordinary people as they adjusted to its impact on their lives. 'Rebeccaism' can be seen as part of an attempt to uphold and defend an established social and economic system – characterised by the historian E. P. Thompson as a 'moral economy' – against the encroaching of a 'market economy' informed by industrial capitalism. Even before the time of Rebecca, there had been widespread disturbances across Wales and the rest of Britain over the high price of bread and grain. In 1816 a strike over wage cuts paralysed the south-eastern coalfield, while in rural west Wales there were riots against enclosure. During the 1820s the Scotch Cattle, a proto-trade union, began to organise miners and ironworkers in the country's industrial belt. In 1831 Merthyr Tydfil, a heavily industrialised and politically radical town, saw an uprising by industrial workers over unemployment, low pay, debt and eviction, which involved, reputedly for the first time in European protest, the raising of a red flag. The first Chartist branch in Wales was set up at Carmarthen in 1837, and the spread of Chartism in Wales culminated in a mass march on Newport in 1839 – the same year as the first Rebeccaite attack on a tollgate. From 1834 Wales had seen opposition to workhouses and the New Poor Law, particularly from the Chartist movement, and Rebeccaites also took part in this opposition. Although it did not contain much clearly defined political analysis or ideology of the kind that would characterise Chartism, and although Chartism and the Merthyr Rising may be more well-known than Rebeccaism, it's possible to see these movements as overlapping, interconnected, or intertwined strands of popular resistance.

Why was 'Rebecca', the symbolic leader of these protests, a woman, and why did her 'daughters' dress as they did? As we see in Eley's story, Rebeccaites were not simply men dressed in women's clothing, but wore a deliberate blend of masculine and feminine signifiers: horsehair wigs but also false beards, white dresses or nightgowns worn over heavy boots and fustian trousers, and shotguns as well as bonnets. The reliance of Rebeccaites on elaborate costume has been explained by previous historians as a method of disguise, but this seems an inadequate explanation when we look at how impractically elaborate their dress could be: protesters often donned highly ornate hairpieces and hats, and even accessorised with jewellery and parasols. This was less of a disguise and more of a uniform – one which allowed the wearer not only to not be recognised as themselves, but to actively adopt a new identity as one of Rebecca's daughters.

Protesters also sometimes adopted female pseudonyms for the duration of a protest, and incorporated female archetypes into their methods of protesting. An example of this is the ritual call-and-response between Rebecca and her daughters described in Eley's story, which publicly – and comically – established that a tollgate had to be dismantled so that the protesters' elderly 'mother' could cross the road. On other occasions, protesters could arrive with their leading Rebecca figure dressed grandly as a noblewoman or 'Lady Bountiful' archetype, occasionally going so far as to use a carriage with protesters dressed as servants. These intricate details of costume and performance, which could reference both pantomime and drama, can lend the retelling of events a dreamlike or surreal quality, which Eley's impressionistic narrative captures. No matter how strange they may seem from a modern perspective, however, at the time these aspects served an obvious purpose which drew on local folk custom, as well as rituals of community discipline like charivari.[1]

Like the prevalence of mythical or symbolic protest leaders, many pre-modern protests which took place before and alongside Rebeccaism also utilised the costume, masks and guising associated with local carnival and festival, using a familiar frame of reference in order to render the events acceptable and understandable to both participants and observers. Staging an elaborate performance or ritual before a protest would have made the event feel both familiar and justified. Meanwhile, dressing up in masks and costumes – particularly costumes which blurred the boundaries of identity – was a way of creating a liminal space and enhanced persona in which protesters could take extraordinary actions which overstepped the bounds of what was possible in their everyday life. It could also allow those who took part to escape responsibility for their actions by claiming it was not them, but Rebecca, who had done these things.

Eley's story stresses the importance of clothing, language and ritual when carrying out acts of protest. These cultural aspects of the movement, and the help they can offer in understanding how it was experienced by participants, have often been neglected by earlier historians who have focused more on its political demands and level of success. Eley also emphasises the disputed or unknown nature of much of the events. We have almost no written personal records from any participants beyond the accounts produced in court reports or trial records – which emphasises the importance of memory, oral history and storytelling in how the events are handed down to future generations. Even the origin of Rebecca's name remains the subject of argument and ambiguity: some explain it as a high-minded derivation from a verse in Genesis, lending divine sanction to the actions of protesters, while others claim more irreverently that the movement named itself after the only local woman statuesque enough to lend a dress to Twm Carnabwth, the leader of the first tollgate riot in 1839. The comical and romantic aspects of this kind of history mean that, although based on real direct action by real people, the events still retain the quality of fairytale or legend.

Finally, it can be interesting to look back at Rebeccaism in the context of recent popular discontent and protest. The Occupy movement of the 2010s, for instance, resembled Rebeccaism in being a mass, leaderless and often spontaneous or autonomous form of protest in which any individual could take part by adopting the symbols or costume associated with the movement. Like Occupy, the methods and tactics used by Rebeccaite protesters could vary, but both were fundamentally a collective response by ordinary people to social and economic problems, combined with a loss of faith in political structures and local or national authorities: rather than 'the 99%', they called themselves 'the children of Rebecca'. Individuals could also take on the persona of Rebecca herself by writing anonymous letters or petitions, which usually demanded lower rents or better treatment in workhouses, and signing them as 'Rebecca'. In this way the name and image of Rebecca could operate as an 'umbrella' name for a group of individuals, a technique which has a long history in protest up to and beyond the 1990's Luther Blissett collective and the use of stylised Guy Fawkes masks by the Anonymous movement. These connections with contemporary leaderless and anonymous movements reminds us both that few historical events are as strange as they first appear, and that many of the social, economic and political problems that our ancestors took action against are still with us today.

Note

1. Charivari or skimmington was a folk custom in which a mock parade was staged through a community accompanied by a discordant mock serenade.

The Children

Lucy Caldwell

TRUMPINGTON STREET IS SCULPTURAL in the sunshine: slashes and rhomboids of light and stark shade. Traffic is heavy and the taxi travels slowly, the driver giving me the tour. The Fitzwilliam, the Pitt Building, Peterhouse. We've already had The Backs, the Mathematical Bridge, designed by Isaac Newton and made, the taxi driver says, without a single nut or bolt. Students took it apart once to see how it worked and were unable to put it back together. I know this isn't true. Newton died a quarter of a century before the bridge was built, and it does have bolts, iron spikes driven in at angles obscured from sight. I walked over this bridge almost every day for the best – or worst – part of three years. But somehow the moment to say this passed, and so I smile and nod and let my mind drift.

I'm writing a story about Caroline Norton, who *changed the lot of mothers forever* with her battle to reform child custody law, or so the blurb on her biography says. I have the biography in a tote bag, though that's as much as I've read of it so far, along with a sheaf of her poems, newly-joined now by a raft of photocopies about marriage and Victorian law and women's quests for equality. I've just come from Girton College, the first women's college in Cambridge; dusty sunlight in high-ceilinged, book-lined rooms, parquet-floored corridors and a lunch buffet (poached salmon, potatoes, mixed sweetcorn and peas) under the patient lights of a hotplate in the Fellows' Dining Room. A communal jug of tapwater, tasting faintly of pewter. Polite tones in respectable surroundings; it all sounds eminently reasonable; Caroline Norton's letters to the Rt. Hon.s, her pamphlets, her famous essay condemning child labour; her Bills presented to the House of Lords. I'll read the texts, write the piece.

The ghost of my former self, indulged all this June day long, weaving on a rusty bike to and from the Sidgwick Site and the UL with a backpack of books, sitting earnestly on threadbare sagging armchairs, is lost to a sudden battery of car horns from behind and an outburst from the driver, who's pulled up abruptly somewhere he shouldn't. We're here. My husband and children are waiting for me in the Botanic Gardens. I pay him and sling the tote over my shoulder and go, all else forgotten.

The following day, I find a lump in my breast.

It's not unduly concerning at first. I'm breastfeeding; it's probably nothing; it will probably go. It doesn't go. A week passes, then another. It is larger now, and definitely there. I Google: breast lumps when to be concerned. Google suggests, as Google always does, that it could be terminal and it could be nothing. I phone the GP surgery, who – uncharacteristically – say they can see me tomorrow, name a time. Ok, great, I say, not sure if I feel reassured or more worried.

The next morning, dodging the breakfast scramble, I grab the untouched tote. The surgery is busy and always running late: it will be a good chunk of reading time. In the waiting room, blocking out the TV giving diabetes advice on a loop, the crying pre-schoolers at the vaccination clinic, the elderly man with a hacking cough, the mother chastising her bored, fighting sons in Bengali, I take out the biography. *Cut off from her children after an acrimonious split, she went about changing the law for wives and mothers.*

Right, I say to the portrait on the cover, a languorous oil painting in an off-the-shoulder dress, gold and ruby bracelets and elaborate lacquered hair, delicately holding a quill. Here we go.

★

I skim through Caroline's parents and her early years until – as she puts it – she accepts a proposal of marriage so that her life can begin.

There's a whole story in the titles of Caroline's songs, the first things she ever wrote. From before her marriage: 'Rosalie my Love, Awake!' 'Dry Up that Sparkling Tear,' 'The Home Where my Childhood Played,' 'Never Forget Me Love.' Afterwards: 'Oh Sad, Sad is the Heart,' 'Why Should I Sing of Days Gone By?' and 'Love Not.' The Honourable – or not so – George Chapple Norton mocks her letters and her ambitions, sets her writing things ablaze. He buys himself a cabriolet with her royalties – the word comes from the French, meaning *caper*, because of its light, bounding motion – a fancy and entirely unpractical vehicle. But when the doctor tells her to get some sea air to relieve the nausea of her second pregnancy, she is forced to share a bed with the landlady to save money. He slaps her face, he beats her. He seizes her by the nape of the neck and dashes her down on the floor. He kicks her in the side so hard that she can't sit down for days. He pulverises her face so badly the sight of it makes her sister vomit. He orders her from 'his' seat at the breakfast table and when she refuses, he takes the boiling tea-kettle and presses it down on her hand. Then he sits in her place and calmly eats his breakfast. She leaves him. He begs her to take him back. She takes pity on him and, for the sake of their boys, gives him another chance. Within two days, he beats her so badly she loses her unborn child. He leaves her bleeding on the floor and goes to shoot grouse in Scotland, refusing to pay the doctor's bill, leaving her to beg her brother for money. For weeks afterwards, she sits looking at raindrops on the window: *I begin to think I must have lost my soul.*

My name is called. But the GP wants a second opinion and asks me to return to the waiting room until her colleague is free. There are no chairs now so I stand against the wall. A weeks-old baby wails in pain and my body responds with the swell and rush of milk. I text my husband, who's meant to be back at work by now, instructions on what to feed the baby for lunch. I fish the book from my tote bag again, then hesitate. A moment: what we used to call *a goose walking over my grave*. This isn't how it was supposed to go. A second opinion. I was expecting, Oh, it's just a milk duct, use hot compresses and a comb. I was even prepared for, Let's aspirate it now, a dab of local anaesthetic and it'll only take a minute. It's suddenly not what I want to read about anymore; mothers, children, loss. I text my husband again. It's all fine here, he texts me back, with a row of Xs. Of course it is. He's a brilliant father. We're equal partners. But still.

Don't be silly, I tell myself, and force my hands to stop trembling and open the book.

Her brother tells her to come to his house in Dorset for Easter, with the children, without George. Her husband forbids it. She doesn't know what to do. She decides to wait until he's at work, and then sneak away. But he makes his move first. She returns home one morning to find the children, and their nanny, gone.

Frantic, she manages to bribe it out of a footman that they've been taken to a lodging house in Upper Berkeley Street, ahead of plans to spirit them up North. She rushes to the house and begs the servants there to let her see her children, just for an hour, just for five minutes, just to tell them she loves them. But their master's instructions are clear and his threats severe, and they refuse.

I could hear their little feet running over my head while I sat sobbing below, only the ceiling between us and I not able to get to them!

Her eldest is recovering from scarlet fever. She doesn't trust her husband with their second, whom he taunts and dislikes, and the youngest is still a baby. She is desperate. But there's nothing she can do. The children are George's property, his to do with or dispose of as he sees fit, until they reach their majority at twenty-one. He sends them to his sister in Scotland. He changes the youngest child's name. When the middle child needs to be 'corrected', he is stripped naked, tied to a bedpost and whipped with a riding crop. She sees them one day in London for a few, snatched minutes. They are nervous wrecks, the middle one *a perfect skeleton*. They do not understand why she has abandoned them. They beg her to stay. Her heart aches with the weight of all that is impossible to explain. The following day, a message from her husband: the boys will not be seeing her again.

The years pass.

The second GP frowns and says carefully that although it is probably nothing, it is certainly something, and she'll refer me to the Breast Clinic at St Bart's. She taps away at her computer. I'll get a phone call in a few days to arrange the appointment. Out in the street, I finish the last few pages of the chapter I'm on. George writes to 'my Carry' that the boys are so grown-up that she would not recognise them if she passed them in the street. He offers to send her portraits he's commissioned. He says she can see them again if she comes back and submits herself to him. He forges letters from her, including one to the children saying their father wants them to die so he'll have fewer of them to keep. He says she can have them back if she engages a female companion of his choice. When she agrees, he immediately backtracks. He tells her she can see them at Christmas. He writes that they have embarked on the steamer SS Dundee. The day after they should have arrived, he tells her they have not come after all. He says they can join her on holiday. She rents a house by the sea, lights fires, airs the rooms. Ten days after they are supposed to be there, they still have not come. George says she can see them in London instead. She abandons the house and returns to London. He says he's changed his mind.

You have made, she writes to him, *an orphanage of our lives.*

I text my husband to tell him I'm on my way home. All ok,

I ask, with you and the children? All fine, he texts back. Ok with you? And my fingers, fumbling, don't know what to say.

*

There is a famous house on Folgate Street in Spitalfields, about fifteen minutes' walk from me (or twenty if pushing a buggy one-handed and trailing a child on a scooter). It belonged to a man named Denis Severs, and he left it as a museum of sorts – part-museum, part-art installation – with the intention that as you walk through the doors, you feel that you are stepping through the surface of a painting. The house's ten rooms are ten 'spells', from the cellar and the piano nobile to the Smoking Room and the boudoir, transporting you back to the Huguenot silk-weavers who first lived there in the early eighteenth century, and on through the Victorian era, following the family's – and society's – fortunes. The porcelain, the portraits, the clink of the old brass clock: it feels as if the house's real inhabitants have just momentarily left the room that you've stepped into. Or so the website says. You cannot wear stiletto heels or heavily-ridged soles on your visit; it goes without saying that you cannot bring a buggy, or a boisterous child. They have night-time openings, which are called Silent Nights, where you leave your phone at the door, and general admission on Sundays and Mondays. My husband leaves work at lunchtime to come and look after the children in a nearby park so I can see the house. But somehow I've misread the website. It's a Wednesday: the house is closed.

They were not like us, the historian at Girton College said. We often think of the Victorians as basically the same as us; a bit stricter, more sentimental, maybe, but they were not like us at all. Imagine that almost everything we believe, all that we take for granted, is overturned. That's how far we are from them, that distance and then some again.

They tell you to allow a whole half-day for the clinic. There are ultrasounds, mammograms, radiographers, registrars to see;

pieces of pink and white paper to be taken to different reception desks on different floors, filed in different buff-coloured folders. I find a corner seat, then move when I realise it's by a rack of leaflets with titles such as: *Cancer and Pregnancy*, and *Preparing a Child for Loss*. The clinic is also the oncology centre and there are women here at every stage of treatment, from potential diagnoses to full-blown weekly chemo. There are women in wheelchairs, bloated with steroids. A woman my age takes the seat beside me and smiles brightly, about to start up conversation. She is wearing a hospital gown and has a cannula taped to the back of her left hand. I look away and make random marks in the margins of my sheaf of papers until I sense her resolve, or solidarity, waning.

In the various waiting rooms, I pore over Caroline's letters in digitised archives online, as she takes her personal loss and transmutes it into something greater than her; something heroic, enduring, revolutionary. Her handwriting elegant and legible even on the screen of a phone, the curve of her uppercase *I* and curlicue on uppercase *C;* the cups of *y*s and *g*s that are dropped when she's writing with haste.

She dreams her husband is dying, attended by two old women who berate her. She dreams an unborn baby has drowned: *I saw him float away and no one would attend to me because I was mad!* Since they were born, I've dreamed of losing my babies, too. I dream that I've left my daughter in a Left Luggage unit and there are hundreds of dully-gleaming lockers and I don't have a key. I get off a long-haul flight and my phone starts ringing: my husband, thousands of miles away, is asking where on earth I am and in the background the baby's crying, desperate for me, and it's too late to undo what I've done. I am dying, and I'm scared, and they tell me to keep calm and hold the hands that reach down for me, and I do, and feel myself pulled from my body. A moment's relief, then the agony of realising I will never hold my children again. I beg for one last chance and am let sink back into my body, sore and clumsy, and I take my boy into my lap and hold him tight, the smooth, warm curve of his back, and know that this is all that matters, ever, ever, ever.

Caroline, without her boys – her Penny, her abandoned chicken Brin, her Too-Too the little tadpole – stays awake all night long, night after night, staring into the dark until visions of their large brown eyes swim up, *as when I looked up from my work and found them watching.*

She would be annoyed with them, then, for interrupting her; for breaking the spell. She writes – has always written – to survive. Her first novel paid for the birth of her son; the doctor's bills and the nurses. She accedes to her publisher's demand and writes a *Bijou Almanac* designed for the Christmas market; an inch and a half wide and sold with its own miniature eyeglass. She tries her hand at plays; she'll turn her pen to anything. She always has and has always had to, children or no.

She tests out guilt and refuses to feel guilty. Refuses shame, too: there is too much fear of publishing about women, she writes. It is reckoned that they wish nothing better than to hide themselves away and say no more about it. *No longer!* She writes. She will tell her truth, and she will change the world.

When I can't concentrate on Caroline's letters any longer, I read Twitter instead, swiping, tapping, swiping. In the US, the children of asylum seekers are being taken from their parents at the border. There are photographs on social media of minibuses fitted with rows of baby-carriers for transporting infants to 'tender age' shelters. There is shaky hand-held footage and anonymous testimony. Children led away from their parents to be bathed, never to come back. Breastfeeding babies pulled from their mother's arms. Sobbing toddlers clinging. A newsreader breaks down on live TV, unable to read the autocue. The US President rants on Twitter, self-righteous, or affecting outrage. I think of George Norton, suspicious, capricious, belligerent, ploddingly unintelligent, an ungovernable child. Foaming and stamping and rambling from one accusation to another, so that it was impossible to make out, wrote a clergyman attempting to mediate, what he wanted, or whom he meant to attack.

Laura Barrera, an attorney at the UNLV Immigration Clinic in Las Vegas, Nevada, tweeting from Paradise, NV.

> @abogada_laura | 5.55PM Jun 28, 2018
>
> My 5-yr-old client can't tell me what country she is from. We prepare her case by drawing pictures with crayons of the gang members that would wait outside her school. Sometimes she wants to draw ice cream cones and hearts instead. She is in deportation proceedings alone.

I read and read the stories online, unable to look away. A six-year-old who is blind, and her nonverbal four-year-old brother; nonverbal, in part, because he's traumatised. An attorney quoted on the BBC: 'Even a five-year-old who wasn't traumatised can't always tell you their address or what their parents look like or their last names. How do you expect a child to do all that? This is not something that the kids or their parents will ever get over.'

They do the scans; in a darkened room they do a biopsy. The results will be back within seven to ten days; the receptionist makes an appointment for exactly two weeks' time for me to come back and speak with the specialist. Back home, I quiz my not-yet four-year-old son: what's your full name? What's mine and daddy's? What's our address? Half of the time, he gets most of it almost right.

*

July. The UK prepares for the US Presidential visit. On the morning of 13th July, I watch over livestream as protesters launch the huge inflatable baby, with its snarling, lopsided mouth and piss-in-the-snow-hole eyes, to float above the Palace of Westminster. My son and I have made our placards, sellotaping pieces of A4 card to sticks of bamboo, and we intend to join the protest march. But at the last minute, the stupefying heat of the day, the thought of the sweltering tube, my husband delayed on the other side of the city, we – I – chicken out. My son is relieved: worried that the man who steals children will try to take him. I will do this, he says, and bares his teeth in a chimp-like snarl. I will do that, and the bad man will run away. Then he buries himself in my side. I want to stay with you for all the days and all the nights.

Yes, I say. Yes.

Later, I look at the best placards on Twitter. Mary Poppins, carrying her iconic umbrella, beside a slogan in rainbow colours: SUPER CALLOUS FRAGILE RACIST FACIST NAZI POTUS. We will overcomb the hate. Orange is the New Nazi. I'm missing Wimbledon for this, you Tangerine WANKMAGGOT. Ours simply said, BREASTFEEDING BABIES BELONG WITH THEIR MAMAS, and, even more simply, NO KIDS IN CAGES.

Caroline to Lord Melbourne: I wish I had never had children – pain and agony for the first moments of their life – dread and anxiety for their uncertain future – and now all to be a blank.

In the evenings, after he's gone to bed, I arrange my son's collection of dinosaurs to look like they're building a tower with his sister's bricks, racing his double-decker bus and her push-along trolley. I think of The Fairies who lived in my dolls' house and occasionally left letters, tiny writing in cards no bigger than postage stamps, and packets of Parma Violets. But my sisters and I were older, then: he will barely remember any of this. Do you remember before your sister was born? I ask him, and he thinks about it and says, No! He thinks some more and says, I hurt my knee in Croatia, which is true, he did, a bad graze falling off a low wall, and the shock of the blood made him howl for an hour.

In good moments, Caroline is convinced that there is still hope. *Let them do all they can about the children,* she writes, *I will undo in two hours what they have laboured to do for ten years – I have a power beyond brute force to swing them round again, back to their old moorings.* But mostly she feels the lethargy of despair. *No future can ever wipe out the past, nor renew it.* The children won't recognise her if she passes them in the street, nor she them. The youngest is no longer the fair, fat baby he used to be: those months, those years, those precious days, are lost forever.

It is unbearable, the thought that a child will not remember its mother.

There is a psychoanalyst who says that at a certain moment in pregnancy, if the mother-to-be is pregnant with a baby girl, five generations fuse together. It comes at around twenty weeks' gestation, when the unborn child, in her tiny, seedling ovaries, makes the hundreds of tiny eggs which will be her future children, or the possibility of them. In that moment, the not-yet-child is already mother; the not-yet-mother already grandmother; just as the mother-to-be was once a possibility inside her own in utero mother, carried by her one-day grandmother. I like the Escher's staircase of it, the sense of nestled Russian dolls. The potential grandchildren that I might never even see joined in a vertiginous rush with the grandmother who only barely met me, the centuries collapsing.

But the psychoanalyst uses the image to explain how suffering is passed down the generations; how we become trapped in the behaviours of our parents and theirs, doomed to repeat destructive patterns unless we find ways of breaking free. The iniquities, as the Bible solemnly tolls, visited unto the third and the fourth generations. The loss of a mother may be played out in the souls of your children's grandchildren.

The lawyers at RAICES, Texas's largest immigration legal service non-profit, estimate that at least a quarter of the children, a number in the hundreds, will never, ever be reunited with their parents again.

I bought the psychoanalyst's book because someone quoted him on Twitter saying that the US President was doing exactly the job he needed to, forcing into consciousness some of our collective unconscious issues. He told us not to look at him, but to look to ourselves. I didn't know quite what I made of this. The notion that we get the people we deserve, or require, seemed to let an individual off the hook; or conversely, to imply that their achievement wasn't that great. I think of Caroline, and Abogada Laura. At night, the children tumble through my dreams. I wake in a tangled sweat. I can't even go to a fucking march. In her cot beside me, the baby whimpers. I sit for hours, years, until my breathing calms.

She changes the law, single-handedly, but it's too late for her. The elder boys at 10 and 8 are beyond the law's reach; the youngest, so long as his father keeps him in Scotland, is beyond its jurisdiction, too. Little William Norton dies of lockjaw – tetanus – one Monday in September, aged just 9, after falling from his horse and cutting his arm. The boys are alone and unsupervised at their uncle's house, the only servant is the gamekeeper's wife, a hunched old woman who opens gates and locks doors. Willie makes his way to the nearest neighbour, Chapel Thorpe Hall, where he collapses and is put to bed. By the time Caroline's told that he's unwell, he has already died. She learns that he was conscious when he died, and begged for her, again and again.

The doctor tells Caroline that young Willie bore the painful spasms *with a degree of courage which he has rarely seen in so young a child*, as if this offers any consolation.

*

I am tired. I try to make my mind let go. This moment, and this, and this. Here, now; my baby's silky hair and milky smell. *A-duh*, she says, when she wakes in the night and wants milk. Online, a mother was alerted to breast cancer when her six-month old started refusing to nurse from one side. Online, another, still nursing twins, died ten days after her diagnosis. It is the night before the biopsy results. Somewhere in windowless rooms, cells have been scraped and splayed on slides, dyed and magnified and studied, pronounced upon. I have finished the biography, and the letters, and now I read the poems until I know sections of them by heart.

THE CHILDREN

If the lulled heaving ocean could disclose
All that has passed upon her golden sand,
When the moon-lighted waves triumphant rose,
And dashed their spray upon the echoing strand:
If dews could tell how many tears have mixed
With the bright gem-like drops that Nature weeps,
If night could say how many eyes are fixed
On her dark shadows, while creation sleeps!

The blue light of my phone gives me a headache. The day slides into dawn.

The hospital again, the staircase, the waiting room; a chair by the window, the rack of leaflets on the wall. The women with gypsy-style headscarves, or attached to IV drips; the occasional solitary man. Another young woman sitting stricken with her silent mother. My name is called. Everything you take for granted may yet be overturned.

And suddenly it's over. There is a name for it, and it's not exactly common, but it's benign. You can go, they say. Come back six months after you finish breastfeeding, or at most a year from now, and we'll re-examine you to be on the safe side. They've changed the boxes on the form so the Registrar can't find which one to tick, and then she does, and then it's done, the flimsy white paper to the ground floor receptionist and out of there, into the merciless, beautiful, stultifying heat. I will make my life matter, I promise to the day. I will use my voice. I will fight for what is right. The promises well up in me. I will spend less time on social media. I will not take my husband for granted. I will never snap at my children again. My children. I will teach them that it's their job, too, to make a difference. I will try to be a good example. I will. I will.

Back in 1863, Caroline finishes a novel in which her heroine refuses to bow to shame. Beatrice Brooke is seduced and then abandoned by the rich, predatory Montague Traherne; alone in Wales, her illegitimate baby boy dies. But Beatrice rebuilds her life: she sells her drawings and handmade lace, she moves back to London, becomes an artist's model. Against all odds and social conventions, *Lost and Saved* has a happy ending: Beatrice marries and has another child. This time, the reviews are split. Some call it a work of 'true genius', her best to date, but others are offended that a fallen women could be so redeemed. Caroline defends her heroine in the Letters pages of *The Times*, then starts work on her next and final novel, although of course she does not yet know it will be her last. Her middle son, *in a dreadful echo of my youth*, becomes increasingly violent; his wild and capricious moods taking dark turns. He flies into irrational rages and blames her for things that are not her fault, so that she is afraid to see him and hides in her room. He shoves her about and tells her to get out of his sight. He berates her in foul language. He hits her, and he hits his wife.

We go on. We endure, and go on. The old battles, the same battles, once again and in endlessly new configurations. On the 24th July it is announced that the inflatable baby will travel to Sydney for the forthcoming US Presidential visit there. RAICES tweets a plea to its followers:

> @RAICES | 7:53 PM, 25 Jul 2018
>
> Keep this in mind:
>
> Children are still in cages. Parents still don't know where their children are.
>
> Some were coerced illegally into leaving the country.
>
> The media isn't writing as many stories but the problem has not gone away.
>
> Please, don't let up.

Afterword: Rights First, Then Power

Dr Ben Griffin
University of Cambridge

THE AGONIES OF CAROLINE Norton echo down to us through her writings: the pamphlets, novels, newspaper articles and letters that flowed from her agile pen record in detail the horrific treatment that men might inflict on their wives.[1] Such horrors persist: the Office for National Statistics reports that, in the year ending March 2017, 1.2 million women and 713,000 men aged 16 to 59 experienced controlling, coercive, threatening or violent behaviour from a domestic partner.[2] And yet there is a gulf between Norton's experiences and those of the present day, because so many of George's actions were legal. It is startling to remember that in the first half of the nineteenth century mothers had no legal right to custody of their children, that married women had no right to own property, that ill-treated wives could not divorce their husbands without a private act of parliament, and that this was regarded as the natural order of things. For many nineteenth-century observers it was not George's behaviour that was shocking but Caroline's: confronting that fact exposes the intellectual and political chasms that separate us from the early Victorians.

As Caroline Norton discovered, a married mother had no right to custody of her children, or even access to them. She had no say in decisions about her child's education or religious upbringing. A father also had the right to appoint guardians for his child after his death, and there was no requirement that the child's mother should be one of them. Even if she were made a guardian, she was legally obliged to raise the child according to the father's instructions. When prompted to justify this state of affairs, nineteenth-century commentators produced a consistent – and to modern eyes bewildering – response: they said that it was to protect household harmony. In a book called *How to Choose a Wife*, written in 1870, we find the author insisting that 'The idea of unity is essential to that of matrimony.' 'Men', he wrote, 'may differ [amongst themselves] on many vital subjects, and still be excellent friends; but matrimonial happiness cannot coexist with such difference.' Consequently, 'Between man and wife there must be only one interest, and one aim.'[3] If arguments were to be avoided then there ought only to be one authority in the household, to which all others should willingly defer. That, it was said, was why wives ought not to be given rights that they might assert to thwart the wills of their husbands. In a debate on married women's property rights in 1870, for example, Lord Hatherley, conceded that 'No doubt it was monstrous to say the husband must be always in the right', but nevertheless he felt that 'somebody must regulate the affairs of the family' and he continued to cling 'to the old-fashioned notion that the head of the family must be the husband.'[4] Male authority then, was deemed essential to a well-ordered household. Moreover, in a culture that was profoundly Christian, it mattered that wives normally made a religious vow to obey their husbands as part of the marriage service, and that scripture unequivocally told wives that 'thy desire shall be to thy husband, and he shall rule over thee'.

But would not depriving wives of rights simply foster resentment against their husbands? It might produce domestic order, but surely not marital harmony? The need to square this circle explains why Victorian marriage advice literature exhibits an obsessive insistence that a good wife would happily surrender her own wishes and desires. So, for example, Elizabeth Sandford wrote in the 1830s that 'Where want of congeniality impairs domestic comfort... it is for woman, not for man, to make the sacrifice'.[5] This literature tackled marital disagreements by urging wifely submission rather than mutual give-and-take: the idea that spouses might resolve differences through compromise is scarcely visible before the final third of the century. Even as late as 1895, we find George Bainton writing in *The Wife as Lover and Friend* that 'The good wife will endeavour to adapt herself to her life companion. She will make her married career a series of adjustments, and, whenever necessary, learn to agree in disagreement.'[6] For a woman like Caroline Norton to disobey her husband, to express wishes of her own that were contrary to his, was at odds with contemporary understandings of marriage itself.

Such concerns are visible throughout the records of nineteenth-century child custody disputes. One of the most famous cases dealt with a wife who had surreptitiously educated her children as Catholics, against the wishes of her husband. The judge, Vice-Chancellor Malins, complained that she had 'entirely forgotten that by the laws of England, by the laws of Christianity, and by the constitution of society, when there is a difference of opinion between husband and wife, it is the duty of the wife to submit to the husband.'[7] To a great extent then, the rights of fathers derived from their authority as husbands, and it is striking that the mothers of illegitimate children had greater custody rights than married mothers (they had a legal right to custody until their children reached seven years of age).

What limits were placed on the exercise of paternal authority? The most important was a belief that a father's paramount duty was to supervise the moral education of his children: where a man conspicuously failed to do this, courts were willing to strip him of custody. It was on these grounds that the atheist poet Percy Shelley lost custody of his children in 1819.[8] In general, judges in the nineteenth century were far less willing to intervene with a father's rights than their eighteenth-century counterparts had been. Victorian judges held that men might be adulterous, or violent towards their spouses, but this was not in itself sufficient cause to strip them of custody of their children unless such behaviour was flaunted in front of the children, such that the father set a bad example. Nor was violence towards children necessarily grounds to interfere with custody arrangements. In an age when corporal punishment was regarded as a normal part of child-rearing, the violence directed towards children had to be extreme before courts would interfere with a father's domestic authority: George Norton's use of a riding crop to chastise his middle child would have been regarded as unfortunate but not illegal. The fact that moral injuries were understood to be more serious than physical injuries explains why disputes over the religious education of children loom so much larger than cases of physical abuse in the recorded cases. At times, this order of priorities produced judicial pronouncements that seem both appalling and bizarre. In 1876, for example, Lord Coleridge heard a case involving an adulterous alcoholic husband who treated his wife with considerable violence. 'He choked her, kicked her, threatened to murder her, threatened her with a pistol, and also used disgusting language towards her.' Coleridge agreed that this man should be deprived of custody of his son, but not simply because he was violent: he was far more concerned about the father's habitual drunkenness and bad language, which he said 'cannot but be seriously prejudicial to the moral safety and welfare of the child.' The crucial detail in this case was not the violence inflicted on the mother, but the fact that the son had 'started swearing at the servants using expressions he has heard his father use.'[9]

It was not enough, then, that George Norton was an abusive husband: that was no grounds to grant Caroline custody of her children. The only option was to reform the law, which is what Caroline set out to do. Throughout her campaign, she insisted that 'The natural position of woman is inferiority to man [...] I never pretended to the wild and ridiculous doctrine of equality.'[10] This, however, was not the lesson learned by the women who read her letters and pamphlets. One such reader was Barbara Leigh Smith (later Bodichon), who was so moved by Norton's 1854 book on *English Laws for Women in the Nineteenth Century* that she began to compile a short pamphlet of her own: *A Brief Summary, in Plain Language, of the Most Important Laws Concerning Women* (1854).[11] This was the seed from which the British women's movement flowered. Faced with such a blunt statement of women's second-class status, a circle of women gathered around Leigh Smith that included Bessie Rayner Parkes, Matilda Hays, Emily Faithfull, Maria Rye, Adelaide Proctor, Jessie Boucherett, Elizabeth Garrett, and Emily Davies. These women (who became known as the Langham Place group, after their base of operations in London), launched their own magazine, *The English Woman's Journal* in 1858, and began a series of campaigns demanding property rights for married women, better education for girls, the opening of professional careers to women, and the right to vote. Whereas Norton's campaign had largely been a one-woman show, the campaigns initiated by the ladies of Langham Place were genuinely national campaigns with their own organisational infrastructures, committees, and petitions.

These women, and the generations of activists who followed them, succeeded in pressuring parliament into improving women's legal and social position, although these reforms usually fell short of equality. As a result of Norton's work, in 1839 judges were given the discretion to award mothers custody of children up to the age of seven (provided that the mother was innocent of adultery – a requirement rarely demanded of fathers), and this age limit was increased to 16 in 1873. The creation of the Divorce Court in 1857 made it easier for wives to separate from abusive husbands, and the new tribunal was able to grant mothers custody or access to their children; in 1861 the same powers were given to the Scottish divorce courts, although Scottish judges initially proved reluctant to use them. Further reforms were passed in 1886 and 1925, but it is striking that neither measure granted mothers the same rights as fathers.[12] Instead, change was justified on the grounds that the law should prioritise the welfare of children above the rights of parents. Lawyers and politicians found it easier to justify granting custody to mothers on the grounds that it was good for the children, than to claim that mothers had rights that were equal to those of fathers. It is salutary, and still shocking, to remember that mothers were only placed on a position of equality with fathers in terms of parental rights in 1973. Before then, the history of child custody law shows that the rights of fathers were not eroded because parliament accepted the case for sexual equality (or children's rights), but because judges were given greater power to consider the welfare of children, and because the welfare of children was increasingly understood to be best served by placing children with their mothers.[13]

The fact that mothers' ability to gain access to their children has been achieved through the expansion of judicial discretion leads us to ask, who were these judges? They were, of course, all men of the educated classes. The first female magistrate, Ada Summers, was not appointed until 1919, and there were no female county court judges until Elizabeth Lane was appointed in 1962; she also became the first woman to sit in the High Court three years later. In 2017, women constituted 24% of the judges in the Court of Appeal; 22% in the High Court and 28% in the other courts (excluding tribunals).[14] A more equal society requires that we have a judiciary that can bring a diverse range of perspectives and experiences to bear when adjudicating disputes, reflecting not least the diversity among women's opinions and experiences.[15] As Baroness Hale, the first female President of the Supreme Court, has explained:

> My view of the law of duress, speaking as a 'reasonable but comparatively weak and fearful grandmother', was slightly different from my [male] colleagues' – I would have allowed the battered wife who stays with her husband although she expects to be forced to cook the dinner, wash the dishes, iron the shirts and submit to sexual intercourse to plead

duress when she is unexpectedly forced to handle stolen goods, store illegal drugs, or commit some other crime.

Engaging with this point requires us to go beyond Caroline Norton's vision of reforming the law while leaving broader political and legal structures intact.

Caroline's story reminds us that male judges have not always been sympathetic to the plight of mothers. Consider the case of William Ebbs, a bootmaker who came before the police court in Lambeth in 1854, having beaten his wife (with her baby in her arms), before attempting to slit her throat with a razor. As the feminist philosopher John Stuart Mill complained in a letter to the *Morning Post*, Ebbs had been treated leniently by the presiding magistrate, who had released him after a week, and had given him money 'sent for his use by a 'benevolent gentleman'. To add insult to the injuries sustained by Mrs Ebbs, who now had to contend with the return of her abusive spouse, the magistrate warned her not to make 'such free use of her tongue in abuse of her husband.'[16] Who was this magistrate? We have met him before. It was Caroline's husband, George Norton. For all the progress that has been made since then, this case reminds us that to have rights without power leaves women dependent on the goodwill of men. To glimpse George Norton wielding judicial power is to confront the implications of this fact. For as long as these inequalities persist, the agonies of Caroline Norton will continue to haunt the present.

Notes

1. The best historical studies of Norton are Mary Poovey, *Uneven Developments: The Ideological Work of Gender in Mid-Victorian Britain* (1988), ch. 3; Diane Atkinson, *The Criminal Conversation of Mrs Norton* (2012). The large historical literature on domestic violence is discussed in A. James Hammerton, *Cruelty and Companionship: Conflict in Nineteenth Century Married Life* (1992) and Ben Griffin, *The Politics of Gender in Victorian Britain: Masculinity, Political Culture and the Struggle for Women's Rights* (2012), ch. 3.

2. *ONS Statistical Bulletin: Domestic Abuse in England and Wales: Year Ending March 2017* (2017).

3. 'H.W.H.', *How to Choose a Wife* (1855), p. 37.

4. *Times*, 22 June 1870, p. 6.

5. Elizabeth Sandford, *Woman, in her Social and Domestic Character* (1831), pp. 2-3.

6. George Bainton, *The Wife as Lover and Friend* (1895), p. 42.

7. *In re. Agar-Ellis, Agar-Ellis v. Lascelles*, 10 Ch. D. 49 (1878); quotation at p. 55.

8. The basis of this principle of intervention to prevent moral harm was set out in *Rex v. Delavel*, 97 Eng. Rep. 913 (1763); it was first reported as being used to deprive a father of custody in *Shelley v. Westbrooke*, Jac 266, 37 Eng. Rep. 850 (1819).

9. *In re Goldsworthy*, 2 Q.B.D. 75 (1876).

10. Caroline Norton, *A Letter to the Queen on Lord Chancellor Cranworth's Marriage and Divorce Bill* (3rd ed., 1855), p. 98.

11. Pam Hirsch, *Barbara Leigh Smith Bodichon, 1827-1891: Feminist, Artist and Rebel* (1998).

12. These reforms are examined in Ben Griffin, *The Politics of Gender*, ch. 5; and Stephen Cretney, *Law, Law Reform and the Family* (Oxford, 1998), ch. 7.

13. Danaya C. Wright, 'The Crisis of Child Custody: a history of the birth of family law in England', *Columbia Journal of Gender and Law* 11 (2002), pp. 175-270; Stephen Cretney, *Family Law in the Twentieth Century* (2003). The 1989 Children's Act was a major innovation which falls outside the scope of this essay.

14. https://www.judiciary.uk/about-the-judiciary/who-are-the-

judiciary/diversity/judicial-diversity-statistics-2017/ [accessed 28 April 2019]

15. For a powerful statement of this case see Baroness Hale's 2007 Maccabaean Lecture, 'A Minority Opinion?', *Proceedings of the British Academy*, 154 (2007), p. 32. Available online at https://www. thebritishacademy.ac.uk/lectures/maccabaean-lectures-jurisprudence [accessed 28 April 2019]. For an extended discussion of this point see Rosemary C. Hunter, Clare McGlynn and Erika Rackley, *Feminist Judgements: From Theory to Practice* (Oxford, 2010).

16. 'A Recent Magisterial Decision', in Ann P. Robson and John M. Robson, eds., *The Collected Works of John Stuart Mill,* vol. XXV (1986), p. 1197.

The Tenth of April

Uschi Gatward

THE WEATHER IS BETTER here, and the air cleaner. I doubt I would have lived so long in England.

When I first saw Hobart, I thought I was coming in to moor in paradise: the bay framed by the mountains. The solid buildings, all quite new, of course. Hobart is younger than I am – as a settlement, that is. We arrived at the end of November, the beginning of summer. No better time to see the place – like an English June. I turned to the man next to me, and we laughed and shook our heads. Van Diemen's Land! He was a silk weaver, from Spitalfields.

Somebody had died on ship. Two people actually: one of the convicts and one of the guards. I think stomach poisoning. They wrapped the bodies up and flung them overboard. The chaplain led some prayers.

We arrived on shore and the clerk asked me my crime. 'Convening a public meeting,' I said, 'and speaking at it. Which in England amounts to sedition.' He wrote it down.

When I am well enough, I visit the reading room – it is just out here and to the left – and when I am not, the superintendent brings me books or old newspapers with my bread and broth. He will sometimes stand and talk a few minutes, local politics or the news from Britain. Sometimes I tell him about the old days there. He knows who I am, of course. Everybody does.

★

My name is William Cuffay, and you know of my deeds if not my name. I was one of the Orange Tree conspirators, but before that I was an organiser of the democratic progress of the Chartist petition of 1848 from Kennington Common to Parliament.

That great petition: how it processed through the streets, four bales of paper bound with string, borne like a royal personage in a carriage – or like a giant coffin – followed by tens of thousands, with thousands more watching – and the police watching, but daring not to impede its progress. How it crossed the Thames like a river itself, the crowds of watchers thronging the bridge; how it was welcomed into Parliament Square by a cheering, shouting, whistling crowd. How it arrived at the gates of Parliament – the seat of government – to a deafening roar of applause …

How it didn't.

How it should have done.

How it would have done, were it not for O'Connor.

★

We had prepared for months. Not just the gathering of signatures – in my sixtieth year I travelled all over London and about the country giving speeches, and O'Connor, not much younger, did much more – but also the planning of the march, deciding rallying points and procession routes for the monster meeting. Then came the news from France and we sped up our work.
My wife collected subscriptions and organised a party to sew banners. She chaired women's meetings and spoke at them. We went round the unions, the public houses and temperance halls, reading the pamphlets aloud to all who would listen. O'Connor hung around the lobby and talked to his fellow M.P.s, though there was not much sympathy, he said (save for the clause about *payment of Members*). Still, it was important to prepare the ground.

We needed a show of force. It is all very fine if the millions petition for change, but a mass of strong, angry people in the street is a more effective memorandum. And if you have the thousands in the street and the millions agreeing with the thousands in the street – and prepared to say so publicly, and put their name to it – you cannot lose. And that is what we had. We could not lose.

The night before the march, we had been making our preparations. It was a Sunday, so there was time enough to call round from house to house. It rained hard, and my coat was soaked through by the afternoon, but at least we found people home when we knocked. We delivered the last of the banners to the leaders' houses, along with final maps of the route and orders of the day. The rain continued all through the evening, drumming against the windows. I made some changes to my speech in the light of current events, while my coat dried by the fire. We retired early, against the long and jubilant day ahead.

I woke several times in the night, troubled by a dream. I heard the rain, which in my dream had been a thumping on wood and a shouting crowd. Eventually I slept, in the hours before dawn, and awoke rested and ready for the day.

*

It dawned rainy; we hoped that it would clear. I took a walking stick and Mary an umbrella: we would be a long time on our feet and, besides, a stick is good to have to hand in these situations. We set out arm in arm, dressed in our best clothes, as were many others we passed on the route. Mary remarked the absence of omnibuses and cabs on Oxford Street; they had heard of our march and, perhaps anticipating trouble, stayed away.

We met a band of women dressed in the Irish tricolour, carrying the flag of Erin. They sang a Repealers' song. We asked if they were Chartists and they said they were.

The streets were lively and excitable for the hour. We passed several knots of police and special constables (on seeing which, the women would sing more loudly and with particular emphasis).

The rallying point for the West Division was Russell Square, and nine o'clock the appointed time. As we drew closer, the street grew busier. By half past eight, the square was already populous, with the police very much in evidence; some musicians (whom I knew to be Soho tailors) led the crowd in a number of Chartist hymns. I left Mary there amongst friends and continued on to our Convention at Fitzroy Square, whence our vehicles would convey the leaders and petition to Kennington. The business of the meeting – *viz.*, the confirmation of existing plans, along with a new letter of prohibition from the police and the provision of contingencies against this – was concluded within the hour. (O'Connor was late: he said he'd been making his will.)

We all climbed into the wagoncar – O'Connor in the front seat with Doyle, McGrath, Jones, and I think Wheeler and Harney. McGrath talked much with O'Connor about the changes he had made to the route plan and how these should mitigate against infraction and disorder. I sat towards the back and spent the time looking out on the streets. The rain was intermittent – suspended in the air rather than driving down – but I was glad to be seated, partially sheltered by a canopy.

Our *cortège* processed through the streets, a vanguard or a herald for the march itself. We stopped at the Land Office to collect the petition and secure it onto the first car, to the accompaniment of much applause from the bystanders. The road was crowded with people, hemming us in, and the pace of the car was fittingly slow.

Some passers-by called out to us as they went about their business, or cheered us on our way. O'Connor joked that it was like the Coronation, and we the Queen. ('Or a load of aristocrats in the tumbrils,' said another.) Some were clearly Chartists going to march – these fell in behind us – and most seemed supportive. Some shouted snippets of news to us, relaying the gossip from other districts. The rain had eased now, and the sun was out. The mood was one of jollity.

Two aldermen were stationed by the Waithman obelisk at Ludgate Hill, but there was no trace of the authorities otherwise. Though the bridge was defended, not the slightest hindrance was offered to our passage towards it. The special constables stood well back, arms at their sides; I could scarcely credit their lack of resistance. Had the government sensed defeat? Was it ceding us the victory? Now I remarked it, there had been a police presence on Chancery Lane but nowhere else since we had left Soho. It was as though the streets were empty of all but our supporters. And yet our information – and indeed the direct communications from the police – had been that there would be resistance. Where was it, then? I felt an unease, for the first time since we had cheerfully boarded the car at John Street. I suppressed the thought and did not share it. It was natural to feel a slight nervousness, and no good would come of infecting others. I put it from my mind.

Just at that moment a cheer went up from the bridge and we saw a battalion of Chelsea pensioners, armed and fully accoutred, landing at the City pier. Then I saw the troop of police, a double line, on the Surrey side of the bridge, and a mounted division with cutlasses come into view at Stamford Street.

'There is artillery at Somerset House,' said someone, grabbing the side of the car and running beside us.

I didn't know whether to believe him. 'Whose artillery?' I said, but he was gone.

★

Elephant and Castle was bathed in glorious sunshine. Here we were joined by another section of the march. Now the route was crammed with spectators, who pointed and called out as they saw our cars appear. Even the ladies waved their handkerchiefs. Many left their place and joined us as we passed. At times they crowded round so that I worried for the horses – or that someone would go under a horse – but for the most part they were orderly even in their crowding. I saluted the gallery – the upstairs windows, stuffed with watching children. And then the fine wide road to Kennington glittered in the sun, clear except for spectators standing respectfully back, and we picked up speed a little. It felt like a victory march.

There was music playing when we arrived, but as the people caught sight of our car the band stopped and the common was engulfed in cheers. A chant started up: 'The Charter, the Charter.' We waved our banners and applauded to acknowledge their applause. The cheering went on for some time.

Amongst the crowd were many elderly people, who had not joined the march but had come to be counted at the meeting. Some were seated on chairs or on the grass. The crowd was peaceful and considerate and there was no disorder (though I saw some boys who looked like pickpockets, moving a little too swiftly and for no clear reason, disbanding and rejoining every so often, whispering and signalling together).

I got down from the wagon a moment to stretch my legs. We could hear the marching band and the distant shouts of the procession – distant but coming nearer. A message came that O'Connor was wanted at the Horns Tavern, to go through last arrangements with the police. He swore, checked his pocket watch, muttered that it would have to be quick, and told Doyle and me to begin our speeches if he was delayed for more than a quarter hour.

'Shall I come with you?' said McGrath.

'No need,' he said, 'or – come if you like and be outside if I want you,' and they followed the policeman across the common to the Tavern, fighting through the crowds.

I got back onto the car. And then a roar started up as the procession arrived, a brass band at its head. The marchers gave up an answering roar and for minutes all was noise and movement of banners, flags and hats. The marchers took their places on the common, flowing out over the green. It was a sight to see. Like the Coronation, in truth.

When the tail of the march had finally come through the

gate, Doyle and I consulted watches and agreed to begin if O'Connor had not arrived within five minutes. I looked out anxiously towards the Tavern, hoping to catch sight of him and Mac running up, but of course it was impossible to see anything now. We could begin without him – we would begin without him. I could speak for ten minutes if need be.

Doyle gave a short but rousing speech about strength in unity and the voice of the working man. I felt a spot or two of rain, though the sun was shining. O'Connor arrived then, I saw with relief, and waited on the ground until Doyle had finished. He looked ashen. The nerves have got to us all, I thought: even Feargus. I gave him a sympathetic smile. As the crowd made their cheers for Doyle he climbed onto the car. 'All of you line up on the platform behind me,' he said to us. When the people saw O'Connor rising to speak they cheered even more, and he raised his hat and put up his hands to quell their applause, to bring silence. They cheered and cheered, and several times over some minutes he had to hold up his hands and ask for quiet.

And then – I thought my ears deceived me – I heard O'Connor, Feargus O'Connor, the physical-force Chartist, the Irish Radical, tell us all to go home. We would not be marching to Parliament with the petition. He was calling it all off. We had shown our strength, he said. There was no need to do more. The petition would travel in a cab to the House, at his expense. No one would follow it. There would be no march: he had told the police there would not be. We must go home quietly now – and it must be peaceably – and patiently await the response.

The message travelled as a wave of dissatisfaction and dissent, from the front of the crowd to the back. I saw people throw up their hands and throw down their hats in disgust and cry out or turn away as they heard the news. Every face took on a look of disappointment. It was like a contagion.

I lost my temper then, and shouted something about it being a trap – a trick – and I'd have no part of it. I shouted at

O'Connor, that he had betrayed us. 'I'll have no part of this,' I told the crowd. 'I wash my hands of it. I am done with it, I'll stay not to hear more.' And I started to climb off the car, with the help of the people below. 'We should be marching on Parliament now,' I said, 'not with a petition but with death's heads and flaming torches.' And I'll make an effigy of you, O'Connor.

'Lead then!' shouted a young man. 'You lead, and I'll follow!'

He wore a kerchief at his neck in the French style and he carried a cap of liberty on a stick. He meant it. He turned to his friends in appeal.

'Aye,' they said. 'Lead, Cuffay!'

'Speak for us, Cuffay – because no one else will.'

It crossed my mind to do it, but in the same instant I knew I couldn't, without a plan and back-up. I shook my head. 'They have betrayed us,' I said. 'They have betrayed us.'

I left O'Connor on the platform, making his excuses with much energy and rhetoric. The crowd was beginning to disperse, turning the common to mud. The heavens opened and the rain poured down.

O'Connor had capitulated. He had an army at his back, and the government on the run, and he capitulated. It was in our grasp and he threw it all away. Coward.

How I got home I don't remember, but I was drenched. Mary helped me out of my wet clothes and boots and placed them once again before the fire and we sat with our heads in our hands, for hours. Chartism was finished. The government would reject the petition – that intention was clear enough – and we would never have the people's trust again.

*

Later, when I asked him what in the name of all damnation he'd been thinking, O'Connor said that the Commissioner of Police had ambushed him before the meeting start – pulled him into a private room at the Tavern, and shut the door – and told him that there were ten thousand troops on the bridges, and eighty thousand special constables lining all routes to the City, and snipers on the roofs awaiting their instructions, and that if we proceeded on our march they would take that as an act of war, and move accordingly.

The room was airless, with a stale smell of beer. O'Connor felt the blood drain from his face and a sickness rising and had to loosen his collar and steady himself (and indeed he looked sick as he related this to me: a failure of courage is easy to see on an Irishman's face – whereas I maintain my native hue of resolution).

'It would have been Peterloo or Newport or Preston again, but ten times worse,' he said. 'They would have opened fire on the crowd and hanged us leaders. They would have hanged us all.'

Well, they might have done. Had they wished to see Buckingham Palace and the Palace of Westminster razed to the ground within the month, and the blaze of Osborne House visible from France, and the Queen, weak with childbirth, and her new infant hauled out into the street, and worse – yes, they might have done.

Did he, I asked him, impress upon the police commissioner that the troops might number ten thousand, but that the petition had near six million signatures, and that many of those were the marks of angry, hungry men? 'We can hold them off for a little while,' I would have said, 'but not for long. They are peaceable – for the moment – but they are impatient. Their demands must be met. I dare not go to them and cancel the procession. I dare not. I would fear for my life – and yours, sir, and those of your men – if I denied them now.'

That is what I would have said, in O'Connor's shoes.

Or why did he not say: 'We make all decisions collectively, sir. So let me call in the committee, and let you repeat to them verbatim what you have said to me, and we will then be in a position to choose our course of action, in line with the constitution of the land, which, as a Member of Parliament, I understand very thoroughly.'

It was not the only tragedy in my life, nor the worst. But the others were acts of God; this was an act of stupidity.

The following day, O'Connor missed Parliament and our own Convention, complaining of pains in his chest. (These pains were not the result of being beaten repeatedly by fellow Chartists shouting 'Coward! Traitor!'– although perhaps in his imagination they were. Perhaps it was the thought of such recriminations that kept him home).

The newspapers – in the pockets of parliamentarians and of those with a vested interest in the *status quo* – gleefully recorded our defeat.

'They had a *cheval-de-frise* at Somerset House,' said O'Connor. 'A revolving *cheval-de-frise*.'

Well. If you say so.

Three days later, in Parliament, when he'd recovered, O'Connor challenged another M.P. to a duel. (O, *now* you want to fight. Now it's too late to fight. Now that the fight is lost.)

We hardly spoke again. I was arrested that summer, and transported the following year. He visited me in gaol to say goodbye. I later heard that he held me up as a monitory tale: what happens when you turn to violence.

You had regrets – I know you had. And they killed you, those regrets. You were mad within three years and dead in seven, the rest of your life spent crazily swinging your fists, fighting with shadows – or demons. Perhaps you're still doing that.

*

Those of us who were not cowed by the police split away from O'Connor, and we organised. One of our number, a printer, acquired some old type that had been broken up. We used it to cast bullets, in the evenings at home, Mary and I – heating it over a candle and pressing it into a mould – distributing these, when they were finished, in packets at the meetings.

I had a pistol, and I practised my shots in a local woodland during those light evenings, shooting at squirrels with the remains of a bad novel, or a seditious pamphlet, as it may be. We ate the resulting fare.

I ran classes at the Chartist Land Office in Soho: an upstairs room with the curtains drawn. I demonstrated loading the pistol with the bullets of print, but did not fire it, of course.

An Irishman came to show us a pike drill. The room was smoky from the lamps and our shadows huge on the walls and ceiling as we ran the drill with broom handles and makeshift sticks, following his lead, so that we could go out and teach it to others. He laid the pike on the floor and we looked at its length and construction (it is heavier than you think) and discussed how we might get more made, cheaply and in secret, and the large but secluded spaces where we might train for battle.

We talked of recruiting arsonists, who on a given day and at a given signal would set light to certain key buildings in the city, which would be seen for miles around like a beacon call to arms. We looked at maps to identify these buildings – some on hills or crossroads for visibility, some symbolic for morale – distributed evenly at the points of the compass.

It was Filden, a new and energetic Chartist, who taught me how to make bombs out of ginger-beer bottles filled with nails and gunpowder, stuffed with turpentined rags.

'Stuff it down, pack it tight,' he said, 'then a match to the rag before you chuck it. Good things for wives to throw at policemen out of upstairs windows.'

He was full of information. He had a fine singing voice and we sang together – 'The Ballad of Ned Ludd'. It was on his evidence that we were arrested, Lacy, Fay and I, and he related the ginger-beer bottles as being my idea. Of course, they made much of the pistol.

*

The night before the march at Kennington, I dreamt I was in Parliament. Robert Wedderburn was there, and my father and mother, and the poet Shelley. This Parliament was filled with working men, and women too: my first two wives, my grandmother and my daughter, all there. Shipwrights and dockers and ropemakers and washerwomen I had known as a child – they all nodded at me, and raised their hand to bid me speak. On the front bench was a boy with typhoid. He nodded and laughed wearily, though he could scarce keep his eyes open. Dark, hollow eyes in a chalky, clammy face. Next to him an old man with his jaw bound up against the toothache. There were slaves whom my father had told me about, from St. Kitts. And a cook he worked with on board ship – a portly man with a ready laugh. He filled his pipe and smiled at me as he puffed away on it.

And I was speaking to the house. I told them about the Charter, and they nodded and said 'Aye' and thumped the bench. Even though some of them had been dead for forty years, they had no difficulty understanding the Charter's aims or appreciating the need for it. Death had not dented their powers of cognition. Not one whit.

*

Well. I have made myself useful here.

A settlement in its infancy is a good place to introduce rights for the working man.

Hobart Town is well laid out, and there are many commodious halls for holding meetings, which, until these last years, I did. The Mechanics' Institute is a fine place, and the temperance halls are also used for political education. All the tools are here to create a strong democracy. So long as the convict labour does not push down local wages.

I have been reading Mrs. Craik. Her stories are good though the politics are not (if more time were allotted me and if I had the means I would begin a correspondence). I would like to finish this one, but I tire easily now and am not sure I will.

Twenty-one years was my sentence, and so it has proved. I smell the hawthorn blossom, though it is July and the dead of winter. Its scent pervaded my dream, cloying white and yellow, stifling the breath. I wonder if others can smell it now.

Bread-and-cheese. Tonight's meal will be frumety. That will be warming, and take away some of the bad taste. I must ask for another blanket.

In England, all male heads of household are now enfranchised. Universal suffrage cannot be far away.

The Hyde Park rally of '67 achieved what the Kennington Common meeting should have done. Twenty years after it should have happened, it did. They called themselves not Chartists but something else. Reformers. Whatever they call themselves, they are pushing for change. Let them call themselves what they like. Progress is made.

The Elementary Education Bill is going through Parliament now, and will soon be law, God willing. All children will receive a schooling paid for by the public purse, to age fourteen. Every child in England will learn to read and write: we can smile at that. An educated workforce will insist on franchise, and it may be the Bill is a witting prelude to it. We may hope.

★

Fellow slaves, brother slaves: there need be no one starving in the midst of plenty (this is an incontrovertible truth: there is no argument you'll put to me that I'll accept). And one day there will not be, if you wish it so. But you must back up your wishing with a fight.

If the government of the day does not serve the working man and his poorest neighbour, then with the vote we may vote that government out. Thank you – thank you.

And whilst we do not have the vote, we must protest that lack.

That men should starve is an active choice we make, and if you do not agitate against it, then you are complicit in it.

They will try to tell you that some are naturally inclined, by birth or otherwise, to be servants, and some masters. You must resist this notion. It is a falsehood and a canker.

We need to rid ourselves entirely of masters and servants. There is capital and there is labour – nothing more. Servitude ennobles no one – not master nor slave.

Thank you, thank you – but more than applause, I would like you to put your efforts into bringing about a just society. I would like you to fight for it.

Yes, yes, yes – thank you – all this clapping is all very fine, but will you fight for it?

Will you fight for it? Will you?

You may not be asked to fight. But you must take off your jacket, and roll up your sleeves. You must put up your fists.

The Charter, and no surrender.

THE GREAT CHARTIST MEETING, 1848

Afterword: Peaceably if we May

Dave Steele
University of Warwick

HISTORIANS CAN'T INDULGE IN speculation, whereas the creative writer is not so constrained. By writing in the first person, Uschi takes the reader inside the head of one of the most fascinating actors on that fateful day, 10 April, 1848, and offers an answer to a question which has long puzzled historians – why at their zenith did the Chartists capitulate?

By the time of his deathbed account, William Cuffay had been living in Tasmania since being transported 21 years earlier at the age of 61. Recalling events decades later is problematic, whether in fiction or real life – memory becomes blurred and events can be changed or embellished. Cuffay's story is no different, but before unpacking the events of that damp Monday in 1848, it is worth looking back at his eventful life.

Cuffay's father was a freed slave from St Kitts who had found work in the Chatham dockyards. His mother was a local white woman. The young William probably suffered from rickets which left him with a lifelong spinal condition limiting his growth to 5ft.[1] Qualifying as a tailor he moved to London where he became active in the tailors' strike of 1834, subsequently losing his job. His radical political journey later led him to join the Chartists where he wasted little time in gaining influence and eventually a leadership role. As a black working class activist he must have cut a distinctive figure but was also a target for racist abuse, the *Times* disdaining the Chartists as 'the Black Man and his Party'.[2]

The life story of our other main protagonist couldn't have been more different – Feargus O'Connor was a wealthy Irishman, having inherited estates from his Protestant father. But there were parallels – both men had roots away from the British mainland perhaps leading the government to treat them both as outsiders.

The roots of the politics of 1848 lie in the radical reform movements arising out of the mass demobilisation after Waterloo. Failure to make headway in the 'mass platform' campaigns for wider suffrage led some, including another black activist Robert Wedderburn, to propose a more violent form of insurgency culminating in the execution of five men for treason following the failed Cato Street conspiracy. The memory of this and the shocking Peterloo Massacre may have later influenced the government to make concessions in the form of the 1832 Reform Bill, which partially extended the franchise but still left unfinished business as most adult males still had no vote.

In 1838 several analogous political campaigns coalesced together to create the People's Charter calling for annual, secret ballots of men over 21 returning paid MPs representing constituencies of equal population size. The Chartist movement united disparate groups such as regional industrial workers with London artisans but more significantly it created an alliance between working class activists such as Cuffay and middle class reformers like O'Connor.

By 1846 the Chartist movement had all but fizzled out having run two mass petitions to no avail. That year finally saw the repeal of the contentious Corn Laws – a form of trade protectionism which had prioritised the financial interests of farmers and grain merchants above the subsistence needs of the poor for the preceding 31 years. Chartists sought alternative means of political expression with O'Connor championing his 'Land Plan', a part-lottery, part-contributory scheme to resettle urban poor on bespoke model farm estates.

In 1847 however corn prices reached a new high and the economy slumped, causing industrial layoffs. These events, combined with O'Connor's election as MP and increased circulation of his newspaper, the *Northern Star,* emboldened the Chartists to float a third petition which was launched in August. Links with Irish radical groups were forged. The turning point came in February 1848 with the proclamation of the French Second Republic, part of a wave of revolutions which spread like wildfire across Europe. As well as catching the Chartist movement off guard, the British establishment were also totally unprepared. As with the prior French Revolution of 1789, the British elite were shaken to the core, prompting them to mis-read the strategy of the resurgent Chartists as planning a violent insurrection. This implies that the usual network of government spies and infiltrators were either incompetent or inactive at that time as they would have quickly reported back the movement's nonviolent intentions (or short-term intentions, at least – the on-going 'moral- vs. physical-force' debate was still unresolved).

Following riotous London rallies in March, the leadership made plans to bring forward the launch of the now-monster petition to 10 April at the grandly-named 'Great Chartist Meeting' and from there the petition would make its way to parliament accompanied by reputedly hundreds of thousands of supporters. The government had banned political meetings within one mile of the Houses of Parliament, prompting organisers to locate the rally south of the river at Kennington Common. In this lay the seeds of their downfall – firstly because they would be separated from their goal by the river and secondly because the Government saw the Kennington meeting as a direct challenge to their authority.

The anticipated attendance was a quarter of a million. This was the hoped-for turnout by the Chartist organisers and clearly they believed their own hype. So did the government, leading them to call in the largest military lock-down of the capital ever seen. I have seen archival provisioning documents, which alone prove that supplies of biscuits, spirits and salt-pork were stockpiled at key locations in the city to keep a garrison of 8,000 troops fed for 10-15 days.[3] There is no question that a serious violent insurrection was expected. The titular head of the army, the Duke of Wellington, together with military secretary, Lord Fitzroy Somerset, presumably with the Peterloo massacre still in mind, agreed to keep troops firmly in the background north of the river. A state of near panic spread right to the top – Queen Victoria and her consort Prince Albert were packed off to Osborne House on the Isle of Wight, even though some members of the government still secretly feared that the Solent wouldn't be wide enough to protect them.

And it wasn't only troops providing security. As Uschi has asserted, the strategy was to allow the Chartist processions to cross the bridges on their way to the meeting but to prevent their return. This was achieved with a massive show of force of 4,000 metropolitan police who closed the bridges in what was probably the first (and largest) example of what would now be called kettling.

In a further tactical move, around 80,000 members of the public were signed-up as Special Constables to keep the peace. Some were middle-class volunteers such as the 36 year-old Charles Dickens but many were workers and artisans conscripted by their employers to guard their workplaces.

Indications from my own research corroborate press reports that the Kennington crowd was significantly smaller than expected – perhaps as low as 20,000. This finding is controversial, as many historians still believe the crowd was nearer 150,000.[4] But, even if the reality was a smaller than expected attendance, there is no doubt of the power projected by the Chartists.

Through Cuffay's narrative, Uschi captures the emotional mix which attendees must have experienced in the confusion, ambiguity and general hubbub – hope, fear, betrayal, anger, and tenacity to name just a few.

Newspaper reports confirm that Cuffay spoke at meetings

of the Chartist Convention at the Literary and Scientific Institution, Fitzroy Square on April 4th, 8th and 11th, so we can assume that, as Uschi suggests, he may also have been present at the convention meeting at 10am on the 10th. Until the Saturday, the leadership had been resolved to go ahead with Monday's Kennington meeting and procession to parliament, but Saturday's Convention meeting was adjourned to allow several delegates to lobby members of the cabinet to allow a reduced procession on the assurance there would be no breach of the peace; this was met with a flat refusal.

By Monday, perhaps with the survival of the movement in mind, some convention members were advocating a pragmatic policy of damage limitation fearing the bloodbath which might ensue were they to flout the ban. However some were undecided or not in agreement. In Uschi's version, Cuffay appears to have been uninformed. Her story shouts indecision, ambiguity and duplicity.

O'Connor would have faced huge opposition to such an about-face, so his primary concern could have been how to break the news to the more insurrectionary members and the crowd as a whole. Although the meeting with Police Commissioner Mayne at The Horn's Tavern has been presented as a surprise summons, it would have provided O'Connor with a face-saving opportunity of a climb-down. This unexpected U-turn, along with other erratic behaviour, could be put down to O'Connor's deteriorating health – by this time he was seriously ill, probably in a fairly advanced stage of syphilitic decline. So he wasn't fully rational. He claimed to have received death threats – perhaps a further symptom of his delusions. Cuffay's incredulity at this capitulation was reported in the press and in a literary account by Charles Kingsley, enhancing his notoriety or heroic status depending on your point of view. Uschi's version captures his feelings of betrayal.[5]

The meeting broke up quickly, partly because of O'Connor's appeal to disperse, but probably also because of a torrential rainstorm and, although a small contingent accompanied the 'cab' carrying the petition to Westminster, several million of the nearly six million signatures were dismissed as being duplicate or fraudulent supposedly having been signed by such dignitaries as the Queen and the Duke of Wellington or downright ridiculous names such as 'No Cheese' and 'Pug Nose'. In the ensuing Parliamentary debate on 13 April, O'Connor conceded that the petition may indeed have contained a smattering of absurd signatories but he asserted that 'there would be left five million of legitimate signatures' adding that a small team of clerks could not have already counted the whole petition.[6] But the point seems to have been overlooked that, even accepting the two million non-contested signatures, this represented 14% of the UK population – an indication of success rather than failure.

The mass event at Kennington was hugely significant for the history of protest for three reasons. Firstly because of the juxtaposition of a concealed military presence with a prominently visible (newly established) metropolitan police force – elements not present at Peterloo 29 years earlier. Secondly, because of new technologies invoked to enhance state power – the railways and the new electric telegraph were both requisitioned to facilitate transport and communications; finally it was the first time a political crowd event was photographed – two daguerreotypes survive in the royal collection showing the crowd in stunning detail.[7] Combined with newly sophisticated press reporting this enabled contemporary readers and historians alike to experience the event as if they were there.

1848 was a power struggle, pure and simple. The ruling elite were not ready to make concessions to extend the franchise and, on that day at least, the Chartists were not prepared to let things descend into violence to further their goals. But in terms of the projection of power of a working class political movement this event should not be denigrated as a failure. For William Cuffay and others, the climbdown on 10 April prompted them to up the ante, ditching the tactic of 'Peaceably if we may' for a more insurgent 'Forcibly if we must'. This led them to lower their guard against infiltration resulting in the mass arrests on 16 August of eleven at the Orange Tree public house in Bloomsbury and thirteen at the Angel in Southwark leading to the transportation of Cuffay along with several others.

But, as Hector Berlioz, present at Kennington, implied in his memoirs, revolution is not the British way.[8] Instead a long game is often played out involving demands, threats, pleas, retrenchment, negotiation and eventually deferred success – in this case in the form of the Second Reform Act in 1867 which effectively doubled the electorate to two million men (though leaving many un-enfranchised for a further 50 years).

So it is fitting that Cuffay's dream on the night before the Great Chartist Gathering was a dream not so different from that of Martin Luther King 120 years later, a dream of hope, a dream in which ordinary men and women of any colour can participate fully in the democratic process. And for Cuffay, the Charter was the weapon to achieve it.

Notes

1. Hoyles, Martin, *William Cuffay: The Life & Times of a Chartist Leader* (Hertford, 2013) p.55.

2. Chase, Malcolm, *Chartism: a New History* (Manchester, 2007) p.308.

3. The National Archives, WO340/111

4. Goodway, David, *London Chartism – 1838-1848* (Cambridge, 1982) p.137; Malcolm Chase, *Chartism: a New History* (Manchester, 2007) p.302.

5. Kingsley, Charles, *Alton Locke* (1850)

6. *Hansard 13 April 1848 Volume 98* (London, 1848) col. 285.

7. Briggs, Jo, *Novelty fair* (Manchester, 2016) pp. 48-50

8. Berlioz, Hector, (Trans. Ernest Newman) *The Memoirs of Hector Berlioz* (New York, 1966) p. 17.

THE LIVERPOOL GENERAL
TRANSPORT STRIKE, 1911

The Good Sister

Jude Brown

LIKE WATER SEEPING INTO a leaking boat, they cannot be kept out. In they stream, one after the other, filling the house with their darkness. Most she recognises, some she does not, but then again maybe she does. Grief turns a person upside down and inside out, Molly told her. The only thing it makes you sure of is nothing at all. But there is one thing Alice does know for certain: they are here because of her. She has done this. She has brought them.

Someone kicks her foot. Ellen, her sister, has had enough. Alice knows she should be helping, knows she should be handing out refreshments, knows Ellen should not be doing it all on her own, even though it's common knowledge she is much better at this sort of thing. Ellen is the thoughtful sister, the caring one. Ellen kicks her again, harder this time, but Alice cannot move. Squashed in beside her father, she is pinned to the settee – not by his bulk but by the heaviness that sits inside her. Growing with every passing day she is now fit to burst, just like the house.

'Go into the kitchen and bring out a pot of tea, cups, milk and sugar,' Ellen tells her. 'It's twelve past the hour and the carriage will be here by half past, so don't take an age, and smarten that face up. Don't make a show of yourself.'

'I can't do it,' Alice whispers.

'Since when are you not able to make tea?' Ellen whispers back.

'This, I can't do this. I can't go through with it.'

Ellen looks around the room then leans into her sister. 'If I have to drag you by your hair to our brother's funeral I will. God rest his poor soul.' Ellen crosses herself and they both look over at the casket in the far corner of the room, at the people queueing to pay their respects. As if the Pope himself were lying there, Alice thinks.

She prises herself up from the settee and now with a better view, can see just how crowded the parlour is. The gathering of mourners reminds her of something but her memory will not release it. She looks at the men lining the walls, the women perched on chairs. Some sit on each other's laps, some on the floor. She sees the Kinsella twins kneeling beside their mother, who has parked herself in the one and only decent armchair. Their skirts spool out in front of them like dirty great puddles and Alice has a mind to pull forward her veil, curl up onto the coal black material and disappear, like a cat in the night. But the thought is as fanciful as John striding into the room, cap in hand, sleeves rolled up, a tale spinning from his lips. 'I got the best job in the world,' he'd say. 'I'm the luckiest catholic in Vauxhall.' *No, John,* Alice thinks to herself, *it was I who was the lucky one. I had you as a brother. Your misfortune was to have me as a sister.*

Murdering bastards the lot of them. If a man can't stand outside and fix the shutters at his window then none of us are safe. The twins' father is talking to another old neighbour. Full of fury, his face is as red as his infamous nose. The heaviness suddenly shifts. Where once it filled her chest, pushed out against her ribs, it now bears down as if she's carrying all four of her children at once. She wraps her arms around her belly instinctively and makes her way out of the parlour into the hallway. It too is heaving and bodies fill the stairs, the landing. Too many in too small a space.

It was the same that day, when she rounded into Vauxhall Road and saw the swollen sea of people. Two blocks away the sight still startled her. The rag-taggle crowd swarming the prison vans, the police escort, the soldiers on horseback, the rifles and bayonets glinting in the bright sun. It took her a second or two to work out what it was. Arrests had been made in the city centre, after the rally at St George's, and the prisoners were being transferred to Walton Jail today, but this wasn't the usual route.

All she had to do was wait and let them pass, then she'd be able to continue to her Aunt's. As the procession approached the corner of Hopwood Street, where she was headed, she caught sight of John. He was outside their Aunt's house, doing something with the shutters at the corner window that faced onto Vauxhall Road. That must be his room. The shutters had never closed properly, and John wouldn't like that. He had tools with him and she wished he'd go back inside, out of the way. She'd tried to call his name but there was too much shouting and jeering from the mob.

The noise grew louder when some managed to get close enough to the vans to rock them. As they swayed back and forth the prisoners inside began shouting encouragement and the soldiers used their rifle butts to keep the crowd back. In the commotion a horse reared and a bottle got thrown, and then all hell broke. Police waded in with their batons and bricks and pieces of fencing rained down. As the chaos drew level with the house, John pressed himself up against the wall and she couldn't make him out. She wished it would all quieten, stop, but a whipcrack of gunfire split the air and stilled everything. It also made her jump and drop the basket she was carrying. All she could think of when she saw the spilled soda bread and smashed blackberry jam was that John would be disappointed.

A bang, loud and sharp as a shot rings out. Ellen has followed her into the kitchen and slammed the cast iron kettle down onto the stove.

'When the kettle's come to the boil, fill it up again and put it back on the heat,' Ellen tells her. 'Think you can manage to do that?'

Alice nods but Ellen is not convinced. 'You're not the only one suffering. Pa's heart is broken and so is mine.'

'It is not heartache Ellen, you know what ails me,' Alice says.

'Shut up with your nonsense and make yourself useful. Put the milk in a jug and the sugar in a bowl and bring everything out on a tray.'

'Ellen, can't you tell them I took sick? Say I took bilious. Please, I beg of you.'

Ellen takes hold of her sister's arm and tells her she will not. 'I swear if Ma was here, she'd tan your hide all the way to Bootle and back, so don't think I won't.'

'Dear Lord, this dress is pure choking the life out of me.'

They both turn to see Molly, Alice's friend, standing in the doorway tugging at the high neck collar, which is as stiff as Ellen's face. 'It's a glorious day for a wedding but not so much for a funeral. I'll be getting buried alongside your John, if I can't get it to loosen.'

Molly's humour has never sat well with Ellen and today Alice is glad of it.

'Oh God forgive me, I'm sorry Ellen. I don't mean anything by it, you know me and my slack mouth.' Molly says.

'Indeed I do,' Ellen replies. 'Why don't you go and stand out in the yard, get some fresh air. Take our Alice with you. You can put that mouth of yours to good use and see if you can talk some sense into her.'

Ellen manoeuvres both of them outside and Alice sees the yard is as full as the house. Full of men dressed in their best, sucking on rolled leaf cigars, supping Irish stout. Ellen has thought of everything but doesn't she always. Everyone knows she is the considerate one, the good sister.

'What was that about?' Molly asks, walking towards a shaded corner of the yard.

'She blames me. She won't say it outright but I know she does. Ma told me to look after him and I didn't. I turned my back, I let it happen. The soldier that pulled the trigger, he didn't kill John. I did. If I'd let him come and live with us, he'd still be alive because he'd have no reason to be there. I know you think that too, as does everyone else.'

'No one's thinking badly of you Alice, everyone here has come to pay their respects.'

'Every time I lay my head to sleep I pray I don't wake up. Regret, I never knew it could pain like this. It's unbearable because there's no end, no way out.'

Molly takes a step closer to her friend.

'It's grief that's all, pure grief got you talking this way. Come on now, your John will be looking down and he won't want to see you like this.'

Alice makes no attempt to hide her scorn.

'You don't believe that any more than I do Molly. I've seen you at mass going through the motions. There is no after life, no world but this one. John's gone nowhere and I wish I could join him.'

Alice hears the sound of the slap before she feels it.

'Stop it! Stop with this mad talk Alice, do not walk into that miserable place. Can't you see how it works? Us taking the blame, us tearing pieces out of each other. We'll never achieve anything that way. They killed him. The people in charge, the ones who tell us we have to work for pennies, the ones who send war vessels up the Mersey to threaten us, those that charge down our streets on horseback, sticks in hand, smashing anyone and anything in their way.'

Molly sees the welt blossom on Alice's cheek. It's like she has taken a strap to her friend's face. 'Oh God, forgive me for striking you. I swear, I don't know my own strength sometimes.'

'It's nothing less than I deserve,' Alice tells her.

Molly flexes her broad hands out in front of her and Alice sees the swollen knuckles, the rough reddened skin. 'Good honest hands, your John used to say, workers' hands. I don't mind they're not elegant, ladylike. They earn me a pretty penny and when the strike's done, they'll earn me a few more.'

'They're not earning you much now,' Alice says feeling the burn in her cheek ebbing and wishing it wouldn't.

'And that's a price I'm prepared to pay. Oh, you should have heard him. Tom Mann. They'll not beat us now we've got the likes of him fighting our cause. See those men over there.'

Molly nods in the direction of the men with the cigars. 'They were at Michael's funeral yesterday. They're members of the Strike Committee, union folk.'

Curls of smoke drift upwards and Alice catches the earthy smell of the tobacco. It was only last Christmas that Pa had bought one for John and didn't he act the role of the gent! Brandy in one hand, cigar in the other. 'Think I could get used to this,' he'd said. 'You'll have to jump a ship to America if you want that kind of life. There's only graft and hard work for the likes of us here,' Pa had told him. 'A man can still pretend,' John had replied, resting back in the armchair.

People keep looking at her and she wishes they wouldn't. She can't take anymore faked pity, empty sorrow and wants the day done and the crowds gone because what she really fears is real concern, genuine sympathy. Punishment, not compassion, is what she needs.

They would play a game as children, take it in turns to be saint and sinner. Whatever the sin the penance was always the same, Alice would lose her sight and John his hearing. John's worst fear was a soundless world and hers a world of darkness. Maybe if she were to strike that bargain, pluck out her eyes, she could be forgiven. She does not seek it from the church, does not seek it from God. This at least has cured her of that pretence.

Molly nudges her and points. 'I think those over there are the carter boys that worked alongside your John.'

Three boys about the same age as John are huddled together like nervous pups. One looks directly at Alice and lifts a hand to his cap in acknowledgement. How young he looks she thinks. Not quite as old as John. Sixteen, seventeen at most. What a smooth perfect complexion he has, what an open face. A laugh escapes her as she realises how inviting that would be. Such blatant innocence would surely stand out in such a riotous mob;

be like looking at the face of an angel. A face just asking to be damned.

'On behalf of the Strike Committee, I'd like to offer my condolences to you and your family Mrs McConnell.'

One of the union men is standing beside her.

'The Committee has organised a collection and a fund is being raised in your brother's honour so if there's anything you need, you only have to ask. We will do our best to bring those responsible to justice. Your brother's death will never be forgotten. Rest assured he did not die in vain; the cause will win out. The whole country is behind us now.'

He takes out a crumpled piece of paper from his pocket, smooths it and hands it to Alice. It's a leaflet, the kind she has seen before. The city is awash with them. It calls for further strike action, for workers to unite. *Join a union! Stand together!* it declares. It is signed by Tom Mann. The man who is forever on everyone's lips. The man Molly talks endlessly about – that eloquent speaker from the south, leader of the strike action, who came in like the Messiah and has now disappeared.

Shouldn't he take some blame as well? Wasn't his arrival the starting point that led to this. If he hadn't given his speech on the steps of St George's there would have been no affray, no arrests, no prisoners needing to be transported. And that day would have been like any other. Children playing in the street, women running errands, John outside seeing to the shutters of his new home.

Alice screws the leaflet up and throws it to the ground.

'My brother was an innocent bystander, that's all. He took no part in any strike or any riot. He broke no law so please do not hijack his good name for a cause he had naught to do with. You can keep your collection, your funds. My family do not need your charity and you can tell Tom Mann his words will never win me over.'

'Hush now, Alice,' Molly says, bidding the union fellow away.

'Hush yourself,' Alice tells her. 'John is no martyr. He's a twenty-year-old boy lying in his own coffin. He had no time for the strike, he was grateful to have work, grateful to have a good job. How many Catholics get to be carters? Who would sabotage that kind of opportunity? Only those that don't know what it's like to be always fighting over scraps. Why should someone's religion, belief, damn you to being poor? Don't see the likes of Tom Mann or the unions fighting that injustice?'

Molly can see the grief behind the anger in the eyes of her friend.

'Surely, if you have more to lose it is more important to fight, Alice. Otherwise nothing changes. If you settle for scraps they'll make sure that's all you ever get. Whether John was for the strike or not, he was a good man and *they* took him from you. Not the strike, not you, them. Let the unions use his name, if it brings change. They opened fire without warning, and they took aim at John and Michael on purpose. Two bullets each they took. How can that be an accident? But they can't kill us all, because it's not just us causing trouble, it's everyone. Like the union man said the whole country's up in arms, there are strikes from London to Glasgow and it's bringing people together Alice. Protestants and Catholics marching side by side. I never thought I'd live to see that.'

Ellen comes into the yard and tells Alice the cortege has arrived. 'It's time. You need to say your goodbyes Alice,' she says. 'He looks at peace. They've covered his head nicely, you can't see a thing. Here, take my arm, we'll go together.'

As they push their way through the dark mass of people the phrase Alice was searching for earlier comes at her like a bullet to her own head. A murder of crows. Of course, that's what they remind her of. For hasn't there been a murder, and hasn't it indeed brought out the crows? Sure, aren't they all here to take their own pickings, feast on this, the saddest of days. Crows take out the eyes first. She knows that, her mother would talk about the farm in Ireland. How the crows would peck out the eyes of the new born lambs, how her father had to slit their throats to give them peace. Maybe she should go there, go back to Ireland, lie down in a bog and let the crows do their worst. But then how could she tend to her children, her husband, and how could she look Tom Mann in the eye and tell him what she thinks? Because she will, one day. She will tell him and the rest of his crew exactly what damage they have done. There must be other ways to do things, to right wrongs. Or maybe she is an innocent herself. Maybe there always has to be blood. Maybe it comes down to good people dying. She has lost a good brother, the best, so all she can do is try and be as good a sister as she can.

Afterword: Green and Orange Ribbons Twined

Dr Mark O'Brien
University of Liverpool

LIVERPOOL BEFORE THE GREAT Transport Strike of 1911 offered poor soil for the growth of trade unionism. Strikes had occurred, of course. Most notably, there had been the dock strike of February-March 1890; part of the wave of 'New Unionism' that swept the industrial centres at that time. Still, the city was very much 'the short straw' for labour organisers. The myriad occupational groups and work-gang culture characterised the labour force on the dock side, and the 'welt' system that meant regular periods of forced idleness during the low tides, stymied effective trade unionism at this time.

More generally across the city, there was the terrible blight of sectarianism between Roman Catholic and Protestant – or 'Orange' – working class communities. One example illustrated above all others just how deep and violent this could become. On the night of 20 June 1909, Orangemen carrying clubs and swords attacked a Catholic procession upon hearing that a consecrated host was to be carried. Tensions continued throughout the rest of the year, with attacks upon churches, priests and nuns in the parishes of Our Lady's, St Anthony's and All Souls in Everton; and with regular clashes occurring along Great Homer Street, that ran between the 'Catholic' Vauxhall and 'Orange'

Netherfield communities. By February 1910 around 3,200 Catholics had left their homes for their own safety.

Religious sectarianism also characterised patterns of work and occupation in the city. The dock labour force was, like those of docks in many parts of the world, mixed and international. However, a large portion of dock labour was drawn from the Irish quarters of the city. These dock labourers were the worst paid nationally and were among the poorest workers in the city. The occupation of 'carter' however, was principally a protected Protestant occupation. The thousands of carters, tending to own their own horse and cart, were crucial to the Liverpool maritime economy, as they took produce unloaded from ships at the harbour-side to railway depots for distribution all over the country. With better wages than the dockers and being usually self-managing, the occupation of 'carter' was desirable; as well as being jealously guarded as a largely Protestant occupational preserve.

It was against this backdrop that the Transport Strike of 1911 erupted across the city and exploded onto the national stage.

During the spring of 1911 union agitation had been occurring on the streets of Liverpool. On 31 May, a demonstration called by the newly formed National Transport Workers Federation saw seamen, galley staff, carters and harbour-side workers gathered at St George's Plateau in the city centre. This emerging solidarity between ship workers from above and below decks, along with dock labourers, carters and other transport workers was a new phenomenon within the Liverpool working class. The strikes by two unions, the National Union of Ships' Stewards, Cooks, Butchers and Bakers and the National Sailors and Firemen's Union, now went to new levels as their demands, initially against medical inspections for crew members, expanded to include wage increases, the right to wear the union button and union supervision of recruitment.

Victory to the ship workers, those 'above decks' and 'below decks', came in late June and was electrifying. Inspired by their success, on 28 June dockers struck for better pay and working conditions. Within hours they had been joined by the multiple trades that made up the harbour workforce. After a week the ship owners, who had once seemed invincible, began to crumble, with each company settling separately; and with each settlement achieving a victory for the unions.

A second phase of the unfolding industrial drama now commenced as successive waves of workers in and beyond the maritime trades went on strike. Warehouse workers, brewery workers, tug-boat men, scalers, rubber factory workers and many more joined the strike movement through the month of July. On the 5 August, railway workers were also striking, paralysing the movement of produce out of the city. Dockers came out once more to join the strike movement. Tensions across the city went to new levels, as fighting broke out between strikers and police.

On the 7 August, extra police arrived from Leeds and Birmingham, supported by divisions from the Royal Irish Constabulary. Soon further police divisions from Lancashire and Bradford would arrive. Troops from the Royal Warwickshire Regiment were now in the city, shortly to be joined by the Scots Greys, Hussars and The Yorkshire Regiment. Liverpool was a city under military occupation. Emboldened, the employers' Shipping Federation announced a lock-out to begin on 14 August.

The strike committee, chaired by Tom Mann, leader of the International Transport Federation, had by now declared a boycott on the movement of all goods (with the exception of milk and bread). Nothing could be moved without a permit from the strike committee. Those goods that were moved required police and troop escorts to get through the city. Responding to the ship owners' lock-out, the committee now called out all transport trades and occupations. From 14 August, ship workers, dock labourers, railway workers, carters, and tram-way workers would join together in a general strike that was to close down the city. A mass rally was called for the

13 August, to gather again at St George's Plateau.

The atmosphere that day was a happy one. It was another bright day in what had been a very warm summer. The photographs of the 80,000 gathering that day show smiling faces and Sunday dress; collars-and-ties and best bonnets. The scene is one of working people, strong in their solidarity but also enjoying themselves under a hot Liverpool sun. That happy mood was about to change; and abruptly.

At about 4pm, police brought a man down from his vantage point on a windowsill. A section of the crowd protested at the use of force and a skirmish with the police ensued. Now, police from Leeds and Birmingham emerged from inside the St George's Hall where, along with troops from the Warwickshire Regiment, they had been secreted by the authorities. After thirty minutes, during which police attacked those present indiscriminately with batons and mounted police charged the crowd, the remaining scene had the appearance of a battlefield. The Riot Act was read, and the crowd forced to clear the area. Bloodied workers lay all around the plateau along with broken glass, scattered bricks and stones. Hundreds of people were injured – with around 350 seeking hospital treatment – as were two police officers, seriously. What had started as a day of determined but happy protest, was to become known as Liverpool's 'Bloody Sunday'.

Further confrontations with police and rioting occurred over the following nights around the city. However, the general strike was now on. 66,000 workers across the maritime and transport industries were out. The two thousand extra troops that had been transported into Liverpool were by this point on the streets of the city. Winston Churchill, Home Secretary, now sent the *HMS Antrim* to be anchored on the Mersey with a second destroyer, the *HMS Warrior* in reserve at Douglas on the Isle of Man. Events took their darkest turn with the deaths of two men on the 15 August. Police wagons carrying prisoners from Bloody Sunday were moving along the Vauxhall Road under guard from the 18th Hussars, fully armed with rifles and sabres. Bystanders began to protest at the passing vans and a skirmish occurred. Without warning the Hussars now opened fire on the crowd, wounding five, two fatally. Michael Prendergast, a 29-year-old Catholic docker was hit twice in the chest. John Sutcliffe, a 20-year-old Catholic carter was hit twice in the head.

The situation had become extremely dangerous for the government. Worker unrest was occurring at a high level across the industrial centres of Britain. On the 17 August, a national railway workers' strike began. The government, now facing difficulties in moving police and troops around the city, began to put pressure upon the railway companies to meet with the unions. After three days, the railway companies did indeed agree to talks, and settled with the railway unions. Days later, on the 25 August the dockers also returned to work. From this point onwards, the various trades concluded their actions, with most having won their demands. With these settlements, nearly three months of some of the most serious disturbances seen on British streets began to come to an end.

The events of the summer in 1911 in Liverpool were dramatic. However, it is in a wider historical perspective that the full significance of the transport strikes of 1911 really stands out. Liverpool had been a graveyard for labour organisers. Thousands of Protestant workers were influenced by virulently anti-Catholic 'Orangeism'. Dozens of separate wharf-side and ancillary maritime trades caused working class solidarity to be constantly undermined by industrial demarcations. Very high levels of casualisation on the docks meant that competition for jobs pitted worker against worker, leading to fights in the day-labour hiring enclosures on the waterfront. Mary Bamber, a giant of the Liverpool labour movement in this era, had once commented that 'Liverpool was the last place God made so far as industrial solidarity was concerned'.[1] In 1911 however, these divisions were overcome in a wave of industrial solidarity that saw ship workers below decks take action with those above decks, the skilled and the unskilled striking together and

Catholics and Protestant workers uniting. On the 13 August, the day of the great gathering at St George's Hall that was to become Liverpool's Bloody Sunday, Protestant carters marched alongside Catholic dockers from Vauxhall and Everton on the west side of the city, from Allerton on the east, and from Birkenhead. Regarding the marching bands that day, Fred Bower, the syndicalist organiser and poet observed:

'From Orange Garston, Everton and Toxteth Park, from Roman Catholic Bootle and the Scotland Road area they came. Forgotten were their religious feuds. The Garston band had walked five miles and their drum major proudly whirled his sceptre twined with orange and green ribbons as he led his contingent band, half out of the local Roman Catholic band, half out of the local Orange band. Now, no longer were they the playthings of 'big business'. This day they were MEN.'[2]

When the funerals of the two Catholic men who had been shot down took place, protestant workers joined the hundreds who gathered to mourn them. Against the backdrop of the violent clashes that had occurred in the city just two years previously, this was remarkable. A process of change was occurring in the context of that momentous industrial struggle. It was not that the changes were instant or complete upon the ending of the strike movement itself. Indeed, working class politics continued to be coloured by religious affiliations long after 1911.

However, the solidarity achieved within the 1911 transport strikes had created an alternative to sectarianism. Now, 'class' was as much as part of worker outlooks and identities as confessional allegiance. For some, it was now their exclusive identification, religion having been put aside to be replaced by deep convictions rooted in working class solidarity. These were the socialists of varying hues, gravitating now to one or other of the competing interpretations of how to put such ideas into practice; the men and women who would go on to give Merseyside its reputation as a forge of general as opposed to trade-specific unionism and as a home of working class socialism.

The deaths of Michael Prendergast and John Sutcliffe were tragedies that were terrible for their families. However, they were of profound historical significance in marking a moment of change in the political emotions of Liverpool's working class; when the violence of the state against workers made a nonsense of religious division, and made standing together the only rational response.

Notes

1.   Quoted by Davies, S. (1996) in *Liverpool Labour: Social and Political Influences on the development of the labour Party in Liverpool 1900-1939.* Keele University Press. p. 17.

2.   Bower, F. (1936), *Rolling Stonemason,* Jonathan Cape. p. 15.

Bright Red

Donny O'Rourke

THE TEENAGE BOY WAS on his knees but in George Square no prayers were being answered. Did his collar bone hurt more than his side? He had never felt such pain. Coshed by a constable who had clearly wished to shatter his shoulder, the lad had no sooner collapsed than a passing sergeant kicked him in the kidneys, the way a keeper would clear his goal, two down in an old firm game. No Rangers Celtic cup final had ever been as noisy as this. It was a pitched battle. Blood was being shed and curdled as if, at any moment, Bruce or Wallace might appear. Trying to get to his feet, it seemed the small of his back ached more than his neck. That adjudication was curtailed before his foal feeble legs could bear his weight. Struck from behind, the sound of his skull cracking was the last thing Dermot Flynn heard until he realised that a comrade must have dragged him to a bench on the edge of the ructions. After a few befuddled seconds – the protesters now routed and in retreat – oblivion was welcome.

'Mr Flynn. Mr Flynn. Dermot?' At five to ten in the midweek morning George Square was tranquil, his slumbers unperturbed. She was about to raise her voice and try again, when all of a sudden, with a slight snort, he was fully alert and upright on the bench, a flummoxed frown giving way to an amiable smile. 'Hello, Mr Flynn. It's Verity.' An actor's pause. 'Verity? Is that the truth?' Twinkly eyes, she was used to. But a twinkly voice? 'Of course, from the BBC, why would I lie?' Two beats. Again, perfectly timed. The teasing smile. 'Oh God, I get it. Sorry. Yes, *Verity*. Truly.' '*Nomen est omen*, as the Romans used to say: name is destiny.'

It was the morning after Mayday, 1979, with a general election looming that would determine working class fates for generations to come. A portentous day to be commemorating The Battle of George Square.

The old man rose and made a gallant little bow, extending a delicate hand. Not tall, but pleasantly proportioned and nattily turned out in a cream linen jacket and navy slacks. Vermillion knitted tie. All this she took her time taking in. He noticed her noticing. 'My apologies. It's a bit warm for a boiler suit and bunnet. And the moths got my muffler.' She laughed, seeing now the silk Paisley handkerchief in his breast pocket.

'This is radio, so the listeners can pick their own props and costume'.

'A top hat and cigar?'

'Probably not,' she agreed.

Gesturing towards the bench, he laughed invitingly. 'Please.'

'Not television then, Verity? Oh and do call me Derry.' She squirmed in her seat, *almost* imperceptibly.

'No, only radio, I'm afraid, and even that's not guaranteed. Busy times, politically.'

'Depressing and distressing in every way.' Flynn's sigh could have won the Oscar for best supporting understatement.

'So, I'm being auditioned?'

'You're being consulted.'

You utter bastard, Nick, she thought to herself. One wine woozy-bonk on the departmental (have it) away day whose only consequence was excruciating social and professional awkwardness, and her lecherous twerp of a boss was attempting to manage her out the door.

For the earth to have moved he would have had to hire a bulldozer.

'No matter'. Blue eyes and a few strands of auburn in his full head of neatly cropped grey hair. 'It's a bonny day and always touching to be back in George Square.

220

'That's very gracious of you, Derry,' she said, removing a spiral notebook from her satchel.

Nick had set this, and her, up via Tamsin, the new trainee whom he was strenuously mentoring whenever his wife and kids were at their cottage in The Cotswolds. Tamsin had refused to waste precious CV-burnishing time on a Scottish commie coffin dodger. She was in Islington battling a fictitious cold. Nick had phoned Dermot but not Verity and was now 'out of the office' and unavailable, doubtless prescribing that Tamsin remain bed-ridden too. He had passed on no details of his (cursory) call to Dermot Flynn. Verity had been in Edinburgh preparing a feature on Thatcher and the Union. Nick had left a three sentence message at her hotel. A colleague in the BBC library had put the 'brief' in briefing before taking a more important call. The rigged referendum on Devolution had not brought out, for Yes, the requisite 40% of those eligible to vote. That calamitous and recent reverse, on the first of March, had closed the door on home rule while opening the gates to Thatcher. Today was May the second; a Wednesday. On Friday, a Tory government seemed certain to be elected.

Verity shuddered. Gathered herself. 'All set'? Her BBC pen was poised.

'You're not recording?'

'Next time. If the pitch is commissioned.'

Derry was easy to offend but hard to hurt.

'Now remember, to tell a story, you have to sell a story, OK?'

'Really? As an engineer I was forced to sell my labour. But I've been retired a long time. There's nothing I'm obliged to sell.'

Verity hadn't blushed since Bedales. But her cheeks pinkened somewhat.

'Quite. My apologies. A glibly chosen word. But my producer, Nick, said you were rather the raconteur.' The blatant fib produced a flush if not a blush.

'Really, *Verity* I've had longer calls from the speaking clock.'

Fucking Nick! How she wished she hadn't been.

'Mr Flynn. *Derry* I'm mortified. Please forgive me.'

221

'Nothing to forgive.' His lightly contoured lilt was as resonantly expressive as a professional actor's. She had worked with announcers whose timbre was not as sonorous as this Clydeside shop steward's mellifluous burr.

'We can begin?'An assenting nod. Gravitas in his countenance and comportment.

'How many people died?'

'Nobody died.'

'And the tank?'

'There *was* no tank.'

'Did the soldiers fix bayonets?'

'The army didn't arrive until the next day.'

'Deployed from England for fear of mutiny?'

'Mostly, but squaddies despatched from Aberdeen obeyed orders and patrolled the streets.'

'Which striker landed a punch on the police chief's jaw?'

'That was Willie Gallacher. But his fist didn't connect. A bit of a romancer, Willie. Mind you, revolutions need their myths.' A sales pitch this wasn't.

'Fiery speeches by James MacLean and John Maxton?'

'*John* MacLean and *James* Maxton. No, prison had broken MacLean. He was away touring the Durham coalfields. Maxton was out of town too.'

'But the ideological underpinning, the efforts to establish workers' councils and a soviet, to emulate the contemporaneous Sparticist uprising in Berlin, the revolution being fomented here on Red Clydeside?'

'Clydeside was as red as a foundry girder but there was no Marxist manifesto. There could and should have been. In 1916, Connolly imposed a theoretical template on a half-arsed nationalist insurgency. But we failed to see, far less seize the revolutionary moment here. We weren't Leninists, merely exploited workers demanding our due.'

His downward glance acknowledged her disappointment.

'There was a police cavalry charge, if that helps...'

Brava Tamsin, you cow. Brava. Artfully dodged. There's no

story here. A scuffle. A fracas. A skirmish. A melee. It's hardly the storming of the Winter Palace.

Derry Flynn watched her doubts file past like a general inspecting a parade. Twenty two? Outfitted from a box in the BBC wardrobe department with RADIO RESEARCHER stencilled on the lid. Serious without seeming solemn. Rigorous yet playful. Ruefully ruthless. Ambitious but likeable with it. Those scarlet, 'ethnic' beads were heading for the top. 'Do you drink coffee, Ms…?'

'Pemberton. I should have said.'

'One barrel? I'd been hoping for a hyphen.'

'I should have offered you a coffee when we met, Mister Flynn. Remiss and rude. The North British Railway Hotel is over there on the left.'

That twinkly smile. 'Things are always better on the left, Ms Pemberton. After you.'

A window table with an unimpeded view of the entire square. 'What can I get you?' the waitress asked.

'Do you have an espresso?' Flynn inquired. An espresso, Verity was nonplussed. In the land of watery instant?

'We have filter coffee,' the young woman retorted. 'Full French Roast from Thomson's. Even faddy fusspots like it,' she averred, staring at Verity as if contemplating the very embodiment of such prissy pretentiousness.

'For two,' the researcher said, handing back the menu. She vaguely knew that the fair fortnight *doon the watter* had been supplanted by cheap charters to Spain. 'Where did you acquire such epicurean tastes? Benidorm? Torremolinos, Marbella?'

He met her gaze and held it.

'Malaga,' he said, so quietly, she could hardly hear him. Verity loved Malaga. 'It's beautiful there by the sea.' One of his pauses. 'Franco didn't let the International Brigade do much sun bathing. I found it tricky to swim with a quarter pound of shrapnel in my leg.'

There's an uncalibratable instant in which embarrassment segues into shame. By the time the single lump of brown sugar had dissolved in the (excellent) coffee, Verity Pemberton's remorse was abject.

'May I make a suggestion?' The engineer leaned forward, pulling his chair a little closer, touching her lightly on the elbow, taking a sip of coffee. 'Why don't I just talk? That's what old men do, we blether.'

Verity nibbled the square of tablet that had been placed, gratis, on their saucers, lowered her head and said, 'Yes please.'

Derry thrust back his shoulders, let his chest swell, took a self-consciously stagey breath, and his delivery soft and low but patently sincere, started to tell his tale.

'We weren't an army on the march spoiling for a fight. Many of the men had been on the western front and were sick to the soul of senseless slaughter. I was born in 1900. As old as this stupid, sordid century. The not so Great War was over before they could mobilise me. I was called up, but wouldn't have gone. My country needed me alright, alive and fighting peacefully for socialism. The only drill we received, from repatriated veterans, before assembling, was designed to get us safely and pacifically in and out of the square. His Majesty's Constabulary had other ideas. There were serried ranks of policemen circling the perimeter.'

He pointed.

'Look out the window and imagine hundreds of hard-hearted, hatchet-faced, truncheon-brandishing, warrant card-carrying, pensionable hooligans. Now picture us, cheerful and orderly, strolling in from the Saint Andrews Halls, a mile west along Saint Vincent Street, our mood good after the speeches, *everything* good, humour, spirits, conduct, news. Aye it was good news we had turned up to hear. We anticipated, expected, were *convinced*, that after the period of reflection he had enjoined our leaders to grant him, the Provost would do the decent thing, and on behalf of the bosses, and the government in Westminster, accede to our demand for a forty hour week, giving way with magnanimity and good grace, setting the seal on the celebration we had been preparing to enjoy. Toddlers gurgled on their fathers' shoulders. Brass bands played. Pipers. Community singing. People had brought picnics. And there was no alcohol. It was a day out, crowded but convivial, like waiting for the steamer with the holiday making hordes, heading for Rothesay.'

No twinkle now, as he nodded toward the City Chambers. 'Until out trots the primped wee plutocrat's poodle in his Provost's chain – which would have looked better by the way on a lavvie cistern, to bark the disavowal he had been bidden to yelp. No oompah music now. *En Fete joie de vivre* gave way to the sullen truculence betrayal begets. The booing was audible in Govanhill and Springburn, miles to the south and north respectively. But the sergeant major had bellowed until we could hold the line, present our grievance peaceably and disperse with dignity. I was waiting to do so when a tram tried to force its way through the throng. Behind Walter Scott there. Mr North Britain. Those nearest risked their lives to prevent a reckless provocation. And a provocation it surely was. With the city at a standstill, the tram drivers and conductors had been cowed into doing their imperial duty by defying picket lines for tram lines. This scab 'caur' was literally stopped in its tracks. The resulting stramash finally furnished the excuse the polis had been waiting for. Now their clubs thwacked not into frustrated palms, but rained down on an enemy they would take delight in crushing. Business *and* pleasure. Bolshie bastard. Away and work. Communist traitor. Sod off to Russia. Biased as a bool, as we used to say. This war was wanted and bespoke. Bloody Friday, the papers would call it. I shed some of my own. They had to hose my 'martyr's gore' from a bench outside this very hotel, a fractured skull, and me calling for calm as the black drapes were drawn. I was only following our leaders from whom not a bellicose syllable was heard. Davie Kirkwood, a gentle giant if ever there was one, rushed out of the City Chambers as soon as he learned of the sellout, determined to restore order. Before he had got two yards, a coward in civic serge laid him out from behind with a blow that could have killed him. The assault was photographed and that newspaper evidence kept Kirkwood from prison when others were scapegoated afterwards. Brave, Willie Gallacher, whom you mentioned, was outraged and came gey close to kayoing that strutting martinet of a Chief Constable, who'd learned his brutality in Dublin Castle, but Willie was bundled to the ground before his uppercut found its target. So off to the dressing station, then the police station in that order, an incarnadined skull to match my own and Kirkwood's. None of this could have happened, had the riot act not been read, which it was, in legitimising part at least. I was within a few feet of the Sheriff and I'd heard louder dialogue in a silent movie. His lips moved; the demonstrators didn't. It was noisy. Machine shops and steel mills howl like Hades. But believe me, Verity, their cacophony was crypt-like compared with the din that day in George Square. A few of the walking wounded sought sanctuary here, in this hotel. Turned away. The emergency regulations stipulated that no protester should set foot on the adjacent pavements. Place a toe on the kerb, and you'd get a side shed that would stay parted until the stitches came out.'

Intermission.

A quick dab with the crimson hankie.

Verity poured Derry some cold coffee.

'Well... Has the scene been set?'

'Vividly,' she said breaking into a mimed round of polite applause so as not to affront the eavesdropping dowagers of Bearsden and Pollokshields primly adjusting their pinkies and prejudices, as the monologue concluded.

'But you need anecdotes and quirky quotes; quips and clips – memories that are memorable. Nick, was that his name? He'll want us to 'doctor' the script?'

Eloquent silence was a career enhancing quality which Verity practiced on occasions such as this. A colleague's coyly curving eyebrow had recently been promoted to Head of Documentaries.

'My dear Ms Pemberton, I do possess a wireless. And most of my faculties. Let's visit the lions in whose marmoreal presence I shall perorate as pithily as possible.'

As she paid, one of the ladies who liked to 'partake' of

elevenses was confiding to her companion, 'a fine looking man for his age. Shame about the politics.'

They were now directly beneath the balcony the Provost had spoken from.

'The speakers addressed the gathering here. And yes, they roared like lions, and were as fearless.' Derry paced back and forth, rehearsing his routine.

He emerged from behind a marble lion, arms akimbo, and stamped his foot.

'At the Glasgow Empire, you always open with a song.'

> *Were you there. In the square? Did you dare. To stand your ground?*
> *Truncheon blows. And worse. God knows. Hurtling hooves began to pound.*
> *Forty Hours. Forty Hours. Though our cause did not prevail.*
> *For all their profit, pride and powers. Our heads and hearts, are not for sale.*

'You sing beguilingly, Mr Flynn. Who composed the song?'

'I did.' A hammy hand to his heart. 'Turns at the Empire move the show along.

'Friends of mine, held a tram driver hostage, working class Tory, would-be toff. Rules this. Regulations that. He lit a disdainful Players. On the lower deck. They bore him aloft, shoulder high, wailing and flailing, made him smoke it upstairs. Or face a fine.

'A lemonade lorry capsizes. Drinks soft, the struggle hard. The crates will serve as providential barricades. Dissidence is thirsty work. God's a Marxist! Free ginger. Each bottle is emptied before being thrown.

'At every rally, a middle-aged woman waves her home-sewn banner. Down she goes, the red flag with her. Trampled under the heels of several spit and polished size tens. An apprentice fitter retrieves it rugby scrum fashion, shimmies up the municipal flagpole and flies the colours at full mast.

'And a wee encore for the pride of Paisley, Comrade William Gallacher. The council has set up an Ypres-style field station in the courtyard of its inner sanctum and Willie's bandage has just been pinned in place, when a man he knows, a clerk and compassionate with it, offers him a recuperative dram, which Willie, like so many of those leading the strike, a lifelong teetotaller, declines, just as the officer responsible for his injury, himself now a casualty, is led in. 'You could have passed that whisky on to me.' 'Had I seen you, I would have and toasted both our healths.' No hard feelings, that was Mr Gallacher.'

Verity was still working on staying volubly schtum.

'Inform. Educate. Entertain.'

Derry said this in a boom-voiced Lord Reith, BBC-as-Presbyterian-pulpit, sanctimonious tone.

'Whatever a Scottish Calvinist means by entertainment?'

She groaned.

'Ahha! It's a love story you're after! OK how's this?

'Lance corporal from Liverpool sent North by overnight troop train. Became a pacifist in the trenches, won over by the poetry and polemics of Seigfried Sasson. Harms or threatens no one in the aftermath of what had happened here in George Square.' Dermot Flynn encompassed the square with a thespian sweep of his hand. 'Sassoon is sent to Glasgow on journalistic assignment. A reading of his verse is organised. Our by now undeluded rifleman brings along a book for signing. A local lass, trainee librarian, is there for the same purpose. Merseyside sees Clydeside across a crowded room. It's Valentine's Day, nineteen nineteen. By the time he's winding down the Southbound carriage window, four days later, they are engaged. And she was my cousin. They live not more than a couple of miles from this lions' den.'

Out, with a flourish, came the carmine hankie. 'Will you be needing this?

'I have a heart of stone. They check at the medical when you join the Corporation.'

He ushered Verity towards a nearby bench.

She closed her notebook.

'Yes, Derry Flynn, human interest stories, every one. But what did that frantic Friday sixty years ago really mean or amount to. What was gained? Why should our listeners care? Yet another glorious defeat for the workers.'

'It was a chapter, maybe a brief one, in the book of protest that eventually got black people the vote in the American south and Catholics the vote in Ireland's North. That narrative includes Castro's Cuba and Allende's Chile where even the CIA can't kill ideas and ideals. Glasgow engineers refused to export engines for Pinochet's British warplanes. The Prague Spring, eleven years ago is one setting; and Budapest in 1956 before that. Brecht was prescient: fascism, that bitch is always in heat. Stalinism is unsustainable, without joy, because life is. George Square, on January, the thirty first, 1919 wasn't a single contested acre, on one discomfiting day. Women had run equal wages campaigns at the Singer factory before the war and rent strikes during it. Clydeside wasn't just geography it was history, history made by workers who knew, but would never be put in, their place. During that whole post-war year, this town seethed with dissent. Despite our fraternal resolve, after all that took place in this square, they forced us back to work; did the same after the General Strike in 'twenty six. But in 1922 Glasgow sent ten ILP MPs to Westminster. Glorious defeat? Verity, I'm with Gramsci: pessimism of the intellect, optimism of the will. The workers, united, will never be defeated. But we might never be united. Capital makes individualism compulsory. Soon, Thatcher will see to that here and Reagan in the US. If I were a sentimental man, I'd say that George Square is a lot bigger than it looks. World-sized in fact. Revolutions invariably begin and end in public squares. Ours hasn't ended. The Scottish Parliament *will* be re-established, out of and to deepen a compassionate consensus every Scot knows to be real and radical and ready to be legislated for. Classic Connolly and MacLean; non-chauvinist, national self-determination, the socialist republic as the basis for international solidarity. No, on this precise spot they beat but did not defeat me. And today we work *fewer* than forty hours. Thatcher's right, poverty *is* a choice, a choice made by the rich. My wife, God rest her, was a primary school head teacher and Labour councillor until her party embarked upon The Lowland Clearances prioritising motorways over tenements. Our daughter is a GP in the poorest postcode in Britain, half an hour's walk from here. Her brother is a human rights lawyer in Edinburgh. When there's a parliament again, he'll stand. Our other girl lives in London and writes for *The Observer*. She'll come back too, I hope, when this country summons up the political self-esteem to be worthy of her, and the millions like her. The youngest boy is a priest and celibately but self-acceptingly gay. I'm not sure he believes in God but he believes in a lot of people who believe in God. He's a proponent and practitioner of Liberation Theology. Sayin' it. And daein' it. Faith doesn't require belief; it demands hope. God and Gramsci agree. What happened here was about faith.'

'Why didn't you go into politics?'

'Because politics went into me. Is this not politics?' Derry joined Verity on the bench. Sat with her in companionable silence for a minute or two. Then stood up, adopting that posture of self-mocking, ironic gallantry again. He took her hand, held it for a few seconds and kissed the air above her fingers. 'Only allow your lips to make contact with a lady's wrist if she invites you to eat caviar from it. A Hungarian count taught me that. Well, he may have been Hungarian; might have been a count. But he died a worker at Jarama. And Franco's gone. When they cheered in the main square of Madrid, four years ago, I didn't feel as if we had lost.'

Her superiors would be the ones to judge. Victory, for them, winners every one, ought never to be ambiguous. Thatcher, now there was a winner.

They embraced.

'Yes, a plane to catch and election coverage to plan. Thank you Derry Flynn. We'll be in touch.'

'Thank *you*, Verity Pemberton. Do you happen to know what the name Flynn means in Irish Gaelic?' A shake of her head. 'Bright Red. Names really can be self-fulfilling prophecies. Those on the left will need to be very bright in the dismal decades to come.'

At Broadcasting House new agendas were being set. Some of the Free Marketeers and privatisers were very bright indeed.

From his pocket, Derry produced a slender pamphlet and proffered it, shyly.

'A wee minding for the journey, something that kept me from brooding on my injuries while I was waiting for the wounds to heal.'

A Vent In Song: James Connolly and the Poetry of Revolution. By Dermot Flynn, Glasgow, 1937. She slipped the tiny paperback into her own pocket.

'Born and brought up in Edinburgh. His last words were a prayer of forgiveness for the firing squad that executed him.'

Verity picked up her bag and walked towards the taxi rank at Queen Street Station. She looked back. Derry's eyes were closed again, a draining morning for an octogenarian. There was a phone box – bright red – on George Street. From her purse she removed a single coin. This would be a very brief call.

Derry Flynn has come to Glasgow from Greenock and the tail o' the bank, his turner's bench at MacArthur's abandoned for a day UP the watter! He is in the second last year of his apprenticeship as a toolmaker and journeymen and time served engineers from Port Glasgow have made this Friday excursion with him. Their cause was just and has been carried. They feel the way football fans allow themselves to feel when the referee is looking at his watch and their team is winning three nil. Chickens are being counted but they are just about to hatch. Everyone is cheering, laughing, basking. The bulbs in the municipal flower beds are in bud and blossom. Tomorrow is St Bridget's Day, the start of the Celtic spring. Socialism feels fresh and fragrant. In George Square, The Red Flag is waved and sung. Seventy thousand jubilant people are not wrong. Everything is about to change…

Afterword: Two Tales of One Battle

Dr Jim Phillips
University of Glasgow

'THERE'S NO STORY HERE', thinks Verity Pemberton of the BBC, as she listens with limited comprehension or empathy to Derry Flynn's eye-witness activist account of the 1919 Battle of George Square in Glasgow. Later, still struggling to understand, she asks, 'What was gained?'

There was indeed a big story behind the Battle, and the Red Clydeside movement more broadly, but its meaning and significance were obscured for much of the twentieth century by the presence of two powerful but conflicting interpretations, which Donny O'Rourke's story shows Verity trying to reconcile. Had there been a revolutionary situation in Glasgow in January 1919, where Scottish workers were poised to seize political power, overthrowing liberal Parliamentary democracy and capitalism? Or did the 40-hour week demand signal instead that moderate trade-union thinking predominated, with the aim of advancing the selfish economic interests of skilled male engineering workers?

The first narrative, the thwarted revolution, was generated by two opposing forces. Initially it was constructed in 'real time', in 1919 and 1920, by Conservative and Unionist politicians. Rushing troops to Glasgow and mustering warships on the Clyde were part of a political strategy geared to preserving the social control of established elites when facing the electoral challenge of Labour. The democratisation of the franchise in

1918 which gave Parliamentary votes to women aged thirty and over also extended this right for the first time to all men aged twenty-one and over. The size of the electorate quadrupled from just over 5 million to around 20 million. Conservative and Unionist strategy isolated Labour by talking up the ways in which it allegedly threatened the interests of the 'public'. The party's 'sectional' trade-union connections were emphasised. So, more damagingly but spuriously, were its 'Bolshevik' tendencies. Derry remembers the words of a police officer in George Square who was gripped by these poisonous ideological stereotypes: 'Away and work. Communist traitor. Sod off to Russia.' Within this anti-collectivist narrative George Square was one in a series of revolutionary-socialist threats averted by British governors acting in the supposed 'national' interest. It followed the suppression of the Irish Rising in 1916, which included the execution by firing squad of leading rebels, notably James Connolly, the Edinburgh-Irish socialist remembered in young Derry's collection of poems. And 1919 then preceded the 1926 General Strike, when the Trades Union Congress was persuaded by government ministers, nine days in, to call off this mass working-class action in support of coal miners in dispute with their employers.

The revolution-narrowly-avoided narrative attained further traction because it was also articulated – although in distinct register and with entirely different political purpose – by those who regarded themselves as the thwarted revolutionaries. A crucial figure was Willie Gallacher, brutalised by members of the Glasgow constabulary in George Square in his role as trade-union activist and leader. Gallacher joined the newly-established Communist Party of Great Britain (CPGB) in 1920, after attending the Second Congress of the Communist International in Moscow, where he met Lenin and other leaders of the Bolshevik Revolution. Gallacher's vividly-written memoir of his war-time activism, *Revolt on the Clyde*, was published in 1936. This important political-literary intervention was designed to establish the CPGB as legitimate successor to the various socialist forces that contributed to the Red Clydeside movement. *Revolt on the Clyde* advanced the claim that the outcome in 1919 would have been completely different if the CPGB had existed. 'Revolt was seething everywhere', Gallacher wrote. 'We had within our hands the possibility of giving actual expression and leadership to it, but it never entered our heads to do so. We were carrying on a strike when we ought to have been making a revolution.'

The second of the two polarised interpretations, that George Square marked the defence of the narrow economic privileges of skilled male workers, was central to a larger political-cum-historical project. This positioned Red Clydeside as chimera, with the protests and protesters of the period and place characterised as both moderate and disparate in nature. Women engaged in rent strikes in Maryhill and Govan, working-class districts to the north-west and south of the city centre, were said to have little in common with the skilled men, led by Gallacher and Davie Kirkwood, Derry's 'gentle giant', who contested wage rates and other conditions of employment in the vast engineering and locomotive workshops to the east and north-east, in Parkhead and Springburn. Neither the skilled men nor the rent-striking women were regarded as having much affinity either with the socialist revolutionaries who were central to the so-called 'legend' of Clydeside. Foremost among these activists was John Maclean, the Marxist educator whose analysis linked the industrial and social difficulties of the city's working class with the broader crises of capitalism and imperialism that had led to the outbreak of global conflict in 1914. Maclean died young, aged 44, in 1923, exhausted by relentless struggle and victimisation by the state. This included two lengthy spells of imprisonment for inciting treasonous actions, illegal under wartime emergency regulations. Red Clydeside-sceptics patronised Maclean and decried his wider influence. Their anti-socialist arguments were often reliant on Gallacher's *Revolt on the Clyde*, which carefully devalued the political legacy of Maclean, who favoured a Socialist Scottish

Republic and had refused to join the CPGB. Coded references were made to the alleged instability of Maclean's mental health, which was the implied explanation for his non-orthodox Communist politics. Red Clydeside-scepticism exerted an increasing influence in the historical literature towards the end of the twentieth century, influenced perhaps by the same anti-collectivist thinking that Verity is detecting at the BBC in the days immediately preceding the UK General Election of May 1979. Within this Red Clyde-as-chimera narrative the Battle of George Square was an accidental but limited public order crisis, arising chiefly from the heavy-handed and panicked response of the city's political leadership to a noisy trade-union demonstration. Red Clyde-as-chimera thinkers applied a very stern test in the 1970s and 1980s when measuring the extent of working-class radicalism in the 1910s and 1920s. Anything short of full-blown Bolshevik commitment tended to be interpreted as evidence that socialism carried limited popular support, and if the people had not been socialists then how could the Clyde have been Red?

These competing narratives frame the dead-end in historical discussion that Verity is grappling with in 1979. In truth, the Battle of George Square was neither a Bolshevik revolution in the making nor a trade-union rally that escalated when nervy civic authority combined with adversarial policing. There is a much bigger and more interesting story instead, that Derry haltingly tells, about working-class people in a major industrial city seeking to impose democratic control over the economic forces that governed their lives. Organised in trade unions, workplaces and communities, these Clydesiders mobilised to protect themselves against market forces in various spheres of everyday life. This was not the defence of privilege by a narrow and male section of the working class, but a major social movement comprising multi-generational family groups. 'Toddlers gurgled on their fathers' shoulders. Brass bands played. Pipers. Community singing. People had brought picnics. And there was no alcohol. It was a day out, crowded but convivial, like waiting for the steamer with the holiday-making hordes, heading for Rothesay.' The movement built working-class solidarity by undermining ethno-religious sectarianism, incorporating Derry and many others of Irish and Catholic heritage, notably the future Labour MP and government minister, John Wheatley. This is the big story of 1919 that Verity found difficulty in seeing: collective action by women, men and children in pursuit of economic security. Affordable rents and decent housing; reasonably-priced food and fuel; fair wages and dignity at work; a share of employment and income. These were not unambitious goals; pursuing them with discipline and determination was revolutionary. Workers were asserting a claim to greater economic and industrial democracy to match the extension of the franchise in political democracy.

The rent strikes of 1915 across Glasgow had pointed the way. Led by working-class women, these were directed against profiteering private-sector landlords who had used the logic of market forces to rationalise increases that their tenants could ill-afford. Glasgow was bursting in 1914 and 1915, its tenement apartments notoriously over-crowded even before the booming industrial-military economy sucked tens of thousands of migrant workers into the city. The Liberal-led UK coalition hurriedly brought forward legislation to limit the operation of market forces in rent-setting, placing fetters on the exploitative powers of landlords. The 40-hour stipulation in 1919 reflected a similar ambition: to limit the hours of work demanded by employers. A regulated week would enable workers to control and share their labour. This was a vital and visionary aim given that Glasgow's industrial economy revolved largely around engineering and manufacturing sectors where employment and production had expanded to supply the state's military needs. These were now in suspension following the Armistice of November 1918, and the 40-hour maximum, had it been passed, would have reduced the extent of unemployment that followed in the 1920s and 1930s.

So what, returning to Verity's question, was gained? Improvement in the short-term was not won by the workers of the Clyde. Employers regained control of their workplaces and communities, and not only in the city of Glasgow. Industrialists likewise consolidated their grip in the mill and shipbuilding towns of Renfrewshire, including Greenock, Derry's hometown, and in the steel and coal communities of Lanarkshire, the Lothians and Fife. In the coalfields the miners' demand for nationalisation of their industry was resisted by the colliery owners in 1919, who found common cause with Conservatives at Westminster. National wage-bargaining in the coal and engineering industries, wartime gains for the workers, were abandoned and employers were able to impose pay settlements and conditions reflective of market forces rather than social needs. Economic insecurity within working-class communities reliant on industry became even more chronic in the hungry 1930s, aptly named in some parts of Scotland.

In the longer-term, however, the ambitions articulated in George Square in 1919 were realised. The unemployed miners of Lanarkshire and Fife who marched for jobs and fought for democracy against fascism in Spain, alongside Derry and hundreds of other engineering workers from Glasgow and Dundee, continued their campaign for nationalisation. This was secured by the Labour government elected in Clement Attlee's great landslide victory of July 1945. Economic and social security were greatly strengthened. Unemployment was eradicated as a significant problem. In workplaces trade-union voice was amplified and health and safety transformed for the better. In mining, for instance, the risk of accidental death underground was halved when comparing the 1950s with the 1930s. The foundation of the National Health Service in 1948, free at the point of use, concretised the redistribution of resources and esteem in favour of the working class. Major public-sector programmes of rehousing followed. Glasgow was rebuilt, losing population and some valuable elements of community life that were mourned, admittedly, but to the betterment substantially of individual and public well-being. Economic diversification followed in the 1960s, under Harold Wilson's Labour government. The industrial staples of the George Square crowd – shipbuilding, heavy engineering and coal – all became less important, with new jobs in assembly-goods factories run by multinationals that were incentivised to locate in Scotland through government loans and grants. These provided many more opportunities for women as well as men, contributing to less unequal gender relations. Welcome progress was advanced too in the expansion of public, social and educational services. This was the better future that the George Square movement had fought for.

It was also a world that remained contested in 1979. Derry laments the fate of the 1974 Labour government's proposals for a Scottish Parliament with devolved powers within the UK. These were blocked after George Cunningham, a backbench Labour MP, an expatriate Fifer representing a north-London constituency, inserted an impossible clause in the relevant legislation insisting that a confirmatory referendum, eventually held in March 1979, required the positive support of 40% of the entire electorate. Maclean's Scottish Socialist Republic remained distant. There had nevertheless been widening political divergence between England and Scotland since 1955, when the vote share of Conservative and Unionist candidates in Scottish constituencies in UK general elections peaked, at 50.1%. At every subsequent general election the Conservative and Unionist share of votes was lower in Scotland than England: by 2.5% in 1959, 14% in October 1974 and more than 20% in 1987. This reflected the popularity in Scotland of Labour's policy agenda in the 1960s and 1970s, defending working-class economic security through public investment along with employment generation and protection. Support for the Labour government in Scotland increased from 1974 to 1979, just as it decreased in England, preparing the ground for Thatcherism's ascendency in the 1980s. Market forces were unshackled after 1979, just as Verity privately feared. Deindustrialisation accelerated. Trade-union voice was diminished. Unemployment and economic insecurity mounted, with minimal attempt by the government to create meaningful alternatives as factories, mills and mines closed. This reckless management of economic and social change from Westminster contributed directly to a renewed impetus for Scottish Home Rule and Independence in the 1990s.

'Revolutions invariably begin and end in public squares,' Derry argues. 'Ours hasn't ended. The Scottish Parliament *will* be re-established, out of and to deepen a compassionate consensus every Scot knows to be real and radical and ready to be legislated for.' In 2019 majority public opinion in Scotland is clearly resistant to the insular and backward-looking dead-end of Brexit that has taken a remarkable cross-class grip in England, straddling ex-coal villages, former-engineering heartlands, struggling seaside towns and plush yet terrified southern suburbs. Scotland's political direction is unpredictable, of course. Independence will probably become more attractive but might also prove harder to attain if the UK leaves the European Union. This is speculation. What can be said with confidence is that most Scots will continue to look outwards rather than inwards, and not backwards but forwards, towards the better future envisaged a century ago in George Square, where the Battle is unfinished.

Further Reading

Bell, Henry, *John Maclean: Hero of Red Clydeside* (London, Pluto Press, 2018).

Brotherstone, Terry and Phillips, Jim, 'A Peculiar Obscurity? William Gallacher's Missing Biography and the Role of Stalinism in Scottish Labour History: a contribution to an overdue discussion', *Scottish Labour History*, 51 (2016), pp. 154-74.

Gallacher, William, *Revolt on the Clyde: an Autobiography* (London, Lawrence & Wishart, 1936).

Kenefick, William, *Red Scotland! The Rise and Fall of the Radical Left, c. 1872-1932* (Edinburgh, Edinburgh University Press, 2007).

MacAskill, Kenny, *Glasgow 1919: The Rise of Red Clydeside* (Edinburgh, Biteback Publishing, 2019).

McLean, Iain, *The Legend of Red Clydeside* (Edinburgh, John Donald, 1983).

Little Bird

Steve Chambers

Wednesday, 30 September, 1936

IT HAD RAINED IN the afternoon and the light from the lamppost pooled in puddles in the alley. In the gutter, a crow pecked at the decomposing body of a rat. Sydney crept up and tried to kick it but the black bird flew up with a squawk and waited for him to retreat. Sydney hated crows; the black iridescent feathers and the pitiless eyes made his flesh creep. He wished he'd brought his catapult with him. He was just thinking about throwing a stone when the side door of the pub burst open and Wally appeared. Ignoring Sydney, he crossed the junction and began to walk quickly down Leman Street. Sydney hurried after him, struggling to catch up.

'So what did they decide, Wally?' It was almost midnight and the street was quiet for once.

'Why did you walk out of the meeting, Syd?'

'All that talking does my head in.'

An emergency meeting of the District Party Committee to discuss Sunday's march by Mosley's blackshirts had met in the back room of the Dog and Duck at Gardiner's Corner. The meeting had been fractious from the start and the seventeen year-old had become bored and then annoyed. When he'd tried to have his say, he'd been instructed to speak through the chair and follow procedure. He'd been close to losing it so he'd upped and left. Gardiner's Corner was part of the problem as far as

Sydney was concerned. The busy crossroads were great for discarded cigarette ends and not just his favourite Craven A's. Sydney had picked up several cigarette ends but given up when they were all sodden. Then he'd seen the crow.

'I thought you wanted to be involved, Syd? I vouched for you. So did Jack.'

'He left before me.'

'He had a union meeting to go to.'

'What's happening about Mosley's thugs, Wally? That's why the meeting was called?'

'The Rally for Spain will go ahead on Sunday as planned.'

Sydney couldn't believe it. 'Twelve hundred blackshirts are going to march through the East End and we're not going to do anything!'

'It was a democratic vote, Syd. Besides, from an international perspective, Spain is more important.'

'What about the petition? They say a hundred thousand have signed up.'

'You don't understand. You have to look at the bigger picture.'

'Mosley wants to drive out Jews like you and me, Wally; that's why they're coming down our streets. We have to stop them!'

Wally stopped and turned to his young friend. 'The rally's been planned for weeks, Syd. What about all the leaflets we printed, not to mention the posters?'

Sydney shook his head and looked away. That's when he saw the slogan. 'Look! Up there!' On the parapet of the railway bridge, written in whitewash. 'Kick the blackshirts up the backside!'

Sydney faced Wally. 'That's been done today. People are getting ready to stand and fight; you can't stop them.'

Wally sighed, 'We don't know Mosley's route.'

'We know where they're planning to end up!'

'We're not ready.'

'What do you mean?'

'Street work without planning and organisation is a waste of time. This is a potentially revolutionary situation. Jack says the dockers are nowhere near being ready and neither are the other unions.'

'Bugger the unions, Wally.'

Wally began to walk again. 'We have to learn from the fascists. Individually we're weak but together we're strong. If we go off half-cock, we could undo all the work we've done.'

'One thing I learnt growing up, if someone wants a scrap, you'd better give it to them because sooner or later it will happen anyway.'

'Not everything you learnt is true, Syd.'

'Is that it then?' Sydney was hopping from foot to foot with anger.

Wally touched Sydney's shoulder lightly with his hand. 'We'll discuss it later.'

Wally's attitude reminded Sydney of the padre at the orphanage and that's when he hit him. Wally wasn't expecting it and went down heavily onto his right hip. At twenty-five, Wally was more than seven years older and half a head taller, but Sydney's blood was up. He understood fascism from the inside. He'd grown up with it.

Seeing Wally on the floor, Sydney's anger disappeared. 'I'm sorry.'

Wally flexed his jaw and got to his feet, rubbing his hip. Distraught, Sydney looked down at the pavement and didn't see the left uppercut that knocked him sideways and sent him to the pavement. Wally looked down at him. 'Now we're even, Syd. Hasn't got us very far, has it?'

A cry and running footsteps alerted them. 'Wally!' Jack Kelly appeared, flushed and breathless.

'What is it?'

'We've just had a phonecall from Frank Lefitte! The line on Sunday's rally's been changed; all branches to rally at Aldgate instead of Trafalgar Square. The slogan is "They Shall not Pass".' Jack bent double, wheezing energetically as he tried to catch his breath. A docker and a union convenor with a Galway accent, Jack had been at the DPC meeting earlier. He was a short, red-nosed man. He watched Sydney get to his feet and saw Wally's bloody lip. He looked from Wally to Sydney and back. 'Not again?'

Wally nodded slowly. Jack looked at Syd. 'What are we going to do with you young feller?'

Thursday, 1 October

As the light began to fade, Sydney watched for coppers and scanned the ground for discarded cigarette ends while Wally daubed 'They Shall Not Pass' on buildings and walls up and down Cable Street and Leman Street. The events of the previous evening weren't mentioned. Wally was preoccupied and Sydney was used to keeping his head down. He was looking forward to Sunday's scrap and spent his time imagining himself rolling marbles under police horses and kicking coppers. After the slogans, Wally suggested a cup of tea at the Sunshine Café. Dark, airless and cramped, the café was poorly named. Sydney was surprised to find Jack Kelly waiting with two women he didn't recognise. One smoked foul-smelling fags, was middle-aged and serious with greying hair and spectacles. The other was young, a bit older than Sydney by the look of her, with short black hair, bright dark eyes and an infectious smile. Wally told Sydney to sit down and went over to Jack. Sydney watched as the two men talked in low tones, occasionally glancing over at him. He used the time to extract the unused tobacco from the nub ends he'd gathered and roll new cigarettes. He'd become expert at rolling his own cigarettes and he'd learnt to sell them when he was sleeping rough. Tobacco was over a shilling an ounce, fags were sixpence for ten. Sydney's going rate for his reconstituted roll-ups was four for a penny. People were always skint and by the end of the week, there were always a few people who sought him out. Cigarettes had been a currency in the reformatory and having a few on him was always useful. Finally, Wally nodded and beckoned him over. Jack spoke.

'The Committee have an important assignment for you.' Sydney said nothing. 'Let me introduce Gabriella and Maria. They've come all the way from Barcelona for the rally.'

'It's cancelled,' Sydney said flatly.

Wally nodded. 'Their return tickets aren't till next week so they're stuck here kicking their heels for a few days. Special Branch would love to know where they are. Our job is to make sure they don't find out.'

The two women, who had been waiting patiently, approached and nodded courteously. Gabriella, the older one, was obviously in charge. Maria was Spanish but Sydney was surprised to learn that Gabriella was Italian. Sydney's job was to keep them off the streets until after Sunday's battle. Sydney didn't respond and remained silent. Afterwards, Jack took the two women upstairs to their lodgings, leaving Wally and Sydney alone.

'Well?' Wally asked.

'I'm going to miss Sunday's scrap because of two foreign women.'

'They're comrades, Syd. They're fighting fascism in Spain and we invited them.'

'What are those fags she smokes? They stink.'

'French; *Gauloises* they're called.'

'French? I thought she was an eyetie?'

'She is.'

'Well, they're fascists aren't they?'

'Gabriella fought Mussolini's fascisti for ten years. She's on one of their death lists. She only just escaped.' Wally leaned closer and lowered his voice. 'They reckon she got romantic with her guard. Then, when he was getting good and excited, she overpowered him. Put on his uniform and walked out the front gates leaving him tied up with his own thermals.'

Sydney was impressed. 'What? The old one with the glasses?'

Wally nodded. 'She went to Spain to carry on the struggle.

We're lucky to get her; she's famous. She was in St Petersburg in 1917.'

'Why are there two of them then?'

Wally shrugged. 'Maria is one of Juan Modesto's rising stars. Jack says they have high hopes for her back home. She's been sent by the party to learn.'

'She's a trainee?'

'I suppose so.'

'I won't do it.'

Wally looked at Sydney. 'Do you want to be expelled from the party?' When Sydney had been laid up, Wally had banged on endlessly about the importance of rigid party discipline in the class struggle. Sydney shook his head.

'This is because of last night. Because I lost my temper.'

'That would be a bloody good reason, Syd, but that isn't all of it. The last time you fought the police, you nearly died.'

'That's why I want another go.'

Sydney hated the police even more than he hated the blackshirts, the way they got away with pretending to be even-handed. They were the reason he had ended up in the East End. Fifteen months earlier, Sydney had joined in a scrap with some of Mosley's thugs who were intent on smashing Steinberg's shop window on Aldgate. The police just stood and watched even when Sydney screamed at them to do something. They'd asked him why he cared about yid shops and he'd shouted back that he was a yid. When they'd tried to arrest him, he'd fought back, socking one of the constables on the jaw but they'd grabbed him and dragged him into a nearby yard. Sydney had struggled like a wild cat but he couldn't escape, and the four burly constables and one sergeant had systematically beaten and kicked him, leaving him with two broken ribs, a fractured eye-socket, a sprained wrist and bruises all over. As they beat him, the sergeant kept time by chanting 'The Jews are the men who will not be blamed for nothing' over and over. Even at the time, Sydney had been confused by this incantation. Later, Wally explained it was graffiti found on a wall at the time of the Ripper murders. In common with the blackshirts, a lot of police believed in a global Jewish conspiracy. When they had finished, the police dumped Sydney at the end of Cable Street where Wally Barnet found him.

Over the next six months, Wally's family nursed Sydney back to health. Wally's father, Jacob, was a tailor and the family lived in the three floors above Barnet's Upholsterers. Wally's parents and grandmother went to the synagogue every week and observed Jewish festivals. Wally paid lip service to keep them happy but ultimately, he was a Marxist and an atheist. As Sydney recovered, Wally spent hours talking about injustice, politics, political economy and the inevitability of the class struggle. Some of it got on Sydney's nerves but he appreciated the care and listened quietly, occasionally asking questions. Wally was short and broad although, like most people in the East End, he was lean. The thing that fascinated Sidney about Wally was that he genuinely believed in the essential goodness of people and whenever he could, he tried to help them. At first, Sydney searched for the catch and didn't like it when he couldn't detect one. Wally was a decent person who acted on his beliefs. He was fun too and for most of the time, he had a calming influence on Sydney. But when he discovered that Sydney couldn't read or write very well and offered to help, Sydney said no. For Sydney, education meant humiliation and he'd learnt to fend for himself.

An only child and an orphan, Sydney had lost his parents in the great influenza epidemic. Newly arrived from the Crimea, their papers were misplaced and Sydney had been passed from one orphanage to another as each charity argued about whose responsibility he was. All he knew about his mother and father was that they were Jewish and that they had fled from Yalta to escape persecution. He didn't even know his own surname. The hospital where his parents had died had named him Smith as a stopgap but the name had stuck. To the teachers and guardians, Sydney Smith was a hothead and a troublemaker. His temper surprised even him sometimes, and once he lost his temper, he found it impossible to rein it in before damage had been done. He despised the orphanage, the bullying from the older children, the casual cruelty of staff, the smell of stale sweat, boiled cabbage and night-soil, the compulsory Christianity. He fought back only to suffer numerous beatings and corporal punishments until, at the age of twelve, he was transferred to a damp, gloomy reformatory called Bleaberry House in the middle of a rain-swept northern moor. After a few days, an older boy called Bear picked a fight and Sydney didn't back down. Sydney was smaller but he was wiry and clever and very stubborn. Bear was so called because of his penchant for crushing opponents in a bear hug. He tried to do the same to Sydney and at first he was successful, lifting the smaller boy clear of the floor until Sydney bit his earlobe. Bear was hospitalised and Sydney punished but no one picked on him again. The staff left him alone too.

At the age of fifteen he was given a postal order for five shillings and released. He hitch-hiked the fifteen miles to Leeds and caught a bus to London where he gravitated to Gardiner's Corner and the streets around Tower Bridge. He kept his nose clean and survived by unloading stock for hotels and bars and selling his scavenged cigarettes until his beating.

For the first time in his life, Sydney was welcomed as part of a family but their unqualified warmth and generosity unsettled him. He couldn't escape the feeling that there would be a price to pay. He preferred it when he felt like an outsider, as when the family spoke Yiddish which Jacob sometimes did to Wally's mother and on Jewish festivals when they all sang together. Sydney enjoyed feeling like an outsider; that was what he understood.

Friday, 2 October

Sydney spent the afternoon on London buses showing Gabriella and Maria the sights of London while Wally took part in a previously planned anti-fascist march from Tower Hill. Wally had given Sydney enough money for bus fares with a little extra just in case. Maria was excited at the sight of St Paul's and the Tower of London. Gabriella smoked constantly, occasionally shaking her head but otherwise apparently indifferent. Sydney struggled to contain his frustration and said as little as he could get away with. Afterwards, as they walked back towards the East End, they passed a bookshop at the end of Royal Mint Street. Maria pointed at a book cover in the window and said something in Spanish. Gabriella snapped back at Maria and the two women began a heated argument. At first Sydney was intrigued as to what they were arguing about but as the dispute showed no sign of diminishing, he became alarmed. At one point, he thought they might come to blows. People were beginning to stare. If a copper happened by or someone alerted the police, they could be arrested. He told them to be quiet but they just ignored him. The sound of a distant police whistle forced him to act. He clamped his hands over their mouths to shut them up. Then he pushed them into the lounge bar of the Kings Arms, across the road, and sat them in a gloomy corner beneath a poster advertising the benefits of milk.

'Sit still, smile and speak English if you don't want to be arrested,' he ordered before heading to the bar. Although under age, Sydney had helped unload beer barrels and was on nodding terms with the barman. He wanted to order spirits but three Buchanan's would have cleaned him out. In the end he ordered three halves of mild but even the one and tuppence they cost took all the money Wally had given him plus some of his own. Someone was playing 'I'm in the Mood for Love' on a piano in the bar accompanied half-heartedly by a few brave souls. It was still early. Sydney took the drinks over to Maria and Gabriella and told them to drink.

Outside, the sound of running feet and another police whistle could be heard. Sydney shook his head and sipped his drink. Gabriella and Maria did the same although Maria grimaced at the taste.

'So what were you two fighting about?'

'The traitor Kamenev,' Maria said quietly as Gabriella shook her head. 'There was a book about him in the window of the bookshop. Gabriella thinks he is innocent.'

Earlier that summer, Lev Kamenev had been found guilty of conspiring with a foreign power to overthrow the Soviet Union and was executed shortly afterward. The trial had been in all the newspapers and everyone in the local party had discussed it at length. Sydney hadn't been that interested but it was big news because Kamenev had been on the first central committee with Lenin, Trotsky and Stalin.

'But he confessed?' Sydney asked, puzzled.

Maria nodded vigorously. 'Exactly. Why would he do that if he was innocent?'

'For the good of the party and Comrade Stalin,' Gabriella said dryly. Maria raised her eyebrows. Outside, the commotion seemed to be dying down. Sydney changed the subject.

'Gabriella, when we were driving round on the bus,' she peered at him through her spectacles, 'why did you keep shaking your head?'

'I was thinking how many fine building to be bombed,' she said in her Italian accent.

'Bombed?'

'From the air; that's what happen in Spain.'

'Your civil war?'

'It will be everyone's war soon,' Gabriella said.

'Tell me about it,' Sydney asked.

'Franco and the army have rebelled against the elected government. Franco is a fascist. Hitler and Mussolini are helping him with men and machines while the so-called democracies do nothing,' Maria explained.

'So you came here to raise money for your side?'

'Not just money; we need volunteer,' Gabriella said

'To fight?'

'Si. Our struggle is yours. If we don't defeat fascism in Spain, it will spread.'

'I'll go,' Sydney said out of the blue. Maria grinned but he was serious. 'I'd like to fight.'

Gabriella lit another cigarette and blew the smoke upwards. 'How old are you, Sydney?'

'I'm eighteen, on Sunday.'

'Why you want to go to Spain?' she asked.

'To fight the fascists.'

'You want to be hero?'

'No, yes. I don't know,' Sydney felt himself reddening.

Gabriella leaned in close to him and he could smell the garlic on her breath. 'It is not adventure. It is war, people are fighting and dying, you can be wounded, killed,'

'I know that,' he blustered.

'Why now?'

'Because you're here, asking for help. I've seen the blackshirts strutting about. I've been bashed up by the police. I'm a communist and I want to fight.'

'You speak espanol?'

'No.'

'You have military experience?'

'No.'

'Allora, what can you do?' Gabriella asked softly

'I don't know. I'm strong. I'm a good fighter. I don't give in.'

For the first time since he'd met her, Gabriella smiled. It transformed her face and he glimpsed the youth and joy that had been there once.

'What's funny?' he demanded.

'Uccellino,' she whispered.

'Youcher what?' Sydney asked feeling foolish.

'Uccellino, little bird,' Gabriella smiled.

'I don't get it,' Sydney felt his anger growing.

'You're not ready,' Gabriella replied. 'You have not learnt yet.'

'Learnt what?'

'You'll know when it happens.'

Their glasses were empty and Sydney had no more money. 'We should get going,' he said, standing. The women nodded.

Maria excused herself and went to the lavatory. Gabriella watched her go and frowned. 'Why they give me this girl? She does not listen.'

Sydney was still troubled over the ferocity of the argument between the women. 'How can you be certain about Kamenev?'

Gabriella lit one of her cigarettes and looked at him. 'I know him in 1917. He never betray the revolution.' Sydney thought about this. Gabriella touched his arm tenderly. 'Be careful.'

'What?'

'There are spies everywhere. Sometimes you have to listen to your heart.'

Saturday, 3 October

At first light, Sydney found Wally having a quiet smoke in the back yard. Despite the hour, the hawkers were already setting up their stalls. The sounds of vehicles revving their engines, of men calling, of animals barking and squealing could be heard. Wally told Sydney that the previous day's march had gone well although the police had still arrested some people without provocation. One of them was Jack Kelly. Wally was going to testify for him at the Magistrates' Court. not that it ever made any difference. The courts always took the police statements as gospel.

'By the way, Syd, I found two more crows in the dustbin.' Sydney nodded but didn't speak. 'What is it with you and crows?'

'Good target practice for my catapult.'

Wally nodded. 'Remind you of blackshirts do they?'

'And coppers and priests.' Sydney replied evenly. In his first weeks at Bleaberry House, he had befriended a stray mongrel. Old and under-nourished, it had been allowed into the grounds and fed on scraps until, on a cold winter night, it had died. The staff had ignored the body and Sydney had seen it with everyone else over porridge the next morning. The other boys had cheered as several crows fought to peck out the old dog's eyes. Logically, Sydney knew it wasn't the crows that were hateful but people who behaved like them but he had never managed to shake his loathing for the birds.

'Oh that reminds me, Syd. Got any change for me?'

Sydney shook his head. 'Had to spend it. They had a big row.'

Wally frowned as Sydney explained what had happened. 'Not great timing, Syd, with Mosley's thugs marching tomorrow.' Sydney turned to go. 'Oi, where d'you think you're off to?'

'To look after Laurel and Hardy.' Wally chuckled and did an impromptu impression of Oliver Hardy while Sydney looked confused and scratched the top of his head like Stan Laurel. Wally laughed and Sydney joined in, pleased that Wally had forgiven him. After a while Wally calmed down.

'You're helping me today, Syd. Soon as I get back from court, we've got leaflets to hand out and barricades to prepare.'

'What time will that be?'

'Dunno. Wait for me in the Sunshine at midday.'

'What about Maria and Gabriella?'

'The women's branch of the Tailors and Garment Workers Union have organised a tour for them for today. We're meeting up with them this evening.'

'OK, Wally. See you later,' Sydney began to walk away.

'And well done, Syd,' Wally called after him, stopping Sydney in his tracks. 'That was quick thinking yesterday, showing them into the Kings Arms. Now get along with you.'

Sydney spent the morning collecting stones for his catapult and organising his marbles. The blackshirts liked to carry potatoes tied to the ends of pieces of string and studded with razor blades which they twirled round in the air as they walked. Sometimes, they'd put the spuds in a sock to hide the razor blades. Even though he wasn't taking part, Sydney couldn't resist going through the motions. Everyone he met was cheerful, reflecting his own mood as he organised his weaponry just in case he was called upon. Wally's praise kept ringing in his head; he remembered the tenderness of Gabriella's touch on his arm.

Wally returned from the Magistrates' court in a bad mood and demanded one of Sydney's roll-ups which he pronounced disgusting on his first drag, before smoking the rest of it hungrily. When Sydney asked what had happened at the court, Wally explained that a policeman had stated under oath that Jack had assaulted him. Jack was so incensed that he'd shouted from the dock at the copper and was given a week in jail for contempt.

Wally's mood seemed to improve in the afternoon as men and women from all over the country began arriving into the district and the street for the coming battle. Groups of coal miners from as far north as Scotland and as far south as Kent marched into the East End carrying their colourful pit banners aloft. Gangs of unemployed workers carried protest banners demanding justice for those without work and they in turn were supported by assorted trade unionists.

Everyone knew that the police would try to force a way through so the blackshirts could march along Whitechapel Road and Commercial Road. Various theories were suggested about what to do if the police tried to use Leman Street or Cable Street and there was no shortage of volunteers to assemble sections of barricade. A lot of them were Jews from beyond East London but there were plenty of gentiles from the Labour Party, the ILP and the unions who'd come because they'd had enough. As darkness fell and the anticipation and excitement began to grow, Sydney's spirits declined. The realisation that he would not be taking part in the big fight began to get him down. By the time he and Wally arrived at the Sunshine Café, it was well after ten and he felt ready to bash someone.

The place was so packed with new faces you could barely make out the regulars. Tables had been pushed to the side of the room and were now heaving with sandwiches and bottles of wine giving the dingy cafe something of a party atmosphere. Someone was playing flamenco guitar and Maria was dancing energetically in the centre of the room, whirling and stamping her feet. Gabriella watched from a corner, nodding in time to the music, a glass of wine in hand, her head wreathed in smoke from her cigarette. The dance ended to applause and cheers. Spotting Wally and Sydney, Maria came over, breathless and flushed from her exertions. She looked from Wally to Sydney and back again, smiled and took Sydney's hand.

'Come.'

With everyone watching, Sydney was embarrassed. 'What?'

'Dance with me.'

'I don't know how to,' he stammered.

'I will teach you,' Maria smiled again.

'Go on, Syd,' Wally added with a grin. 'You can't refuse such a beautiful comrade. You could cause an international incident.'

Wally gave him a shove and Sydney found himself in the middle of the café facing Maria. The guitar began a slow rhythmic beat accompanied by a handclap from those watching. Maria took hold of his hands and began to step sideways, encouraging him to follow so as to start turning slowly together in a circle. The tempo began to speed up and they kept time with it until they were whirling faster and faster. The exotic flamenco rhythm was new to Sydney and he struggled to copy Maria's intricate footwork but Maria laughed and encouraged him and he became more confident until he felt as if he were flying. It reached a climax and ended in a loud cheer, Maria falling into his arms. They were both dizzy and reeled slightly as they looked at each other. She held his gaze for a moment, kissed him softly on the lips then straightened up and pushed him away. The café broke into loud applause. An accordion appeared and began to play 'The International' and everyone joined in. Sydney took his wine and went outside and stood listening to the excitement within. Maria appeared by his side in the darkness.

'You have cigarette?'

Sydney shrugged and offered one of his roll-ups. She lit it and inhaled deeply. He followed suit.

'You are a good dancer Sydney,' she whispered.

'My first time.' She turned to him, wide-eyed with surprise. 'It's true; I've never danced before.'

'No?'

He nodded. 'Not much call for it in Bleaberry House.'

'You are a natural.'

'Don't think so.' In the distance, a clock chimed. He listened to it striking and sighed.

'What?' Maria asked.

'It's Sunday.' Maria looked at him quizzically. 'I'm eighteen today.'

'It is your birthday? Why are you sad?'

'Just because.'

Maria drew near and examined his face as if she were appraising a painting. Sydney was thinking about kissing her when the door of the café flew open and Wally appeared. 'Come on you two, we're all doing the Hokey Cokey.'

Sunday, 4 October

The day was clear and unusually warm for early October. Groups of people hurried back and forth past Gronofsky's Outfitters shouting and calling excitedly. By mid-morning, word came that Gardiner's Corner was already blocked by demonstrators and that traffic was at a standstill. Wally set off up Backchurch Lane to help organise resistance, shouting back to Sydney as he walked. 'Catch a bus out east and take them downriver for the afternoon. Don't come back until after six.'

Sydney watched Wally hurry away before turning and walking slowly towards the café, all the time feeling his blood rising. In an attempt to cool down, he stopped to help move one of the three Cable Street barricades into place before going to collect the two women. Maria met him at the entrance and pushed him back outside. She was smiling coquettishly but there was also something purposeful and organised about her.

'Come on, we've got to catch the bus,' he said shaking his

head. 'It's getting late.'

'We don't want to go, Sydney.'

'We've got to. Orders from the District Committee.'

She shook her head. 'Go and fight your coppers.' In her Spanish accent, the suggestion sounded almost exotic.

'I can't do that, Maria.'

'We will be fine. We will stay here in the café and if it gets dangerous in the street, we will go to our room. It is one day.' Sydney shook his head. 'It is our birthday present to you.'

Sydney peered through the glass into the cafe. Gabriella was smoking heavily as usual and reading a newspaper. She looked up and smiled at him. He turned back to Maria. 'Why?'

'We know you do not wish to be our chaperone.'

'But what if the committee finds out?'

Maria shrugged. 'We won't tell them. Wally is at Gardiner's Corner and Jack is in jail. The rest of your precious Committee will be pretty busy today.' In the distance, a crowd began chanting. 'What are they shouting?' she asked.

'The slogan. 'They Shall Not Pass'.'

Maria nodded, '¡No pasarán!' She took his face in her hands and kissed him. 'Go on, Sydney. We will be fine.' Sydney looked at her for a moment, then turned and walked away.

It was after five when Sydney bumped into Wally. 'We won! We beat them.'

Wally nodded. 'Where were you, Syd?'

'I started off up a lamppost on Leman Street but then it all kicked off at the junction of Royal Mint Street and Cable Street. The fighting was savage but we managed to hold them for a while. The first aid stations did a tremendous job, considering the numbers of injured coming back all the time. When they started down Cable Street, we hit them with everything we had. Bricks. Hoardings. The police were trying to clear a path for the blackshirts who were massed at Tower Bridge but we didn't let them through. My marbles upset five or six horses and I used up all my catapult ammunition in minutes. The police kept on coming and broke through the first two barricades but with the street being narrow, they found themselves boxed in and we managed to stop them at the third barricade. All sorts of people were fighting; proper Jews with hats and beards, dockers, party members, trade unionists all scrapping like demons, pelting the police with stones, bottles, anything they could from doorways and the windows above the street. I saw one old lady empty her chamber pot over a mounted copper from her bedroom window. When they started pulling back, we knew we had done well but then we heard that Mosley had abandoned the march altogether; it was fantastic.' Sydney was beaming with excitement at the memory then noticed that Wally wasn't smiling. 'What is it?'

'You abandoned your post.'

'Gabriella and Maria stayed in the café. Maria said it would be OK. The fighting didn't get that far.'

Wally stared at him, stony-faced. 'Gabriella has been arrested.'

'What?'

'A Special Branch squad took her from the café at midday.'

'How d'you know?'

'Someone saw them.'

'How did they know where to find her?'

'A little bird must have told them.'

Sydney struggled to comprehend. 'It wasn't me, Wally.'

'I know that, Syd.'

'What about Maria? Was she arrested?'

Wally shook his head. 'No.'

'Where is she?'

'Search me. Look, I've got things to do. I'll see you later.'

For the next three hours, Sydney wandered the devastated streets trying to make sense of what had happened. Shop windows had been shattered and broken glass was everywhere. Bricks and cobbles used as missiles and debris from the barricades littered the street in the aftermath of the battle.

Despite the devastation, there was a carnival atmosphere as people began to tidy up but Sydney wasn't cheerful. He couldn't even summon the energy to scare off the crows and pigeons picking among the debris. His elation had been replaced by a terrible empty ache, the kind he hadn't felt since his darkest hours at the reformatory. He set out to find Wally and discovered him, inevitably, in the Sunshine Café in the midst of a celebration. Unable to join in, Sydney stood on the doorstep. Wally spotted him and came outside.

'If you've come to say you're sorry, it's too late, Syd. You left your post.'

'What's going to happen?'

Wally sighed. 'There'll be a disciplinary hearing and, in all likelihood, you'll be expelled.'

Sydney stamped his foot. 'Not to me; what'll happen to Gabriella?'

'She'll be deported, sent back.'

'To Spain?'

Wally shook his head. 'To Italy.'

'Will she be put in prison?'

'I told you. She's on one of their lists. She'll disappear.'

'And there's nothing we can do?'

'Don't think so.'

Sydney turned away then turned back to his friend. 'You think Maria told them?'

'It would certainly tie up a few loose ends.'

'So she's a spy?'

'No, she's one of us,' Wally sighed deeply. 'Gabriella is not afraid of saying what she thinks. She's made it plain that she doesn't revere Comrade Stalin. That can be dangerous. This way, her silence can be blamed on the fascists.' Sydney moaned in horror. Seeing his young friend in distress, Wally took pity on him. 'Don't be too hard on yourself, Syd. If they wanted rid of her, it would have happened sooner or later. They sent Maria with her for a reason.'

'What can I do? It's my fault.'

'Keep fighting. That's all any of us can do.' Sydney looked at Wally and shook his head. 'Go home and get some sleep. We'll talk in the morning.' The eighteen-year-old nodded and turned to go.

Monday, 5 October

When Sydney didn't appear on Monday morning, Wally assumed he was still licking his wounds somewhere. Wally had his hands full helping with the clean-up. Despite the victory, there was a tremendous amount of damage and little money for repairs. Old Mrs Corman's sweet shop door and window had been smashed and trampled by a charge of police horses. Wally spent a couple of hours trying to repair the front door and board up the window. Then he organised an impromptu repair gang and helped make a list of the most urgent repairs. When Sydney still hadn't appeared by tea-time, Wally went looking for him.

Sydney's bed was a narrow cot high under the eaves of their house. It was a small space surrounded by old suitcases and clutter. There were a few nails on the rafters where Sydney hung his clothes but they were empty. The noise of crows skittering and cawing on the roof tiles was amplified in the small roof-space. On the cot was a note addressed to Wally. Inside it said,

> *Sorry.*
> *Tar for lukking arfter us.*
> *Gon to Spane to keep fiteing.*
> *Luv*
> *Syd.*

THE BATTLE OF CABLE STREET, 1936

Afterword: They Shall Not Pass

David Rosenberg

STEVE CHAMBERS'S COMPLEX AND engaging story is set in the febrile atmosphere of London's East End in the days before the Battle of Cable Street – an iconic confrontation between fascism and anti-fascism in 1936 that brought hundreds of thousands of people on to the streets and saw violent clashes and multiple arrests.

Fascism was rising in Europe and chalking up a series of victories. In Mussolini's Italy it had already ruled for more than a decade, and by 1936 its army was flexing its deadly military muscle in Abyssinia. In Nazi Germany, where Hitler came to power in January 1933, a reign of terror against Jews, communists, socialists and trade unionists was in full swing. In central and eastern Europe, fascist and right wing antisemitic movements were gaining strength, attacking Jews politically with highly charged rhetoric, economically through discrimination and boycotts of shops, and physically through violent assaults. News of pogroms in March and June 1936 in the Polish village of Przytyk and the town of Minsk-Mazowiecki made Jews across the diaspora fearful of what the future would hold for Jewish people in Poland. Jews had lived there for 1,000 years and in earlier times had enjoyed a 'golden age' in that country but in 1936 dark clouds were gathering above Europe's largest Jewish community.

The most pertinent international development that Steve

refers to in that year, though, took place in Spain. General Franco launched a military rebellion against Spain's democratically elected Republican government, initiating a three year bloody civil war that ultimately established his fascist dictatorship. In that war, Franco called on professional military and political support from Germany and Italy. The Republicans recruited International Brigades – a brave untrained force from more than 50 countries comprising 35,000 'Volunteers for Liberty', including roughly 200 volunteers from London's East End.

The Spanish republicans revived and popularised a defiant slogan: '¡No Pasarán!' (They Shall Not Pass!), which originated in a First World War battle. Anti-fascists in London's East End enthusiastically adopted it when they heard that thousands of uniformed blackshirts from Oswald Mosley's British Union of Fascists (BUF) had threatened to invade their area on 4 October 1936. Mosley's posters promised 'four marching columns' and 'four great (open air) meetings'.

'They Shall Not Pass' was chalked on walls and pavements in the days and nights preceding 4 October and chanted by massed ranks of protesters on the day. It is a testament to the power of these words that anti-fascist mobilisations against Mosley's political descendants from the National Front of the 1970s to the followers of Steven Yaxley-Lennon (a.k.a. Tommy Robinson) today continued to use this slogan in their propaganda.

But why was Mosley so keen to invade the East End? What was the area's socioeconomic and ethnic profile? And what was the connection between Spain, fascism and this district, in the period that Steve Chambers writes about?

Sir Oswald Mosley – the 6th Baron of Ancoats – was a relatively young and charismatic political figure when he founded the British Union of Fascists in October 1932. He won a parliamentary seat in Harrow for the Conservative Party in December 1918 when he was barely 22 years old, but soon fell out with the party over its policy towards Ireland.

Unusually for a right winger, Mosley believed in a united Ireland guaranteeing self-determination for the Irish people. He strongly condemned the brutality displayed by the Black and Tans to suppress Irish struggles. After fellow Conservatives attacked his leftist perspective on Ireland, Mosley quit the Tories, adding in his memoirs that he had preferred to face his enemies rather than be surrounded by them.

He retained his seat as an Independent before joining the Labour Party in 1924. In 1926 Mosley returned to Parliament as a Labour MP in the Midlands, and was a rising star in the party. But he fell foul of the party's hierarchy, who rejected his bold plans for addressing the economic crisis of the late 1920s. Increasingly fascinated with Mussolini's Italy (Mussolini had once been a revolutionary socialist), Mosley left the Labour Party in late February 1931, at the height of the economic crisis, and at a moment of great disillusionment with conventional politics. He announced the formation of the New Party, an odd mixture of left wing economics and ultra nationalist, anti-democratic rhetoric, which rebranded itself eighteen months later as the British Union of Fascists.

As a political movement the BUF advanced radical policies for a 'Greater Britain', alongside its development of a menacing street army with barracks, a uniform, and a trained defence force to guard its public events. This new force drew enthusiastic support from Viscount Rothermere, the publisher of Britain's largest circulation daily newspaper, the *Daily Mail*, who saw in Mosley's movement the voice of patriotic youth that could replace the 'tired old gang' of politicians.

As it grew in strength across all classes nationally, aided by a gushing spread in the *Daily Mail* written by Rothermere himself, proclaiming: 'Hurrah for the blackshirts' and advising 'young men' about how to join the movement, the BUF planned a series of spectacular indoor rallies in London.[1] The first, at the Albert Hall was a considerable success. The second, packed with 15,000 people at Olympia Exhibition Centre, was a PR disaster. In the face of heckling from anti-fascists, who had obtained tickets through a clever deception, the stewards, with knuckle dusters hidden under their gloves, openly displayed their brutality in the hall and left 80 bloodied anti-fascist hecklers needing medical treatment after they were ejected.

Whatever the fascists' political appeal, these brutal methods proved unpopular with most of their wealthy business backers, and the movement began to decline. A few months later Mosley unveiled a plan to revive their fortunes. They would build a patriotic working class-based fascist movement. He looked towards London's East End, where just beyond the impoverished Jewish ghetto of Aldgate and Whitechapel, tens of thousands of unhappy and increasingly embittered, unemployed or low-paid workers yearned for better times. Mosley saw them as potential foot soldiers of a movement that could sweep him to power. The antisemitism that he had cautiously expressed in the movement's earlier period, gave way to full-throated scapegoating and hatred.

In October 1934 he opened his first East End branch in Bow. By early 1936 his East End powerhouse consisted of four branches, with thousands of members and supporters in Shoreditch, Bethnal Green, Bow and Limehouse, that almost encircled the Jewish ghetto, where some 60,000 Jewish tailors, shoemakers, cabinetmakers and market traders eked out a living.

While Mosley himself still preferred glamorous central London venues, his movement consolidated its local base by establishing open air speaking pitches that edged closer and closer to the Jewish areas. Many of the party's local street corner speakers came from the Irish community. Mosley consciously sought to to turn one poor community – the Irish – against another, depicting Jews as the barrier to Irish locals obtaining better jobs, better housing, better access to services. In truth, both communities were suffering. Solly Kaye, a Jewish anti-fascist who later became a Communist Party councillor locally, described how the fascists played on fear and envy, by saying 'Over there the Jews have got your houses, over there the Jews, they've got your jobs – even though we were living in bloody poverty with bugs crawling over us in the night.'[2]

But Mosley was smart. He knew that as well as the poor Jews in the East End, there was a smaller community of wealthier Jews in the West End. At an Albert Hall rally in March 1935 he described them as the 'nameless, homeless and all-powerful force which stretches its greedy fingers from the shelter of England... grasping the puppets of Westminster, dominating every party of the state... the enemy which fascism alone dares to challenge.'[3] He concocted propaganda which portrayed the poorer Jews of the East End as somehow in league with the wealthy Jews, and therefore fair game for fascist assault. The threat to local East End Jews peaked in 1936 after the BUF changed its name to the British Union of Fascists *and National Socialists* (the name that Hitler gave his party in Germany). Until that year Mosley had been more partial to Mussolini than to Hitler. Mussolini's fascism was dictatorial and oppressive but it was relatively free of antisemitism until the late 1930s. Hitler's fascism was more wild, and his antisemitism more zoological. He cast Jews as a lower species, akin to animal life.

At fascist street corner meetings in East London from early 1936, you would hear Jews described as 'rats and vermin from the gutters of Whitechapel', 'simians with prehensile toes', 'Oriental sub-men [...] an incredible species of sub-humanity', and a 'pestilence' or 'cancer'.[4] When hundreds of people at a time were whipped into a frenzy by propaganda depicting Jews as taking their jobs and homes, and were then told that these Jews were sub-human, they felt that *any* kind of action against them was permissible and justified. Through the spring and summer of 1936 there was a wave of physical antisemitic violence.

Despite Mosley's vivid imagining of the relationship between East End and West End Jews, the reality was that the latter showed little interest in the former. Their origins had been in Germany, Spain and Portugal rather than Eastern Europe; they were preoccupied with breaking through the glass ceiling into the British establishment, and showed little concern for their poorer co-religionists.

East End Jews looked for local allies among non-Jewish anti-fascists who they found in the fast-growing Communist Party, the Independent Labour Party and the Labour League of Youth. These organisations had political differences but combined very effectively against fascists. East End Jews also created their own grassroots organisations, the most prominent one being the Jewish People's Council against Fascism and Antisemitism. This was the ad hoc alliance that put paid to Mosley's plans by mass propaganda which helped to swell the numbers who were spontaneously coming out to teach the fascists a lesson.

The largest of these groups, though, was the Communist Party (CP), whose remit stretched more globally than Aldgate and Whitechapel. From July 1936, Spain – where actual fascists were murdering actual anti-fascists – was the CP London District's prime concern. They launched an Aid Spain movement which gathered material support to be shipped out to embattled comrades in Spain.

Mosley may have played a deliberate spoiler by calling his show of strength in the East End on the very day when the Young Communist League (the CP's youth section) had already planned an Aid Spain rally in Trafalgar Square. Steve's story provides a colourful account of the arguments that were raging in the party. Ultimately, in an organisation more used to top-down discipline, the grassroots rebellion of local branches prevailed. The Aid Spain rally in central London was abandoned, and comrades across London were urged to rally in the East End. The party produced a special London supplement with the *Daily Worker* newspaper on the Saturday, identifying key points where it directed its supporters to mass. Some 4,000 fascists assembled near Tower Hill. A larger force of police, including every mounted policeman in London, turned up to ensure the fascists could exercise their right to march. (The Home Secretary had been unmoved by a petition of nearly 100,000

East Enders put together in two days by the Jewish People's Council, calling on him to ban the march on the basis that it would seriously damage community relations and result in disorder.)

However, the combined numbers of fascists and police – a Venn diagram with some crossovers – were no match for the numbers of anti-fascists, women as well as men, that had been mobilised. When the police failed to break through at Gardiners Corner, Aldgate, the focus shifted to Cable Street, but the anti-fascists were one step ahead and had already built barricades. The most heartening aspect of this event, according to several Jewish veterans I had the privilege to converse with since the 1980s, was that despite all of Mosley's efforts to win support among the Irish community, many Irish dockers and railway workers helped to defend the barricades alongside the Jews.

Like the character, Sydney, a number of people who took part in the determined and bloody protests against the fascists on 4 October, took their anti-fascism one very large step further by heading to Spain to join the International Brigades. At least 36 of those who went from East London never returned. We owe so much to that generation of fighters for a better world.

Notes

1. *Daily Mail*, 15 January 1934.
2. www.csb-berlin.com/berichte/battle_of-cable-street_interview.htm
3. *The Blackshirt*, 29 March 1935.
4. Quotations are from reports published in the *Jewish Chronicle* between July–November 1936.

THE NOTTING HILL RIOTS, 1958

The Whistling Bird

Karline Smith

To the Memory of Kelso Cochrane
(26 September 1926 – 17 May 1958)

Friday, 29 August 1958

BEFRIENDED BY A JAGGED beer bottle, a rain-sodden armchair lies sideways on the hop-scotched pavement, like a dying soul awaiting its last rites. An old lady pauses as she sweeps the grey steps leading up to her three-storey tenement house on Bramley Road. Cocooned in leathery white skin, pushing back straggly hair behind her ears, her eyes catch mine as I pass. I cast my head back, watching her thin creased lips curl upwards in a wavering smile. As I mirror her smile, I imagine her inwardly lamenting her own long-lost youth at the sight of me: sixteen, gregarious, floating past in my black stiletto heels, blue pencil skirt, and a yellow cardigan over my shoulders, like the world is mine for the taking. I hug the library books closer to my bosom, uneasy with my own acknowledgement of her. She has never smiled at me before. The old lady heads inside where two large families live packed together side-by-side. A scruffy dog scampers in behind her, barking, whipping its tail in behind it just in time as she slams the paint-shredded door behind her.

My house is three doors down from the old lady's. The front door is newly painted blue, and the tiled steps polished red, a tradition that came with us from Jamaica. I skip lightly up the steps, feeling the warmth of the day's summer sun fading on my back, removing my cardigan as I enter the house. The back living-room door swings open after a gentle push. Three pairs of different coloured eyes jump up from the food laid out on the table to greet me. My eyes settle on the most commanding set: light brown, surrounded by sandy-brown Caribbean skin, sprinkled with grainy-brown freckles, and briefly I see the relief in Poppa's pupils as he realises his last born is home.

'You're late,' Poppa says. 'Where have you been, Pansetta?'

His job as a vinyl stock assistant at Oxford Street's colossal HMV store brought him enough money to buy music at a discount as well as his first portable record player, an RCA Victor Victrola 4-speed encased in a beautiful tan alligator case, costing a full week's wage, at £6. He'd been working at the store since leaving school at fourteen. Reggie loved music and now he was 21 he could afford to buy, everything: 45s, 78s, and 33s. When he covered one of the shop floor staff's shifts, he also had the opportunity to listen to new music in the listening booths. After he finished work, with a new batch of vinyl wrapped in brown paper tucked under his arm, he couldn't wait to get home, jumping on the bus at Oxford Street all the way to Westbourne Park Road, and the terraced house he shared with six brothers, sister Elsie and parents. On a summer's night, like tonight, he'd walk, taking in the mixture of people, through Mayfair, passing Hyde Park and Edgware Road, on to Bayswater Road and then cutting through the side streets. But this particular summer night had an edginess to it, a tense atmosphere Reggie couldn't tell if he was imagining since the race disturbance in St Ann's, Nottingham, that he'd read about in the *Daily Mail* earlier that week. Where he had, until recently, walked quite unnoticed as a young white male through the West Indian communities of Notting Hill, scrutinising eyes now cut through him; Reggie felt a discomfort rise in his throat. For the last few months, summer was bright, boiling, nothing like last year. The rain had poured heavily back then, denying him walks like this one. But this year was so hot. And when the rain finally came last night, he welcomed it. Lying in bed next to his brother, Archie, a cigarette balanced on his lips, he listened to it bouncing off the roof and stared through the open window, thinking about the change on the streets.

'You know we won't say grace without you.' Poppa's voice sounds tired. Placing my books on the side unit, I walk over, hug him from behind and kiss his curly black hair, my nostrils full of the scent of Pears Soap and Jamaican Caster Oil. Then I join him and my sisters at the table.

'And dinner barely warm now. We take it outta the oven well over twenty minutes ago.' Iris, my eldest sister, has an edge to her voice, and I see her left eye flickering like a crazy butterfly. 'Who do you think you are, making us all wait on you like you're the Queen of England.'

'Alright, there's no need for all this vexation.'

'You keep spoiling her. She needs to know her place.' Iris turns her face sideways, as if it pains her to look at me, and I wonder why she hates me, what torments her so.

'And it's not your place to give orders in this house or make rotten comments.'

Iris rolls her eyes, pursing twittering lips.

'Where have you been, Edie?' Serving the boiled potatoes, Poppa switches from my pet name Pansy or Pansetta to my birth name, resting his chin on his hands, leaning on the plastic-covered dining table. I fix my napkin on my lap, lowering my eyes from the inquisitive faces staring at me, waiting for an answer.

In the room he shared with his eldest brother Archie – after a wash, but not yet ready for sleep, lying on his bed, smoking a cigarette, glad that it was Friday – Reggie played his music. It was so loud he had no idea when Archie came in until a scratch on the vinyl brought the sound of The Rays' 'Silhouettes' to a halt. Swallowing, Reggie stood up quickly, and stared at his brother, narrowing his blue-green eyes at him.

'Why'd you do that? That record cost me 6s.8d.'

'Listening to nigger music again?' Reggie had been a fan of rhythm and blues ever since two West Indians, James and Linford, had asked him to get some records for them, and rewarded him with an invite to a blues party over at The Gate. This was three years ago, but Reggie still remembered how welcome everyone had made him feel there.

A rage tore up inside Reggie, hot, burning, making him shake. The record was ruined. A large scratch ran from the outside to the label.

'I can bloody well listen to what I like. It's *my* money.'

'You're getting soft, Reg. Need to come out with me again, like you used to, and show those spades what for. Me and Joe were outside Latimer Road tube yesterday. Saw this commotion and this spade arguing with a white bird. Ain't having that kinda lark. Tried to give him a good kicking, we did, other spades came out the woodwork and she turned on us. Fucking nigger arse-licking traitor bitch.'

Reggie was looking forward to the hot summer bank holiday weekend, resting, playing music and meeting his girl in the usual place, maybe taking her for a picnic in Hyde Park, but Archie had muddied his vibes. Sat in front of the mirror, Archie primed his hair in the Boston style greased straight back and cut square across the nape. He pulled on his drain pipes, fastening the front, talking all the while.

'Do you think Elsie would ever disgrace this house and bring one of those currants home – I'd give her a good kicking and boot that darkie back to his banana boat.' Archie grabbed the cigarette Reggie had been smoking and put it to his lips, blowing a long smoky curl, before slipping on a high-necked loose-collared white shirt, slim tie, beetle crusher shoes and a draped jacket, all paid for in weekly instalments to the tailor on the high street.

'So you're not blackberrying with us tonight?' Archie opened his drawer and took out a ratchet knife, knuckle duster, belt and hammer, the cigarette pinched between his lips. 'We'll soon get the message to them. Go back fucking home.' Reggie let out a long breath, half-closing his eyes. He wanted to say. *Don't.* He wanted to ask *Why?* But his lips remained shut.

Archie left, slamming the door.

A cold breeze wafted around Reggie, sinking deep into his blood, turning it cold.

'North Kensington Library.' I finally answer.

'Again?' Iris says, incredulity weaving with irritation in her tone. 'Do you eat those books, spit them out and bring them back?'

Laughter sputters from my throat.

'Imagine a coloured girl bringing back chewed-up bits of paper,' I say. 'They'd put me in a circus.'

'Except, they don't think you're coloured, do they?' Iris replies.

Golden, my other sister – two shades darker than me but still light enough to be recognised as a mulatto West Indian – takes my hand in hers and reaches to take Iris'. With her free hand Iris takes Poppa's and their fingers, the same dark chestnut-brown, entwine.

'Pansy, say grace for us.'

I look at my sisters' bowed heads and see Poppa smiling gently at me.

'Heavenly Father, thank you. Thank you for another day in the Wetherburn household. Thank you for the food you have given us, the roof over our heads where many have none, and the opportunity to be together as one family in the Mother Country, to continue this new life Poppa began for us ten years ago. Please bless the family we left behind, especially Grandma Ginny, and Auntie Lou and keep them safe… Lord, keep us all safe.'

As the Blue Spot Radiogram started up, playing the harmonious voices of The Platters singing 'The Great Pretender', the kitchen began filling with people, and Alphonso's mind drifted back to the winter three years before. February. Three hundred and sixty Brixtonians had assembled at Lambeth Town Hall on Acre Lane, half of them West Indian brothers and sisters, half local white residents coming together to dance. Not that black and white people weren't living alongside each other already. They were, but this was the cherry that would finish off the cake. He was glad to be out of the cold, amongst warm bodies, even if the music was not his type; at least 'Knees Up Mother Brown' was bringing them all together. As he watched the couples dancing, his heart ached. He missed Lynette so much. The last time he had seen her was on the wall of Kingston Harbour in '48, waving goodbye to him as the SS Empire Windrush slipped from the harbour. She was kneeling, as she waved, comforting their crying girls – thirteen-year-old Iris, ten-year-old Golden, and six-year-old Edie. She had promised to join him a few months later. But in '52, his mother wrote to tell him Lynette had run off to Montego Bay with the widower Ezekiel Johnson, their neighbour and a fellow lawyer, leaving the girls with his mother.

The sound of dominoes crashing down on the kitchen table brought him back to the game. High-pitched laughter reverberated off the kitchen walls. Winsford and Randolph had won the round again. This meant more beer and Guinness. The room was full of the boys, *his* boys, friends from back home and new ones he'd met in London. Smoke, in undulating layers, circled the bodies in the room like a hazy aura. More boys would arrive later, after the pub. Friday nights were always like this: dominoes, smoking, music, food, the front door open to anyone wanting to reminisce about back home, or catch up about who was left in the district, and of course Alphonso being teased about Gloria Davies, the woman from Savanna-La-Mar who could beat all of them at this game without even trying.

The girls were asleep in bed. Almost eleven o'clock. Whatever was out there on the streets could stay. Over the heads of the others, Alphonso watched Gloria, aproned, bringing plates and serving out curried mutton and rice. Occasionally she'd return his glances with a wide gap-toothed smile, her hair pressed in curls, her satin-brown skin glowing in the light from the kerosene lamp. Alphonso's heart beat like the crickets of her lush Westmoreland homeland. Then suddenly Gloria's expression changed, her eyes glazed as she stared beyond him. Two plates of food fell from her hands and smashed onto the floor. Then silence. No music. No nothing. Alphonso turned around in his chair, slowly.

Gilbert 'Gilly' Donaldson stood in the kitchen doorway, blinking. Blood poured from the side of his face, saturating his clothes with its darkness.

His body twisted and, as it folded downwards, Winsford and Randolph were able to catch him.

Lifting the apron to her face, Gloria screamed.

'What happen, Gilly?' Alphonso asked, flying to kneel by his friend's side.

'Teddy boys. Teddy boys. Outside. Teddy boys.' Gilly's voice wavered before unconsciousness covered him like a black blanket.

Four of the boys carried Gilly to the Ford Escort estate parked out front, all eyes straining in the lamplight for signs of the Teddy Boys that did this as they made for the hospital. The car was large enough to fit five inside, but Alphonso knew he couldn't go. He would stay behind with Gloria. Clean the place up and get rid of the blood so the girls would not have to see it in the morning.

He would never let them see this.

Saturday, 30 August 1958

I wake up early to find Poppa in the back living-room, sitting in his armchair by the radio listening to nothing, smoke curling from his pipe. Poppa doesn't smoke in the morning, unless he's worried. I thought I would be the first up, but I'm wrong. Poppa has cooked fried dumplings and cabbage and two boiled eggs – still warm on the stove – waiting for the rest of us to rise.

'Are you alright, Poppa?'

He looks at me quizzically, his forehead wrinkling like little ocean waves. 'Where are you going so early in the morning?' he asks.

'The library. I've got to study, remember?'

'I don't want you out late.'

'It's OK. I have a friend there. He keeps an eye on me.'

'What is he? Jamaican? Small Island?'

'Poppa I want to get the seat by the window before anyone else. That's why I'm up early. I've got to go.'

He is silent for a moment, looking as if he just drifted off into the empty space between us.

'Things are happening out there. White boys acting crazy. Just make sure you are back before 5pm.'

'OK, Poppa. I won't be late.'

If you cut open my mind you will see the colours trapped in the melting waves of my deep consciousness. Green-blues of Negril on the west coast where Grandma Virginia, aka Momma Blessed, used to take us on vacation in the Summer before Poppa wrote to say we were coming to England to join him. I miss the green palms and the fruit trees. I miss the kaleidoscope colours of the flowers there, such as the beautiful fern-like Poinciana and Hibiscus that Momma Blessed brewed as tea. I still long for the sound of the whistling bird that perched on the red polished veranda steps every morning.

Strangely, I see a little blue bird this morning. It stands lightly on the doorstep of the old lady that smiled at me yesterday, then ascends into a cloudless sky. A car pulls up, white people walking into the house, people hurrying out, neighbours whispering audibly on doorsteps. 'She passed yesterday.' My heart spirals, like something unable to fly anymore, as I try to contemplate the soul that has departed that smiling, nameless lady.

Reaching the top of the road, clutching my books as tightly as ever, my own soul nearly departs from my body as I hear a familiar whistle. He leaps out and grabs me, pulling me around the corner and behind some bushes. He kisses me all over, then pulls back and looks at me.

'Do I sound like your whistling bird?'

I have been teaching him the pitch and rhythm of the whistling bird, watching and laughing as he tries to reproduce the exact sound, failing miserably at first. He must have been practicing really hard because now it sounds almost authentic.

'Yes. You really do, I say, feeling emotional.

'I've missed you, Pansy.'

'We saw each other yesterday!' A giggle escapes from my mouth and I start to laugh and shake.

'It's not enough.'

I remember when I first saw him at the library, after joining two months ago. I had discovered the library on the bus journey from the West End. I love everything about books, the smell, the covers, the anticipation. I particularly love crime and mystery, and Agatha Christie is my favourite author. I was waiting anxiously as the librarian issued my new adult borrower ticket, explaining the book lending rules to me. Becoming aware of his burning gaze, I turned around and caught him smiling; he held a book out to me, and I glimpsed the title: *The Great Gatsby*.

'It's an old book but it's a good one, I promise. It was made into a film in '49. I've never seen it. I like to read a book the way it's meant to be and not somebody else's interpretation.'

He had a kind-looking face, pale-skinned, wavy blonde hair and round blue-green eyes that seemed to see right through me. He put out a nervous hand for me to shake.

'Reggie.'

I took his hand.

'Pansy, but my real name is Edie.'

'Nice to meet you, Pansy.'

'Likewise.'

Reggie walks with me and talks hurriedly, like he always does, as if time is a stolen commodity. We walk side by side, our bodies brushing together slightly from time to time. I can't stop thinking about the smiling lady, as people hurry past us shopping. We decide to head up to Bayswater, into the West End, to buy coffee, talk some more, wander around the shops, and maybe go to his store and listen to jazz and rhythm and blues in one of the booths. Then we'll walk in the afternoon sun and talk about books, the stars, the universe, radio, history, where I'm from, and about his family. Time will pass and eventually he will walk me home. When we get to Bramley Road, he will stop at the top of the road, an invisible barrier preventing him from walking any further.

The house was so full, people were spilling out of the downstairs rooms into the hall and the stairway leading to the first floor where the girls' bedrooms were. The air was stale with cigarette smoke; even the open windows, allowing a fresh breeze from the road outside, couldn't disperse the smell. Alphonso had opened up the front room, the best room, and as many people as could squeezed themselves onto the sofa and chairs. The rest stood. By immigrant standards, Alphonso Wetherburn was quite well off. Back home he had been a lawyer working in Savanna-La-Mar, so wealth was not unknown to him. His family were descendants of plantation owners and their white European ancestry was evident in Pansy's fair complexion and green eyes. The kink in her hair gave away her African bloodline and she often pressed it straight with the hot comb. Alphonso had come to the Mother Country because it was his right. He was its heir. And no one could or would tell him otherwise.

His arrival in '48, however, taught him he was just another black man and there was no work for him as a lawyer. Reluctantly, he learned to drive London's trains, begrudging white lawyers and other professionals boarding his train to their offices in the city. That was a long time ago. Now he accepted his destiny. He couldn't go back. Notting Hill was his community, and there he was known as the 'loans man' because he lent money at a reasonable interest rate to fellow countrymen shunned by banks. The extra income allowed him to purchase, decorate and furnish the three-storey house where around 30 people – men, women and some children – now assembled.

He was glad the girls were out. Pansy at the library and the others with friends two streets over. Celeste Brown, a teacher from Spanish Town, and her husband Patterson had called the meeting after two nights of rampaging by the Teddy Boys, following the attack on Raymond and his Swedish wife Maj outside Latimer Road Station. Tea and coffee were available for those who wanted refreshments, and some of the women had brought pots of cooked rice and peas with chicken, or curried mutton.

'They mash up the restaurant last night de Teddy Bwoy them.' Celeste began, with a tremor in her voice. 'When the police come from Harrow Road after we call them, I never hear such dutty language in my life and you know what they did… they raid the shop for offensive weapons, take the machete we use to chop meat and shut down the shop. Now we scared the Teddy Bwoy them gon come back and bun it down like the house pon Latimer Road. Is all we have. Me and Patterson put all we life savings inna it. Bwoy, if me did know me was a come to this me woulda ah never step foot in this Godforsaken place.'

'Don't talk like that, Celeste.' A young Trinidadian woman called Syreeta said. 'God see the afflicted and He will deliver us.'

'Cousin, did you tell the Caribbean Welfare Service?'

There was a buzz in the room, a hum of discontented voices in unison.

Celeste kissed through her teeth harshly.

'Is what them can they do? We've been telling the police long time and they are not listening, and they don't care. Instead of picking up these filth, the Teddy Bwoy, they standing back and watching. Is like they don't care. Look w'happen to Gilly.'

'I think we should fight back,' Patterson said, tilting his trilby over his dark face glistening with perspiration. 'This is a war now.'

Trusted by so many in the community, Alphonso felt people

were waiting for him to speak. 'No. No need for that,' he said raising his hand. 'I have been advising people to get out early, do what they need to do, shopping, work, whatever and come into their homes and lock up them doors early, till it passes over.'

Suddenly, Alphonso thought about Pansy.

'Why should we hide like cowards?' Hissing, teeth-kissing and growl-like noises rose from the guests. 'Not a day goes by when the police don't pick up any black people just for walking in the street. Nobody cares. Nobody doing *nothing*.' Celeste brought her fist down on the arm of her chair with each word. 'I hear seh them white people mek a plan for us next. Then Brixton. I hear there's going to be big trouble like Nottingham. Look at this leaflet they push through me door.' Celeste handed the leaflet to Alphonso.

He knew what it was without looking at it: a leaflet from those fascists, Oswald Mosely's Union Movement, spouting its usual garbage. He screwed the paper up and threw it on the low table in front of him. 'Nobody should panic,' he continued, keeping his voice as calm as he could. 'The storm will ride over. Everything will be...'

Alphonso heard a smash. From the corner of his eye he saw the object hurtle into the room, heard the whip of it through the air, and felt its breeze as it flew past his ear, landing on the table, sending the cups and plates flying, before crashing to the lino. The screams and shouts that followed almost deafened him. Bodies surged and crushed. Before he could catch his breath, he was clambering to see what had caused the commotion. A large stone lay on the floor, in the corner. Broken glass lay sprinkled over most of the guests.

'Still think we shouldn't fight back?' Patterson asked, mouth twisted in a scowl, fists clenched his into balls of anger. 'I think it's about time we gi' dese people a good rarsing.'

Reggie and I reach the top of the street where we hug, and he kisses my cheek. I look into his eyes and know that my life has been transformed. He *is* my life, my everything. Tonight he decides to walk me to my door but half-way up the street we hear it. A large group of Teddy Boys have gathered on Bramley Road, a few doors down from my house: hovering, drinking, throwing their beer bottles to the ground to watch them smash. I feel Reggie freeze as one of them walks over.

'What the fuck are you doing here?'

'Archie, I'm walking my girlfriend home.' Reggie stutters and swallows as if his throat is dry.

I've never met Archie, or any of Reggie's family, and it's obvious he doesn't know who I am. I can tell by the look on his face he is puzzled by my presence. His eyes root me out, check me over, register my hair, my pale brown skin, my green eyes. I know he sees it. He sees the hint of colour and he knows that all he has to do is get my mouth to betray me. The Caribbean lilt that Reggie loves, that tickles him when I whisper sweet nothings in the library, will cut through Archie like a knife.

'What's your name?' Archie asks.

'Edie.'

'You live here? On *this* street?'

My head drops to my chest.

'You don't have to say, Pansy,' Reggie mutters.

I see the anger flash in Archie's eyes as more smirking Teddy Boys gather around him. Behind them I see my own front window broken and people pouring out of the door. I see Poppa striding towards us, screaming at me to get in the house, only he seems to be moving slowly, as if in a dream. Turning, I see Archie launch himself at Reggie who collapses to the ground, scrunches up into a protective ball. Feet and fists from all directions pummel him and boots stamp down on him. I am screaming. I am screaming for Reggie. I am screaming for my love. I feel myself being lifted, hoisted inside the house, upstairs to my bedroom as I continue to scream, and Poppa flings me on the bed, glaring down at me. But it's not Poppa. It's like someone is wearing a mask with Poppa's face on it. The man inside is spitting and frothing and bellowing with his fist raised in the air.

'You? How could you do this to me?'

'Poppa they are going to kill him. Please… please save him.'

'I don't care. Let them kill him.'

'Poppa I love him. I love him. Please help him!'

I try to rise, but Poppa pulls the belt from his trousers.

'Pansy, if you leave this house and try to see that white boy again, I will kill you, you hear me. Stay in this house. Do not move.'

Poppa slams the bedroom door and locks it with a key. For a while I bang on the door and walls and scream. After a while I just fall to the floor.

Monday, 1 September 1958

As he filled each bottle, the words of an old Jamaican proverb rang in Alphonso's head: *Every day bucket go a well, one day the bottom must drop out.* This weekend was the last time the Teddy Boys would try and carry that bucket and fill it with West Indians. There would be no more terrorism. No more white mobs running through the streets with bricks, sticks or stones. Still angry with Pansy but seething for justice, Alphonso was putting the plan into action. Over the last twenty-four hours the women had collected empty milk bottles from doorsteps, washed them out and brought them by the box-load into houses, churches, clubs, anywhere where West Indians gathered. Each milk bottle was now being filled with petrol and a rag stuffed in its neck. Ex-service men set up a headquarters in Totobags Café on Blenheim Crescent, devising strategies for combat, organising groups of men to escort and protect families if they were out. Not even the hurricane of '44 could compete with the gale-force tensions surging through Notting Hill.

The HQ stocked an array of weaponry: stones, fencing, metal bars, machetes, knuckle dusters, and rachet knives. Alphonso sat with the ex-service men, listening. The Teddy Boys said they were coming. But that was alright. *Every day bucket go a well, one day the bottom must drop out.*

They waited in darkness. Late in the evening, the murmurs of a crowd congregating outside alerted them. Gathered round the HQ's third-storey window, Alphonso, Randolph, Patterson and Winsford could see the size of the crowd; 400 at least, marching down the Crescent. Most of the other houses on the street were in darkness. As they drew closer, Alphonso sensed confusion growing among the Teddy Boys; they had expected crowds of West Indians to be waiting for them, ready to fight. But besides them, the Crescent was empty. Silent.

'Let them have it!' Randolph's voice bellowed through every floor of the HQ, as petrol bombs poured out of windows. Molotovs rained out of the third-storey windows, just as the crowd was passing. Other domino regulars threw bottles from the second storey, whilst West Indian youths bombarded from the first. From nowhere, the police screamed into action, filing down the street. They lit more milk bottles and when they heard the police starting to batter at the front door, they formed a wall, burst through and dispersed into the bloody, fighting crowd.

This was the night Alphonso saw the hell on earth his mother had talked about from the Book of Revelations. It was a long night. A long battle but they did not, and never would, lose.

Summer 1960

Golden says I am a fool for trying, but I still visit the library every week, hoping to see him. And sometimes I stand at the top of Bramley Road, in case he passes it on one of his evening walks. I go to HMV on Oxford Street as well, even if the staff there seem to think he has a wife now, or that he's moved to Essex.

The riot that week spewed hate but also love. From the ashes of those Molotovs, an American lady called Claudia Jones organised a Trinidadian Mardi Gras at St Pancreas Town Hall, sixteen months ago, January '59. A festival where black and white folks enjoyed the music and culture of the Caribbean in the neighbourhood together. Iris and Poppa, and other West Indians, attended. Poppa described the cabaret with exhilaration; the beauty contest, the crowning of the Carnival Queen, limbo dancing, bongo and tamboo bamboo. He particularly liked when a young jazz singer named Cleo Laine performed with Guyanese pianist Mike McKenzie and his trio. The climax to the evening was a jump up around the building, outside then back in again. I wish I'd been there. Instead I have the details and photos cut from the *West Indian Gazette*, noting that the British Broadcasting Corporation had filmed it, and pasted in my scrap book to save forever.

Today is my long-awaited chance to experience the second carnival, this time at the huge Lyceum Ballroom. It is almost magical as the light tinkles and melodic sounds of the steel drums sway me, filling the whole building like hypnotic chimes. Bunting and the flags of all the colonies hang over the walls and from the chandelier lights. I smile as I see my homeland flag in the middle, flapping and waving away. The vibrant costumes and masks are so beautiful I feel tears well up. Exotic Caribbean food fills my nostrils and there is so much on offer I can't keep up with the names of the dishes from all the other islands. Joy and happiness rebounds from one face to another as black and white people mingle together. In the centre of the Ballroom, children run around with streamers, mini flags, whistles and balloons. My beautiful blue-eyed, curly-haired boy lets go of my hand and runs off to join them. *He* is the reason I was unable to make Claudia Jones's first carnival. My son, Kingsley Reginald. Born five days before it. With Gloria melting his stance, Poppa has learned to accept his grandson and Iris and Golden are also supportive. I am lucky, yet I don't *feel* lucky. In the midst of all this joy, my heart is in pain. Still in pain.

It is 5pm already. I say goodbye to my friends, leaving the steel drums and dancers in the hall, and scoop baby Kingsley up to take him home. Pushing past crowds of people on the wide carpeted stairway, struggling with my handbag and my baby, I head to the exit onto Wellington street. Outside in the sunlight and the light summer breeze, I close my eyes in despair. Tears threaten to weaken me. I'm happy there is a change in the community but unhappy that it's too late for me and Reggie.

Kingsley is holding on to me tightly. I raise my hand to hail a black cab on the other side of the road when I hear a chirping sound behind me. It's high-pitched, delicate and persistent. My hand drops. I freeze for a second then my senses catch up. There are no whistling birds in London. Kingsley is asleep on my shoulder and I am about to raise my hand again for the next passing taxi, when I hear the bird chirp again. I turn around slowly, my heart thrashing against its cage. At first, I think that my mind is betraying me but as a smile spreads across his face I know the moment is real. My breath almost stalls in my lungs. *Reggie!* Reggie is leaning against one of the Lyceum's huge pillars, a cigarette dangling in his hand, still chirping. He walks over slowly, relieves me of the weight of Kingsley and puts his sleeping son against his chest. I watch him kiss Kingsley's hair before putting his arm around me, pulling me close, holding me tight.

Afterword: Don't Believe the Gentrification

Dr Kenny Monrose

University of Cambridge

ALTHOUGH POST-WAR BRITISH governments for a short spell adopted a *laissez faire* attitude to new commonwealth migration from the British West Indies, the ever-increasing appearance of black people from 1948 was frequently seen as a cause for concern, in both the public and political life.

A mere ten years after the arrival of the Empire Windrush, we witnessed racialised civil unrest on the streets of Britain, arguably for the first time since the Cardiff conflicts in 1919.[1] The first incident of note occurred in St Anne's area of Nottingham (23 August), and then less than a week later in Notting Hill, London. Both were said to be spurred by public disapproval of inter-racial relationships between black males and white females. Indeed the latter riot is thought to have been triggered by a public argument between a Swedish woman, Majbritt Morrison, and her Jamaican husband, Raymond, at the Latimer Road underground station, which led to a group of white men intervening and a fight breaking out between them and Raymond Morrison's friends.[2]

At the time, black people – men in particular – were often constructed, in the popular consciousness, into bearers of ascribed characteristics which were seen as a threat to British society. A number of white supremacist groups such as the

White Defence League (WDL), saw miscegenation or 'interbreeding' as a potent and present danger to 'Britishness', that had to be curbed in order to prevent the country from being over-run by 'a mulatto population'.[3] This was an era of British history when unofficial colour bars and lines were still unapologetically fixed within public spaces that included not only streets, roads and squares, but also applied indoors to lodgings, pubs, churches, even barbers, with no parliamentary legislation yet in place to address discrimination of the basis of race.[4]

While the congress of a black man and a white woman was unmentionable, the kind of relationship explored in Karline Smith's story – between a black woman and a white man – was frankly unthinkable. And, while bearing distant echoes of Basil Dearden's award-winning 1959 film *Sapphire,* Karline's story provides an original contribution to the literature on the event, bringing to life the real human dynamics that underpinned racial tensions associated with intermarriage in the 1950s.

The 1958 Notting Hill riots act as a crucible for post-war race relations in Britain. Notting Hill, known locally as Ladbroke Grove, or as simply 'the Grove' to its denizens, had a higher population of blacks in residence than most other areas of London and was one of the few places where West Indians could secure living accommodation, albeit at the hands of questionable slumlords – Peter Rachman being the most well known. This, we will go on to see, caused discontent amongst whites, and led to parts of the area, particularly the Colville quarter, being dubbed 'Brown Town', in a gesture that contrasted it to the long-established parish that stood nearby in Hammersmith and Fulham – White City. Tropes such as this coupled with the promiscuously daubed graffiti slogan 'KBW' (Keep Britain White), highlighted the sentiments held in reference to black presence.

Of course, these ill feelings had been exploited by a number of nationalist groups located in the area for decades. Through much of the 1930s, Oswald Mosley's British Union of Fascists

(BUF) or 'blackshirts' had appealed to the basest human instincts, directly targeting working class communities across London (see The Battle of Cable Street, pp. 241-268). During the 1950s however, the fascists began disseminating their hateful propaganda to a completely new socio-economic class that had emerged as part of the post-war cultural revolution: the teenager.

Karline does well to capture this moment of genesis for youth counter-culture in post-war Britain, and how this was epitomised by a white working-class spirit of rebellion: a vision of a new youth, decked out in 'brothel creeper' shoes and 'bum-freezer' jackets: the Teddy Boy. For many of the mild-mannered, family-oriented West Indians in Britain, the Teddy Boy was a byword for racist white youth 'out to get niggers', armed with flick knives, bike chains, iron bars and shillelaghs. Indeed they were later characterised by sociologists Stan Cohen and Paul Rock as 'atavistic monsters'.[5] Mosley's BUF had been outlawed in 1940, but he was attempting to re-enter British politics through his new party, the Union Movement, and in 1959 declared he was standing for parliament in the local constituency of Kensington North. Other British fascists in the 1950s were gathering under another banner: Colin Jordan's White Defence League. WDL was bankrolled by Mary Leese, widow of Arnold Leese, founder of the Imperial Fascists League, a sometime rival to Moseley's BUF. The fact that WDL was headquartered at Mary's house, at 74 Princedale Road, just a stone's throw from Totobag's Café in Blenheim Crescent – a popular meeting place for the black community – did little to help. Racial hatred was stoked by local residents receiving WDL pamphlets with strap-lines such as 'Black gets white girl', 'Negroes lead in VD' and spurious claims that a local woman had been raped by a black man. This polluted the minds of disaffected youth, and older white men, and prompted them to take to the streets in late August with the intention of attacking any black person they happened upon.

Historically Notting Hill had been an area with a gruesome

reputation. Charles Dickens's magazine *Household Words* described the district as a 'plague spot', unequalled by any other location in London for its insalubrity.[6] Seediness, exploitation and murder seemed to be an ever-present fixture within its streets. The recent case of the serial killer John Christie, who had operated out of 10 Rillington Place, cast a macabre spectre over the area well into the mid 1950s.

But as the decade drew to a close, in the year following the riots, it was another murder case that drew the nation's attention back to Notting Hill; this time the murder of a young, black carpenter Kelso Cochrane, to whom Karline's story is dedicated. Kelso's tragic, unsolved murder is thought to have been a turning point, and one of the reasons Moseley's support suddenly waned, and his attempt to re-enter parliament in the 1959 election failed (polling less than 3,000 votes). Also, as tensions grew around Kelso's murder, the British government realised for the first time it had to take the matter of race seriously.

The ongoing denial that Notting Hill was a polarised, indeed garrisoned community, and the attempts to put the blame for Kelso's murder at the doorstep of outsiders, was trashed by locals, who easily saw through coded messages of the media's propaganda machine, as well as the ill-placed comments from parliamentarians such as Home Secretary Rab Butler who blamed anything but racism for his murder. These feelings were validated by the sheer turnout and intermixture of community members who mobilised to attend Mr Cochrane's funeral on 6 June 1959.

The events of 1958 and 1959 still leave an indelible stain on Notting Hill today, despite several decades' worth of perfuming, peroxiding, pomading and re-defining the district in the name of 're-gentrification'. However, in the light of the history of the white community here and the clarity offered by Karline's story, the question remains: how gentrified was Notting Hill in the first place?

A positive outcome of the riots of 1958 and tragic passing

of Kelso in 1959, is the great work undertaken at various junctures by Claudia Jones, Rhaune Laslett, and Leslie 'Teacher' Palmer, in establishing what is now globally known as one the world's greatest celebrations of muliculture.[7] However this too carries with it a thinly veiled subtext, which applies to the carnival more than any other festival in 'post-racial' Britain, namely a subtext of racialisation – ascribing ethnic or racial identities to a group that may not have identified itself as such.

Notes

1. One of the earliest documented violent conflicts involving black people occurred in Cardiff in June, 1919. The 'Cardiff Conflicts', as they became known, were the first mass black declaration of resistance to racist attacks and discrimination in the UK. In particular they were a response to a tide of violent racism that had been passing through the length and breadth of Britain, fueled by post-war unemployment. Areas of Cardiff such as Butetown, and Tiger Bay, where significant numbers of blacks resided, as well as the nearby town of Barry, experienced disturbances. Mobs of whites, (ironically, led by Australian immigrant soldiers) mobilised, and carried out armed attacks on the lodgings and homes of what were mainly ex-black servicemen, killing at least three: John Donovan, Mohammed Abdullah, and Frederick Henry Longman. No plaque or statue has ever marked these events.
2. Majbritt Morrison was subsequently attacked the following day by a group of white youths who recalled seeing her the previous. According to various reports, she was attacked with milk bottles and an iron bar, and called such things as 'Black man's trollop'.
3. See Colin Jordan, interviewed by Billy Symon for Pathe News: https://www.youtube.com/watch?v=aGi_wIWRYys

4. When it finally arrived the 1965 Race Relations Act banned racial discrimination in public places and made the promotion of hatred on the grounds of 'colour, race, or ethnic or national origins' an offence. This was followed by the wider-reaching 1968 Race Relations Act, which made unlawful acts of discrimination within employment, housing and advertising.

5. Paul Rock and Stanley Cohen, 'The Teddy Boy,' in *The Age of Affluence, 1951-1964,* edited by Vernon Bagdanorand Robert Skidelsky (Macmillan, 1970), p. 289.

6. Cited in 'Riots and Rachman to New Reality: the Notting Hill Effect', *The Independent*, 21 September 2010.

7. The very first event, at St Pancras Town Hall, was designed by Claudia Jones not only to 'wash the taste [of racism] out of our mouths' but to raise funds to cover the legal costs of people caught up in the riots the year before.

The Done Thing

Luan Goldie

GRAN PICKS UP A pair of heart-shaped sunglasses from the sea of crap on sale. The stall holder lifts a tiny mirror and smiles encouragingly.

Ben whistles, 'Looking good Mrs A.'

Mrs A? Why has he started talking like The Fonz? He never talks like this when we're back in America. It's one of the hundred annoying habits Ben's taken up since we arrived at Heathrow.

'You don't think I'm too old for them?' Gran asks, tipping the glasses down her nose, doing her best Lolita impression.

'You? Old? Never.' Ben tries a pair too, with eyes shaped like flamingos. He nods along to the whiny Drake song from the stall holder's phone. Ben's being goofy, but Gran seems to like it, to like him. At least someone does. He's gone down very badly with my dad the last few days.

'Five quid,' Ben shouts in a fake British accent, 'bargain.'

Again, Gran chuckles. 'Told you, it's cheap here. Everything is cheap.'

She's right, Dagenham Market is cheap. It's also shit. I had forgotten that and now I can't believe I suggested coming here.

They lay the sunglasses back on the tablecloth and walk ahead of me, arm in arm, past all the semi-decent things I want to look at; knock off handbags, vinyl, mini-doughnuts.

'Do you have markets like this in America?' Gran asks.

'Of course there's markets in America,' I say as I catch up. 'But where we live they're a bit more artisan you know? Handmade soaps, truffles, limited prints, that sort of thing.'

'Oh no,' she says, 'truffles. Sounds all a bit pretentious.'

Pretentious. She's talking about me.

Gran slows, she's getting tired. I take her other arm. 'Are you okay? Do you want to sit down?'

She tuts, 'Oh calm down. I can walk fine.'

'Oh Mrs A,' Ben throws his arm around Gran, 'You would love Seattle. You've got to come and visit.'

'Yes, I've always wanted to go. I do like *Fraiser*. They show the repeats on Channel 4. Was it really filmed in Seattle? You never know, do you? Like *Eastenders* is actually filmed outside of London. Cockfosters I think.'

'Really?' Ben says.

Even though he has no idea about *Eastenders* or Cockfosters.

We stop in front of a stall selling 'bespoke' furniture; a mannequin in a sequinned evening gown sits on a three piece purple velvet-effect couch.

'Very posh,' Gran says. But it's hideous.

Maybe I *am* pretentious.

'Ben, you're right love, I could do with a sit down now. Let's find the others and get a cuppa.'

They hobble off ahead to find Dad, who insisted on getting a chicken chow mein as soon as he arrived at the market, even though it was only half nine. He sits with his 'new wife' Elaine in the make-shift food court around a table covered in empty polystyrene bowls. Another Drake song plays through a tiny speaker propped against a large pan of jumbo prawns.

'How was your breakfast son?' Gran asks.

'Perfect,' Dad says as Elaine wipes at a yellow stain on his shirt with a paper napkin.

'Didn't buy anything then?' Dad asks me.

I wish I bought something, to prove I'm not a snob. 'I was

going to get some toothbrushes, they're so cheap here. But I didn't have the correct change.' I say.

'Not your sort of thing anymore is it? Now you're all *living abroad*.'

'What's living abroad got to do with buying toothbrushes?' I ask, but hold off on asking him what exactly he means by it. I promised myself I wouldn't argue with him this week.

Elaine leans across the table, showing too much of her freckly cleavage, and says, 'I'd love to live in America, I'd get my teeth done.' She runs a finger along her top row of teeth then drops out of the conversation to swipe about on her phone.

Dad nods over to Ben and Gran, their heads close to each other giggling about something.

'1968?' Ben says, 'No way. You must have been a baby.' And again Gran laughs.

'What's so funny?' I ask.

Instantly she stops and her face falls back into neutral. How can she do that, go from vital and bright to pissed off and dull whenever I ask her anything?

'Your Gran was telling me about her anarchist past,' Ben says.

Gran slaps him on the knee. 'Oh, stop it.'

'What's this about?' I ask. But no one answers and Dad shrugs.

'I didn't know Ford made cars in England,' Ben says.

'They don't anymore,' says Dad. 'We don't make anything in England anymore.'

'Right, shall we make a move?' Gran wobbles as she stands and Dad rushes to catch her. 'I'm fine. Stood up too fast that's all. Blood ran right from my head.'

As we walk back to the car Gran falls behind with Dad and Elaine.

'So weird,' I say, 'I never knew she worked for Ford. Can't believe Dad didn't tell us either.'

'Sounds cool though. She said when all the women went

on strike it brought the company to its knees.'

'Yes, I know that,' I say, frustrated with the history lesson. 'Everyone knows that. They even made a film about it. I just didn't know that she was part of it. She never told me.'

But then she never tells me anything.

★

Downstairs, Gran sleeps propped up by cushions in an armchair, a half done Sudoku on her lap. I step close and put my face in front of hers until her nostrils flare slightly. She's so still. Dad and Elaine are in the kitchen, whispering about something. Maybe they're talking about Ben. About how much they dislike him. I creep towards the door but what I overhear is to do with appointments, injections and check-ups.

'Everything okay?' I ask.

'Yep,' Dad says. 'Where's Lover Boy?'

'Asleep. He's exhausted. The airbed kept waking us up last night. It deflates every few hours.'

'Best I could offer I'm afraid.' Dad takes the last bite of what looks like a ham and cheese sandwich. I thought when he remarried he would stop eating bread-based evening meals.

Elaine, in her too tight vest and leggings, stands by the sink, tapping away on her phone.

'So,' I rap my nails on the table. 'It was interesting that Gran was telling Ben about the Ford strikes right? I've never heard her talk about that before.'

Dad laughs.

'What?'

'Nothing, it's funny how your accent keeps changing. You sound like him.' He jabs a thumb up, then mimics '*like, right, whatever you guys.*'

'I don't sound like that.'

'Yes, you do.'

'Anyway, well,' I stop and make a conscious effort to sound how I imagine my old self used to sound. 'I've never heard Gran talk about Ford and the strikes before.'

But he's not listening. 'Elaine, can you make me another sandwich? Jam one this time please. There's Hartley's in the fridge.'

'Dad, did you know?'

'Everyone knows. There's a film about it and everything.'

'About her being involved. I never even knew she worked for Ford.'

'Most of the old lot from round here worked for Ford at some point. It had the best wages in the area. It's not a surprise. You've got to remember she was a single mum. She was always working. The chemist, the garage, the big Tescos, the mini cab station.'

'Mini cab controller is the worst,' Elaine says as she slops jam across four slices of bread, 'I lasted about two weeks in that job. Couldn't understand what most of the drivers were saying to me.' She plops the plate down in front of Dad.

'But to be part of the strikes must have been amazing. Don't you think? I was reading about it. People credit it as kick starting the gender equality–'

'Bloody strikes,' Dad says, 'Can you believe there's another tube strike coming up? They walk out every time someone throws themselves on the tracks.'

'That's not why they strike.'

'The teachers are the worst. They already get half the year off but they're always pulling a strike about pensions. It's ridiculous. You got a job, do it. Plenty people in this country desperate for work and can't get it. Then the people with all the jobs don't want to even show up to them.'

'Tony,' Gran's voice from the living room calls, breaking him mid flow, 'what you shouting about?'

Dad takes a bite from his sandwich and shakes his head, 'Nothing Mum. Right, let me help the old bird to bed. I'll leave you two ladies to chat.' He walks out with the sandwich in his hand, leaving a trail of crumbs at which Elaine sighs before grabbing the *Dirt Devil* from the wall.

I don't have a clue how to *chat* to Elaine. What can I say to try and bond us? To allude to what Gran did all those years ago so that women of my generation, which incidentally is also Elaine's generation, could have equal rights at work?

The hoover stops and Elaine smiles at me, 'She really appreciates you coming back to see her.'

It's not true, Gran couldn't care less if I'm here or not, but I nod along with Elaine anyway.

'And it's so nice that you've brought Ben here too. He's very,' she clips the hoover back onto the wall, 'well Gran likes him doesn't she? Bless her.' Elaine glances at her phone, which sits blinking on the table. The conversation has officially died and it's only a matter of time before one of us throws in the towel. 'Do you play *Candy Crush*?' she asks.

Online gaming. My worst nightmare. 'Oh, not tonight. I'm a bit tired. Going to head up to bed.'

She smiles with relief and I go upstairs where I lie awake for hours on the wheezing airbed.

★

The next day all five of us are squashed on a bench at Leigh-on-Sea eating chips and drinking Ribenas. My diet always plummets when I come home. Carbs and sugar. Salt and grease. Surely, this kind of food can't be good for Gran either, but she's enjoying it, squashing the last of her chips onto the tiny wooden fork before raising her wobbly hand to her mouth.

'Stop gawping at me,' she says. She always catches me. It was the same when I was a kid, at her house after school, trying to watch how she cooked the dinner and ironed shirts. I didn't have a mum growing up so figured Gran would be the woman to teach me what I thought I needed to know, but instead she would scold me for staring at her.

'I was just thinking...' I trail off.

'What? Go on, spit it out.'

'Well, I'm trying to work out how you got involved with the strikes?'

'Oh, you do go on don't you?' She opens her handbag and pulls out a bottle of sunscreen.

'No, I don't. I want to know more about it, that's all.'

'Wish I'd never mentioned it now. It was only a strike. The film probably made it more glamorous than it was. Ben, here you go, put some Factor 30 on. You're very fair aren't you? My late husband was like you. People used to think he was Scandinavian.'

I lean forward, breaking her view of Ben. 'I read a few articles about it. There's loads online, I can show you. You might recognise some of your old friends. Maybe you could get back in touch with them?'

'So, what was this strike for?' Elaine asks as she begins collecting up everyone's chip papers and handing out wet wipes.

'Something about wages weren't it?' Dad says 'The girls doing the sewing wanted a bit more money.'

'Did you just say *the girls*? Dad, they were skilled machinists and the company paid them like cleaners.'

'We only stitched seat covers,' Gran says. 'Ben, you look very distracted, what is it? Do you need a break from the sun?'

We all follow Ben's eye-line out to sea. But there's nothing other than brown waves.

'Is that France?' he asks.

Dad laughs, a big roar of it. 'No, you silly sod. It's Kent.'

'Leave him alone, he's foreign.' Gran says. 'Come on Ben, walk me up the road and buy me a stick of rock.'

He helps her up and together they walk off towards the small parade of shops while Elaine strips down to a bikini and sunbathes a few feet in front of us.

'I think you're making too much of this Ford thing,' Dad says.

'Why? What do you know?'

'I know that women of her generation don't like talking about themselves too much. Not like now. Women these days, they're different aren't they? Need to shout about everything all the time.'

299

'Actually no, women are the same. We're just speaking up more.'

He laughs, 'I've noticed.'

'What's that meant to mean?' I look back to the waves and try to calm down. I will not argue with my dad. I will not let him wind me up. I'm not sixteen anymore.

'To be honest sweetheart, I don't know where I stand with any of it.'

'Any of what? Fairness? Equality? Women having a voice?'

'Feminism,' he says with a laugh. 'I'm surrounded by women but still never seem to say the right thing. Complimented a girl in the office the other day and my manager came down on me, going on about sexual harassment.'

'Oh come on Dad. This is ridiculous. Also, we prefer to be called *women*.' I can feel myself losing it.

'You've always been like this.'

'Like what?' I'm definitely shouting now, even Elaine sits up and looks back at us.

'A little know-it-all.'

We sit in almost two hours of traffic on the way home, me squashed in the awkward middle seat in the back while Ben snores on one side and Gran hums off-tune on the other. The air-con's on too high the entire journey and by the time we get back to the house I'm convinced I'm coming down with a cold. I wash the smell of chips and sea from my hair and climb onto the airbed, waiting for the slow process of deflation to begin. Ben clatters around in the bathroom for long enough to save me from having to pillow talk with him. But he wakes me up anyway. 'Hey, I thought of something.' His breath tickles my ear.

'I'm asleep.'

'Maybe something else went down with your Gran during the strike. It was London in the swinging sixties right? Lots of bra burning. Free love. Women standing together in solidarity. Maybe she had a fling with someone.'

I definitely don't want to talk about this anymore. Not now.

'She must have gotten lonely over the years. She told me she was widowed in her thirties. I didn't know your Granddad died so young.'

So, she's even spoken to him about Granddad. She's never once spoken about Granddad with me.

'Anyway,' he carries on, 'I told Gran we'd do an early lunch with her tomorrow. What time are we meeting your school friends?'

I can picture it already. Ben asking for vegan options at the pub, my friends smirking across the table at his accent and wondering how I ended up with someone so alien. 'You know you don't have to come tomorrow.'

'Why wouldn't I come tomorrow?'

'Well, it's just that it's going to be a lot of talk about people you don't know. Wouldn't you rather do something touristy? I know you wanted to see the Tate Modern.'

He doesn't say anything, but the sheets rustle as he turns away. When he speaks his voice is quieter, 'You're right. I'll go to the Tate. Leave you to catch up with your friends. Night then.'

'Night.'

Despite my earlier exhaustion, I can't sleep.

★

Ben hardly speaks to me the next morning, except for some complaints about the British weather while he rubs Aloe Vera on the back of his sunburnt neck. Then he's gone, without a goodbye, off to the Tate, just like I told him to. And I feel gutted.

Elaine is in the kitchen in her short-shorts, crop top and marigolds.

'Morning,' I say as I flick on the kettle.

'There's no milk. Your Gran's gone to get some.'

'Oh, I don't drink cows' milk anyway. Black is fine for me.'

Elaine runs the cloth under a tap, 'I didn't realise how smeared my cupboards were until the sun started shining on them. Filthy.'

I nod and make a kind of agreeable noise. 'Do you mind if

I put the radio on?'

'No. Of course not.'

It's a talk show, a caller passionately defends a Head Teacher's right to ban skirts from its school uniform policy and I laugh. 'Lucky them, I always hated my uniform. It was the tights really; I could never get on with tights.'

The front door opens and Gran comes in, she plonks the milk down on the counter and looks around the kitchen. 'Where's Ben?'

'He's gone to the Tate.'

'What? What for?'

'To see a world class collection of modern art maybe,' I laugh, and she rolls her eyes at me.

'Well, he could have told me. I thought we were going to the new café in the park together. I've got a BOGOF lunch voucher.'

'Well, I haven't gone to the Tate and I'm not meeting my friends till later. I can come with you?'

'Oh,' her face falls.

'Actually Gran, should we have a walk up the high street first? Do some shops then lunch?'

'No love, bit hot for that today. It's already scorching out there.'

'Okay, well I'm happy with the park café then. We could go early, have brunch instead.'

'I don't think they sell that. It's mostly burgers and stuff.'

The kitchen falls silent and a caller explains how a genderless uniform will make transgender young people feel more comfortable. Elaine gasps.

'What *is* this drivel you're listening to?' Gran stands and switches off the radio.

'It's a debate Gran. People discussing issues that matter. Remember, you used to be interested in things like that?'

'Right now I'm only interested in eating. Elaine, are you bothered about going up to this café? Bit hot to be walking about I think.'

Elaine snaps off her marigolds and throws them in the sink. 'I've got some ham in the fridge, needs eating. I can make us a few sandwiches instead?'

I give up. 'You know what, I don't really fancy eating another sandwich, so I'm going to go up to the café by myself.' I know I'm being stroppy and that I should rein it in. But I can't help it and before I can calm down I've already slammed the front door leaving my phone and money behind. But I'm too proud to go back in and get them. So instead I walk towards the park and the café I can't even eat in. Gran was right, it is hot and I feel my nose burning so hide under a tree. Two Romanian men sit on the bench opposite laughing with each other and sharing a bag of sunflower seeds, the ground below them is covered in empty shells. I remember Dad said the mess of sunflower seeds in the park was in his 'Top ten reasons for voting Brexit.'

I've never agreed with any of them on anything, not Dad or Gran or Elaine or even the school friends I'm meeting later.

I miss Ben. I feel bad for how I've treated him, and for the fact that right now he's probably looking at modern art with no one to make fun of it with. I can't even message him.

When I get back to the house no one is there. I pick up my phone but I don't want to apologise to Ben over text. I cancel my friends and spend the afternoon eating jam sandwiches and watching *Made in Dagenham*. It's stupid but I find myself looking for Gran in it, for the woman she must have been, one so determined and full of will that she walked out of her job until the right value was put on her skill. But the women in the film are plucky and homely, all 'saucy' jokes and sixties clichés. I feel even more deflated.

Dad tries to call me a few times but I don't pick up. Then finally, Ben calls and I rush to answer, keen to say sorry straight away but he talks first.

'Where are you? Your dad's looking for you.'

'I'm home. Well, not home, I mean back at the house.'

'Your Gran's in hospital. She collapsed.'

★

I see Ben first and he grabs me for a hug, but I pull away, embarrassed that I was watching a film and eating Hartley's jam from the jar while everyone was here, with Gran.

It doesn't even matter but I have to ask him, 'How did you know what happened?' Did they call him before me?

'I went back to the house to speak to you, then the ambulance arrived.'

Dad comes over and raises his eyebrows at me. 'I tried to phone you.'

'I'm sorry.' I hold Ben's hand, as if he can protect me.

'What happened this morning? Elaine said you stormed out the house in a mood about school uniforms?'

'Are you blaming me?'

He puts his palms up, 'Don't start an argument with me now. Go and see your Gran. She was asking after you.'

Ben lets go and nods me ahead, and I walk slowly down towards her bed at the end of the ward.

'Oh Gran.' I burst into tears and take her frail hand.

'Stop it,' she waves me away from her. 'Sit down will you.'

'I'm sorry. I'm sorry.' I sit in the chair and pull a tissue from a box on the side.

'I'm fine. It was only a fall, so stop bringing the theatrics in, alright?' She lies back on the bed and puts the air mask on her face. The sound is slow, deliberate and long and I wish someone else was here now, to fill the silence.

She puts the mask down and rolls her eyes, 'You're doing it again.'

'What? I'm trying not to do anything.'

'You're gawping.'

'Sorry. I'm sorry.' I'm useless.

'So, how was the new café in the park then?'

'I didn't go. Well I did, but I forgot my purse. So went home when I got hungry, but you were all gone. I must have just missed you.'

'Everyone was trying to phone you. But they couldn't get through.'

'I was watching *Made in Dagenham*.'

She chuckles, I actually made her laugh. 'Oh, why are you so obsessed with this?'

'Because you were part of it, and I think, well I think that's so amazing.'

'No, it wasn't. It was ordinary. Ford was a rowdy place to work back then, there were strikes all the time. It was the done thing. Anyway, I would never have got involved with that one if I'd known.'

'Known what?'

She sighs and turns away, up to the ceiling.

'All those hours on that bloody picket line, standing there trying to fight for something I wasn't even that bothered about. It was a job at the end of the day. I should have stopped working altogether and gone home to spend time with him.'

Him? I have to think about. The strike was in the summer of 1968, why hadn't I made the connection?

'Some of the women's husbands were getting embarrassed, you know, that we were out on the picket lines. Especially when Ford shut down production completely and everyone was out of work. But your Granddad wouldn't hear of it. He was a union man and really encouraged me. Believed in it and pushed me to continue. And then a week after we went back to work, he walked out in front of that van and that was that.'

'Sorry. I never realised. I wouldn't have kept asking if I did.'

'Course not. You weren't to know. Just like I didn't know what was round the corner back then. You never have as much time as you think. Oh, listen to me, now I'm the one being theatrical. Here, pass me one of those.'

I pull a tissue from the box and look away while she wipes her eyes.

'So, now you tell me something.'

'Me?'

'Yes, you. Why are you being so horrible to that lovely man you've dragged all the way here?'

★

I find Ben sitting near a bank of vending machines eating a *Sesame Snap* bar.

'You know those things are over 50% sugar?' I say.

'It's the only vegan thing I can find.'

He offers me a bite as I sit down next to him and for what seems like a long time the only sound between us is crunching.

'Your dad gave me a very impassioned speech about the National Health Service earlier.'

'Sorry about that.'

He laughs. 'No, it was great; it's the longest he's spoken to me all week.'

'I don't know why I've been such a bitch to you these last few days.'

He puts a hand on my knee and I feel worse.

'Ben, I'm sorry.'

'It's okay. Families make everyone act weird.'

I put my head on his shoulder and we sink back into the vinyl plastic chairs together.

'You were in there for a long time,' he says. 'Did your Gran finally tell you what you wanted to hear?'

'Yeah,' I nod, 'I guess she did.'

Afterword: A Victory for All, but Not Some, 1968

Dr Jonathan Moss

University of Sussex

ON 7 JUNE 1968, the 187 female sewing-machinists at Ford's River Plant in Dagenham, Essex, walked out of their factory and 'into the pages of history' as they went on strike against sex discrimination in their job grading.[1] Ford had introduced a new wage structure in 1967 that separated the workforce into five standard grades, ranging from the least skilled Grade A, which included non-production workers, to Grade E, which comprised the most skilled craft jobs. The sewing-machinists, who produced car-seat covers, were placed in the second-lowest, semi-skilled B grade. They believed they were entitled to the higher C grade because of the levels of experience and training required to perform their work. They argued that the company undertaking the job evaluation scheme failed to recognise the skilled nature of their work because it was performed by women and they voted to strike until Ford re-graded them.

The strike lasted for three weeks and brought Ford's entire British production line to a standstill. The women gained official support from the National Union of Vehicle Builders (NUVB) and Amalgamated Union of Engineering and Foundry Workers (AEF). They were joined by the 195 women at Ford's Halewood plant in Merseyside two weeks later. The dispute was resolved when Ford asked Barbara Castle, the Secretary of State for Employment and Productivity, to intervene and 'do whatever it takes' to persuade the women to return to work.[2] Instead of recognising the sewing-machinists' demand for skill recognition, they were offered a 7% pay increase, a court of inquiry into their grading grievance, and the promise of equal pay legislation in the future. As a result, although the women did not gain the re-grading they desired, the strike has been seen as a landmark in British industrial relations, widely associated with prompting the 1970 Equal Pay Act, which made pay discrimination on the basis of gender illegal.

Consequently, the strike occupies a key position in British political history. It is generally associated as a turning point in British attitudes towards women's work and gender equality. Feminist activists identified the strike as an important moment in the formation of the women's liberation movement. It has also been cited as evidence of the effects of women's growing presence within the labour movement. The strike is an unusual example of an industrial dispute from the post-war period that has publically been remembered, even celebrated for its national impact. The idea that the strike was a decisive victory in women's fight for equal pay was popularised by Stephen Wooley and Elizabeth Karlsen's 2010 feature film *Made in Dagenham*, which has been adapted into a West End musical. The film was a box office hit and has been described as a 'feel good movie' that portrays the strike as a progressive campaign for women's rights that acted as a direct catalyst for the Equal Pay Act.[3] The subsequent publicity generated by the film has proceeded to weave the place of the dispute firmly within the public history of women and gender equality in Britain. Gregor Gall wrote in *The Guardian* in 2010:

> But make history the Ford women machinists did. Their action was the inspiration for the Equal Pay Act 1970… the Dagenham women workers were among those that laid the foundations for something bigger – women starting to play

a much fuller part in deciding how their workplace relations were determined.[4]

From the opposite end of the ideological spectrum, *The Daily Mail* concurred, claiming the women 'changed the course of British history by going on strike in 1968, demanding the same wages as the men and paving the way for the 1970 Equal Pay Act.'[5]

While not necessarily denying the wider impact of the strike, by focusing on how it influenced equality legislation, feminism and the representation of women in the labour movement, the existing accounts of the dispute have generally centred on its effects upon women who worked outside of Ford at the expense of the sewing-machinists' own interpretation of the strike's outcome. This is significant considering they interpreted the initial outcome of the strike as a defeat at the time and had to wait until 1985 to have the skilled nature of their work recognised after another seven-week strike. The sewing-machinists' disappointment with the strike's outcome was captured in an interview with shop steward Lil O'Callaghan in 1978 when she reflected:

'We mucked it up. We should have left it open to fight another battle on another day... The girls felt they were in B Grade because of sex discrimination. It wasn't the money, it was the principle involved – our skill was not recognised, and we are skilled. Today we still feel it isn't fair'.[6]

Looking back on the strike in 2013, a former worker expressed a similar view in an interview with me:

'I mean, really Fords had won, if we're being honest, after we had gone back to work Fords had won because we never got our grading. We hadn't got what we wanted... All they had given us was a rise. And not an equal pay rise, not equality.'[7]

This failure to account for the personal meaning of the strike within the participants' life stories raises issues about how class and gender inequality in the past are publically remembered and interpreted, and whose memory of such inequality is accepted and portrayed in the public sphere. It is a literal example of the 'Hollywood epic view' of history, which emphasises the individual's capacity to produce social change while downplaying the fact they do so within conditions not of their choosing. The women's continued experience of class and gender inequality after their strike spoils the 'feel good' narrative and is thus ignored.

Luan Goldie's 'The Done Thing' alludes to the 'ordinary' nature of the strike, which reflects two important themes. Firstly, it highlights how trade union participation was accepted as a quotidian aspect of working life in post-war Britain – something which is perhaps underplayed in the film itself. The sewing-machinists were representative of the growing number of women joining trade unions during this period. Trade Unionism and workplace militancy represented a central aspect of working at Ford, Dagenham. The militant collective culture at Ford and social practices that went with it – electing shop stewards, attending meetings, voting and going on strike – were accepted as a normal part of their work experience and not considered extraordinary – both retrospectively and at the time. This stands in contrast to popular narratives that characterise the 1960s and 70s as a period when unruly unions and working class greed caused economic decline. Such accounts appear to imagine trade unions as opaque institutions with tyrant leaders and fail to recognise the values, ideas and identities of the individual people involved seeking to improve their working conditions.

Secondly, Goldie accounts for the sewing-machinists' initial interpretation of the strike as a defeat and the limited impact of the dispute on the lives of the women involved. There was a divergence between the public memory of the strike as a milestone event in the evolution of the women's movement, and the sewing-machinists' self-understanding over 'what they had done'. In 1972, socialist-feminist activist and historian Sheila Rowbotham suggested the sewing-machinists had provoked women on the left to 'feel that they could do something' and made it easier for women within trade unions to discuss women's specific oppression.[8] By contrast, a former worker said to me in an interview: 'Speaking honestly, it was just like another day's work and then we just carried on... Nothing changed for us. Being honest... I didn't think that we achieved all that much until everything that's happened'.[9]

This raises a significant tension with the historical meaning of the dispute. On the one hand, the strike is a great example of people making change from below: the strike stimulated a significant debate about equal pay in the labour movement, and its impact upon equality legislation and the origins of second-wave feminism is undeniable. On the other hand, the former sewing-machinists interpretation of the strike as a defeat illustrates the ineffectiveness of the strike's resolution and how the government, company and unions involved militated against them to preserve the interests of capital and male workers in the factory. The value of their work was not recognised until 1985.

It is important not to downplay the importance of the sewing-machinists' activism and its impact on forcing the government to address the issue of equal pay, yet to celebrate it as a victory of and for 'all' woman and 'all' workers side-lines the protagonists' own reading of events and continues to deny their specific agency in the present.

Notes

1. J. Friedman and S. Meredeen, *The Dynamics of Industrial Conflict: Lessons from Ford,* (Croom Helm, 1980) p. 1.

2. *Ibid.* p. 96.

3. T. Brown and B. Vidal (eds.), *The Biopic in Contemporary Film Culture,* (Routledge, 2014), pp. 11-13.

4. G. Gall, 'Women didn't just strike in Dagenham', *The Guardian,* 4 October 2010.

5. M. Paton, 'The Dagenham Girls: Meet four friends whose crusading work inspired a new film', *The Daily Mail,* 11 September 2010.

6. Interview with Lil O'Callaghan and Rose Boland in Friedman and Meredeen, *Dynamics*, p. 176.

7. Interview with Gwen, Eileen, Sheila and Vera, 21st June 2013.

8. Sheila Rowbotham, 'The Beginnings of Women's Liberation in Britain', in *Dreams and Dilemmas: Collected Writings* (Virago, 1983), pp. 33-34.

9. Interview with Eileen and Gwen, 11 August 2015.

Inner State

Irfan Master

Dawn

THE STREET LAMPS IN Southall flicker then flash then die as dawn unravels, solemn, silent. And silence makes the most of this moment, stretching its arms, enveloping the streets and for the briefest of moments, Southall is safe. A catch of breath before the first pan is scraped on the stove, the first eggs cracked, the first cry of a hungry child, the first embrace of husband and wife, the first song heard on the radio. Tired streets, old roads, weary avenues waking to lorries lumbering slow on Dominion Road, to a thousand voices speaking in tongues foreign and fantastic. A sudden crash, milk bottles, scuttles the silence away, the broken glass, the spilt milk, the shock of sound brings a violence to the day that is unexpected.

The light, when it comes is mottled and reluctant to offer its true nature. A woman, sari-bound, shuffles across the pavement stopping at each shop front to whisper a prayer of protection, willing the glass to hold. The unwilling light follows in her wake, painting its own picture, settling on roofs. A safe distance from what is to come. In a low-ceilinged factory, a man flicks on a switch and a loom kicks up, the shuttle relaying too quickly until the thread snaps. The man swears, shutting the loom down, and starts the long process of removing broken threads.

And here we come to rest, a woman with tired eyes gently guiding her son along the street, coaxing him to keep up,

313

whispering to him to be careful in the world the light and silence has created.

As dawn hastily leaves to settle on some other place less heavy with portent, the people wake, unaware of the battle between light and dark, sound and silence.

Southall wakes.

Dominion Theatre, 12 June 1979

Manjeet stood in line patiently, moving forward one short step at a time. The long line wound its way out of the theatre and spilled onto Dominion Road. A hum of prayer settled on the gathering and, lulled by the low cadence, Manjeet swayed with the crowd. Looking over his shoulder, he saw specks of saffron, white and yellow, leading all the way down the road. The turbans flickered, small flames blurring against the grey sky. He touched his own turban and grimaced. His mother had laid it out on his bed that morning, starched and ready to wear. Folding the stiff material in his hands, it had taken him three attempts to tie it. It seemed to weigh heavier than he remembered. He was just reaching the threshold of the Dominion Theatre when he hesitated. What was he doing there? What was it he wanted to say? Or do? He felt a hand on his shoulder and turned to see an elderly man smile at him. He was wearing a white turban, and the absence of colour in the crisp, unbleached material startled Manjeet. Made him self-conscious of his deep saffron. The colour of blood.

The old man, sharp, alert, noticed.

'I am past colour, my child. White is easier for an old man like me. I was angry too, once. Rebellious, wanting to burn bright. Now, I don't mind glowing dimly.'

'Saffron doesn't feel right today. It's too rich,' said Manjeet shaking his head, embarrassed.

'Maybe that's precisely why it's right.'

'Why are you standing here? Why am I, for that matter?' Manjeet replied, turning to leave.

'To pay our respects,' the old man intoned. 'It's important.'

'He's dead. He can't hear our respects. Why else?' asked Manjeet taking a step over the threshold.

'To bear witness,' said the old man putting a gentle arm around Manjeet.

'I'm struggling to bear it,' said Manjeet looking at his feet, unable to look at the photograph of Blair that was in the foyer.

'Courage. We must bear it.'

'I walked past him. He was alive. He was smiling. And then everything happened,' said Manjeet touching his turban, reliving the moment.

Gently shepherding Manjeet over the threshold, the old man nodded, 'Tell me. What happened?'

★

Manjeet walked along The Broadway, carrier bag in one hand. Tall, trousers already too small, ankles exposed. 'Stick to the back streets,' his brother Rana had said. 'Stay away from the Town Hall. Don't get involved. Run if you see a blue uniform.' Alright for him to say. Manjeet knew where his brother would be. In the thick of it, giving those fascists hell. Loud, angry, strong. Why couldn't Manjeet be a part of it? Southall born and bred, he'd barely left the borough in his fourteen years. Rana had always kept him away from any aggro. He'd never seen these fascists up close. He wanted to see what the fuss was about. He was miles away from the action. Taking a left onto Norwood Road, Manjeet walked toward the high street. It felt different, the air, the colour of everything. He noticed that he was gripping the carrier bag too tight and took a breath to release some tension. A fluttering flash of blue and red caught his eye and made him stop. On top of the council building was the Union Jack. St George's day. The flag looked pristine. The colours insultingly bright. As Manjeet had stopped, so did others and each one noticed the flag. A splinter lodged in the translucence of the sky.

It was noon, and already there were vans everywhere. Full

of police. Waiting. There were people everywhere too. People from everywhere. What did these people care about Southall? Why had they come all this way to a world that wasn't their own?

As he started getting closer to the town hall, the crowds swelled. There were police in large numbers lining the road. A dark wall of grim faces, tense bodies. Already small groups of elders were trying to talk to senior members of the police whilst the younger ones were waiting, standing off, bristling.

Manjeet moved closer to the growing crowds and searched the faces for Rana. He knew his brother would be annoyed with him for coming so close to the action, but Manjeet felt compelled to see. To understand why a group of people who hated him and his people wanted to hold a meeting here in Southall. He couldn't spot Rana and stepped back from the street. That's when Manjeet sensed it. A feeling of dread. The air close, stifling, still. Southall was holding its breath. Manjeet's palms felt clammy and he switched the carrier bag to his other hand, swearing under his breath, annoyed at his mother for asking him to go to the shop on this day of all days. His eyes blurred. The blue, the dark ominous block of colour the police wore, seemed to multiply and to organise itself into lines and grids, creating around itself a negative space. No mans land. An invitation – in the form of a blue wall – for the bustling crowd to try and scale.

Some of the elders were stepping back from the frontline. Something in the way they moved suggested they had seen this before. Their old bones remembered. Some others held up their arms, placating, trying to reason with the officers in charge. Manjeet couldn't read lips, but he could read two opposing views. He could read the anger in the crowd, as those elders still at the front pleaded with the officers to call the meeting off. And he could read the stubbornness, the set of the jaw of the officer in charge. Manjeet's ears began to close off the world around him and only pick up the sound of his own heart. A fist thumping against his chest from the inside. He looked across at the lines of young Asian men and saw fury. This would not stand, their clenched fists said. Even the elders who were trying to mediate shook their heads, resigned knowing that this community had reached its limit. Manjeet saw the crowd ripple, as if a long fuse had been lit from a distance. Behind the police, in the space they had created around the entrance to the town hall, a small handful of men and women appeared. They raised their fists at the crowd, smiling in their direction, a couple lifting their arms in short sharp motions aping the Nazi salute. This was it? This small gathering, less than a hundred! Manjeet noted the smug faces, swaggering, self-assured and totally safe. They looked so... ordinary. On the walk here, Manjeet had made monsters of these men. Contorted faces, tall as trees, wild eyes, barbed skin, clawed hands, but these were men he saw on the streets every day. Ordinary. Men he saw driving buses, selling fruit, council men, teachers at his school, police. And this, more than anything filled Manjeet with fear. Monsters, he could spot a mile off and avoid. But ordinary people, living alongside him, walking down the streets, going about their lives, and all the while with this inside them. This rage and anger towards him, his family, his people. Manjeet stepped back from the fray, the realisation filled him with so much panic, it made him stagger. As the members of the National Front walked into the town hall, he felt a wave of frustration crash forwards from the front line, exploding against the shield wall.

The police lines broke and charged the protesters where they stood. Batons and shields raised, the blue block surged against the amassed crowd. Manjeet heard the sharp clap of hooves on concrete and, out of the confusion and mass of bodies trying to get away, horses charged and on them men with heavy truncheons. For a moment, Manjeet stood and observed the chaos objectively. He was not really there, none of them were. Manjeet didn't move an inch. Like a pebble on the ocean bed, he felt the force of water sweep over him. Through a break in the crowd, he glimpsed a woman, dressed in a white shalwar kameez sitting on the floor, refusing to move. An older boy hurtled past him and grabbed Manjeet by the collar, dragging him along. He was propelled from his reverie into a sprint, heading for an alleyway. Manjeet looked back for the woman in white, but she was gone. The older boy looked over at Manjeet as he ran and shook his head.

'What's wrong with you? Standing there like that?'

'I didn't think they were after me.'

'It doesn't matter does it. You're in the way. You've got a big red turban on your head. Like baiting a bull. You know they can't see anything else.'

'Where are we going?'

'Away from the action. The SPG are on the prowl,' said the boy, shivering.

'Who are the SPG?'

'Special Patrol Group. You'll know them when you see them. Big bastards. They kick first, ask questions later. If you see one, don't hang around like back there. They're not interested in having a chat. Find a safe spot and stay there until things calm down. One thing we've got over them is we know these back streets. Home advantage, isn't it.'

'Doesn't much feel like home today,' said Manjeet doing his best to keep up. The boy looked at him properly, slowing his pace. The high street was far behind them now, as they picked their way through residential backstreets. Manjeet walked past houses seeing anxious faces in windows.

'Are you Rana's kid brother?'

'Yeah. Manjeet.'

Chuckling to himself and pulling Manjeet with him, he said: 'He's going to kill you, man.'

'Not if the police get me first.'

The spill from the town hall went in all directions – police horses charging to clear a path, followed by hundreds of officers hitting, grabbing and wrestling men, then marching them away to waiting vans. As the second wave of police charged, the violence reached into the back streets. This time Manjeet didn't stand around staring, but jumped over a garden fence and took cover. In these quieter streets, the atmosphere was different. Manjeet could taste blood in his mouth and spat. He'd bitten his tongue as he'd leapt the fence and a bitter taste swirled around his mouth. From behind the fence, he heard rushing feet and a shout. Looking through a gap, he saw a man stumble to the ground and a police officer standing over him. Only he wasn't dressed like a normal officer with the usual dark blue uniform. He was tall, wearing heavy boots, a padded jacket and he didn't move like the others either. The fallen man held up his hands and stayed kneeling. Grabbing the man by his shirt, the plain-clothes officer punched him repeatedly in the head and, when he buckled, kicked him in the stomach, continuing to kick him until the man stopped moving. Manjeet stopped breathing. He shifted his weight snapping a twig underfoot and saw the helmeted head turn. Crawling back away from the fence, Manjeet clambered up a wall and broke into a sprint as he landed in a side alley, desperate to get some distance between him and the dark blur he still sensed behind him. People were running down the street ahead of him, but it felt as if the numbers were dwindling, so he slowed his pace, the carrier bag still in his hand. He took a right onto Beechcroft Avenue, where it felt like people had chosen to take refuge. Manjeet scanned the street – a row of blocky terraced houses on either side – and saw mostly strangers. It was an ordinary street where most days, nothing much happened. He took in the faces and walked past a small group sitting on the kerb. They were talking amongst themselves. One of them, a tall man, noticed Manjeet's enquiring eyes and smiled at him. But the smile stopped short of reaching up to his eyes.

Heavy boots thundering into the quiet street broke the eye contact. He felt them before he saw them, like an icy hand on his shoulder. Manjeet didn't even turn to look. He just ran, his long strides taking him further down the street. Don't look back! Don't look back! Turning a corner at speed, he crashed into what felt like a brick wall. He landed hard on this knees and struggled to get up. A police officer stood calmly in front of him. Face covered, wearing a padded jacket, it was what rested in his hand that really caught Manjeet's attention. He'd seen a lot of the police officers wielding standard issue coshes before, but this looked different. It was thicker, longer, heavier. Like a pipe. The heavyset police officer was also different. There was no anger in his eyes, just a brutal reckoning. A familiarity with the weapon in his hand and his right to wield it. As he saw the weapon swing towards him, Manjeet held up his hands weakly in surrender.

The thick lead pipe swung and caught Manjeet across the top of his skull. He was already ducking when it made contact but sensed the blow knock him to the ground. He felt his turban slip off his head and unravel as he fell, the dark saffron unfurling and spooling around the officer's feet. The carrier bag he'd been lugging around all day left his grasp and split sending its contents across the dull grey slabs of the pavement. Reaching up to touch his skull, Manjeet expected a bloody mess, but there was nothing. The turban had taken the brunt of the swing. Deflated, scared, helpless, Manjeet dropped to his knees, his long black hair unravelling in a slow pirouette that transfixed the officer. On the floor between the officer and Manjeet hundreds of brown grains of rice were scattered, falling into the gutter, crunching under the officer's feet.

*

The old man listened. Age had taught him patience. He looked at the young boy in front of him, saw the tremor in his hands and heard the rawness of his voice. He had been a soldier in India before he had come to the UK. He had seen violence and heard death whisper in his ear more than once, so he knew the look in the boys eyes. He had stood back that day and watched as things unravelled, and despite the horror and tragedy of it, he had also seen the passion with which the community had spoken as one. They had felt humiliated, ignored. After years of trying to ignore the worst of the insults, they had made a stand.

To stop hate from assembling on their doorstep. To stop bigots smirking in their faces one too many times. To stop the police from siding with those who believed they did not belong.

'I could have died. The turban saved me. I could be lying there too. I saw him. I saw Blair in the moments before I was hit. We were probably both struck at the same time, but I survived. Why?'

'To live. To speak out against this sort of thing. This violence, this hate.'

'But now I hate them. I want to hurt them.'

'That won't make you feel better, my son.'

'What do you think he wanted? Blair, I mean.'

'I know very little about him, but we are here as witnesses to his life. I have heard he was a teacher at a primary school. I guess he wanted to change things.'

'Do you think it will? Change things?'

The old man looked at Manjeet and smiled. He did not believe it would change things. It might make people pay attention, but it wouldn't change things. They would not apologise, they would not accept responsibility. There would be no justice. Not for Blair and not for others like him to come. He considered sparing Manjeet these thoughts, lying to him, but the bruised look in the boy's eyes stopped him.

'No, it won't,' the old man said. 'It won't change anything.'

Manjeet flinched at his bluntness.

'But it will make us stronger,' he added.

'What will I say to him?'

The old man put a hand on the small of Manjeet's back and gently led him into the room where Blair was lying in state.

Manjeet stood beside the coffin staring at a point on the wall opposite. There were some men ushering people in and out of the hall, while women in the corner prayed – a low cadence that set the tone for the space, over which no one raised their voice. Manjeet switched his attention to his shoes. The old man squeezed his shoulder and moved away.

'I wanted to come today. I wanted to see you. I wanted to

say something that meant something. But now that I'm here, I'm not sure I have anything to say. I was there. I saw you. I ran past you. I don't know why I was even there. I just wanted to see. Everybody told me to stay at home, but I wanted to see the hate for myself. But that's not all I saw. That was only a part of it. A small part. I saw something else too. People from everywhere came to Southall, for us. People came from different parts of the country, a lot of them weren't even allowed in. People came to stand alongside us and say that we wouldn't allow hate to organise in our own backyard. People from everywhere, people like you. There was no victory that day, no winning. You died, and there was nothing in the world to celebrate. We had to make a stand, but the cost was too high. I wanted to say that, to let you know that even if they never admit their responsibility. Even if they never hear our voices in the courts, even if those who murdered you are never brought to justice. We will never forget you. Your name is with us now. Forever.'

Manjeet finally looked at Blair's face, and without a moment's hesitation, he began to unravel his turban. His hands moved quickly to gather the material, roll the cotton up and hold it for a moment. Taking one last look at Blair, Manjeet lay the dark saffron turban on top of the coffin and walked from the hall.

*

Midnight

Southall staggers, punch drunk. Bandage and gauze hastily swaddled on tired and bruised limbs. Silence reigns but for the static from a thousand radios. Waves that bring bad tidings. Of one lost. One not of them, but who will now always be with them. A chain of prayers for Southall mourns as the longest day turns into the longest night. Tears muffled in bloodied handkerchiefs, candles flickering in the cold places, in the old places, mouths opening, closing in testimony to a life lived and lost. The beginning of songs, 'Southall Kids are Innocent', 'Reggae fi Peach' already written in waking nightmares, as Southall weeps.

The silence is complete. Broken buildings keep their own secrets, empty streets hushed, the long limbs of lampposts bowing, swaying, blinking light filled tears for the day, for the night. The story spreads. Of protest, of resistance, of gods and children. Southall is closed for business, open for justice. Closed for the night, open for the unforeseeable future.

It stops. Silence imposes its will on the borough. In a bid to start the healing, start the grieving, the silence is a clamp. A litany of whispered complaints lost in the darkness. Nothing to see here. Nothing to witness. Nothing of note. Silence claims all. The baby hushed in its crib, the wounded man's cuts treated, the youths, fire spent, herded into safe houses, the death of a man signed and delivered and sworn to secrecy, the story already written, a sign of the times, and in the span of years, in the distance from death to truth, the cloud of silence takes all.

Afterword: What Free Speech Needs Martial Law?

David Renton

ON THE EVENING OF 23 April 1979, more than 2,800 police officers, 94 of them on horseback, confronted an anti-fascist protest outside Southall Town Hall, in order to protect a meeting taking place within that building for a National Front election candidate. By the end of the night, 700 protesters had been arrested, of whom 340 were charged, mostly with public order offences. Sixty-four people were receiving treatment for injuries at the hands of police officers, including several with headwounds. And one anti-fascist demonstrator, a New Zealand-born schoolteacher, Blair Peach, was dead.

Perhaps the strangest thing about the fighting was the near invisibility of its seeming protagonists: the two dozen or so members of the National Front. One NF speaker, Joe Pearce, records in his memoir, 'I was shuttled to Southall Town Hall, the location for the meeting, with a large police escort. As I gave my speech, I could hear a riot outside.'[1] Clips survive of the NF's supporters descending from their shuttle bus, waving their right hands briefly in the direction of the television crews, and then striding into the town hall, out of sight of the anti-fascist demonstrators. The protection of the bus and the police was needed because in the days leading up to 23 April, the people of Southall had demonstrated peacefully and in huge numbers against the National Front. There had been a public meeting against them, several hundred strong, and a march against them on the previous weekend before with 5,000 people taking part.

That demonstration – in common with the crowd on 23 March 1979 – was largely composed of first and second generation British Asian men and women, many but not all of them of Punjabi Sikh heritage. In the popular culture of the time, Sikhs were timid and deferential: the turbaned natives of *It Ain't Half Hot Mum*. The real-life people of Southall were rather better equipped to deal with the Front's racist threat.

The largest community organisation in this part of West London, the Indian Workers' Association (IWA), had been set up by supporters of the Communist Party of India. Its historian, John De Witt, estimates that by 1966 more than half of all Punjabi-born men in Southall were members of the IWA. Thirteen years later, the IWA remained a formidable presence, its members steeped in a tradition of political radicalism and a memory of colonialism and of anti-colonial struggle. They were part of a black working class and living in a decade of trade union struggles. Not only were the shops of central Southall closed on 23 April but so were a number of local factories: Ford's truck plant at Langley, Sunblest bakery, Wall's and Quaker Oats.

The events at Southall represented a collision between a radical black community and official opinion which may well have distrusted the Front but preferred nonetheless their right to speak over the rights of local residents to live without fear.

This part of West London had long been a target for the far right: a successful election campaign in 1964, when the British National Party's John Bean stood for election in the constituency and came third with 9% of the vote, had been a key moment leading to the adoption of an electoral strategy across the British right, and the formation of the Front in 1967 as a coalition of Britain's hostile and fissiparous far-right parties.

In 1976, a sixteen year-old man, Gurdip Singh Chaggar, had

been stabbed and killed in Southall by two white men, Jody Hill and Robert Hackman. Within days of Chaggar's death, a Southall Youth Movement was launched at the Dominion Theatre.

The younger generation in Southall may have learned from their elders a tradition of protest, but they were trying to create yet more radical forms of struggle, and this inter-generational conflict could be seen on the 23 April. The IWA was preparing for a National Front meeting which was due to take place in the evening. As the day wore on, and the scale of the police preparations became evident, the older generation urged anti-fascists to be patient. The younger generation were, however, unwilling to wait.

Stories circulated from house to house, warning that the police were planning to get around the sit-in by smuggling National Front members into the town hall early. Members of the Southall Youth Movement began to assemble outside there from around noon. Balraj Purewal of the Youth Movement led a march along South Road to the town centre. According to one participant interviewed by the BBC, 'This is our future, right? Our leaders will do nothing... our leaders wanted a peaceful sit down but what can you do with a peaceful sit down here? We had to do something, the young people.'

Before 7:30pm, police tactics focused on controlling the streets immediately surrounding Southall Town Hall. Anti-fascists tried to guard the areas just beyond the police lines. Peter Baker was with them, 'A roar went through the crowd. People turned and looked westwards down the street. I saw, to my amazement, a coach being driven fast straight into the back of the crowd. At a cautious estimate, I would put the speed of it at 15 m.p.h., which is murderous when it is being driven into a crowd.'

Once the police had forced a way through for the National Front coach, their tactics changed and their objective became the dispersal of the remaining crowd from the vicinity of the Town Hall. Balwinder Rana was the chief steward on the anti-fascist side, 'The police used horses. They drove vans into the crowd, and fast, to push us back. They used snatch squads. People rushed back with whatever they could pick up.'

During the evening of 23 April, three main groups were the victims of aggressive policing. First, many people were arrested for being on the protest. A large number were teenagers. Several were simply abandoned by the police in the roads beyond West London and told to make their own way home. In the days that followed they suffered a particularly aggressive form of summary justice, with Ealing magistrates convicting at unprecedented rates. The following report, in the *Guardian*, was typical: 'A 14-year-old Sikh boy appeared before a magistrate at Ealing juvenile court. He had been charged with "threatening behaviour" and being in possession of "offensive weapons" at 6.20pm on 23 April 1979... [A] white doctor, a white solicitor and a white ambulance man... all testified that the boy, at the time, was being treated for a hand wound and had suffered a severe loss of blood... The boy was found guilty and fined £100.'

Second, police officers broke into the Peoples Unite building which was being used as a medical centre to treat wounded anti-racists. Dozens of eye-witnesses complained that police officers aimed their batons at the heads of doctors, nurses and solicitors, as well as the protesters who had sheltered there. Clarence Baker, the manager of reggae band Misty and the Roots, was among those hit on the head by a police baton. He was so badly hurt that he spent five months in a coma.

Annie Nehmad, a doctor helping as a volunteer in the centre, recalls treating the wounded, including one man Narvinder Singh who had a three-inch wound in his right hand following a police attack. As the police came closer, she saw people running in the street outside and closed the windows and the door. The police demanded to be allowed in. Attempts were made to keep the door closed before the police succeeded in kicking the door in. She and a nurse were forced from the room. Nehmad herself, although identifying herself to the police as a doctor, was struck on the back of her head. So heavy were the blows that she stumbled and had to be rescued by other demonstrators. Looking back on the events, Nehmad insists that 'On 23 April, not only were heavier than normal truncheons used but police throughout the demo used these heavy truncheons to hit people on the head. Someone somewhere must have said this was OK. Someone somewhere was prepared to see people killed on a demo in Britain.'

Also caught up in the events at Southall on 23 April was Blair Peach, a teacher at the Phoenix School in East London for children with special needs. Twice in 1978-9 he had been attacked by supporters of the Front as he cycled home from teaching at the Phoenix School and suffered black eyes and cuts to his hands.

On the fateful evening, Blair Peach travelled to Southall with a group of friends, Jo Lang, Amanda Leon, Martin Gerald and Françoise Ichard. He was part of the crowd that tried and failed to block the Front's coach from entering the town hall. Shortly before 8pm Peach was on Beachcroft Avenue, where he was attacked by a member of the police's Special Patrol Group and struck on the head – either by a police radio or by some unauthorised weapon. Another police officer Constable Scottow saw Peach stumbling after the blow. Scottow shouted at him to move on. After being taken in by a local family, the Atwals, Peach died in hospital, shortly after midnight.

The Special Patrol Group was a mobile unit within the Metropolitan Police Service, and was used against large demonstrations, such as the one at Southall. After Peach's death, Ken Gill of the Trades Union Congress spoke at his funeral telling the 15,000 mourners that the SPG must be disbanded, 'Every one of us must take up this call.'

As part of the police investigation into Peach's killing, the lockers belonging to the half dozen SPG officers who had been in Peach's vicinity when he was struck were raided. Some 26 unofficial weapons were found, including a leather-covered stick, two knives, a large truncheon, a crowbar, a metal cosh, a whip and a whip handle. The fatal wound had been large – larger, the pathologists advised than an ordinary truncheon – but had not broke Peach's skin, as a wooden truncheon would have done. But the discovery of these weapons raised wider questions even than Peach's death. How was it possible for officers to go on demonstrations with their own private weapons such as coshes or knives?

Peach's death is remembered, among lawyers, for the manifest injustice of the inquest, and above all for the refusal of the Coroner John Burton to permit the jurors to read the report of the inquiry which had identified the probable culprit for Peach's death, or to allow Peach's family or their lawyers to know that one had been found. Three decades would pass before the report was finally disclosed.

Blair Peach was a socialist, an anti-racist, and an English teacher in his thirties who had fought all his adult life against an almost-disabling stutter. Singers Linton Kwesi Johnson, Mike Carver, Hazel O'Connor and Ralph McTell all released songs commemorating Peach's death. He has also been remembered by other writers: Chris Searle, Edward Bond, Michael Rosen, Louis Johnson, Sean Hutton, Tony Dickens and Siegfried Moos all published poems in his memory.

Peach was a deeply private person, more comfortable in political rather than literary circles. No more than one or two of these writers can have known that in his youth Blair Peach had also been a poet. At the University of Wellington he had helped to edit a literary magazine *Argot*. Against the overwhelming horror of his untimely death perhaps a tiny satisfaction can be found in the way he has been remembered since: by the people of Southall as a man who fought alongside them, and by his fellow writers.

Note

1. This chapter is an abbreviated and rewritten version of the relevant chapter from David Renton's book, *Never Again: Rock Against Racism and the Anti-Nazi League 1976-1982* (Routledge, 2018). Full references are provided there.

THE LIVERPOOL DOCKERS DISPUTE, 1995-98

¡No Pasarán!

Lucas Stewart

North America, 15 December 1995, 8.04am

'GOD BLESS YOU BOYS, but I haven't got a clue what I'm doing?'

'Who the hell is that, lid?' Jam Jar asked, 'Is that the Bishop?

'They're trying to get the radio working,' Peter Pan answered.

'I've never done this before,' a second voice came. 'Can they hear us?'

'That'll be The Virgin,' Jam Jar said, unclipping the mobile transceiver, 'Oy, Gary, wrong channel, lid!'

'Is this thing even working? Fuck sake, Rob, am talking to myself here. How's them down there supposed to know what we doing?'

There was no answer.

'Try again,' Peter Pan said.

Jam Jar clicked to another channel, 'No one can hear you except us, lid.'

The two men waited and heard nothing except more cursing.

'I fucking hate heights,' Peter Pan muttered.

'We know, lid,' Jam Jar answered. 'Everyone knows, "He 'aint no Peter Pan." That's what everyone said first day you came on the books. Who ever heard of a docker afraid of heights?'

'Then what am I doing up here?' Peter Pan peered through

the thickened windows of the box at the top of the port control tower. Steel booms leered over the wharf below though neither men could see the cradle lines and hooks as a curtain of sleet crossed over them.

Somewhere below them, standing too, floating unsure, untied, unable to berth and held in place by a single tug, was The Poseidon.

The curtain drew back for a brief moment.

'That's why, lid,' Jam Jar said. 'Those pickets at home aren't working, we all know that. I've been in many fights, but none has gone on as long as this, nearly three months already. Alan was right, if we can't hurt them at the Port, then we hurt them abroad.'

Peter Pan raised the collar of his coat around the nape of his neck and sunk lower into the plastic seat. Flecks of ice lacerated the box.

'I know that. I was at the shop stewards meeting. What I meant is: why aren't I down there? John-Michael must need some help.'

'He knows what he's doing. Like he said last night: pick up the gear, line up for the muster, go through the gates, don't say a word, get up the control tower. He'll do the rest. Police will come soon, no doubt. Some reporter from the local rag is down there too, John-Michael promised.'

'So we just sit here and wait till then?' Peter Pan rubbed his gloved hands together. 'I'm just saying it's baltic up here.'

'You're not on your jollies, lid, nevermind what some of them back home are saying. Every minute, every hour we stay up here is costing them money. Lads below 'aint going anywhere. That scab ship won't be worked on as long as we are up here and...'

Jam Jar leant forward and heaved. He coughed, gasped then spat on the metal floor.

'You good?' Peter Pan asked, shifting in his seat to give Jam Jar more space in the box. Though Peter Pan was taller, he was also thin and his narrow shoulders and slight legs could turn and twist in the box more easily that the shorter and heavier man next to him.

'Like you said. It's the cold, lid. Nothing more.'

Jam Jar sat back in the plastic chair and wiped his mouth clean of the spittle that had caught on his chin. The two men sat in silence.

'You got that letter?' Jam Jar asked Peter Pan.

'Not opened yet, she told me to not to until it was time.'

'Time's now, lid.'

Peter Pan reached into the pockets of his trousers. The single piece of paper had curled and creased in the days since he had left Liverpool. He had kept his promise and not looked at it.

'Read it to me,' Jam Jar said. 'It'll be good to hear her.'

Peter Pan took the paper from his pocket. It was still dark so he held the letter close. He thought, just for a moment, that she was there with him, somehow, in the way the paper was folded – as small as possible, five times or more – so that it couldn't unfurl accidentally, just as her notes to him at school had been. He peeled apart the layers, one by one, and Lynn came again, quicker this time, until a wind, having skulked till now, suddenly tore her away.

'Read it, lid.'

'I know you haven't gone yet, but we already miss you. Christmas won't be the same. Sian will ask for you. I don't know what to tell her. She is young. Some are saying we shouldn't say anything, but she learnt to read between the lines before she learnt to read. She knows something is different. This is why you are there, don't forget that, for her and us. I don't know what to do. You have gone and I'm here. I can't just sit here. Look after him. He's not as strong as he thinks is. This is not like before, when he was younger. Look after him. And yourself.'

Peter Pan folded the paper and slipped it back into his pocket. Jam Jar had closed his eyes. Somewhere below, blue lights flashed and men started shouting.

Liverpool, 25 September 2022, 2.04pm

Sian grinds a cigarette into a plant pot of sand. Though autumn is just around the corner, it is a late summer, and the sun coats the streets in a heat neither women are comfortable with.

'That's my last one, I promise,' she says to Lynn.

Her mother snorts. 'I've heard that before.'

The two women stand outside the Casa. The red brickwork announces its age. Edwardian. A sign, a white five-pointed star on a red background extends over a narrow, split, wood-framed door. To the left of the door is a chalkboard advertising in tidy, white letters appointment times for the next welfare advice officer.

The two women look up and down Hope Street. The Anglican cathedral to the south. The Roman Catholic cathedral to the north. An Amazon drone whirrs nearby then drops into view, landing on the steps of a solicitor's office next door.

'Wonder what they're getting,' Sian asks and peers over the small brick wall.

'Nothing exciting,' Lynn answers, 'divorce papers probably. Or a will.'

The mention of a will stills the two women and they stand in silence. The drone clicks into life, rises and then banks north.

'That's not how I received his,' Lynn says to herself, as the drone passes the Everyman Theatre and skirts around the spired crown of Paddy's Wigwam.

'I Whatsapped him on the way,' Sian says, and slides her Samsung XV out of her pocket, unfurls it and looks at the screen. The phone powers up. 'I'm not changing the subject. I'm just saying, he knows we're here.'

'Lynn takes the phone from Sian's hand, 'I still can't believe you managed to teach him how this works.'

Sian smiles and gently takes the phone back, 'I taught you, didn't I? Anyway, he hasn't replied.'

'He'll come. You know what he's like. He still can't drive past Seaforth without remembering. This anniversary's not helping. I've been hiding the *Echo* from him over the last few weeks. Told him it hadn't been delivered. Thank God no one else is writing about it.'

'You don't mean that'.

'You're right, I don't. Come on, let's go inside. It's too hot out here.'

Asia, 23 April 1996, 11.37am

Ali's office occupied the third floor of a squat four-storey building erected in 1919; the former headquarters of a Scottish-owned company exporting timber, teak, mahogany, sandalwood and the 150 foot hollong mostly. Small shrubs and green shoots sprouted through the exterior red brickwork, crumbled by nearly a century of monsoon rains. Green and black mould crept over the tea shops and notary stands that lived along the edges of the ground floor.

Jam Jar and Peter Pan walked slowly up a staircase, wide with cracked porcelain tiles spiralling around a broken cage-lift, deadened by age and swathed in thin sheets of dust resting on spider webs.

'It's not far now. Just up here, my friends,' Ali said, scratching the hair under his jaw then looking back at his visitors, a few steps behind him. 'My apologies for the lift, we don't have the money to fix it.'

Peter Pan glanced at Jam Jar. He took the steps slowly. His breathing was laboured. It occurred to Peter Pan how much his father-in-law had aged just over the last few months. Lynn blamed his lifestyle, too many cigarettes and not enough walking, but he was walking now and it looked like it was killing him.

The three men passed through a set of double doors and into a wide room. Twelve windows opened on both the east and west sides and though it was nearly midday and the sun was directly above them, it was bright compared to the dull stairway and Peter Pan blinked and let his eyes adjust. A silent group of men sat at tables arranged along the centre of the room facing south to a small dias backed by red curtains and a wooden seal hanging above: a dockers hook, bent with its cylindrical grip intertwined with motifs and a script Peter Pan didn't recognise. One by one, Ali, through a translator, introduced the gathered men who now stood, dipped their heads and extended their hands to the two dockers from Liverpool. The seniors came first, their names and positions, and Peter Pan nodded, trying as best he could, to remember their names and faces.

Lines, drawn by marbles of sweat, raced down Peter Pan's chest, some quicker than others, darkening his shirt. He looked down, uncomfortable with the stain that had grown around his stomach. He placed his right hand over the mark, growing, in his imagination, every second he stood there and hoped no one would notice.

'I was one of 50 men who refused to work on a ship unless we were paid the overtime we were due. We were sacked that morning in the canteen. Another 300 men were ordered to work the ship, my father-in-law among them...'

Thirty-one heads waited for the interpreter to finish and turned to Jam Jar who nodded but said nothing. Peter Pan continued. He spoke one sentence at a time, giving the interpreter time to consider and speak himself:

'They refused to take jobs away from their sons, their nephews, their family. They were sacked too. All we want is our jobs back.'

'First Liverpool', a voice came, stilted, excited, as if he was surprised he spoke, 'then us'.

'It's true my friends,' Ali said, sitting in a mustard-stained chair at the front of the gathered.

Ali continued. A call to action. A stoppage of all ships loaded in scab ports in the UK that made their way east. Union members would wear badges signifying their intent. The design to be decided at a later meeting. Further meetings would be held. Resolutions would be passed in support of their brothers in Liverpool. Donations given for their families.

Peter Pan turned to Jam Jar, 'I bet you never saw anything like this back in the day, eh?'

The ceiling fans above Jam Jar swirled then halted. A dense air hung and wrapped around Jam Jar, layer upon layer, stifling, suffocating.

He propped his arms on the chair-rests and rested his head close to Peter Pan's shoulder and gasped, 'I think I need to leave, lid.'

Peter Pan placed his right hand on Jam Jar's shoulder, 'What's wrong?

'Nothing,' Jam Jar said, gripping his son's left hand. 'It's probably the heat. Yeh, that's it. It's too hot. Am tired as well. It was a long flight. I just need to cool down somewhere.'

Jam Jar rose and the rest of the room stood up with him. Peter Pan motioned to Ali with his closed hand raised twice to his lips. His dad needed a drink. That was all.

The corridor was cooler. A wind blew, pulled through the narrow walls. Jam Jar sat on the floor. Peter Pan stood over him, unsure of what to do. Someone, though he forgot who, had given Jam Jar a cup of water, but the water was warm. Jam Jar drank it but it was not enough. His face was pale. He ducked his head between his knees, his mouth open, loose. Peter Pan squatted beside him and rubbed Jam Jar's back, just as he did whenever Sian was unwell. He was sure it would make no difference, but there was nothing else he could think to do.

'I'm sorry,' a voice said from above the two of them, 'but a fax has come for you.'

'I'll read it later,' Peter Pan said, without even looking at the curled scroll Ali held.

Jam Jar raised his head. He spoke, though his voice was thick and lumpen: 'You need to read that. Jimmy and Chris are on their way to Nagoya. It might be important, lid.'

Peter Pan stood and took the fax from Ali.

Hi Love,

I don't know if you will get this. Ricky at the Merseyside Trade Union office helped me. He said the machine will get this to you, but I don't know. I hope you got there alright. Sian asked me where you are. I showed her a map. Even I don't believe it. How's the weather? What are you eating? I was on the radio the other day, City FM. Didn't know I could do it. But I had to. Some idiot was on saying us lot had to get with the times. It's a different world and all that. Like the Port is dead. The Port is the heart of Liverpool. If the Port is dead, then Liverpool's dead.

Some journalist from down south was listening. Spoke to Alan, said she had heard about the Women of the Waterfront movement and wants to help us in dealing with the media, you know, like what to say, how the papers will try and spin it. We're meeting next week.

Sian is good. I tell her everything now, like we agreed. Some of the other mothers don't agree. They reckon politicising the kids is bad for them, like they don't know what is happening anyway! She's been talking about you to her mates at school. Her and the other kids, Maureen's son, Caroline's twins. Don't know what their teachers' think. She misses you. We all do. How is he? He looked different last time I saw him home. He was thinner. Does he know yet?

Peter Pan rolled the paper up and handed it back to Ali. He looked down at Jam Jar,

'Well,' Jam Jar asked, 'what does it say?'

Peter Pan paused and looked to Ali. He nodded and walked away.

'Nothing,' Peter Pan said crouching down, 'It's nothing important.'

Liverpool, 25 September 2022, 2.17pm

It's cooler inside. The bar is quiet. Two students from the nearby School of English sit on a table towards the back. Alex, the

Casa's day manager, is standing by the corner of the bar signing off on casks of beer from a new brewery after her previous supplier refused to honour their promises of overtime pay for their workers.

A mirror lines the bar, and Lynn is reflected next to her daughter. *She looks just like me when I first met him*, Lynn thinks, *and also like him, of course.* Lynn's hair is lighter and shorter than her daughter's, but Sian has his height, and his frame and she turns away from the mirror and looks down ruefully at her own figure and brushes imaginary dots of nothing from her trousers.

'Now then, Lynn,' says an older man in his sixties sitting on a stool at the bar. He knows her. All the men from then who come to the Casa know her, though she doesn't come as often as before. It's harder without him there. It had gone on so long, it had become normal. And then one day it was suddenly all over. A settlement was made. And then what? Pretend the last two and a half years had never happened? Then the Casa opened. A cast-line was thrown and they had both grabbed it. The Casa found what they had lost. A community.

Then he died. And Sian left, went to university somewhere else to become a teacher. So she stopped coming.

Lynn and Sian take a table in the corner, away from the two students and facing the grey entrance doors.

'They've painted it,' Lynn says looking around the room.

'When were you last here?'

'Do you remember the funeral?'

'Of course. I had my first drink that day. I was sixteen.'

Lynn laughs, too loud and places her hand over her mouth in embarrassment, 'That wasn't your first drink.'

'How do you know?'

'Coz them boys from Holland drank the bar dry. There was nothing left after they got here. Good of them to come though. They never forgot.'

'That was over 20 years ago. The Casa was only open a year or two by then. Seriously, Mum, when were you last here?'

Lynn takes a moment.

'Let's see…'

The walls of the Casa hang heavy with memories of those like him, people no different or more important or special than him. To the left, over the tables and chairs, their images framed in black and white. Tokens of their struggle. A leather bag in a glass case. It belongs to a man who showed Liverpool the way. Sculptures nestle in the corners of the ceiling gifted in the guise of a docker from Liverpool, nameless, an everyman.

'… Maureen's 60th, I think. We had drinks in the back.'

The two look at the narrow corridor that splits the main bar area. Lynn knows what lays beyond. An annexe, built after the dockers bought the Casablanca and renamed her the Casa, and a room where people could remember.

But she is not ready to see him.

Not yet.

'Come on, Mum,' Sian says, placing her hand on her mother's knee. 'Let's at least have a look before he comes.'

Europe, 8 August 1997, 10:41pm

The room was dim. Round ceiling lights filtered weakly through separated layers of smoke that grew, light at first to a heavier pall that hung over the bar. Neon lights burned red, green and white for beers Jam Jar and Peter Pan had never heard of. Tables set against long, cushioned pews looked onto a set of a six frosted windows. In the corner hung a dartboard. Outside, though it was August, a rain fell. The street was quiet. A couple of cars parked under yellowed street lamps. Dark, red-brick buildings all boarded up. Garages and store-houses. Beyond, the city's edges grew bright again, as the sea met the land and ships came and went. Peter Pan shifted on his stool.

'What's wrong with you?' Jam Jar asked.

'I don't know. Feels like I've been here before.'

'Been around over the last year or two. How many countries now? Twenty. Twenty-two. You've met them all before. Many came up to Liverpool for the conference in '96.'

'I know, but this is their home turf. You know what I mean? This is their city. But it feels like home.'

Jam Jar smiled. 'There's more in common between us and them than there is between us and lads in Manchester, son. You've seen enough by now. Doesn't matter where you're from. You work the ports, we're brothers.'

'My round,' a voice came from the table the two men sat at.

'Don't be daft,' Peter Pan said rising. 'This one's on me.'

'You see,' Jam Jar called at the back of Peter Pan. 'Ain't no difference.'

Hans wiped speckles of beer from his stubbled cheek with the back of his wrist, 'Jorgen called me in and told me he's not happy you're bypassing them and going straight to the rank and file. You know Jorgen, he got voted on the regional board last year. He told me, twice, we should be nice but to back off.'

'And?' Jam Jar said, sitting back in his chair.

Hans smiled and twisted his palms to the smoky air, 'Fuck them. Comrades don't abandon each other.'

The other men around the table grinned.

'Seriously, though,' Hans continued, his eyes flicking to and from Peter Pan and Jam Jar, 'how much longer can you hold on?'

'As long as it takes,' Jam Jar said.

Peter Pan coughed and shook his head. 'We thought we had them. When C.A.S.T. threatened to pull all their ships from the Port last year. They blinked. But there was no support, mate. Calls were made. People had meetings. And they knew. The Port, the shipping lines, they knew we had no support from the union.'

'What about back home?' Hans asked.

'Nobody cares, do they? Didn't then, don't now.'

'One more push, lid, that's all it'll take,' Jam Jar said, slapping Peter Pan on the back. 'We've already got word from the Swedes, the French and the Italians. Kaliningrad, Mombasa and

Yokohama will support us. Canada, America and South Africa too. They can't sack the whole world. Isn't that right, Hans?'

Hans looked at Jam Jar and nodded, understanding. 'Like you said in the Charter, on the 8th we will stand together.' He thumped his fist on the table. Bottles and glasses wobbled.

'You're right,' Peter Pan said, sitting up in his chair. He shook his head again, as if disagreeing with himself, 'You're fucking right. Next month will show them.' And then, 'Hang on, where are you getting the Charter from?'

'There,' Hans pointed to a computer terminal sitting on a low table next to the bar. 'No-one's got the internet at home yet. I come in here and print out your updates for everyone.'

'You got email on that thing?'

Hans nodded, 'You can check if you want.'

Peter Pan booted the computer up. Only one message was waiting for him:

Hi Love,

How's it going? I hope you got there alright. Did Hans meet you at the terminal? Don't let him keep you up all night. I know what he's like. And don't forget to thank him for what he did last Christmas.

Alan came round yesterday with the books. When W.O.W asked me to be treasurer, I wasn't sure. What do I know about numbers? But Alan's been good. I'm learning and I'm actually good at it. Guess they didn't teach this kind of maths at school. I ran through the figures last night. I don't know how much longer we can go on. Fifty pounds a week doesn't go far and Maureen's on her final demand. If she loses the house, Alan says it's time. Honestly, I agree with him.

Thank God I'm working, it doesn't bring in much, but it's better than nothing. At least Sian has a roof over head and food in her belly.

She's different since you took her to London. That march made her older somehow. She went round Alan's the other day. She asked him why none of the kids get to have their say seeing as they are just as affected as their mums and dads. She said the children should have their own rep. She's got a point. They all come to the Friday meeting, they hear everything, they know what's going on. They're not stupid.

Anyway Alan agreed. They had a vote last night, and Sian was elected. Alan says she can speak at the next action. Apparently Scargill will be there. We'll help her when you get back, of course – what she's going to say and all that – but she says she not scared.

One more thing. I didn't want to, but you said I should. The hospital results came. I opened it. It's not good.

We love you. We wish you were home.

Lynn

Peter Pan considered replying, but what could he say? He had drawn his lines, he had made his stand around the world, but now those lines felt thin and narrow. *It's been too long*, he thought, *this can't go on.*

'Hey,' a voice shouted, 'something is wrong.'

Peter Pan turned, 'What happened?'

Hans shook his head. 'I don't know. He was telling us that story again about the time you both went up a control tower and stopped work on a scab ship for a shift and then he, well, he fell down.'

'It's nothing, lid,' Jam Jar said, his voice weak. He sat on his elbows and raised his head and looked at Peter Pan, 'It's nothing, lid. Too much drink. That's all. Went to my head. Just help me up and I'll be good.'

Several hands grabbed Jam Jar and put him back on his stool.

Peter Pan looked at Jam Jar, 'Perhaps it's time we went home, mate?'

And Jam Jar agreed.

Liverpool, 25 September 2022, 3.36pm

'Sorry about the mess,' Alex says. 'We haven't had time to clear up after last night.'

'Who did you have?' Sian asks.

'A fundraiser for the Taiwan Solidarity Movement. The community's grown over the last year. Since the invasion.'

Alex takes one of the many chairs and lifts it aside. 'We've also got a virtual reality play on tomorrow, local school's putting it on. A wedding tomorrow and you're back next week aren't you, with the National Education Union?'

'Could be a larger crowd than normal,' Sian confirms. 'First Brexit, now Scotland's going independent. We have to know how this is going to affect us. I need to talk to you about that, by the way.'

Alex nods, 'We kept today free. Some of the lads are coming in. They're having drinks in the bar later, if you're interested?'

Sian looks at Lynn.

'I think he would like that,' Lynn says and then looks around the room. 'So where is he?'

'Over here.'

The three women face the north wall of the annexe. Hanging, like bricks one on top of each other, are hundreds of brass plates, each 10 by 5 inches. Stamped on each plate is a memory, of someone, for someone, who stood together at the lines drawn across the world.

Alex slips her hand into Lynn's, 'I know it's not the best, but we've not got much room these days.'

'No, it's perfect. He would want to be there. All of his mates next to him.'

She turns to Sian, 'See, there's John-Michael, "International Longshoremen's Association, Local Chapter 134 – Only the People Matter". He helped your dad get onto that control tower back in '95.'

'Here's Ali,' says Sian, pointing, '"The All Amalgamated Union of General Transport Workers – Unity is Strength". You remember when he came back from that trip? He was so fired up, talked about nothing but Ali for weeks.'

'Where's Hans?' Lynn asks and scans the wall, 'Oh, there he is "Hans Beckmann – No Surrender". I still can't believe he sent over those food boxes at Christmas. We would have had nothing to eat then if it wasn't for...'

'You could have waited,' a voice interrupts her.

The three women turn to a man behind them.

'Didn't think you would come.' Lynn says, greeting and kissing the man on his cheek.

'What do you think?' Sian asks.

He pauses. Alex leaves and the three stare at the brass plate, screwed high above them where the wall meets the ceiling. Four lines are engraved on the brass.

The first is his name: Sean Miller.
The second how everyone knew him: Peter Pan.
The third what he was: A Liverpool Docker.
The fourth what he believed in: No Pasaran.

'Looks good,' Jam Jar says, and then, 'but he never did like heights.'

THE LIVERPOOL DOCKERS' DISPUTE, 1995-98

Afterword: A Series of Betrayals

Mike Carden

ON THE EVENING OF Monday 25 September 1995, five young Liverpool dockers were sacked by a small stevedoring company called Torside Ltd. for refusing to work overtime on a ship. The workers had challenged Torside's overtime demand because, in their view, it was in breach of recognised agreements made between Torside and their union, the Transport and General Workers' Union (TGWU). By the next day, the five sacked workers were joined by 75 more, and two days later by a further 420 dockers – mainly employed by the port authority, the Mersey Docks and Harbour Company (MDHC), and including myself[1] – all sacked for refusing to cross a Torside dockers' picket line. In evidence provided to the House of Commons Employment and Education Sub-Committee in May the following year, Torside's Managing Director Bernard Bradley claimed he had told the local TGWU of an offer he made to reinstate the Torside dockers on Tuesday 26 September. But this critical information was never conveyed to the dockers by their union who were to claim later that the offer was never made. Either way, the struggle of the Liverpool dockers to get their jobs back – a 28-month long campaign that would become one of the longest disputes in labour history – had begun.

This wasn't a strike though – the men had already been sacked. This was a dispute, although what kind of dispute – in particular whether it was an official or unofficial union dispute wasn't immediately clear. No official repudiation from union leadership was immediately forthcoming (as required by The Trade Union and Labour Relations (Consolidation) Act 1992).[2]

Reflecting on the complexities of creating a film about the dispute several years later, writer Jimmy McGovern echoed this sense of complexity, concluding that the best way to structure a narrative about it was through 'a series of betrayals. Betrayal by your employer, betrayal by your friends, betrayal by the Labour Party, betrayal by your union.'[3]

The first betrayal was the betrayal of the state. In 1989, the Thatcher government passed a bill scrapping the National Dock Labour Scheme. Introduced by the Atlee Labour government in 1947, the scheme was intended to end the scourge of casual labour by giving dockers the legal right to minimum work, holidays, sick pay and pensions. It also protected wages and meant that registered dockers laid off by any of the 150 firms bound by the scheme would have to be taken on by another firm or be paid compensation.

With the abolition of the Scheme in 1989, the Conservative government opened the sluice-gates of casualisation in every port in the UK. It enabled port bosses to impose new contracts on their dockers, and constructively dismiss them, replacing them with casual labour. Dockers' jobs were replaced by sub-contracted workers under different working conditions. Between 1989 and 1992, 80% of dockers left the industry, whilst direct (un-subcontracted) employees fell by over half, from 1100 to 500, between 1989 and 1995.[4] Despite this, volumes handled by a port like the Mersey Docks continued to increase, from around 20 million tonnes in 1988 to over 30 million tonnes in 1997.

Deregulation also turned out to be profitable for port bosses, personally. The management of Mersey Docks had long realised the potential of the huge land assets they controlled as they observed events in other ports that rushed towards privatisation in 1989. It was a time of easy pickings and easy money for these bosses.

The acquisition by Mersey Docks of the Medway Port, in Kent, in 1993, offered a porthole for Mersey Docks bosses into quite how much money was to be made in the new deregulated climate. In the takeover process, they saw how Medway CEO Peter Vincent had imposed rigid contract changes on the Medway dockers and then dismissed them when they took industrial action to defend their original contracts. The direct outcome of this was Peter Vincent and some of his financial backers made millions on their purchase of the sacked Medway dockers' shares at £2.50 each and their re-sale to the Mersey Docks at £37 each. Vincent was given a directorship on the board of the Mersey Docks with the new owners no doubt realising now how *they* had missed a trick when they didn't fully privatise (buy the government's remaining shares out) or dismiss all workers in 1989.

Mersey Docks CEO Trevor Furlong confided to the *International Freight Weekly*: 'I suppose in hindsight we were too soft in 1989. We should have got rid of the lot of them and recruited.'[5] But they were keen to make up for this mistake. Shortly after the Medway takeover began, Mersey Docks started imposing harsher employment contracts that asked for longer working hours and required dockers to be available 'at any time', knowing these demands would be resisted. To ensure dockers accepted the revised contracts, Mersey Docks started advertising new jobs locally, receiving thousands of applications and interviewing hundreds of candidates, although none of them would actually be employed. As casualisation took hold, company profits went up and the bosses themselves started to reap enormous personal rewards, through pay rises and share options.[6]

The second betrayal in this story was that of the unions. TGWU leader Bill Morris, despite voting to establish a hardship fund for the dockers,[7] and famously telling a mass meeting at Liverpool's Transport House, 'Comrades you in Liverpool will never ever walk alone,'[8] went on to ultimately dismiss the conflict as unofficial because a ballot had never been taken between the 25 and the 28 September over the initial picket and walk-out (despite three subsequent Electoral Reform Society postal ballots being organised for the dockers to take part in, all three of which delivered a vote overwhelmingly in favour of continuing the struggle).

Eighteen months into the dispute Morris used his union's official publication, *The TGWU Record*, to set the record straight on why he decided not to act in solidarity with its Liverpool membership: 'The MDHC workers had broken their contract of employment without first holding an industrial action ballot, the TGWU became vulnerable to legal action for damages by MDHC or any ship owner… the TGWU has an obligation to all its 900,000 members, which must include avoiding action which could render the union unable to operate on behalf of those members.'[9]

This strategy was subsequently described by Len McCluskey (later to become leader of the same union, rebranded 'UNITE') as an example of unions seeking 'to hide behind anti-trade union legislation as a reason not to act'.[10] Jimmy McGovern summarised the decision as follows: '[Morris] had argued that [...] It was better for 50[0] dockers to rot than for [nearly] one million members to lose their union'. But, McGovern added, 'What are unions for? Why do people form them? They do it because they know that the strength of the many will protect the few. That is the fundamental principle of trade unionism. Lose that, as the TGWU has done, and there is no reason to join or remain in a trade union.'[11]

Indeed in July 1997, at the TGWU Biennial Delegates Conference (their key lay-member policy-making forum) Bill Morris appealed, 'for unity and a course of action within the law.'[12] This was rejected by a clear majority despite the General Secretary's warning that Conference faced a straight choice between 'unity or oblivion' (if it supported the Liverpool dockers).[13] The General Executive Council's policy and that of the General Secretary was overwhelmingly rejected (182 for, 283 against). However this rejection was ignored both at the conference and after it. It was ignored by the GEC, whose role, under the rules of the union, was to carry out the decisions of the membership as determined by the BDC. The members had spoken, they wanted their union to support the Liverpool dockers but, like the dockers themselves, their decision was ignored by the union's leadership.

What was so ironic about this betrayal of the dockers, by the TGWU and subsequently other unions, was that the modern British trade union movement owed so much to the dockers for the way 'new unionism' emerged in the late nineteenth century. 'The Great London Dock Strike of 1889 was the foundation stone,' McCluskey writes, 'on which the modern trade union movement is based. Before 1889, trade union membership was largely the preserve of skilled craftsmen. The dock labourer's achievement [...] lay in convincing other unskilled workers that improvements in pay and working conditions could be won through trade union activity. Nothing was to ever be the same again.'[14]

But Thatcher's anti-union legislation had succeeded. It left only the second half of the popular slogan dying on people's lips: *Divided we fall.*

The third act of betrayal in this saga was undoubtedly New Labour's betrayal of both the dockers of Liverpool and the left generally. With the election of Tony Blair in May 1997, there had been some glimmers of hope (perhaps among those that hadn't been watching Blair closely enough) that the new government would intervene in the dispute. It didn't.

Instead of respecting and championing all that Liverpool dockers had done throughout the Thatcher era (and before) – raising wages across Liverpool, and supporting international progress movements[15] – the incoming Labour government decided to characterise the dispute as belonging to a bygone '*Old* Labour' era, a monochrome past of burly men bullying their way into management decision-making. The media –

following Murdoch, in whose pocket Blair was by now deeply nestled – followed suit. Even the mischaracterisation of the dispute as a 'strike' helped to distance the dockers from the supposedly 'modern' New Labour world-view – Blair's soundbite-strewn vision of neoliberalism, globalisation, and a 'third way'.

This representation of the docker's dispute as 'out-dated' ran deep across the entire spectrum of the media. If the journalists covered the dispute at all, they kept to this New Labour line. Even local press coverage was infiltrated by it. When the dispute finally came to an end, the *Liverpool Daily Post* ran an article under the header 'The Dog that's Had its Day', saying, 'The dispute [...] seemed to symbolise something from another era [...]. It was as though an old yard dog, wearied and weakened by beatings, managed to bare his teeth once again, and in so doing recalled the lost years when he was young and strong.'[16]

Consequently, these three great betrayals left the Liverpool dockers completely isolated, cut off from those who would traditionally support them, 'walking alone'. For most of the 28-month conflict, the dispute was largely ignored by the British media (despite the irony of ITV's prime ratings show *This Morning* being broadcast live from Liverpool's Albert Dock, just down the road from the site of the dispute). Liverpool dockers had to go elsewhere for solidarity, and think more creatively about how they communicated, as Lucas's story shows.

As early as April 1997, Oasis's songwriter Noel Gallagher agreed to play an unbilled concert for the dockers at the Mean Fiddler venue in London. Gallagher and the Beautiful South performed other fund-raising gigs through the year. On 16 October 1998, at London's Sound Republic, some of the biggest names in British music joined forces to draw attention to the ongoing plight of the sacked dock workers in, what was called, the 'Rock the Dock Concert'. Gallagher and Who guitarist, Pete Townshend were the headline acts. The campaign also found support from celebrities such as actors David Thewlis and Dexter Fletcher as well as singer/TV producer Bob Geldof. Oasis, Primal Scream, Dodgy, Cast, Chumbawumba, Chemical Brothers and Paul Weller who all featured on a compilation CD, also called *Rock The Dock*, released by Alan McGee's Creation Records to raise money for the dockers.

On 20 March 1997, Liverpool Football Club played in the UEFA Cup against SK Brann Bergen, winning 3-0. Robbie Fowler scored two goals and in celebration of his first goal he lifted his team shirt to uncover a 'Support the Sacked Liverpool Dockers' t-shirt – a now famous design that played off the 'CK' (Calvin Klein) logo. Despite leading to a UEFA fine of 2,000 Swiss Francs (approximately $1,400), a week later, this simple act of solidarity made the front and back pages of every newspaper in the UK, and put the dispute on the world stage.

The premature euphoria that followed the General Election saw New Labour deliberately cosy up to the stars of the mid-'90s Brit Pop phenomenon, culminating in the now infamous photos of Blair sharing a glass of champagne with Noel Galagher himself at a Downing Street party in July 1997. Against this backdrop of mutual appreciation and 'Cool Britannia' cross-branding, what happened in February the next year at the Brit Awards should be seen as quietly revolutionary. Chumberwumba, whose song 'Tubthumping' had debuted at No. 2 in the charts in August and become the unofficial theme tune of the dispute, chose to amend the song's chorus in their primetime performance, to include the now prophetic line: 'New Labour sold out the dockers, just like they'll sell out the rest of us!' With a number of dockers, including Micky Tighe, and his wife Silvia, on the guest-list, drummer Danbert Nobacon completed the protest with what he called an act of 'drench warfare', tipping a bucket of icy water over Deputy Prime Minister John Prescott's head, saying: 'This is for the Liverpool dockers.'

In an era before social media, the Liverpool dockers realised that the task was to get around a mainstream media that had all but blocked them out. The above-mentioned pop culture interventions were just the beginning of a new type of campaigning, which would also see filmmaker Ken Loach come to Liverpool to shoot his documentary *A Flickering Flame* (1998) for Channel 4, and Jimmy McGovern and Irvine Welsh work with sacked dockers and their wives to co-script the abovementioned feature film for Film 4.

Another groundbreaking element of the campaign was its internationalism. Support was shown from comrades in ports across the world, from North America to New Zealand. Transport House – effectively the dockers' campaign HQ – saw international delegations from Nigeria, South Africa, Iran, the Indian continent, Argentina, Brazil, Australia, France, Sweden, Denmark, and so on.

As Lucas's story illustrates, dockers used the new technology of the world wide web to spread the word and organise internationally, operating well under the radar of a British police force more used to the physical side of suppressing disputes. Dockers in New York were the first of these international comrades to respond, in December 1995, when they refused to cross a picket line set up by three Liverpool dockers – an act that nearly cost Liverpool the business of American shipping company Atlantic Containers, who threatened to pull out of the port.[17] Two years into the campaign, on 8 September, 30 ports around the world (across 16 countries) halted work for 24 hours (around 50,000 dock workers in total),[18] bringing the US East Coast to a standstill.[19] Other ports in Japan and South Africa also came to a halt during the campaign, with dockers in the latter stopping their work 'in solidarity with the Liverpool dockers who stood by us during apartheid.'[20]

Both in their methodology, and in the way they raised awareness of casualisation and what would come to be called 'zero-hour contracts', the allegedly 'old school' dockers were, in fact, well ahead of the curve.

Although, ultimately the dockers lost, with their campaign coming to an end in January 1998, the legacy of the dispute would be multifaceted and long-lasting. Ever since the dispute, the International Transport Workers' Federation (ITF) has had to organise alongside, or in competition with, the International Dockworkers' Council (IDC) which the Liverpool dockers established in 1995. Two of the sacked dockers now organise the permanently employed Liverpool dockers under the leadership of convenor John Lynch at Peel Ports. Mike Morris, who had worked with fellow dockers and McGovern and Welsh on the film, *Dockers*, went on to set up the Writing on the Wall literature festival. Other sacked dockers involved in the film (including Tony Nelson and Terry Teague) who shared the co-production rights used the £127,000 they received to buy the three-storey Casablanca Club to establish the CASA (the Community Advice Services Association) in Hope Street, which has given legal, welfare and employment advice to thousands of residents over the years.

Perhaps the most important legacy of the dispute was its impact on the TGWU, now UNITE, which experienced a seismic transition with the elections of Tony Woodley (as Joint General Secretary) and Len McCluskey, himself a former Liverpool docker (as General Secretary) in 2007 and 2010 respectively. Their leadership of the largest union in the UK radically altered the political direction of the organisation they inherited from Bill Morris. In 2015, Len McCluskey was to prove instrumental to the socialist transformation of the Labour Party under the leadership of Jeremy Corbyn who had been one of the few Labour MPs to address the Liverpool dockers and their supporters from the steps of St.George's Hall back in 1996. And following the 2017 General Election, Corbyn's precarious support among Members of Parliament was bolstered, at least by one vote, with the arrival of a newly elected MP for Liverpool, Walton: one Dan Carden, a man who at the age of seven had once stood on the picket lines along with his brother John, with his old man, me.

Notes

1. I happened to be off sick at the time, recovering from accident driving a stacker truck on the Timber Berth.

2. The Trade Union and Labour Relations (Consolidation) Act 1992: 'An act shall not be taken to have been authorised or endorsed by the union if it is repudiated, [...]. Repudiation is completed by a trade union when the action of its members are repudiated by the executive, president or general secretary as soon as reasonably practicable after coming to the knowledge of any of them.

3. As quoted in the documentary *Dockers: Writing the Wrongs* (1999), directed by Solon Papadopoulos.

4. Marren, Brian (2016). *We Shall Not be Moved: How Liverpool's Working Class Fought Redundancies, Closures and Cuts in the Age of Thatcher*, Oxford University Press, p. 213.

5. See also *Liverpool Echo*, 18 Jul 1996 ('Dockers should have been sacked years ago'), and *The Morning Star* ('We should have sacked the lot of them'), 18 Jul 1996.

6. 'Managing Director, Trevor Furlong, took an £87,000 pay rise just before the company sent 329 men to the dole. Furlong's 38% increase brought his earnings to £316,000 a year. He also had a £293,000 share option over the next two years.' John Pilger, *The Guardian*, 23 Nov 1996. See: http://www.labournet.net/docks2/9611/PILGER.HTM

7. Marren, Brian (2016), p. 217.

8. Speech by Bill Morris, Gen. Secretary of T&GWU, to Liverpool Dockers, 14 Mar 1996. http://www.labournet.net/docks2/9608/MORRIS.HTM

9. The TGWU Record, Feb-March, 1997.

10. 'Community Spirit will never be defeated' Len McCluskey Speech at the Adelphi Hotel 26 September 2015, Unite Live, 3 September 2016 http://unitelive.org/community-spirit-will-never-be-defeated/

11. 'When You're a Liverpool Docker, it Never Rains But it Pours,' *The Observer Review*, 1 Feb 1998.

12. Merseyside Port Shop Stewards, International Update, 9 Jul 1997

13. *Ibid.*

14. Len McCluskey, Foreword to *The Great Dock Strike of 1889*, Unite Education, 2015.

15. Liverpool dockers accommodated Chilean political refugees during Pinochet's regime, refused to handle ships or cargo from South Africa during the Apartheid era, and blockaded Namibian Uranium Hexaflouride (again in protest against Apartheid).

16. 'The Dog That's Had its Day', *Liverpool Daily Post*, 29 Jan 1998.

17. 'What was the 1995-1998 Liverpool docks dispute all about?' *Liverpool Echo*, 20 Sep 2015.

18. Mukul (1998). 'Liverpool Dockers; Making and Un-Making of a Struggle,' *Economic and Political Weekly*.

19. 'No going back at Liverpool docks,' *The Independent*, 21 Sep 1997.

20. 'Keeping the spirit of solidarity alive 20 years after Robbie Fowler backed Liverpool dockers,' *The Mirror*, 16 Jan 2015.

198 Methods of NVDA

Gaia Holmes

1. Public Speeches; 9. Letters, Pamphlets and Books[1]

ACTUALLY, I'M A COWARD. I'm scared of woodlice. I'm scared of wet York stone pavements, motorbikes, dark water, big dogs, ladders and tinned lychees. I'm scared of ice, rats and sewer covers. I'm scared of pain, policemen, bridges, beansprouts and conflict. I'm scared of crying and not being able to stop. I'm scared of saying what I feel. I'm scared of things, people, dying and I'm scared of heights.

This morning I'm feeling a little anxious. My mum makes me toast and coffee with an inch of rum and five drops of Bach Rescue Remedy in it. I am shaking. Although from when I was a baby in a pushchair, right up through my teenage years, I've accompanied my parents on many a protest – sat hand in hand with strangers, run out of newsagents clutching slippery stacks of top-shelf magazines, stood outside banks, town halls, supermarkets and council offices in the pouring rain for hours, holding up banners on bamboo sticks or soggy placards and bashing a tambourine – I've never done anything like this as an adult. But I need to do this for Stella, for the corms and keys and seeds she kept under the sink in red string bags and little brown dinner money envelopes, for the leaves she pressed in the dictionary, for the saplings she planted in the garden that I left to the rabbits, for the last crop of cherries that I allowed to rot in the grass. I need to do this because Stella would have done this, without question, without fear or fuss.

'Try not to fret, love. You're doing such a good thing,' my mum says. 'You're doing the right thing. I think it'll be good for you to do something proactive, to focus on something else. When you're my age you'll be able to look back at your life and feel proud that you did your bit for the planet... and anyway, things are a bit more civilised now... I doubt you'll get trampled to death by a horse if you just keep your head, stay calm, don't panic...'

And then, for the second time this week, she tells me about Amrita Davi of Rhajastan, the original 'tree hugger', a woman of the Bishnio people who, after hearing that the prince of the region had ordered soldiers to clear all the trees in her village to make space for a palace, hugged a tree, held on as they came with machetes, said, 'Anyone wishing to cut down a tree will have to first cut down me,' and they did, they chopped off her head. Then, impassioned by their mother's sacrifice, her two daughters followed suit, wrapping their arms around a tree and refusing to let go. They too were beheaded. More of the Bishnio people, 363 of them, did the same thing and were slaughtered. After the massacre, shocked by the bloodshed and overwhelmed by the dedication of the villagers, the prince relented and passed a decree legally protecting the trees, which stands to this day.

'It can be good... empowering to leave your comfort zone. And though sometimes it seems that the law's always against us protesters, sometimes it works in our favour. No one's going to chop your head off... not these days... well, they might but it's highly unlikely.'

She's put together a protest bag for me: a multi pack of Peek Freans biscuits, plasters, a Swiss army knife, firelighters, a very tatty photocopy of a list called '198 methods of NVDA', stained with mud and cup rings. *The Art of Knots*, by Marc P.G. Berhtier, four blister packs of paracetamol, a green tin mug, stock cubes, candles, three clipper lighters, a tube of Germolene, some Damart thermals, a bottle of TCP, a mini sewing kit, a bicycle lock, a torch, a bundle of blue propylene, five tins of baked beans, five tins of mushroom soup and what she describes as her 'Greenham Scarf', a slightly faded purple silk affair patterned with turquoise peacocks which she tells me she hasn't washed since she left the peace camp over ten years ago. It has a strange heady smell – woodsmoke, mildew and patchouli.

We set off in the afternoon and drive to Newbury, through the downs, along the A34 looking for diggers or smoke in the trees. She pulls up into a lay-by.

'I'll leave you here love,' she says. 'I think they're over there.' She points to the glow of a campfire in a copse across the fields.

She kisses me and strokes my cheek, says, 'Think of it as resisting rather than fighting... and don't feel you have to swear... remember to brush your teeth... keep your hair tied back and try not to have anything dangling... earrings, necklaces, anything that could get caught in the trees or machines... anything that they could grab... and sing loudly... remember, do whatever you do loudly. You're much stronger than you think you are.' She drives off. I hoik my rucksack onto my back and start walking across the fields towards the sound of hammering, dogs barking and the shrill tones of a penny whistle.

47. Assemblies of Protest and Support

When I hobble into the camp, struggling beneath the weight of all these books and tins of beans, someone comes to greet me, eases the straps of my rucksack off my shoulders and asks me if I'm an undercover security guard, bailiff, detective, journalist, climber or member of the police force. I say no and he shakes my hand and ushers me to a big, dirty white bender full or pans, bread, bundles of rope, mud-caked boots and sleeping bags. It smells of wax and damp socks. There's a glowing stove in its centre around which dogs and people lounge or sit on wooden pallets covered with army blankets. Someone hands me a chipped cup full of cider and someone else kneels in front of me, unfolds a creased map of the proposed Newbury bypass, points out the bull-dozed camps (Skyward, Kennet, Rickety Bridge, Granny Ash, Camelot, Quercus Circus, Gotan, Sea View, Babble Brook) and the camps still standing – nine down, twenty to go – and recites a long list of casualties: 69 ash, 82 oaks, one broken ankle, 115 pine, three cracked ribs, 48 alders, one split lip, 227 arrests, 57 beeches, two pneumonias, four hyperthermias, 16 bat roosts, 31 Sweet Chestnuts.

50. Teach-Ins

There's a lot to learn before I can get up into one of the twigloos or tree houses and I spend the next week being taught about my rights as a protester, how to avoid arrest and what to do if I get arrested, familiarising myself with Section 6 of the Criminal Law Act, learning about harnesses, cow tails, karabiners, knots and winching. I'm taught how to scissor my way along the walkways from tree to tree, how to breathe, how to use a D-lock, an arm tube, how to make a chainsaw whip, how to 'dress' a tree with chicken wire and bitumen to delay the tree surgeons. And after my practical learning, Evie, a woman with a huge Yggdrasil tattoo on her upper arm, teaches me about the more earthy, spiritual side of things. She teaches me that ash sap's a tonic. Hazel knows. Aspen trembles. A hacked alder bleeds deep orange when it's cut and never forgives the axe. The lilac tree has purple heartwood. Oak will not forget. She teaches me which wood bends the best, which bark heals, and which leaves are good for a poultice. I love this lore. I gorge on it, and finally, on the eighth day, with my head full of new knots, cures, wisdom and druids, I am deemed ready to ascend.

18. Displays of Flags and Symbolic Colours

As soon as I 'move in' to my tree house I tie my mum's purple Greenham scarf to the tree top, let the chilly breeze draw out the old smoke to charge the air above the camp with its energies. In the wind, after rain, it hisses, flickers and lashes the sky – a bright dragon's tongue speaking for the bare, black trees, warning the world away.

158. Self-Exposure to the Elements; 173. Nonviolent Occupation

It's my twelfth day here and the fires aren't as bright as they were when I arrived. All the tunes the penny whistler plays seem to be in a minor key. Down in the communal bender, a heavy sense of despondence lingers in the air along with the smell of our eternal cabbage stew. So many of our camps have been cleared. All day the yellow jackets burn the butchered trees in huge pyres whose thick smoke makes us, and the security guards, cough up blood. No one's saying it, but we all know that we're not going to stop them building the road and now our job is to merely delay the inevitable. I don't think that's enough of a reason to stay for some people. Every day, two or three protesters leave, scrape the mud off their boots and go back to their other lives. For some, this has become their only life and it's a hard one. It's not all happy prusiking and bird song. It's damp and cold. Constant shivering. Bluing fingers. Running noses. It's waking up to a frozen water bottle and frosted blankets. It's thin soup and pot noodles and flapjack and not enough proper food. It's wet socks and trench foot, pneumonia, scabies, lice and impetigo. It's 'donga belly', the shit pit, rope burns, bruises. It's being called 'a fucking dosser' and holding your tongue. It's smiling at the cameras, being polite, trying to keep your knuckles slack, trying to 'keep it fluffy' when you want to kick and bite the bloke that's dragging you through the mud. It's hoping the rope won't snap, the harness will hold, the clips won't buckle. It's trusting the police won't trample you under their horses. Trusting the bailiffs won't cut the walkway with you on it. Trusting the security guards won't let you fall. Trusting the climbers will stop pulling before your shoulder pops out of its socket. The things that keep us here, fighting the green fight, are small things: the smell of the woods after rain, the contrast of fresh white snow on the bare black branches, 87 year old Mabel who comes limping into the camp on her stick bearing a basket full of chunky doorstep cheese and onion sandwiches, the gentle Quakers with their urns of tea and tureens of soup, the widower who gives us all hugs and warm freshly baked shortbread, and the suited, court-shoed lady who stops by on her way home from work to chuck Mars bars and KitKats up to us in our houses in the trees.

162. Sit-Ins; 173. Nonviolent Occupation

Since my fifteenth day, when they nailed an eviction notice to the silver birch at the edge of the camp, I've been up here full-time, reading, smoking, learning knots, thinking about the things I've been trying not to think about; those awful months before I realised I couldn't cope anymore, left the cottage and went back to my mum's – the shadows I lived with, and allowed to breed, in that cold, mould-riddled place. I remember the mass of mail I left to pile up behind the door which made leaving even harder, the mug I wouldn't wash whose coffee dregs had grown a thick layer of pungent white and green fur. I remember all the husks I surrounded myself with: the bleached spider plants, the dead roses I never got round to binning, Stella's books and boots and coats with things still in their pockets that I couldn't bear to give away, those tortured Bonsais forcing their crippled limbs back into their seeds, starving cacti eating themselves, those poor goldfish slowly turning white, pots full of desiccated soil, dying things whispering all the time, crying out for water. The only thing I had the desire to water was my grief and it grew until it was tall and monstrous, nudged the roof off and let the sky leak in.

I think I'm going a little bit mad. I have to keep reminding myself that this is not some kind of weird purgatory I'm putting myself through. I have to keep reminding myself that I'm here to try and stop them filleting out another precious chunk of the countryside. I am here to try and stop another mile of trees being felled. I become fixated on words for falling: felled, fallen, befall, fell, tumble, fall. I wonder if, after Stella, I had been felled or had I fallen? And, if I had been felled, was it the death, the dying, or the lack, that felled me, and how could something that wasn't there have a blade strong or sharp enough to chop me down?

Evie comes up to bring me tea and sandwiches and keep me company. I tell her I'm feeling a bit wobbly. I tell her about Stella and she talks about being in limbo – the limbo of grief, the limbo of waiting. Evie knows about death. She says grief may stop growing but it never goes. It just becomes different. And sometimes it leans towards the light, becomes a strange companion. It roots in you. You learn to sway with it. You learn to name it.

33. *Fraternisation*

They arrive at 8am this morning – that awful caravan of security guards in their day-glow jackets, and police and chainsaw operators. I say good morning to them and they don't look up or acknowledge me, just drop down their visors, pull the starter cords of their machines and start lopping off the lower branches of my tree. Legally, they can't cut down the whole tree with me still in it, but this is a tactic they employ to bring us down without forcibly having to remove us. Their whirring, buzzing blades are getting closer to me branch by branch. I tremble as my tree trembles and sweet clouds of sawdust drift up to me. All I can smell is wood: woodsmoke from the camp fires and the bender stoves, the wet bark that cradles me and those fresh, dry wounds, those raw new sores. Protesters on the ground are getting roughed up and dragged away as they try to intercept. The camp dogs are going mental, yapping and growling, and people are shouting, 'Shame, shame on you,' each time another branch is butchered.

They start with words, try to talk you down as the tree surgeons lop off the branches below you. If that doesn't work, they send up the bailiffs in a cherry picker. They can be rough but generally they have boundaries. They know when to stop and they're a little bit frightened of falling. If the bailiffs can't get you down, they send up the hired climbers who have no fear of heights or falling, and that's when the really bad stuff might happen. Arms and noses might get broken. Lips might get bloodied. Ropes and cow clips might be used as whips. Rumour has it from the other camps that the hired climbers don't know when to stop. Rumour has it that they have tricks. They know about pressure points and the science of holding on, the science of clutching and clinging, the science of balance. Rumour has it that they're paid five hundred pounds a day and it seems that's enough to smother the consciences of these mercenary soldiers of the sky.

133. Reluctance and Slow Compliance

They tried talking me down for a while but I told them I'm not budging so they've sent a bailiff up in a cherry picker.

He says, 'I don't want to hurt you love so I'm going to ask you very nicely to come down.'

'Thank you for asking me, very nicely, to come down,' I say. 'But I'm telling you, very nicely, that I'm not coming down.'

'You do realise that the longer I'm up here trying to get you down, the more I get paid?'

'Well then, that's good for you, isn't it? Why don't you hang around and make a day of it, make a bit of easy money?'

'This isn't easy money… having to deal with your lot.'

I start asking him questions, talking rubbish just to delay the proceedings and I reel off my new cache of tree facts and folklore. I tell him about Yggdrasil and Odin. I tell him about oak gall ink. I tell him how leaves filter our poisons and stop the stars from falling. I tell him about Stella and how she collected acorns, saved all our pear and apple pips, wanted to grow an orchard. I tell him about the Judas tree and I call him Judas, ask him if he ever has nightmares about tarmac being poured down his throat or his wife and his children being buried alive beneath asphalt.

He's getting agitated. I can tell by the way scarlet flushes his neck and starts creeping into his cheeks. I wonder if it'll seep into his eyes and turn them red.

'You might soon be the devil himself!' I say.

'Look, love,' he says. 'I've been reasonable with you so far. I've given you a chance, but now I'm going to have to bring you down by force.' And he lunges forward, gets me in a head lock and starts to pull, tries to prise me off the tree.

37. Singing

Five minutes is a long time when you're holding on to something with all your strength. Already I am aching, cramping up, bruising. I keep thinking about what my mum said when she dropped me off, 'You're stronger than you think you are,' and, 'Do whatever you do, loudly,' so I start to sing, loudly. I sing my favourite hymns from my school days. I sing, 'All Things Bright and Beautiful', and he's still pulling at me, getting rougher, trying to peel my fingers off the branch I'm clinging to. He's saying 'Fucking let go,' and fumbling with the karabiner on my harness and I'm terrified and I hurt but I keep singing. I sing 'Jerusalem': 'And did those feet in ancient time, walk upon England's mountains green?' And he grabs my ponytail and yanks it. I get to the second verse when something cracks: a bone, a tendon or just my resolve. Whatever it is, it's agony, and I remember that line from a poem that Stella stuck on the fridge, 'A strong woman is a woman who loves strongly, weeps strongly and is strongly terrified' and how, when I was with her in the hospital and they were upping her morphine, she kept saying it was ok for me to cry. And then, afterwards, my mother coming round to see me at the cottage, buttoning me into my coat saying 'Come on love. You need to get out, and you need to let it out,' and driving us through the pouring rain to the windfarm, telling me to scream. Both of us screaming out all the dead things, making the turbines roar. And, back in car, her telling me about the legendary Greenham scream, how her voice was part of the tender weapon that freaked out the American soldiers and stopped things for a while when the women unleashed their collective keening, and up here, in my state of limbo, I begin to scream.

28. Symbolic Sounds

I scream strongly, loudly, apocalyptically. I scream and my scream is the scream of banshees, dryads, sirens. I scream because I'm scared of being felled or falling and I ache. I scream for Stella. I scream for Amrita Davi and her severed head. I scream for the sawn off branches at the bottom of the tree. I scream for the green miles being buried alive. I scream until I can hardly breathe and I'm gasping, choking, and the bailiff starts to look worried, lets go of me, says 'Can you please try to calm down?' and this makes me scream even more. After a few minutes my scream of fear becomes a scream of power. I pack it full of my sadness, my anger, my questions. It hums through the trees and they bellow back an answer and though there is no breeze they begin to creak and sway. Things knock through the wood. Things mutter from the mud. Things creep out of the bark: wispy, uncertain things with wings, pine needle teeth, huge burl eyes and twigs for fingers. They hang howling and hissing from the branches. Down on the ground my tree friends are yelling, 'Leave her alone!' some of them are crying. The bailiff is looking terrified. He shouts something into his CB and the arm of the cherry picker begins to sink. The platform is lowered to the ground.

Note

1. The story's title and headers are taken from the 198 methods outlined in Gene Sharp's seminal work, *The Politics of Nonviolent Action* (3 Vols.) (Porter Sargent, 1973).

Afterword: The Third Battle of Newbury

Dr Chris Cocking
University of Brighton

FOR ME, READING GAIA'S chapter was an evocative reminder of the Newbury protests, despite it now being nearly 25 years since they happened. The character's experiences that she describes, and even the specialist terminology used (carabiner, prusik, poly-prop, cow-tails, etc.) brought me back to the crazy world that we inhabited in the trees above Berkshire and Hampshire. It was a life-changing, high-intensity experience for many involved. At the time, I was an idealistic twenty-something PhD student who was fortunate enough to get UK Research Council funding to do an ethnographic study of direct-action anti-road protests (so I was effectively being paid by one government department to protest against another!). Therefore, I decided to get down and dirty at the Newbury protests. Gaia's chapter brought a lot of those memories back, so I owe her a debt of gratitude for that.

The Third Battle of Newbury[1] raged from 1996 to 1998 and was the biggest direct-action anti-roads protest seen in Britain thus far.[2] The Newbury bypass connected a major arterial route linking the South Coast to the Midlands and north of England. The nine-mile route bypasses Newbury to the west and its construction involved the felling of large areas of ancient woodland and the building of road bridges in environmentally sensitive areas and Sites of Special Scientific Interest (SSSIs). The clearance work to make way for the road was regularly disrupted by protests including: occupying trees and machinery; targeting companies involved in the clearance work; and then resisting the evictions of over 30 protest camps that had been set up in the path of the road. The final eviction was completed in April 1996, and the main contract to build the road began in August 1996. In November 1998, the bypass was finally opened. In January 1999, during a demonstration to commemorate the third anniversary of the campaign, over 250 protesters occupied the completed bypass.

Newbury attracted many seasoned activists (myself included) who were veterans of the Twyford Down, M11 and Solsbury Hill road protests, and their tactics had evolved over these campaigns into quite sophisticated defensive actions to defend the land and houses threatened. This in turn required extensive resources by the state to remove them (costing around £35m in total), such as: private security, police, bailiffs and professional climbers. Newbury was no stranger to direct action either, as in a bizarre historical coincidence, the route of the bypass was very close to Greenham Common airbase, which saw mass protests against the introduction of cruise missiles throughout the 1980s (my own mother used to attend these protests with her friends who volunteered at the local Women's Aid refuge in West London). Some former Greenham women also came to protests against the road. However, Newbury also happened in the broader context of the campaign against the Criminal Justice Bill (CJB) that threatened to criminalise squatting, free outdoor raves, and most direct-action protest activity, bringing together diverse groups from the UK counter-culture scene that had previously not had much to do with each other. The campaign against the CJB culminated in the 1994 Hyde Park Riot,[3] where the media latched on to a rather artificial distinction between the tactics of non-violence and more militant forms of protests (often caricatured rather simplistically as the 'Fluffy/Spiky' debate).

There certainly were those from an avowedly pacifist perspective at Newbury and getting arrested for tree hugging was something of a badge of honour if this description appeared on your charge sheet (although my favourite arrest was the case of two people charged with aggravated trespass after dressing up as a pantomime cow and invading the site!).[4] However, I think it was also largely accepted that not everybody agreed with an entirely pacifist approach, and it wouldn't have worked to rigidly impose such an approach during the campaign, as a lot of people would have simply left. Nevertheless, I felt there still tended to be a pragmatic (rather than ideological) approach to non-violence as it was generally recognised that during the Newbury protests, the power dynamic usually rested with the authorities, and protesters would have been unlikely to win any 'violent' confrontations as they were usually outnumbered and/or surrounded (especially during the camp evictions). One exception to this was the Reunion Rampage in January 1996, a year after the protests began, where over 1,000 protesters stormed a construction site, physically forced police and security to withdraw, and then caused over £250,000 worth of damage to machinery, with some being set on fire.[5]

The efforts to prevent the route from being cleared saw the largest and most dramatic protests, as this was when the camps were evicted, and this is rightly focused upon in Gaia's story. These were incredibly intense experiences for those involved, with some people putting themselves at enormous risk to defend the camps. For instance, one person at the Snelsmore camp threw off his climbing harness, stripped naked and covered himself with grease when the bailiffs came in to get him from his tree house (this was during one of the coldest winters of a generation, note). During the eviction of my own camp (Kennet), my line was cut from under me, which nearly resulted in my girlfriend and I falling 40 feet to the ground. Afterwards, I noticed the first white streaks in my hair, so I blame Newbury for eventually having to start dyeing my hair black! The clearance of the route was completed within a relatively short time (from January to April 1996), but the campaign didn't end there, and protests continued until the opening of the road.

My PhD looked at the role of empowerment in those engaged in protests to combat climate change, and so I was very interested in how the protesters viewed the effectiveness of their actions.[6] What I found particularly interesting was that this failure to stop the clearance work being completed wasn't necessarily considered a defeat. It was fairly well accepted among the protesters I spoke to that they were unlikely to prevent the land being cleared and the bypass being built (I'm not aware of any road project that has been stopped by direct action protests once construction work has started). Indeed less than 5% of the participants I surveyed felt the outcome was an outright defeat, with many describing a sense of success in raising public awareness of road building and/or broader environmental issues (such as climate change) through their actions and/or through the costs generated from the increased policing and security for the protests. Some even contrasted their noisy defeat at Newbury, with the quiet victories they had in decimating the Tory government's road-building programme during the early 1990s. The 600 road projects that were originally planned were reduced to 150 by the time of Newbury because of the increased financial and political costs of policing the protests, and the programme was scrapped altogether when Labour came to power in 1997.[7]

The protests at Newbury also had a long-lasting legacy that has endured to this day. Newbury was a largely defensive battle, but in its wake the anti-roads movement adopted more pro-active tactics, such as Reclaim the Streets actions,[8] where busy roads were reclaimed and turned into massive outdoor street parties. The tactics used in these protests are still evident today, and the recent fracking and Extinction Rebellion protests in the UK have used the same tripods[9] and other road blockades that were seen at Newbury (I have even recognised a few familiar faces at the protests). Probably one of the most heart-warming aspects of this legacy for me though is that as I write this afterword, the 16-year-old climate activist Greta Thunberg[10] has just arrived in New York after crossing the Atlantic in a yacht, so she can attend the UN Climate Summit in Chile by carbon neutral transport. I feel in some way proud that someone who hadn't even been born at the time of the Newbury protests is putting our efforts to shame by spending a couple of weeks in a tiny boat to raise awareness of climate change, as most evictions at Newbury were done within two or three days and at least we had a pub we could go to afterwards!

Notes

1. Newbury had previously been the site of two major battles during the English Civil war.

2. https://en.wikipedia.org/wiki/Newbury_bypass

3. https://www.independent.co.uk/news/uk/the-park-lane-riot-how-park-lane-was-turned-into-a-battlefield-1442203.html

4. https://www.newburytoday.co.uk/gallery/nostalgia/17429/Newbury-bypass-protests-in-1996.html

5. Anon (1996a) 'Newbury: An Adrenaline Junkie's Idea of Heaven'. *Do or Die: Voices from Earth First!* pp. 24-26 http://www.eco-action.org/dod/no6/newbury_description.htm; Anon (1996b) 'A Critique of Newbury'. *Do or Die: Voices from Earth First!* pp. 27-32. http://www.eco-action.org/dod/no6/newbury_critique.htm

6. Cocking, C. & Drury, J. (2004). 'Generalisation of Efficacy as a Function of Collective Action and Inter-Group Relations: Involvement in an Anti-Roads Struggle', *Journal of Applied Social Psychology 34 (2)*, pp. 417-444.

7. https://www.bbc.co.uk/news/uk-england-berkshire-35132815

8. https://en.wikipedia.org/wiki/Reclaim_the_Streets#United_Kingdom

9. Tripods are a very effective way to blockade roads, made by attaching three scaffolding poles together to form a tall pyramid, with a protester dangling from the apex who is then very difficult to remove safely.

10. https://twitter.com/GretaThunberg

Seeds

Zoe Lambert

FOR A MOMENT, the court was silent. Jo squeezed Andrea's hand. She could see her parents sitting at the front of the public gallery. Behind them, the six other members of Seeds of Hope sat together – Ricarda giving Jo a small smile – and every seat taken, all eyes on the foreman of the jury.

The foreman stood, coughed, pulled at his shirt collar, then started to mutter something.

'Can you speak up for the benefit of the court, please,' the judge said.

'The jury returns a verdict of not guilty,' the foreman bellowed, still looking at the paper in his hands.

There was a collective intake of breath, then cheers erupted, applause, as people jumped to their feet. Jo flung her arms around Andrea, then Lotta and Angie, as they all hugged and cried. For a moment their sobs were all she could hear until more cheering and whooping broke through from somewhere above, and the judge demanded: 'Order in the court! Order in the court!'

'Look,' Andrea said, pointing over Jo's shoulder. Jo's mum was climbing over the barrier of the public gallery, her skirt catching and pulling on the railing, as two court officials scurried over to stop her. Releasing herself, she ran over to the dock to hug her daughter, pressing her cheek into Jo's jacket, saying she couldn't believe it, just couldn't believe it. 'Dad is so proud!'

It seemed then as if Jo and the others were carried aloft, borne by the surge of people, and before she knew it they were passing through the public entrance, without time to go back for her bags – but it was OK, someone said they had Jo and Angie's bags, the others' were back in the cells – and they were conveyed, pushed, propelled through the revolving doors, out into the bright sun of the July afternoon. How strange it was – July – two seasons on from the action on that snowy January night. Even stranger that there should be hundreds of people here, the whole of Derby Square outside Liverpool Crown Court full of people. At the front of the crowd, a bank of microphones and a huddle of cameras, photographers and journalists vying for the best position.

Jo grinned at the other three as the microphones were held in front of them. Angie raised her hands to quiet the crowd. 'Following this bold verdict, it is imperative that the government act swiftly to ban all arms sales to Indonesia and end their complicity in the genocide in East Timor.'

Her mother was still holding Jo's hand. 'I'm so proud,' she said. 'Look,' and she pointed to Dad standing on the steps, speaking to a journalist and camera.

There were so many people for Jo to hug: the six members of the support group, friends, and others she didn't even know, and then, a few minutes later, hands grasped waists, and people set off in a spiral dance around the square. Jo held on to Lotta's top and Andrea grabbed hers, as the line began to spiral inwards until everyone in Derby Square seemed to be a part of it.

When the dancing stopped, Jo was told that there were three men in suits waiting to speak to them near the steps. Jo and the others went over; the suits said they were acting on behalf of British Aerospace and had been instructed to serve injunctions on all four women, requiring them to stay away from all BAe sites. Breaching the injunction could incur a penalty of up to two years in prison.

Several stacks of paperwork were dumped on the steps by their feet, one for each defendant. Angie just smiled at the men, thanking them profusely and shaking their hands. When they had gone, someone shouted, 'Tear them up!'

'Should we not keep one, just to check?' Jo asked.

'Never mind that!' And the next thing she knew the documents were being passed around the group, with everyone pulling out pages, ripping them up, and throwing them as high as they could into the air, the pieces floating down onto the steps like confetti.

On that January night, the security guards had finally arrived at five in the morning, shocked to find three women in the hangar. They escorted Jo and the other two hammerers after hours of waiting and telephoning, leaving a message on John Pilger's answerphone, his number found from directory enquiries, then calling Angie whose role was to openly do press work and make a second attempt if theirs failed. They finally got through to the Press Association, who were incredulous when Jo asked them to call BAe.

One of the guards sat Jo, Andrea and Lotta down in the lodge to wait for the police. 'You're the women who've been leafletting at the gates.' They nodded, still shivering despite their body warmers and heavy coats. 'This will warm you up.' He handed them steaming mugs of tea as if they were the victims of a crime, not activists who'd just hammered on a Hawk Jet, causing £1.5 million of damage, before arranging pictures of smiling Timorese children around it, turning it into a shrine with seeds and ashes.

It felt like an age since they'd caught a train to Preston at 6pm, then waited in Pizza Land for the last bus to Warton, barely able to eat the garlic bread and pasta they'd ordered, a holdall of crowbars, bolt cutters and hammers tucked under their table. The court hadn't believed they'd travelled by public transport, but after the bus dropped them at Warton, they had taken up a position behind a hedge not far from the perimeter fence, waiting for the security patrol. Snow still lay on the ground, crisp beneath their boots, their noses already cold. On reccies, they had learned that the Sunday patrols only passed every two hours, whereas other nights, it was every half an hour, as if BAe didn't expect trespassers on the day of rest.

Once the patrol had gone, Lotta fished the bolt cutters out of the bag and cut a small, discrete hole in the fence. Andrea and Lotta climbed through while Jo took one of her peace cranes from her bag and tied it above the hole. The floodlit hanger was barely a hundred metres away. As the others ran up the steep bank towards it, Jo checked the crane, took a deep breath, and ran after them.

The morning after their acquittal and release from Risley Prison, Jo boarded a yellow underground train to Liverpool Central and sat clutching her rucksack to her chest as if someone might at any point snatch it to search its contents. Once they had escaped the media attention outside the court, they had gone for a meal at a community centre – she hadn't caught whose idea that was – and over 200 people had turned up. Then she slept at a friend's flat in Crosby, the others staying at the Campaign Office at Jude's in Princes Park. The office from which Lyn had organised the prison visits and the six-woman support group had run a high-profile media campaign, liaised with the legal team, printed posters and leaflets, and arranged a march every morning of the trial from the bombed out church to Liverpool Crown Court, culminating in a remembrance ceremony outside the court with a hundred people including a Catholic priest and Buddhist nun.

She rubbed her eyes, leaning her head against the window as the train rattled through the tunnel, the yellow carriage packed with commuters, people going to work, happily travelling from one place to another. How strange it was to be able to go somewhere, anywhere, without having to ask permission first. Her eyes were sore. She had lain awake on a roll mat in her friend's box room most of the night, her head spinning with it all. It seemed as if she'd been given a fresh start; her life opened up in front of her. And the trial. The jury had actually done it. They'd gone against the judge's direction and listened to the four expert witnesses. East Timor's Special Representative to the UN had begun to tell the jury about the Hawk attacks on villages in the mountains of Timor, of how many people had been slaughtered, but the judge had tried to stop him speaking. Angie, who was defending herself, had apologised to him for this. But for the jury to go against the judge! No wonder the foreman had looked so uncomfortable. However, there had been a legal justification for the acquittal: they had used reasonable force in the prevention of a crime, only this crime was genocide. Surely, this would change things, really shake things up. The first Ploughshares acquittal ever! And they'd been the ones to pull it off. Ten women had won.

The train burst out of the tunnel into the underground station. Jo got off and ran up the escalator, grabbing the handrail to steady herself. At the entrance, she stepped outside, momentarily blinded by the bright sunlight. She stopped at a newsstand, blinking. There they were! Their faces on all the front pages: the photo of them outside the court, smiling, laughing, announcing their acquittal. She bought one and hurried to the community centre over on Mount Pleasant. She could run down this road, she thought, if the impulse took her. No one would stop her – unless she knocked into someone, of course. The feeling she'd had in the train grew more intense outside. Everyone else was just plodding along, looking their usual, slightly miserable selves. But they didn't appreciate that they could go where they chose. This might only be these grey city streets, but they went there of their own volition, at their own pace, no one was hurrying them or looking at the clock. There was no barbed wire on the horizon.

And there it was, the community centre. She walked inside, past the people queuing to take their seats and the camera crews, momentarily confused by the crowd. All these people, all together. Then she saw Angie, Andrea and Lotta already standing near the stage where four chairs were set behind a table, with conference mics. She hurried over. They were all talking together, going over what they needed to say, the message that the action had been legal, that they had had no choice; they had exhausted all other means – contacting their MPs, signing petitions, writing letters about BAe's contract to sell 24 Hawk jets to Indonesia. They had substantial evidence the jets previously sold had not only been used for training purposes but also to bomb civilians including children in East Timor as part of the ongoing genocide.

'Here you go,' Ricarda said, handing her milky tea in a polystyrene cup.

'Thank you,' Jo replied, and as she took her seat next to Lotta and the others, she could sense the strangeness she felt on the street leaving her.

She didn't get back to her flat in Kirkby until a couple of days later. Setting her plastic prison bag on the floor, she was relieved by the sight of her clean, bare kitchen. It made a difference coming home to a defrosted fridge and a tidy flat after six months' absence.

The weekend of the action, she had taken all the perishables out of the fridge and lined them up on the counter, then scrubbed off the spots of congealed jam and brown sauce from the trays, and washed out the vegetable box. Now, peering inside the fridge, there was only the smell of damp and old plastic to greet her.

Andrea and Lotta had stayed with her, Andrea for two months since she'd given up her privately rented flat, and Lotta came for the last couple of days so they could make final preparations together. They finished off all the food, the last apple, the rest of the cheddar and the final scrapings of her mother's homemade pickle. Then they wrote letters. First, Jo wrote to her old friends, who had no idea what she had been planning, only that she'd been spending all her time with this new group, Seeds of Hope. Then to her parents, her father's words – 'I can't condone anything illegal' – ringing in her ears.

Dear Mum and Dad, she'd written. *By the time you read this letter, I shall probably be in prison, having decided to take personal responsibility for disarming a Hawk jet.*

Please try not to worry. I'll phone when I can. I've taken care of my flat and bills, left my house plants with a friend, along with my valuables, photo albums and address book.

She leaned over the counter to switch the fridge back on. The rumble – always the white noise of living in this flat – began to shudder into life, making more noise than a small refrigerator had the right to make. She'd had this same fridge since she moved in ten years ago. That was before she became active, setting up the tenants' association, then later running as an independent councillor, which she won by a comfortable margin. She wouldn't re-stand now, though.

The flat next door was empty too. Jo's neighbour, who always used to pop round – calling, 'Got any sugar, love?' or 'Can I borrow some tinfoil?' – had bumped into Jo in Risley. Her face: 'I didn't expect to see you in prison! What you in for?'

'Criminal damage.'

'Really? But you're a councillor. I'm in for burglary, love.'

But now the fridge was officially on. And Jo was officially home. Sitting down beside a pile of bills and letters on the kitchen table, she half expected them to be already opened like they had been in prison.

She looked at her hands, the letters shaking in her grip. She hadn't expected to feel so wobbly afterwards, that being in prison would be something to get over. But then it had been impossible to prepare for actually winning. Who wanted to jinx it by booking holidays and making plans while still in a cell?

It was so quiet up here on the thirteenth floor. Jo had been alone in her cell, but the experience had still been collective; they were in there as a group and with a purpose. She had always been able to hear the footfall on steel staircases and landings; prisoners shouting conversations through walls and windows. Sometimes, Angie's voice arguing with the guards over the cancellation of education and association time, of not getting their statutory hour of exercise, the guards claiming they didn't have the staff to take them out: 'I'm writing a report, you know,' she'd say. 'We've made an application to the governor.' This wasn't Angie's first time in prison, and each time she'd written a report on the conditions.

Jo's flat needed some air. Opening the door to the small balcony, she peered down to the carpark thirteen floors below. In front of her, the familiar row of tower blocks, each with what seemed like hundreds of windows and tiny balconies identical to hers. Andrea was determined to stay on in Liverpool; the others had all gone home to different parts of the country to start their lives up again, get things back to normal, leaving her in her flat with its empty cupboards and lonely-looking kitchen. No Lotta or Andrea here with her now. She looked at her hands again. They were still shaking.

Three years had been on the cards. The same as doing a degree. That's what she'd told herself during the prison preparation workshop. She'd learn a lot, perhaps more than her degree in Biology! And for a year everything had been geared towards the action, ten women working together, each weekend planning and organising.

During the Seeds of Hope meetings, they worked out who was prepared to go to prison: Jo, Andrea and Lotta had no dependents, and Angie's children were now adults so they felt able to. The other six had caring responsibilities, jobs they loved, or they preferred to work in a supporting role. They decided on their name by a consensus process, which resulted in: *Seeds of Hope East Timor Ploughshares: Women Disarming for Life and Justice!*

The Hawk Jet had looked so peaceful when they draped the two purple banners on its wings. Around them, they arranged the photos of Timorese and British children and then scattered the seeds and ashes.

They had taken care to leave no doubt that this was an arrangement. It should not look like a piece of everyday vandalism; this wasn't criminal damage, this was disarmament.

The banners had taken months to make, as had the film and book that Jo placed in the cockpit. They set out the story of the

Indonesian invasion and occupation of East Timor, the complicity of the British government and the arms companies and the case for ordinary citizens to take up their hammers. Finally, they left calling cards, with their three names and Angie's.

And once they'd done this, Jo, Lotta and Andrea looked around the hangar. 'What now?' Andrea said. They had always expected to be caught, not to get this far. 'Listen!' They could hear a patrol vehicle, so they ran outside and called, 'Hello!' But it had already disappeared off around the perimeter. Time for some more hammering, then Jo suggested they call the press, so they found a telephone in a small office.

In the weeks following the trial, Jo and Andrea were booked up with visits to universities, churches, peace and amnesty groups, while Angie threw herself into her ongoing forestry campaign. A four-day tour of Wales was planned for later in the year, then presentations in Glasgow, Edinburgh, Manchester, Leeds, Sheffield. As well as talks about Indonesia's brutal occupation of East Timor and the arms trade, they gave workshops to get people thinking about what might motivate them in their own activism.

They had their final Seeds of Hope meeting at Angie's house in Norfolk. As always, they had cake, everyone usually baked something. All ten of them were there. Andrea, Lotta, Angie, and the six support members, Clare, Emily, Jen, Lyn, Ricarda and Rowan.

They sat in a circle. It seemed like only five minutes ago they'd spent New Year's Eve together, Rowan designing a ceremony for them where 'the hammerers' were presented with decorated tools. They had all brought seeds, then they had each written regrets on pieces of paper, and burnt them in the garden. Then all the seeds and ashes had been mixed together, ready for the action in January.

So, now, over cake and tea, they decided that their work together as Seeds of Hope was complete. They had never planned to be a permanent group, and they had achieved what they had set out to do. Some might continue in other related support groups – the Merseyside East Timor Support Group had grown while the four had been in prison; the last meeting had over forty people squeezed into a small room.

Angie talked about her plans to set up Trident Ploughshares and how she wanted to build a mass movement. She placed her cup back in its saucer, and said that in Risley she'd received a letter telling her of the historic decision of the International Court of Justice at the Hague about the Advisory Opinion on the Legality of the Threat or Use of Nuclear Weapons. This explained that the threat or use of nuclear weapons would, in general, be contrary to the rules of international law applicable in armed conflict. Angie looked around at them. 'Don't you see what this means? It means the burden of proof is on the governments with nuclear weapons to justify how using them could be deemed lawful. How could a 100 kiloton nuclear warhead discriminate between a supposedly legitimate target and a school and hospital?' She picked up her teacup and put it down again. 'This is what could be done with Ploughshares next.'

'Yes, of course. But that will be a new group. This group has done its job.'

Jo scraped the last of the walnut loaf off her plate. 'This is delicious, by the way.'

'It really is…'

The group discussion seemed to have come to an end and been replaced by individual conversations, more tea being poured.

'Did you ever watch the news reports?' Ricarda asked Jo.

'I didn't.'

'My friend taped them for me. Your Dad is on there.'

Ricarda got the VHS and put it in the video player. They all quietened down to watch. First the news reports, then the film of them outside the court. The final clip was of Jo's father standing on the steps, saying at first he'd been against breaking the law, but after sitting through the trial, he now passionately believed it had been the right thing to do.

Angie placed a hand on Jo's. 'See,' she said. 'I told you he would come round.'

'Yes, you did.' She smiled, but then she paused, closing her eyes to the sound of the voices around her. It was an end. An end of this group, this camaraderie. It was a loss. And what she was feeling was a kind of grief.

She opened her eyes and said, 'Remember what the judge said?'

'Ha! Yes. "Women like you,"' Angie said, in a posh old man's voice, craning her neck and wagging a finger at the group as they cleared away the plates and teacups, '"should be locked up for a very long time."'

Afterword: Taking Responsibility

Jo Blackman

ZOE LAMBERT'S STORY BRINGS to life the key moments of the
Seeds of Hope action, trial and its aftermath, and although
fictionalised, is faithful to the essence of our story. For me, it all
began in the autumn of 1993, when I read in *Peace News*
magazine about the forthcoming trial of Chris Cole, a Christian
peace activist who in January of that year had broken into a
British Aerospace (BAe) weapons factory in Stevenage, and
'disarmed' the nose cone of a Hawk jet as well as damaging
other equipment[1] – all with a household hammer and in the
tradition of the ploughshares movement. Chris had been
charged with criminal damage, the cost of his action being
estimated at £500,000. Intrigued, I attended the first day of his
trial, at which I underwent a crash course in the UK's complicity
in the genocide in East Timor.

East Timor is a former Portuguese colony, the eastern half
of an island lying east of Bali and due north of Darwin, Australia.
Days after Portugal withdrew from East Timor in 1975,
Indonesia, under the dictatorship of President Suharto, invaded
in pursuit of its rich natural resources (including oil), and to
offer a stark warning to the diverse peoples of its island
territories: there was no room for small, independent nations in
this archipelago. In the weeks that followed the invasion, tens of
thousands were massacred. Those who could fled to the
mountainous interior, with many managing to eke out an

existence within a fragile, autonomous zone defended by a small armed resistance, called Falintil (allied to Fretilin, the deposed political party which had enjoyed majority support).

Despite numerous UN resolutions condemning the Indonesian occupation, the UK and the US entered into lucrative contracts for the sale of ground-attack aircraft to Indonesia. These jets were nimble enough to manoeuvre through steep valleys and were decisive in forcing a mass civilian 'surrender' in 1978-79. Eye-witness accounts emerged of BAe Hawk jets bombing villages during and after this period.

In 1983, the Head of the Catholic Church in East Timor estimated that at least 200,000 people – a third of the population – had died as a direct result of the Indonesian occupation. Six years later, Bishop Belo[2] wrote to the UN Secretary General saying: 'We are dying as a people and as a nation'. He received no reply. It is now estimated that during Indonesia's quarter-century-long occupation, up to 180,000 civilians were killed or starved to death.[3]

In 1993, BAe signed a new deal to supply a further 24 Hawk jets to Suharto's government, with an export licence and an export credit guarantee from the Department of Trade and Industry (DTI), and a target delivery date of January 1996. A campaign to 'Stop the Hawk Deal' took off, with thousands of people signing petitions and lobbying their MPs. Together with Andrea Needham and Emily Johns (who I'd met at Chris's trial), I became involved with the campaign and took part in demonstrations at BAe sites and outside the DTI.

Meanwhile, I followed up on my curiosity about the ploughshares movement, learning about its origins in 1980, when – inspired by the Old Testament prophet Isaiah's call to 'beat swords into ploughshares'[4] – eight people entered a nuclear missile plant in Pennsylvania, and used hammers to disarm nose cones. In ploughshares actions, participants take personal responsibility for disarming weapons (sometimes including computer control systems) in a nonviolent, peaceful, safe and fully accountable manner. By the end of 1995, around

130 individuals had participated in 55 ploughshares actions in the UK, US, Australia, Germany, Holland and Sweden.[5]

In November 1994, I went along to a ploughshares support network gathering, at which we discussed why there had been so few women involved in ploughshares actions until then. Andrea, Emily and Lotta Kronlid had all previously been part of ploughshares groups – but in support roles, while most or all of the 'hammerers' had been men. We concluded that there was probably some unconscious gender stereotyping taking place and that women were more likely to be constrained by the responsibilities bound up in caring roles. As the discussion wound up, someone playfully threw out the question: 'So who wants to be part of the first women-only ploughshares action?' A quick round of responses revealed that four of us were interested: Andrea, Lotta, Lyn Bliss, and myself. We agreed to meet in the new year.

At our first meeting, we decided to focus on the Hawk deal, with a twin-track strategy of continuing to call on the government and BAe to take moral responsibility and cancel the Hawk Deal (we even had a meeting with BAe's Director of Communications), while at the same time preparing to personally intervene and disarm the Hawk jets destined for Indonesia.

We soon realised that we would need more support. So, very discreetly, we set about recruiting another six women by word-of-mouth. We met for a long weekend each month, all squeezing into someone's home, getting to know each other over the cooking and washing-up, going for walks and planning. We discussed everything, from huge questions of principle down to tiny practical details. We initially focused on working out our different roles: Andrea, Lotta and myself would be the 'first wave' of hammerers – a covert attempt to disarm Hawk jets; Angie Zelter and Ricarda Steinbrecher[6] would make up the 'second wave' – an open approach to disarmament; while Emily, Lyn, Clare Fearnley, Jen Parker, and Rowan Tilly would be the 'support activists' – sharing in the preparation work and taking responsibility for communications and media, prison support and organisation around the trial. We aimed to value all roles equally and agreed that we would be collectively responsible for decisions about the action, while taking great care to avoid revealing the existence of the support activists in order to protect them from potential conspiracy charges.

In between meetings, we collated evidence about the role of the Hawk jets in enforcing Indonesia's illegal occupation of East Timor and wrote personal statements expressing our intention to disarm the weapons of genocide. We found out the serial numbers of the jets being sold to Indonesia by simply browsing military aircraft magazines in newsagents and became experts in identifying Hawk jets. Andrea's autobiographical account of the Seeds of Hope action, *The Hammer Blow*, includes a helpful appendix listing the many tasks we undertook.[7]

One of the most important parts of our preparation process was considering the possible consequences if we were convicted: imprisonment (hypothetically up to ten years), court orders to pay compensation to BAe and in Lotta's case, deportation to her home country of Sweden. We shared our fears, often finding that the simple act of expressing them to an attentive listener loosened their grip. With the more persistent fears, we gently probed what was underneath them – what stories and assumptions we had about how things might play out. Some of these fears focused on the more personal impacts of imprisonment, for example on health, relationships, employment prospects and life opportunities. Other fears related to difficult conversations to be had with family members or potential confrontations with security guards or possible violence in prison. We role-played a range of scenarios, trying out different approaches and practising de-escalation techniques. We also addressed practical concerns by finding out all we could about prison – even phoning up a local prison to ask what items could be handed in to prisoners.

There were no easy reassurances, but we tried to mitigate these various fears by taking heart from the stories of others who had actively resisted injustice. We were particularly inspired to hear of several groups of Timorese students who had taken great personal risks to draw the world's attention to the Indonesian regime's brutal occupation of their country. They had scaled high fences to occupy the grounds of embassies in Jakarta, risking arrest, imprisonment and torture.[8]

We were inspired and emboldened by how civil disobedience challenges the culture of obedience, disrupting the habit of fitting in and following the rules, while exposing the lie that ordinary people have no power to bring about a quantum shift towards a more just and sustainable society. This in turn reveals an important limit to a government's power: its dependence on the compliance of its citizens.

Per Herngren, a Swedish writer and ploughshares activist, argues that: 'Since fear is the final obstacle for us in creating a more just society, punishment is the most important part of civil disobedience.'[9] He adds that the main function of the punishment is 'to make citizens internalise control – so that they become their own jailers.' However when we overcome our fear and are prepared to accept the likely personal consequences of our actions, the threat of the punishment loses its power.

For the Seeds of Hope group, the power of civil disobedience lay in the following components:

1. A Commitment to Nonviolence

For us, nonviolence meant acting in a way that was consistent with our vision of a just and peaceful world, and also prefigured it. We took great care to try to ensure that our action would not harm or endanger any living being and also sought to relate to security guards and police with respect, acknowledging their humanity. We were often asked whether damaging 'property' could really be considered nonviolent.[10] Our response was that weapons were not the kind of property that deserved respect, and that we had used proportionate force in a safe and controlled manner with the aim of rendering these weapons harmless.

2. Telling the Truth

By acting at the site where the Hawk jets were assembled and test-flown, and taking full responsibility for our action, we were able to make injustice visible, revealing the links between British economic interests and genocide, and exposing the ways in which arms companies and governments routinely dehumanise and oppress 'other' people. Our arrest process and court hearings offered the opportunity to put BAe and the British government effectively on trial, as well as creating space for dialogue about the responsibility of citizens. During the trial itself, there were several powerful moments of truth-telling: A video we had made was shown to the jury including a clip of a 1993 parliamentary debate, in which the Minister of State for the Armed Forces, Archie Hamilton, was questioned by Alice Mahon MP about British arms sales to the 'murderous dictator' Suharto. He responded without hesitation: 'The point of selling Hawk aircraft to Indonesia is to give jobs to people in this country.'[11] This cynical and immoral stance was not lost on the jury, and contrasted starkly with the moving testimony of Jose Ramos Horta, East Timor's Special Representative to the UN. Horta described the devastating impact of Hawk bombing raids on villages in Timor and spoke with emotion about relatives who had been killed, with the whole court hanging on his every word.

3. Confronting the Culture of Obedience

Our involvements with the ploughshares and wider peace and environmental movements challenged us to overcome our conditioning to live quietly as compliant subjects, afraid of the consequences of stepping out of line. 'If I really believe that this jet will be used to bomb civilians,' I asked myself, 'then what is my responsibility as a human being?' Accountable actions highlight our everyday complicity in injustice: the degree to which we all live in a state of denial and disconnection; the ways in which we acquiesce in the immoral actions of our governments and our passivity and learned helplessness in the face of corporate greed.

4. Inviting Fellow Citizens to Take Responsibility

As soon as Andrea, Lotta and myself had been arrested, Angie embarked on the second wave of action, with the primary aim of mobilising others to continue the disarmament work. She spent a week darting around the country, publicly announcing her intention to disarm further Hawks and inviting others to join her – including politicians, journalists and campaigners. She was finally arrested on her way into a public meeting in Preston, BAe's 'company town'. During our trial, the prosecutor questioned me about the effectiveness of our action – we had only damaged one jet, surely not enough to stop any genocide. I replied that we had started the job and it was up to others to continue the disarmament work.

5. Community Building and Solidarity

A key element of ploughshares actions is building communities of resistance and solidarity. At the heart of the Seeds of Hope action was our affinity group of ten women, including disarmers and support activists. At the same time, we were part of a wider resistance community: the anti-arms trade campaign, the ploughshares movement and the rapidly growing support network within the Liverpool area. From the first day of the trial, hundreds of people took part in processions, vigils and public meetings, as if our action had suddenly taken on a life of its own. Following our acquittal, further resistance communities were formed including a group of four Timorese refugees, a Catholic priest and three parishioners, who on Easter Day 1997, boldly climbed the fence at BAe Warton and entered the site to demand the immediate cessation of work on the Hawk deal.[12]

Ultimately East Timor won its freedom after 24 years of occupation. In 1998, riots and demonstrations in Indonesia –

many led by students – forced Suharto to resign after three long decades as president. The following year, under the pressure of renewed lobbying from Portugal, the EU and Australia, as well as sustained campaigning by the international solidarity movement, the new Indonesian president, Habibie, requested the UN hold a referendum in which the population of East Timor would be given the choice of either greater autonomy within **Indonesia** or independence. On 30 August 1999, 98% of the electorate turned out to vote, with a resounding majority (78.5%) in favour of independence. Immediately following this clear mandate, Indonesian troops and paramilitary gangs launched a campaign of bloody and indiscriminate revenge on the general population, leaving 1,400 dead and hundreds of thousands displaced from their homes. UN staff withdrew swiftly, while journalists were expelled from the country. For a couple of weeks, virtually no news reached the outside world. It was smoke from burning villages that alerted meteorologists and eventually the UN to the extent of the destruction. The arrival of a UN Peacekeeping Force three weeks later brought an end to the violence and paved the way for a UN **transitional administration** (UNTAET), which oversaw recovery and reconstruction until independence was formally declared on 20 May 2002.[13] Jose Ramos Horta, the man who had testified so movingly at our trial, became the first foreign minister of the new nation.[14] On 27 September 2002, East Timor was renamed Timor-Leste and became a member state of the UN.

As mentioned in Zoe's story, Angie went on to set up the Trident Ploughshares mass campaign, which includes a variety of types of action from peace camps to blockades to DIY disarmament.[15] To date, the Trident Ploughshares campaign has seen more than 2,700 arrests, 650 trials and 2,300 days spent in prison (not including days in police custody).[16] Fines and compensation orders totalling over £88,000 have been imposed – the vast bulk of which remain unpaid as a matter of principle, leading to bailiffs confiscating property and to the threat of more prison sentences.[17]

Ploughshares actions focused on the Trident system have included dismantling equipment on the conning tower of HMS Vengeance (the fourth and final British Trident submarine),[18] emptying the contents of a floating laboratory into the loch (the lab was concerned with maintaining Trident's invisibility from surveillance whilst underwater)[19] and disarming a nuclear convoy truck.[20]

The first two of these actions resulted in acquittals while in the latter case, the activists were found guilty and sentenced to a year in prison. The 'Trident Three' who disarmed the floating laboratory were acquitted by Sheriff Margaret Gimblett on the grounds that their action was justified since Trident presented an active threat that was illegal under international law, and that they were acting as global citizens, preventing nuclear crime. This was the first time that a British judge had accepted a defence of the illegality of Trident nuclear weapons based on international law.

Some ploughshares actions in the UK have focused on disarming British military equipment within the context of wars being pursued by the UK government. In March 2003, after Blair ignored the largest demonstration in UK history and prepared to go to war against Iraq, three separate groups of activists entered RAF air bases to attempt to disarm jets destined to be used in bombing operations. Two groups were successful, damaging a Tornado fighter jet and bomber support vehicles.[21]

More recently, on the 21st anniversary of the Seeds of Hope action, Methodist minister Reverend Daniel Woodhouse and Quaker activist Sam Walton entered BAE Systems' Warton site intending to disarm fighter jets bound for Saudi Arabia. They were intercepted by security before they were able to do so and subsequently charged with criminal damage to a perimeter fence and hangar door. At their trial, District Judge James Clarke found them not guilty, concluding that the defendants honestly believed that their action was justified for the immediate protection of property and lives. In a joint statement, the two men said: 'We did not want to take this action, but were compelled to do so in order to stop the UK government's complicity in the destruction of Yemen. Thousands of people have been killed in the brutal bombardment, while companies like BAE Systems[22] have profited every step of the way.'

Reading Zoe's story takes me back to the profound sense of purpose that accompanied my decision to take part in an act of DIY disarmament, and the strange sense of freedom that I sometimes experienced in prison, the palpable sense that 'another world is not only possible, she is on her way'.[23] It was if the old, ossified structures of an unjust society were indeed capable of being torn down.

Reconnecting with these feelings also brings me firmly into the present. In the early autumn of 2019, as this book goes to press, we stand at a crucial moment for humanity. There is a consensus among climate scientists that we have only a very few years left to pull off a rescue mission, if we are to avert the collapse of our societies, mass starvation and global descent into violence and war, and limit the mass extinction of species, which could eventually include our own. This requires us to change course drastically, with the ambition and urgency of a war-time mobilisation. However despite three decades of international negotiations, global carbon emissions are still rising. Governments of industrialised nations are wilfully complicit in the surge of climate disasters around the world and the consequent human misery and death. The same governments are also abjectly failing to safeguard the future for their own citizens, as they cling to the old paradigms of unlimited growth and competing nation states. Swedish activist, Greta Thunberg challenged world leaders at the 2018 UN Climate Summit saying: 'Until you start focusing on what needs to be done rather than what is politically possible, there is no hope. We can't solve a crisis without treating it as a crisis. We need to keep the fossil fuels in the ground, and we need to focus on equity. And if solutions within the system are so impossible to find, maybe we should change the system itself.'[24]

In April this year, I participated in Extinction Rebellion's fortnight of resistance in London, risking arrest for the first time in over two decades. I was reminded all over again of the lesson we knew back in the Warton arms factory in the mid 90s, that deep structural change rarely happens without civil disobedience. As Greta Thunberg says: 'We can't save the world by playing by the rules... It is time to rebel.[25] So let's rise to the challenge of our lifetimes!

Notes

1. Chris Cole also damaged a radar dome mould and a computer running software for deploying the Hawk's ALARM (anti-radar) missile.
2. Bishop Belo was awarded the Nobel Peace Prize in 1996, together with Jose Ramos Horta.
3. The Commission for Reception, Truth and Reconciliation in East Timor documented a minimum estimate of 102,000 conflict-related deaths in East Timor throughout the entire period 1974 to 1999, including 18,600 violent killings and 84,200 deaths from disease and starvation; Indonesian forces and their auxiliaries combined were held responsible for 70% of the killings. http://www.cavr-timorleste.org/updateFiles/english/CONFLICT-RELATED%20DEATHS.pdf,

http://www.etan.org/etanpdf/2006/CAVR/07.2_Unlawful_Killings_and_Enforced_Disappearances.pdf
4. Isaiah 2:4, 'and they shall beat their swords into ploughshares, and their spears into pruning hooks: nation shall not lift up sword against nation, neither shall they learn war any more.'
5. Arthur Laffin & Anne Montgomery (editors), *Swords into Plowshares* (1996), and https://www.kingsbayplowshares7.org/plowshares-history

6. A few months into the preparation phase, Ricarda's father fell ill and so she reluctantly withdrew from the second wave of hammerers and joined the support group.

7. Andrea Needham, *The Hammer Blow* (2016).

8. In November 1994, 29 East Timorese students occupied the US Embassy in Jakarta: https://www.youtube.com/ watch?reload=9&v=V5ogoUUyXu4

9. Per Herngren, *Path of Resistance* (1993).

10. *The Economist* described Seeds of Hope members as: 'Vandals in Sandals', 4 Jul '96.

11. https://hansard.parliament.uk/Commons/1993-01-12/ debates/19d2d2f0-55cf-42e9-9b8e-12f88b8eeee9/CommonsChamber

12. The group of eight people who entered the BAe Warton site on Easter Sunday, 31 March 1997, were charged with trespassing on a civil aerodrome.

13. The United Nations Transitional Administration in East Timor (UNTAET) was established at the end of October 1999 and administered the region for two years. On 20 May 2002, control of the nation was turned over to the new government of East Timor and independence was declared. On 27 September 2002, East Timor joined the United Nations as its 191st member state.

14. Jose Ramos Horta later became President of East Timor from May 2007 to May 2012.

15. In December 2001 the 'Trident Three' were awarded the Right Livelihood Award (known as the alternative Nobel Prize) for their Trident Ploughshares disarmament work. In her acceptance speech, Angie noted: 'We have learnt by now that if we want nuclear disarmament then it is no good waiting for our governments to do it. They have signed many international treaties and agreements promising to disarm their nuclear weapons... But what do these promises mean when, at the very same time, they are researching the successors to the Trident system and continuing to say that they rely upon nuclear deterrence? If we want nuclear disarmament then we, the people, have to take on this responsibility ourselves. This is what People's Disarmament is all about.'

16. These figures are for actions taken as part of the Trident Ploughshares campaign over the period 1998-2018, including

blockades and trespass actions as well as disarmament actions. Most of the arrests took place at blockades and during disarmament camps at Coulport and Faslane.

17. https://tridentploughshares.org/introducing-tp/

18. On 1 February 1999, Rosie James and Rachel Wenham ('Aldermaston Women Trash Trident group') swam to and boarded the Trident submarine, HMS Vengeance. They painted slogans on the sub, damaged test equipment on the conning tower and draped banners.

19. On 8 June 1999, Ellen Moxley, Ulla Roder and Angie Zelter (the 'Trident Three') disarmed the floating laboratory 'Maytime'.

20. On 3 November 2000, Catholic priest Martin Newell and Dutch Catholic Worker, Susan van der Hijden ('Jubilee Ploughshares 2000'), entered RAF Wittering base in Cambridgeshire, where they disarmed nuclear weapons convoy trucks.

21. See (#79) RAF Leuchars Disarmament Action and (#80-81) RAF Fairford Disarmament Actions at:https://kingsbayplowshares7. org/plowshares-history/

22. In 1999, British Aerospace merged with Marconi Electronic Systems to form BAE Systems.

23. Arundhati Roy, *An Ordinary Person's Guide to Empire* (2005).

24. Extract from Greta's speech at the United Nations Climate Change Conference (COP24) in December 2018. Transcript in Greta Thunberg, *No One is Too Small to Make a Difference* (2019), p.16.

25. Extract from Greta Thunberg's speech at Extinction Rebellion's Declaration of Rebellion, 31/10/18. Thunberg, *Ibid.* (2019), p. 12.

Two for One

Nikita Lalwani

PARSLEY, CREAM, POTATOES. HE wanders the aisles, a tourist at a mausoleum. 'Hazelnuts, not too many,' she said. Some cuts from the reduced section of the fridges, anything that might be deemed good value. He turns a corner and is confronted with a whopping long lane of desserts: fairy cakes, meringues, jam tarts, coffee and walnut, the big icing caterpillar for a kid's birthday in its docile cocoon of marzipan and smarties. He looks down at the small wire basket that is hanging off his arm and is overcome with a violent fatigue that threatens to crack his bones in one short, sharp moment, like you do with walnuts. Who are they trying to kid? It is a bit pointless, though isn't it, when it's just the two of them eating tonight?

She takes a piece of gold tinsel and wraps it around the lower layer of the tree. It's her third attempt to make it look good, she's never liked tinsel – the squeaky thin metallic touch of it, so straggly, the way it feels like it will get stuck in your teeth somehow. When she's done she steps back and takes another picture. The pinpricks of light are very small in the cheap new fairy lights that she's put on this year. Battery-powered and weak for it. They make it seem unfinished in the picture, like you still need to join the dots. She hears herself wheeze out a sound of frustration even though she has no audience, thinks to herself: Well, that's properly middle-aged behaviour, making that noise, isn't it? Forty-one, and feeling old today. She moves some baubles and takes another photograph on her phone. It's not like she can send them to him right now, it's not even going to be Christmas any more by the time of her next visit. But she persists in recording the scene so she can show it to him on her phone. The boy does love all the trimmings.

★

'Hiya', he says when he gets in, as is their custom, releasing the word through the door hopefully, like a talisman of sorts, wanting it to do a job way beyond its worth. *Hiya*. The hallway is the most vacant part of the house since the kid went to prison. It used to be that you'd use it as a place to collect, dismantle, rebuild, disperse – shoes, scarfs, coats, words. A hub of noise and fuss even though they have only ever had one child. Now he can hear the small snuffles of her movements in the front room and the flame of resentment in him is fanned up high, dangerous, like a gas flare, because she doesn't reply. She'll pretend that she couldn't hear him. Part of him wants to dump the carrier bag in the hallway there, right now, and leave. Instead, he goes into the room, sees her fiddling with that tree and when she turns around, suddenly his heart is unexpectedly breaking in his chest, she looks so vulnerable, and that is why he says what he does:

'He's coming back. It's not like he's gone forever. He'll be back in a month, though, won't he?'

The look she gives him is a mixture of bewilderment and accusation. Or so it seems. He knows that they take turns with paranoia all the time these days. Rain is spraying a deranged rhythm on the window as he speaks, spitting on the silence with a reminder of the world outside. Fuck this, he thinks, I'm not getting sucked into it like her, this whole Christmas thing. I'm not.

'I know he's coming back,' she says. 'But he isn't here.'

'No shit,' he says, and it's too late to say what he should have which is *You know I love you, so why won't you just let me love you while we wait this out together?*

'Oh,' she says, standing and gathering herself together as the crimson blotches itself under the skin of her cheeks, a fury straining against her tears. 'Oh, you want to make this about us.'

'No,' he says, quick as a nail in plaster. 'No, that's the point, isn't it? I don't want to do that.'

'But you do though, Jay. You think that I give a shit about us.'

Oh, but it hurts when she says it! Even though she's said as much with her whole way all day, and she can surely see it's a blow to him as she pushes past and leaves, running up the stairs with a muffled wail as though she's the only one who loves the kid, as though she is carrying all the pain for the both of them.

He goes out in the hallway and looks at the lumpy bag of shopping lying on the cold click-clack floor. There's so little in it.

★

There's nothing I can do about it, she thinks, sitting on top of the toilet seat and screwing up her eyes to get a handle on the tremors of her body. He'll have a bloody criminal record and there's nothing anyone can do. Sam will have a criminal record. This is the thing that gouges at her insides more than anything, a cleaver in meat every time: that there's no way of erasing this fact, not really. And him being so desperate to go to college, getting through his first year of the course and everything, but what for? On his own in that institution tonight. She holds on to the latch while she cries, although her husband is hardly the type to come and try to invade her privacy here. Part of her wishes he would, of course. Part of her wishes so much for it.

★

She's right, he thinks, laying a blanket on the sofa and positioning a tinny on the table next to it. Sam shouldn't have gone to prison. But it's not because he shouldn't have been out there, protesting, though, is it? Surely they are agreed on that? Let's get this straight. He has to get it straight because his mind is doing somersaults all over the memory of it and it's very confusing. So, he makes it out as a list in his mind. This is how it goes:

1. Police kill a 29-year-old man called Mark Duggan. Thirteen police in four cars pursuing one boy in a cab. They actually kill him – shoot him twice – once in the bicep, once in the chest. They claim that Mark was pulling a gun on them but the gun they are talking about is found twenty feet away from the scene, wrapped in a sock. There is a bullet found lodged in an officer's radio but it's police ammunition and couldn't have been fired by Mark.

2. After killing him, they don't tell Mark's family what happened – the police – they hide it from the mother, brother, all of them, not even visiting the family until the riot is two days in. When protesters arrive at Tottenham police station, they physically lock the door on them instead

3. The crowd builds, it swells with threat while they wait for answers, and why not? It's a terrible thing, and the police don't seem to give a shit. There's something deeply suspicious and familiar about all of it.

4. Jay encourages his own son Sam to go out and join the crowds outside the police station. Yes, he even gives him a speech about what happened in 1985 right here in Tottenham, how police terror led to a fatal heart attack, killing a woman in Broadwater. About dignity being a human right, and having the courage to take action. Yes, he did do that. *There comes a time when silence is betrayal.*

5. The protest turns into something else. The television pumps fear into homes, like petrol into the flames. The animal scum rioters are coming to get you. There's them and there's us. The crowd roars with the taste of power, unrepentant. People screaming down that accommodating megaphone of live TV that they've

been fucked over their whole lives and they aren't going to stop, they've got nothing to lose, and then they either smash or try to set fire to all the places that have kept them out: the magistrates court, the job centre, the solicitors, before they hit the shops. Where are the police now?

6. People get hurt, and there are even some dead. It's awful scary for him and Lisa watching it on TV here in Tottenham now. Pretty much the end of days, in Technicolor. They can't get through to Sam's phone. Jay goes out looking for him, unsuccessfully. He does this again the next night.

7. On the third night, the kid is picked up for looting an ice cream shop. Yes, that's right. Sam has a cone in his hand on CCTV, two glistening fat scoops of Maraschino Cherry and Salted Caramel, is brandishing them in a fancy place in Notting Hill. And yet there is no way to unpeel the comedy from this absurd moment, or the relief that he is alive and unharmed. There is nothing hilarious about him being wheeled along to the police car with an audacious grin on his 19 year-old face, lips wide open to show the full goofy gap between his front teeth. No, they send him to prison for five months. Like most of those arrested in the riots, the sentence is much longer than the normal length.

8. It's Jay's fault.

9. Lisa can't forgive him.

★

She is full of the opinions of others. Her mind is a slipstream of call and response, and this is how she lives her days at the office at the moment, in this constant argy-bargy with herself. She knows she should pierce this bubble, let the pus seep out in a conversation with Jay, but she can't, she's not like him, she can't be so self-righteous and convinced and besides, she's not worried about being right. She's worried about Sam. But she can't think straight, her mind's all soaked up with those other dizzying views like a sponge full of sherry.

Sam's told her that he didn't just steal ice cream, he also had two t-shirts at one point in the night, plus a random single boot which he'd taken on a whim and left in the middle of a road somewhere. It doesn't matter, is how she sees it. He's still screwed up his record and it doesn't matter how much he explains that in the rules of the crowd, the thieving was not just thieving, but also symbolic, itself an act of revenge, she really doesn't care. Her child tarred as a thug. It was not supposed to be this way.

'Mum, I can't explain it,' he said when they first discussed it, giving her these big doleful eyes and a cartoon frown, as though he was making an effort to get it authentically correct. It was the first visit she made to that god-awful place. He was muted, all his usual acid humour neutralised out of him but he wanted to relive it still. 'People were shouting for justice. It felt like things could change, something could happen. There was this power at the centre of the crowd and it was coming out in waves to the edges, it was electric, Mum, I can't tell you, a proper once in a lifetime takeover. People were shouting. *Whose streets, our streets! Whose streets, our streets!*'

Yes, it was like he'd invented rioting when he could have been describing any protest, any march, any big disturbance in the history of this country – the poll tax, Brixton, Greenham, it's a long list. But this was so degrading in comparison. All that footage of them throwing baked bean tins and Tesco wine bottles, not just at police but at innocents too. The burning of buildings without thinking that people were living in the flats above. Poverty linked to stupidity in the news.

'They were bricking boss cars, Mum – Beemers, Mercedes, and all the police cars, it was like a movie. People saying that this was the best day of their lives. These girls ripped out a police radio from a car before setting fire to it. They were shouting all this stuff into it, actually confusing them on the other end and sending them the wrong way, I could hear the whole thing.'

Yes, there's hatred for the police and their harassing ways.

But it's the focus on looting that gets her. A lot of people nicked stuff because they could, of course, something opened up once they realised it was possible. Like the award-winning film-maker who turned up to film a smashed-up shop and couldn't resist taking hundreds of pounds of clothes once he saw how easy it was? He got four months himself, that guy. That posh student that Sam knew, who got six months for taking a case of Evian water from Lidl, and the other rich girl from Kent, police found five grand's worth of gear in her car, nicked from Comet. Or those commuters hovering near the crowd in their car, saying to eleven year-olds near Richer Sounds, 'Get us a TV, mate and I'll give you hundred quid.'

The thing is, he's not wanting for anything, Sam. He wasn't one of those taking nappies and bread and milk for the coming days. Or those carefully scanning clothes and batteries at unmanned tills at Asda, so they could return them when the riots were over.

There's some statistic they had in one of the presentations at work, that over 30% of people regularly steal at supermarket self-checkouts because they see it as a victimless crime – all classes, mind, from Waitrose to Morrisons – and that it doesn't matter to top management because it's still cheaper to use machines rather than people, so they just absorb the costs.

She wants to scream at those around her. You think you're better? These kids don't have jobs, same for their parents, no college for them, all the cuts instead. Shit schools, slashed grants, no more free travel. Hungry half the time. They want the Ralph, the Gucci, the Nikes for a reason. Because it takes about two seconds to recognise one of those brands. The iPhone, the Blackberry. They terrify you but actually they are terrified themselves. And aren't they right? About having nothing to lose?

You expect them to march like middle class people and break for a nice lunch before resuming? Like people who are used to being heard and know their rights? It's septic, this country – how we live side by side, so much to so little.

But she can always see the other side of the story, is her problem. And people were hurt, is the thing.

*

He lies back, his head against a flimsy silk cushion that is inadequate against the hard edge of the sofa where he is trying to position his neck. He wants to avoid his shoulders cramping up. Deep purple, the silk, with a black tree imprinted on it, and too thin to be of any use. The black space is bloated full of shifting shapes around him. They've got these thick velvet curtains in the living room, and the blots of light from the tree are still visible against them, blurring, he can't help but keep looking at them. It's too early to sleep, but there's no sound of her moving upstairs, which bothers him.

Of the darker images that come back to him, the most brutal is Carpetright, burning on his conscience like a visitation, an emissary from the same place as the twin towers. All those people in the flats upstairs, scared for their lives. There is no getting around the fact that what happened at Carpetright was wrong, awfully wrong, no surprise that it split the crowd, a lot of them didn't agree and filtered off once it began. People are saying that when rioters went up to help people escape the smoke, many of the residents sealed their doors against them, thinking that the mob they could see on their screens had come to kill them.

There are several of these images that aggravate him, based around the terrorising of ordinary people going about their business – the bus hijacking, petrol bombs, lighter fuel and knives, robbing small businesses and the like – that he can't just relegate to the bin entitled 'collateral damage'. Someone saying six boys took a policeman down an alley and beat him. Bad. But isn't that always the way with any mass action, though? People who spin out, go off-road. Tainting it for the rest.

He hears himself make a small sound as the leather creaks underneath him, something like a groan, something that wants to be louder. Sam is in prison, and the house is unbearable. It's a failing in him and Lisa that they can't cope without him. It's something broken between them that has cracked in such a way that it refuses to fit back together. They've stopped seeing everyone – family, friends – it doesn't help. There are so many people around them with similar – look at that teenager three doors down, she must be around eighteen, nineteen now. Her mother took the rap for the stolen goods her daughter had stashed in the house – H&M, FootLocker, Curry's and more. But Lisa doesn't want any part in bonding with people over this, and he has to agree, that he finds himself instinctively keeping his distance most of the time.

Meanwhile, Mark is still dead, and it's horrible seeing his brother around the place with that look in his eye. Like he has to apologise for what happened, and the trial still stretching out ahead.

But Sam is coming back. In a month, the long bony obstinate joy of their son will walk back through that hallway. To what, though?

★

There are good years and bad in marriage. She shivers as she gets changed, does not want to go downstairs and past the living room door to put on the heating, but it's what the house needs. People talk about a house having good bones, well this one is a skeleton that is cold and rattling out its horror in the most unsubtle of ways. She sits in the bed and huddles her knees, weak from the crying. Outside she can hear cars, sirens, the odd muttering couple of voices as people walk past. The world is unchanged. And that's because it's the same, is what Jay would say.

Husband. Father. Two words that couldn't be more straightforward.

They've never told Sam that the man whose seed went to create him is someone other than Jay. She wrinkles her nose at this way of putting it, it does sound wrong, as though she got it from a donor. But these words: *father, dad,* they are something for Jay and no one else in this instance. Ben was already in prison when she was pregnant, and her own violation in being with him was breaking on the rocks of her mind every morning like surf. She didn't tell Ben either. She was working at the front of the hotel in Bournemouth then, straight off the bat after her course in event management, and she had come home to Tottenham and lain down in the enormous quilt of Jay's kindness like it was a boutique service itself, something special, a deep dive in featherdown to forget yourself for a weekend.

He was working as a postie back then, and she began coming back for his ministrations every Friday, lying sated in his bed the next day as he did his rounds, the roll blinds down and filtering the sun to mush while she pressed pause, held all thoughts of the future away. In the evening... those big, persistent eyes, the way they made her the centre without weighing in on her, their conversation dancing out gleeful rhythms like a sampler over the hubbub of whichever pub they were in. Carefree. She would be sitting there clutching her lime soda like it might evaporate at midnight, and Jay turn into a frog, imagining the effect of her belly swelling up to carry this bowling ball inside her. Instead, he just stayed right there, next to her, nothing seemed to faze him.

Good years and bad years for marriage. What's yours is mine. They've had their fights. When Jay was striking with the union and money squeezed down to a drop. Those months when he went from silent to bellowing and back because his mother was dying. But nothing like this. He thinks she cares about prison, Jay, because it fits in with her mission for self-improvement, the way she cares about getting five a day and eight glasses of water. That she wants to always be stepping up a level and looking after number one. It's so insulting, and yet something has changed because she doesn't care to go into the ring and fight it out – the individual over the group, the family over the community – whatever philosophy he's got about it – she just wants her baby back, free from scarring or infection.

Jay sent him out that night while she was working late, unawares, and now Sam is lying in a sewer. No one looks at you the same after prison. Employers, college, banks, the list is endless.

★

There was a theory in the introduction of one of those self-help books Lisa kept in the bathroom, that the story of a marriage is all laid out in the beginning, like the first page of a good book. Foreshadowing, it's called. That you can look back to early conversations and see it all, plain as can be, like a mystery story – the hierarchies, the tensions, the way it's going to pan out. The answer to who will hide the body in the carpet.

In their case you could always see that he was going to love her more than she would him.

'Baboom!' she had said in that first week, with an operatic giggle, when he had his hand over her heart in bed. He was feeling the rhythm of it for a clue to her emotions, but also just for the miracle of it, the way it was hot-skipping under his palm. 'Baboom, baboom, baboom!' He had tried to look her in the eye, let her know he was submerged, that the sensation was overpowering, but she had continued the giggle, turned over.

And then there was their first argument, about three or four weeks in. He didn't remember what it was about, but it had got unnaturally heated. He remembered the critical moment, when he had gone to leave the room, and she had run to the door and stood in his way with this look in her eye, as if she couldn't believe that this was the same man who had just been dowsing her hair with apricot conditioner in the shower and holding her wet body against him as he whispered out all his love. This is not part of the deal, her eyes said, when she was blocking his way. This whole thing relies on you sticking to the deal.

What was the deal? It was difficult to unpick it, looking back, but it was something to do with being as passionate in action as in word. A man who spoke like that of love should not threaten to leave her. The two things would not work in tandem.

But in reality, it was a correct assessment, of course. He's never wanted to leave her. He can't even sleep a bloody night apart on the couch like this without feeling like he's been bleached through, away from her warmth.

*

She is shaking again, it's so bloody cold, even with part of the quilt wrapped right around her body to help trap the air like a sleeping bag. She's wondering about the temperature in prison. Too hot, too cold? Do they have decorations, a special meal for tonight and tomorrow? They must do, of course, but it's impossible to think of them doing it without imagining a picture of the inmates all decked out at the table with a big fake smile for the camera – people going *Aw look… innit lovely.* The same condescending shit that is reserved for a children's ward or hospice at this time of year. The staff with baubles in their ears, singing along to the Christmas songs on the radio. This is her point, she doesn't want him to be the subject of anyone's pity. Not Sam, the kid who was always coming home from school with more goodness, more garlands of pleasurable facts and ideas, life opening out in front of him, behind him, all sides, year on year. There has to be a way to escape it. The only answer is to move, of course, she knows that, it's what she comes back to again and again every night when she thinks it through. But he's nineteen years old, not running around in his nappy and waiting to be scooped up. He'll take some convincing. And Jay will never leave Tottenham, but that's something else.

*

He stands in the garden with a rollie. There's a sprinkle of gear in it, not much, just enough to help lull him down. A concrete yard, but a garden still, that coveted piece of outside space, big enough for a sand-pit and two deckchairs to watch Sam roll around in the golden, sugary sludge, that summer of 1993. Lisa, again, pushing for more with them buying a whole house when the council was selling them off on this small estate, against his natural caution. A row of houses from the seventies facing the Victorians on the other side rather than more of the same. It seemed inconceivable back then, that mortgage, so much debt it made his eyes sting to think of it, but she worked out the figures, that the bank wouldn't give it to them if they didn't think they could pay it, and somehow convinced him.

People are saying that Bruno Duggan is seriously ill and he's given up against the disease now, after this. It was someone at work who knows them well that brought it up. He said he went round and the man wouldn't speak, other than to say the same that we all know: 'They killed my son, they killed my boy.' Another guy in the post room with the statistics. Only two trials in the last twenty years where the police have been held to account for shootings in this country. And both times they were found not guilty. Not a single fucking conviction.

He looks out over the fence and sees the high-rise looming, then the mistier one behind it, thinks of the others even further away, repeating and linking themselves across London like dominos. Living down here, on the ground, you could just see the pattern of those distant squares, lit-unlit, and forget that each life in each room counts itself for something, each mind is playing the lead part in their own days. He squints. The lights are blurring in his vision, just like those on the tree.

It's 2am when he walks into the room. Inside himself he feels a clenching as he lies down. She's right at the edge of her side, almost brushing the bedside table with her nose. He lies on his back, inches away from her, listening to her breathing, although it is regular, it sounds light, as though she is awake. It's a risk, when he turns, and their feet touch, but she doesn't pull hers away, part of his right leg is against her too, and this is how they lie, without him pushing it further, the rest of his body back and away, but the feel of their skin together.

Afterword: Untidy Freedom

Dr Roger Ball
Keele University and University of Sussex

When I first met Nikita to discuss the historical background to her proposed story about the Tottenham riot of August 2011, we laughed about getting the 'short straw' in this volume. If only we had been given an eighteenth century 'uprising' or a contemporary, 'worthy' series of protests like those concerned with funding and access to education in 2010. Instead we had to analyse and interpret, from our different perspectives as creative writer and historian, one of the most contentious events of twenty-first century Britain.

Our worries were partly derived from popular understandings of the concepts of 'riot' and 'looting' – highly charged terms which are problematic, fluid and contingent on political perspectives. For example in 2003, according to US Defence Secretary Donald Rumsfeld, the new found 'freedom' of the Iraqi people after the fall of Baghdad was being expressed in a massive wave of collective looting. Rumsfeld claimed: 'Freedom's untidy, and free people are free to make mistakes and commit crimes and do bad things'.[1] Contemporaneous to the August riots in the UK was the 'Arab Spring' which was feted in much of the British press. Didn't this wave of revolts which challenged despots and dictatorships across North Africa and the Middle East originate from a series of riots in Tunisia?

In Nikita's story, Sam's parents are struggling to reconcile the dichotomy between 'protest' and 'riot', trying to understand how one developed into another and how that concluded in arson and looting, and the imprisonment of their son. As they both realise, attempting to hammer the square peg of the August 2011 riots into the round hole of 'political protest' is problematic, despite the help of Martin Luther King and his over-used soundbite 'A riot... is the language of the unheard'.[2] Similarly, it is difficult to force the August riots into a hole designating them as 'criminality, pure and simple', as Prime Minister David Cameron attempted before the disturbances had even concluded.[3]

Pathologising the August riots or reducing them to mere criminality was a popular activity among journalists and politicians in 2011. Terms such as 'feral youth', 'mindless thugs' and 'career criminals' were being commonly used to characterise the crowds of people who took part in the rioting and looting.[4] Alongside startling images of massive fires in commercial and residential properties were numerous reports in the media of corner shops being attacked and looted. The impression was being given that the target of 'psychopathic' rioters was the local community, 'you and me', creating fear and anxiety in much of the population. But how true was this characterisation, and how well did it explain the behaviour of the rioters?

Mark Duggan and the English Riots

The shooting dead by a police firearms unit of a 29-year-old mixed heritage man, Mark Duggan, in Tottenham Hale, London, in the early evening of 4 August 2011 precipitated four days of urban disturbances across England. Beginning with a major disorder in Tottenham on Saturday 6 August, over the following two days rioting and looting spread across the capital and on the Monday evening appeared in several other cities including Birmingham, Liverpool, Nottingham and Bristol. On the Tuesday evening, while London quietened, disturbances developed across the east and west Midlands and occurred in Manchester, Salford, Leicester, Gloucester and again in Liverpool and Bristol. In all, it was estimated that 66 areas experienced around 100 disorder events. Five people were killed during the disturbances, over 200 police officers were injured and more than 5,000 people were arrested for riot-related offences. The financial cost including compensation claims, loss of trade and policing was estimated to be in the region of £500 million.[5]

Duggan's death at the hands of the Metropolitan Police Service (MPS) is recognised as the 'trigger' incident for the collective violence that followed, but is this a good description of what happened? There were no riots in the immediate aftermath of the shooting. So his death was hardly a 'trigger' instantly 'igniting' the supposed 'combustible material' in Tottenham. Instead of an immediate paroxysm of violence, suggesting impulsive and mindless behaviours, Duggan's family, friends and eventually wider community came to terms with their loss and began to challenge the narrative that was being propagated by the authorities and the media. The false story that was being 'fixed' over those crucial hours was that Duggan was armed, had 'come out shooting' and wounded a police officer before being killed. This behaviour was explained by portraying him as a dangerous 'other', a 'well-known gangster' according to police sources, a 'gunman' according to journalists, who had apparently been 'threatening passers-by with a firearm'.[6] The problem with all this was that the people who knew Duggan best did not buy the story that was being spun. They found it hard to believe that he would have behaved in this way.

To add to doubts about the story of the shooting in the media, over the crucial 48 hours after Duggan's death, neither the MPS nor the Independent Police Complaints Commission (IPCC) provided an adequate explanation of the incident to his close relatives. While the IPCC gave a press conference and vacillated with the MPS over who was responsible for family liaison, anger and frustration grew in Duggan's community.[7] By Saturday lunchtime, plans were afoot for a protest. In the late afternoon, a group of about fifty people, including the family and friends of Duggan, left Broadwater Farm estate to walk the half mile or so to Tottenham Police station. As they walked they chanted 'We want answers' and 'Justice for Mark Duggan'.

This march had significant historical resonances with the deaths of other innocent Black Londoners at the hands of the MPS, which were not lost on those present and are recalled in the story by Sam's stepfather. In October 1985, after police burst in to search her home, Tottenham resident and 48-year-old mother of five, Cynthia Jarrett, collapsed and died. A week earlier another black mother, Cherry Groce, was shot in her bed and paralysed for life during a bungled police raid in Brixton. In both cases protests at the local police station in the immediate aftermath developed into extremely serious riots. The former, centred on Mark Duggan's home estate of Broadwater Farm, led to the death of Police Constable Keith Blakelock.

From Protest to Riot

On arriving at Tottenham police station, the majority of the protesters gathered outside, while inside members of Duggan's immediate family attempted to get some answers. News of the demonstration filtered via social media and word of mouth into the community. Like Sam in the story, a number of local residents who either knew Mark Duggan or identified with him joined the protest. The crowd blocking Tottenham High Road grew to several hundred, while lines of police began to form to guard the police station. After nearly three hours of frustrating discussions, the Duggan family left Tottenham Police Station without satisfaction, implicitly signalling that the negotiations were over. Within minutes, some protesters began throwing missiles at the police lines, while others dragged an abandoned police vehicle into the middle of the main road and set it alight. However, the violence did not become collective until an hour later when a Territorial Support Group (TSG) police unit charged forward and knocked a young woman protester to the ground. Angrily citing the 'beating of the girl', a large number of protesters advanced down the High Road past the burning police vehicles and attacked the police cordon, launching a volley of missiles. The protest was now developing into a full-scale riot. As the violence escalated, photos of burning police vehicles and a double-decker bus began to circulate on social media and then featured on national TV. These images, which were being associated with the police shooting of Duggan, attracted those who identified with his plight, as a working-class black man, subject to police violence.

For the following eight hours, serious rioting involving hundreds of people took place along a mile stretch of Tottenham High Road. Among targets damaged or destroyed by fire were a duty solicitor's, Neighbourhood Police Office, Council office, Job Centre, Magistrates Courts and the Probation service. However, the most dramatic instance of arson was the huge blaze set in the Carpetright department store which eventually destroyed 26 flats above the shop. In the early hours of Sunday morning, hundreds of people broke away from the rioting to loot a nearby retail park in Tottenham Hale and Wood Green shopping centre. The violence in Tottenham eventually petered out at dawn after the deployment of mounted police, low-flying helicopters, an armoured vehicle and significant numbers of public order units.[8]

From Protester to Looter

In the story Sam's mother Lisa struggles to understand how her son could transform from a respectable protester into a violent rioter and then to a base looter. To understand this transformation, we need to examine shared social identities of the protesters, perceptions of legitimacy, and the interactions between the crowd and the authorities. The shared identities which caused the protesters to gather at the police station were related to ethnicity, social class, police-community relationships, and local history. Jay, Sam's stepfather, references Tottenham's history of protest against police violence to encourage his son's attendance at the demonstration. His mother describes hatred of police harassment as normal and thus legitimises the reason for protest. It is also likely that as a young (black) male in Tottenham, Sam would have experienced Stop and Search by the police which may have been why he and many others saw Mark Duggan as self-relevant. The perceived illegitimacy of the shooting thus brought a section of the local community onto the streets who shared anti-police feelings. Once gathered together as a crowd, however, new identities and behaviours can arise, dependent on the situational actions of the authorities.

A number of key events helped unify the crowd and transform the protest into collective violence. When the small march arrived at Tottenham Police station the police declared it a 'critical incident' and immediately asked for reinforcements including public order units. Most of the crowd were barred from the police station for the duration of the protest. The visible failure of the negotiations after several frustrating hours of waiting allied with the growing numbers of police apparently there to defend the police station enhanced the 'us' and 'them' feeling. Finally, the assault on the teenage girl by the TSG unit was perceived as an illegitimate action, and collective violence against the police was therefore legitimised and generalised. The protesters, including Sam, had now transformed into 'rioters'.

At this point, the reversal of power relations becomes important as it can determine the longevity and severity of a riot event. Two main processes of empowerment can be discerned from accounts by rioters.[9] The first concerned existing divisions among young people in the borough of Haringey through 'postcode rivalries'. Although the potential for violence between these groups dissuaded some from travelling to the Tottenham riot, for those that did the experience was uplifting. Seeing themselves as 'the same' people in relation to the police, enmities were transcended, creating a larger ingroup united in common purpose. The second empowerment process was a consequence of the aggressive action of the TSG unit. This was carried out without having the police numbers present to sustain dispersal of the crowd. As a result, for several hours police responses were perceived by those present to be absent or ineffectual and in some cases they were even defeated by crowd action. This empowered the rioters by reversing the day-to-day disempowerment they felt historically in relation to the police. This created feelings of excitement and joy, as Sam recalled in the story: 'it was electric… a proper once in a lifetime takeover'.

The reversal of power relations experienced by the rioters opened up new possibilities for action. Seeing the inability of the police to react, a crowd set off to Tottenham Hale Retail Park where they began looting major chain stores. While some continued to fight the police in north Tottenham, others headed for the Wood Green shopping centre. However, these episodes of collective theft should not be reduced to merely acquisitive crime. The looting appeared to be a public and collective act of defiance and celebration; for some it was revenge on the 'establishment' for taking away their educational opportunities;[10] for others it was an expression of power to be flaunted in front of the 'weak' police. Many participants spoke of the surreal nature of the plundering, and Sam was certainly not alone in being arrested and jailed for helping himself to something as trivial and absurd as an ice cream.[11] The looting was also a way for people to take collective power over familiar public spaces, such as retail parks, malls and shopping centres, in which they experienced their everyday lives.[12] As Sam recalled, the crowds chanted 'Whose streets, our streets!' and then acted out this desire. Very few people who went to the protest or joined the rioters on Tottenham High Road planned to be 'looters' that night in August. Instead these behaviours emerged out of the changing power relations in the transformation of the protest into a riot. Sam was one of those who was both affected by and part of this collective process.

However, the collective empowerment which transformed protest into riot and then into looting was not open-ended; it was not the 'free for all' or 'chaos' that the media portrayed. Rather than some pathological loss of self in the crowd or 'criminal instinct', this was a process marked by limiting behaviours – that is, what the crowd *did not do* is as important as what it did. For example, throughout the events in Haringey the vast majority of violence was directed at the police. Members of the public were not in general targeted. Press and TV journalists were tolerated for long periods as long as they did not film people engaging in crimes. There was also little or no violence directed at the police during the long period of negotiation with the Duggan family and when it did generalise it was only after the 'beating of the girl' by the TSG unit. Also, many rioters refused to engage in the emerging looting, stating that their 'beef' was with the police over the killing of Duggan; they continued to fight the police through the night while others left to loot Wood Green.

Although fires, which were so prevalent in the media coverage, were set in certain shops, of the hundreds of potential targets in Tottenham, most of those chosen related to the police, magistracy, local government and employment services. And as Jay recalled in the story, when the fire in the Carpetright department store began to endanger the families living in the flats above, rioters broke into the building in order to warn them and some helped rescue children. Even one of the most iconic images of the August 2011 riots, the burning double-decker bus on Tottenham High Road, has a sub-plot. As Jay recalled, it was hijacked by some rioters; one passenger remembered 'the guys who did it come on the bus first to warn everyone to come off the bus, we're setting the bus on fire'; hardly the psychopathic or feral behaviours that were being propagated by the mainstream media.

I hope in this short article looking at the anatomy of the Tottenham riot I have explained some of the processes which transformed Sam from 'respectable' protester to rioter and looter. Of course, examining just one of the numerous riots of August 2011 does not explain them all, but recent research has demonstrated that many of the processes and patterns that appeared in the Tottenham riot were replicated across the country.

Notes

1. Loughlin, S. 'Rumsfeld on Looting in Iraq: "Stuff happens"', *CNN.com/U.S.*, 12 April 2003.

2. Rothman, L. 'What Martin Luther King Jr Really Thought About Riots,' *Time*, 28 April 2015.

3. 'London Riots: Prime Minister's Statement in Full,' *Daily Telegraph*, 9 August 2011.

4. For examples, see Crick, A. et al. 'Descent into Hell as London Burns,' *The Sun*, 9 August 2011; 'They Stole Everything! Shelves Stripped Bare and Shops Ransacked as Looters Pillage London High Streets,' *The Daily Mail*, 9 August 2011.

5. *Five Days in August – An Interim Report on the 2011 English Riots* (London: Riots, Communities and Victims Panel, 2011), p. 28.

6. Hughes, M. and Wardrop, M. 'Officer Saved by a Radio as "Gangster Fires"', *The Daily Telegraph*, 5 August 2011; Sales, D. and Pollard, C. 'PC Hit as Cops Kill Gunman; BULLET HIT RADIO,' *The Sun*, 5 August 2011; Chalk, N. 'Gunman Shot Dead after Policeman is Saved Because Bullet Hit his Radio,' *The Express*, 5 August 2011.

7. Milsom, T. *Independent Investigation Final report: Report of the Investigation into a Complaint Made by the Family of Mark Duggan about Contact with them Immediately after his Death* (London: IPCC, 2012) Reference: 2011/016449.

8. A comprehensive account of the riots in Haringey in August 2011 researched and written by the author can be accessed at the Beyond Contagion project website: 'Haringey Riot 2011,' Beyond Contagion, University of Sussex, http://www.sussex.ac.uk/beyondcontagion/projects/haringeyriot2011.

9. More than 200 accounts of participants in the August 2011 riots gathered by the *Guardian*/LSE Reading the Riots project were made available to researchers. Stott, C., Ball, R., Drury, J., Neville, F., Reicher, S., Boardman, A. and Choudhury, S. 'The Evolving Normative Dimensions of 'Riot': Towards an Elaborated Social Identity Explanation,' *European Journal of Social Psychology* 48, (2018), pp. 834-849.

10. 2010 saw numerous and sometimes violent protests concerning funding for higher education.

11. Sam's five months in jail for petty theft was not unusual. In the aftermath of the riots exemplary sentences were handed out to participants across the country. In London 'the immediate custody rate tripled from 12% to 36% in magistrates' courts and rose from 33% to 81% in crown courts...Sentences were on average approximately two months more than the 13 months received by similar offenders the previous year'. Doward, J. 'London "Riot Crimes" Fell in Months After Courts' Tough Sentences, Study Finds,' *Guardian*, 11 May 2014.

12. Tiratelli, M. 'Reclaiming the Everyday: The Situational Dynamics of the 2011 London Riots,' *Social Movement Studies* 17, no. 1 (2018), pp. 64-84.

Fear in Your Water

Julia Bell

I HAD BEEN READING FOUCAULT – and not understanding it properly; I was too distracted to concentrate. But I got the gist of it, at least what I thought was the important stuff, what he was saying about madness and how it has been civilised out of us, how back in the day it used to be that sane people and mad people all lived together and there wasn't so much of a difference. And 'mad' people were often seen as visionaries with special access to God. It was only when people got all Jane Austen and mannered, that it was suddenly embarrassing to be unhinged and people got shipped off to asylums. Like George III who thought he was dead and started talking to the angels so manically he foamed at the mouth and they strapped him to a chair.

I let my mind wander, imagined all kinds of upsetting scenes, which made me feel uneasy, so I went out to look for something else to do. I'd had four sessions on the phone with a woman who spoke too quickly, who was supposed to help with intrusive and paranoid thoughts. 'Distract yourself,' the voice said. 'Go for a walk, or a swim.' But I wasn't sure that helped either. Sometimes, I heard things. My dead mother talking to me, or ex-lovers would appear in the night. I was supposed to be taking medication but I found it hard to know what day of the week it was and often forgot. In the end, I ignored the messages from the doctors about renewing my prescription. In other circumstances I probably would have been in a hospital, but there just weren't enough beds.

I had a girlfriend, once, and we lived in this flat together. She still checked in from time to time, but she was mostly gone, with someone better and healthier. 'I just can't look after you,' she said, crying.

I didn't blame her really, most of the time I could hardly get out of bed, but it did make me lonely to think of her, happy with her new partner. 'You can stay here until you sort yourself out,' that's what she said. But I didn't want to move out, I was safe there, next door were alright – Mrs Obidike or her son sometimes brought her leftovers and in return I would feed their cat. People looked out for each other, were generally kind, whatever they liked to say in the papers about council estates being rough. Then my ex helped me take over the contract and set it up so the housing benefit paid the rent. But now there was something going on with that, letters that I didn't want to open piling up by the door. I'd been meaning to take them over to Mrs Obidike, but speaking to people was getting increasingly hard. Whenever I tried, my mouth became dry and sticky and I trembled with nerves. Thinking about this made me feel sick. I needed to get out, get some fresh air, although the weather was heavy and hot, there were storm clouds looming east, though it was hard to separate them in the haze of the polluted sky.

I took the stairs because only one lift was working and the hallway was full of builders. The tower had become like an island, marooned in a construction site, cut off from the world by a sea of scaffolding. Regeneration: what a bullshit word. They were just covering the building in some fancy tiles to make it look smarter for the people who had to look at them. Why should poor people live in a rich area? That's what they thought. But it wasn't always this way, this area wasn't always rich, this tower wasn't always stuffed and crumbling. As if it was *their* fault that property was now worth so much money. I had been putting off thinking about it for a while, but there were protest posters in the hallways and leaflets in the mailbox. One of the neighbours had started a campaign, but even he was sick with the stress of it. Every day it seemed there were random men in suits taking measurements, meetings behind closed doors. People from the council, who now worked for the management and development companies. But what could we do? No one was listening. It felt like a siege.

A few hours later after wandering around for a while, I found myself at a bus stop in Marble Arch. There was a person next to me that I didn't pay attention to at first. But then the woman coughed and the sound was so weirdly familiar that it startled me. There was a pile of Big Issues at her feet, and I heard a voice in my head: *I know who you are.*

'Hello.' I said. 'Have we met before?' I said. Too stiff and formal, as if I were not herself, but a reflection of myself.

The woman didn't answer, she had long grey hair like Patti Smith, the kind I thought I might have one day when I got older. I thought the woman was probably younger than she looked although I am bad at guessing people's ages. Sometimes when I look at people, they all seem like children, old men still have the bellies of babies, old women carry a girlish hope in their eyes only made perverse by their grey hair. If I had made the world, everyone would stop growing old at about nine years old, which was probably the last time I ever felt safe in my life, and a part of me had been trying to find my way back to that place ever since.

'Do you know James?' I asked. Perhaps we'd met at a party or something, years ago when I was better.

'Know lots of them.' The woman smiled, cheekily, like she had a secret. 'You got any tobacco?'

'Sure.' I gave the woman my pouch and stood and watched her roll one, then another which she put behind her ear. When she gave it back, I rolled one for myself and we sat next to each other smoking in a weird silence watching people come and go, as if we'd known each other all our lives. The woman didn't seem to mind me sitting there quietly, and I was glad to have the company.

I looked at the woman's stuff, an old floral shopper on wheels ripped on one side and half-bursting its contents, grey clothes, plastic bags, lots of plastic bags, and some papers that were covered in dense lines of writing. I had once wanted to be a writer, though I did pretty much everything I could to avoid actually putting pen to the paper. I spent most of my time thinking about what I might write, formulating sentences that I never wrote down and then forgot. I could never find my voice, that one position that would hold the whole world together, it fragmented every time I tried. The writer's voice seemed like a dictatorship, something that organised and bossed reality. Maybe I just wasn't that bossy.

The traffic moved around us, people, catching buses, rushing, no one paying any attention at all. The woman tried to sell a few copies of the Issue, but people just hustled past, shoulders braced.

I picked out one of her copies and flicked through it, an eco-special, full of articles about the frightening state of the planet. The woman watched, then started talking about how there are so many pollutants in the water we have no idea how much dirt we are putting into our bodies, the whole time pulling on a cigarette.

'They're trying to kill us,' she said. 'Everything is full of poison.'

She talked about this artist, Emoto someone, who did experiments with water. She said he had proved that water molecules take on the emotional resonance of whatever is directed at them. That basically, when you project feelings at things they change.

'I mean if you direct hate into something long enough, that's what you'll get. Fear. Fear in your water.'

Apparently, this Emoto person had studied the crystal components of water after it had been subjected to various sounds, from loud thrash rock to Beethoven to love poetry to recordings of Hitler.

'The ones that had been hated on were all fucked up! Makes sense if you think about it.' The woman spoke in a low growl, smoking another of my cigarettes down to its nub, squinting as the smoke drifted into her eye. 'In fact, you could say it explains my whole life.'

The truth of this flowed through me with the force of a revelation. 'Mine too.'

I could still see his face, his sadistic leer when I knew it would be happening again. Living around him poisoned them all. Especially my mother. My heart started beating hard, I didn't want to remember, to go back where the air was thick with the stench of his selfishness. Sometimes it was so close it could have happened yesterday. I groaned with the weight of the memory. Hit my arms against my thighs, slapped myself on the head a few times until the woman told me to stop and she held my hand until I felt calmer.

Time passed, the air got closer until suddenly a huge thunderclap made us both jump and a woman at the bus stop screamed. I tried to ignore it because I was in a really intense phase where everything seemed like a warning. I could read things into the weather, or the graffiti on the streets, every moving thing had so much significance it was overwhelming.

'At last!' the woman said, 'the air pressure's been giving me a headache all day.'

And it started raining, at first spatters, then heavy and soaking. I loved the smell of it, the way the water sluiced the dusty streets. But the weather was bringing a temperature change too, colder, wetter. The heat was breaking.

'Have you got anywhere to go?' I asked her, shivering from the cold. The rain was splashing our feet. 'This is going to go on.'

'Course! I got a palace on the Goldbourne Road!' The woman laughed, and for a moment I thought that this could easily be true. Maybe she was one of those who lived on the streets because she couldn't stay indoors, like the gypsies, who couldn't bear to live in a house, were always leaving doors open, wandering outside because they felt confined.

The rain got still heavier. 'My place is just nearby.'

'So's mine,' the woman pointed to the bushes. 'But I never sleep in the doorways of Mayfair. If they see that you're a woman, you'll wake up with spunk on your sleeping bag.'

The woman drew herself up tall, and I could see that once she had been beautiful. She had haughty cheekbones and when she wrapped her hair in a scarf she looked almost elegant, posh, perhaps. Even to me, who by that point was as close to the edge as it was possible to go without falling off, it was shocking to think that someone like her could be homeless. It would have been wrong to have left her outside on her own in the pouring rain.

We half ran, half walked back through the streets of fancy houses, dragging all her stuff behind us. All around us, the white stucco, the landscaped front gardens, the brass door knockers. I always felt like a tourist when I walked past these houses. Sometimes I could see inside to the fancy kitchens or living rooms, like photos from a magazine. And it always made me feel suffocated, like I was underwater, looking up at something far above, how was it even possible to reach the surface, to have any small part of that for myself? I couldn't imagine it.

By the time we got to the tower, we were both soaked to the skin. The woman looked at all the scaffolding and the builders sheltering in the entrance on one of their perpetual breaks. She tutted.

'How long has this been going on?'

'Months.' I thought about it and corrected myself. 'Years, actually.'

'All across London,' the woman shook her head.

'I know.'

'Property. The biggest scam there is,' the woman said, loudly nodding at a group of three builders smoking under the

NO SMOKING sign. 'Question is, who are they working for?' and as we passed them, watching them sneerily in their high-vis jackets, she started singing a riff from the Lou Reed song 'I'm waiting for my man' except she changed it to 'I'm working for the man.' One of the men whistled at us. I looked at the floor, but inside I was laughing.

But the moment we crossed the threshold into my flat, something changed. The woman darted like a sniffer dog, nosing in every corner of the room, eyeing up my stuff, dripping water all over my books. She even sat on my spot on the sofa, the one by the light with the best view and made a damp patch. I felt invaded and immediately regretted inviting her in. I wanted her to leave but I didn't know how to tell her.

I had that feeling again, sick-scared and dizzy. It came on so quickly it gave me vertigo. I was sure of it now, the woman wasn't homeless at all, but she was here to spy on me from the council, I was sure of it. The woman had tricked me, and now I had invited her into my home. Why should someone like me live here? That's what they were thinking. They were going to throw me out. Panic coursed through me. I fetched a towel, hid beneath it, rubbing my head until my scalp tingled.

'It's OK,' the woman said. 'Don't be scared.'

But I was scared. And I didn't know what to do except grit my teeth and pull the towel harder over my head. If I could do that then I could make the woman go away.

'Listen to me. In a few hours the police and the bailiffs are going to come and throw you out of here,' now the voice sounded like my ex. 'Do you understand? They stopped paying your benefits weeks ago. You need to call your social worker and pack up your stuff in boxes. You need to find somewhere to go.'

I didn't understand, it was too confusing. Peeping out through the towel I navigated to the wet patch on the sofa, and lay there, listening to the sound of my own heavy breathing.

The knocking was so intense that at first I thought it was just more construction noise. Under the towel it was hot and humid. And there was more shouting, someone yelling through the letterbox. And that's how they found me when they rammed in the door, hiding on the sofa with a wet towel over my head. I screamed when they touched me and someone used my old name, one that connected me back to the past and made me feel sick when I heard it.

'That's not my name,' I said, but they weren't listening. My name was just a part of the procedure.

'Jesus, it stinks in here.'

'You need to take that towel off your head.'

When I peeped out there was a broken door and two men in suits and a policewoman there.

'Is there anyone else living here?'

'I have a visitor, but she's going soon,' I said.

'But there's no one here.'

'She must have gone out the window.' I said this so matter-of-factly that they actually went to the window and looked out, even though, being on the 17th floor the windows didn't open wide enough for someone to get out. And then they gave me *that* look, the one that is a mix of pity and fear.

'Where's my social worker?'

The man with the papers shrugged. 'She's off sick. We've got you a bed in a hostel, just 'til we can sort out you with something else.'

In the end I took just one rucksack. Some clothes and a few books. I left Foucault behind because when would I have time to read that? I was going to live under the bushes in the park, or later, out in the countryside, I would find an abandoned caravan for a few months, I would travel to the seaside, find a hostel in another town. I would be cold and hungry and dirty and I would get very sick.

Then, in another town, I saw it on the TV in the day centre. All of us crowded around one of the volunteers ipads to watch the news. At first I couldn't believe how quickly it went up, there was something about the flames that was almost starving, the way they consumed the building. Those fancy tiles might as well have been firelighters, the way they accelerated the fire. After a while I couldn't look. Mrs Obidike and her son. Their cat. All of that waste. Everyone in the day centre was pale and shocked. Some of us who had come from there, muttered about going straight to London to show solidarity. I pressed my nails into my palms, overwhelmed by a helpless rage. It just seemed so... *inevitable*, that of course this was going to happen, this disaster had been happening for years, the neglect, the carelessness, the slow, cruel hardening. And it confirmed what I already knew, that for those of us who have to swim in this water, everything is fucked and everything is on fire.

Afterword: Grenfell Never Fell

Daniel Renwick

THE DATE THAT GRENFELL burned is scorched in our minds. On 14 June 2017, we were shown just how far market-state logic has encroached upon our right to life. The market-state corrupts, corrodes and kills. It has torn up the fabric of this country, by which I mean the social contract that underpins it. Innumerable people now sleep in death traps. Tower blocks up and down the country are crammed with human life and are just as likely to light up like kindling at any point, or befall some other tragedy that cost-cutting has made inevitable. And yet, the state does nothing but the bare minimum and has to be forced to do even that. Through Hobbesian logic, the government, in collusion with the market, has created the necessary and sufficient conditions for a revolt, because the one reason people have to obey the laws of the state has been voided. If those in power put your life in danger, it is your natural right to defend yourself.

Yet Grenfell has not been a cause of mass protest. There have been many small actions, meetings and demos in its wake; a bit of pushing and shoving outside (and inside) Kensington and Chelsea Town Hall. But where mass action, protest and potential political violence were once expected, there is only stoicism, silence and dignified remembrance. At the time of writing, the Metropolitan Police Force have interviewed eighteen people under caution, but no individual or company has been charged with criminal liability. Seventy-two dead, including at least 18 children, and no charges. The Public Inquiry's attempt to unearth the truth has contaminated the pursuit of justice. If a criminal investigation were given precedence, justice might be on the horizon. However, the Public Inquiry has meant that the *what* has displaced the *who,* making the *how* irrelevant. The state want us to remember a tragedy, yet forget the crime.

What is now known screams gross criminal negligence. The local authority were non-compliant with fire safety regulations. The tower did not even have proper fire doors, as detailed in Barbara Lane's expert report to the Public Inquiry.[1] Grenfell fell foul of the flimsy regulations that allowed the fire to travel at speed internally and externally. The spread on the outside of the building was due to deregulation allowing combustible materials – the equivalent of 30,000 litres of petrol – to be used to clad the building. The spread on the inside of the building was due to a policy of managed decline and needless austerity. Investment from the UK's richest local authority into the purchase of proper materials would have saved lives. Proper fireproof cladding would have prevented the propogation of the fire; protection of the gas pipes would have also prevented it; fire doors too. Instead, the council's negligence and lack of care killed.

The corporate bodies complicit in the start and spread of the fire – Arconic, Whirlpool and Celotex – all removed the products from the market while the Tower still smoked.[2] Soon after the fire, they also set aside billions to cover compensation. A class action lawsuit currently being pursued in the US should see a substantial payout. But, of course, it won't be enough. These companies knew of the risks and they ignored them. In the case of Arconic, their own brochure said the Reynobond PE cladding should not be used above 10 metres.[3] Grenfell was 67 metres tall. Their sales team targeted the local authority for the sale, knowing the risks. Cellotex has admitted falsifying data it provided to Building Research Establishment (BRE), masking the fact that the RS5000 insulation it used on the Tower was more flammable than the one that had previously passed safety tests.[4]

Yet the reason Grenfell remains a state crime is because government ministers were warned of the risks and did nothing. Gavin Barwell, the Housing Minister at the time (recently made a life peer for his services to Theresa May) was warned in seven separate letters of the dangers of Grenfell; the last letter was just weeks before the fire.[5] Government inaction when the risk of high loss of life was known is criminal, is it not? Yet all complicit walk free.

The tragedy of Grenfell was that people knew and articulated the dangers, but they campaigned in vain. They were not voiceless, but purposefully ignored, as if someone had hit the mute button on them. The Grenfell Action Group (GAG) and the Grenfell Community Unite group tried to hold the council, the developers and the Tenant Management Organisation (KCTMO) to account over the redevelopment. These are the 'posters in the hallways and leaflets in the mailbox' that Julia's story refers to. Yet the campaigners were treated like the usual irritants and impediments to 'progress'. When they spoke up, they were shouted down. When they put in freedom of information requests, they were ignored. Their calls for independent safety tests across the redevelopments would have saved lives if they'd been listened to, but instead, meaningless placation was undertaken. The work being done by contractors was inexplicably praised by the Royal Borough of Kensington and Chelsea's director of housing, Laura Johnson, who merely called for inconveniences to be mitigated. There was even a blog posted by one of the GAG founders, Edward Daffarn, six months before the tragedy, warning: 'It is our conviction that a serious fire in a tower block... is the most likely reason that those who wield power at the KCTMO will be found out and brought to justice!'[6] These words should haunt. The local council, the Grenfell Action Group contended, were more concerned about property development than their duty of care.

The feeling of being besieged by developers and future planners was very real in the community of Notting Dale, more colloquially known as 'Latimer,' before the fire. Julia Bell's story of eviction makes one think of the council's decant policy, issued in a statement in March 2017,[7] described by local activists as a 'fascist document' because of its unapologetic agenda for social cleansing. The council had decided to start moving people out as part of their redevelopments, but were not legally compelled to bring them back. As the document states, 'Where there is no suitable property available within the redeveloped area the secure tenant will be offered a suitable property elsewhere.'

The land that was providing a home for working class people was worth more on the private market than in its current function and this discrepancy of value was the primary consideration for the council. A firesale of local assets preceded the fire, and the two were inextricably bound. The auction block and the chopping block are struck by similarly crude weapons. The Westfield extension of the Imperial College development got closer and closer to the area daily. The cranes became ominous, destabilising residents' futures. Reis Morris, a local resident politicised by the fire, compared the cranes to guns pointed at the blocks. If it were not for the tragedy, the blocks would no doubt have been demolished by now. Silchester Estate – a social housing block just across the road from the Tower – only remains standing because Grenfell burned.

But Grenfell never fell. It stands as a tombstone. It haunts us in ways unimaginable, because there were so many opportunities for things to have gone differently. We can all conceive of a different sequence of events, in some parallel universe where this never happened; where zinc had been used instead of plastic for the insulation; where sprinklers had been a legal requirement (95% of social housing remain without this safety mechanism); where second fire escapes had been compulsory; where flimsy regulations had been tightened and where developers acted

433

with a duty of care. But that is not the world we live in. The one we live in now is one of despair, because to all attuned, what happened at Grenfell 'just seemed so... inevitable,' to quote Julia's story. If there is to be more widespread loss of life as a consequence of market-state greed, we will have even fewer excuses than before for not seeing it coming. And what will we do if there's another fire? The instinct to revolt, the impulse to rise up, the rationale for physically overturning those responsible will no longer seem so unreasonable. This is the understanding on which the social contract is predicated. If the state don't want that smoke, they must stop the fires now; they must stand up to business, they must defend our right to life. As the rapper Lowkey put it, as tens of thousands gathered to mark two years since the inferno, 'Regulate them before we regulate you.'

Notes

1. https://www.grenfelltowerinquiry.org.uk/evidence/dr-barbara-lanes-expert-report

2. https://uk.reuters.com/article/uk-britain-fire-arconic/arconic-knowingly-supplied-flammable-panels-for-use-in-tower-emails-idUKKBN19F05C

3. https://www.constructionenquirer.com/2017/09/14/celotex-recalls-five-insulation-product-lines/

4. https://www.architectsjournal.co.uk/news/grenfell-tower-insulation-never-passed-fire-safety-test/10031286.article

5. https://www.insidehousing.co.uk/news/news/pms-chief-of-staff-did-not-act-on-multiple-warnings-about-fire-safety-in-months-before-grenfell-new-letters-show-61883

6. https://www.bbc.co.uk/news/stories-42072477

7. https://www.rbkc.gov.uk/sites/default/files/atoms/files/Tenant%20Decant%20Policy%20March%202017.pdf

About the Authors

Julia Bell is a writer and Director of the Creative Writing MA at Birkbeck, University of London. She has published three novels, most recently *The Dark Light* (Macmillan, 2015). Her essays and short fiction have appeared in *The White Review, Times Literary Supplement, Paris Review, Mal Journal*, the BBC, and numerous anthologies. She is the co-editor of the newly re-issued *Creative Writing Coursebook* (Macmillan, 2019). She divides her time between London and Berlin.

Bidisha is a writer, TV and radio broadcaster and film-maker. She specialises in human rights, social justice, gender and the arts and offers political analysis and cultural diplomacy tying these interests together. Her most recent book is *Asylum and Exile: Hidden Voices*, based on her outreach work with asylum seekers and refugees. Her most recent film is *An Impossible Poison* which has been highly critically acclaimed and selected for multiple film festivals internationally.

SJ Bradley is an author and short story writer from Leeds, UK. She is a K. Blundell Trust Award winner, and a Saboteur Award winner for her work on *Remembering Oluwale*. She is director of the Northern Short Story Festival and Fiction Editor at *Strix* magazine. Her second novel, *Guest*, is now available from Dead Ink Books.

Jude Brown has had short stories published in several anthologies and her work has been shortlisted for the Bridport and Raymond Carver Short Story Prizes. She is a winner of a Northern Writers' Award and her debut novel *His Dark Sun*, supported by a grant from Arts Council England, was selected for this year's New Writing North's Read Regional campaign. Originally from

Middlesbrough, she has lived in London, Liverpool, Reading and Sydney. She now lives in Sheffield and has an MA in Creative Writing from Sheffield Hallam University.

Lucy Caldwell was born in Belfast in 1981. She is the multi-award-winning author of three novels, several stage plays and radio dramas, and two collections of short stories (*Multitudes*, 2016, and *Intimacies*, forthcoming in May 2020). She is also the editor of the anthology *Being Various: New Irish Short Stories* (Faber, 2019). Her story 'The Children' was shortlisted for the BBC National Short Story Award 2019.

Steve Chambers is an experienced writer and dramatist. His political thriller, *GLADIO: We can Neither Confirm nor Deny* (Zymurgy), won a Newcastle Journal Culture Award. His feature film, *Hold Back the Night* (Parallax Pictures), won the Prix du Public Forum at Cannes while his adaptation of Graham Swift's *Waterland* for BBC R4 won the WGGB Best Radio Dramatisation. Currently, he is writing a novel, *The Dark Months*, and developing ideas for radio and stage.

Martin Edwards's latest novel, *Gallows Court*, has been nominated for both the 2019 eDunnit award for best crime novel and the CWA Historical Dagger. He was recently honoured with the CWA Dagger in the Library for his body of work and has received the Edgar, Agatha, H.R.F. Keating and Poirot awards, two Macavity awards, and the CWA Short Story Dagger. He is consultant to the British Library's Crime Classics and President of the Detection Club.

Uschi Gatward's stories have appeared or are forthcoming in *Best British Short Stories 2015* (Salt), *The Mirror in the Mirror* (Comma), as a Galley Beggar Press Single, and in the magazines *The Barcelona Review*, *Brittle Star*, *gorse*, *The Lonely Crowd*, *Short Fiction*, *Southword*, *Structo* and *Wasafiri*. She was shortlisted for *The White Review* Short Story Prize 2016.

Luan Goldie was born in Glasgow but has lived in East London for most of her life. She is a primary school teacher, and formerly a business journalist. She is the winner of the Costa Short Story Award 2017 for her story 'Two Steak Bakes and Two Chelsea Buns'. Her short stories have also been long and shortlisted by Spread the Word and the *Grazia*/Women's Prize First Chapter competition. Her debut novel *Nightingale Point* was released in July 2019 by HarperCollins.

Gaia Holmes lives in Halifax. She is a cat/dog/house sitter, freelance writer and creative writing tutor who works with schools, universities, libraries and other community groups throughout the West Yorkshire region. She runs 'Igniting The Spark', a weekly writing workshop at Dean Clough, Halifax. She has published three collections of poetry, *Dr James Graham's Celestial Bed*, *Lifting the Piano with One Hand*, and *Where the Road Runs Out* (all with Comma).

Nikita Lalwani is the author of three novels – *Gifted*, *The Village* and *You People*, which will be published in June 2020. Her work has been longlisted and shortlisted for the Man Booker Prize, the Costa Prize and the *Sunday Times* Young Writer of the Year, and she is a winner of the Desmond Elliot Prize and the Edoardo Kihlgren award. Her novels have been translated into sixteen languages. She is a Fellow of the Royal Society of Literature and lives in London.

Zoe Lambert's first collection of short stories, *The War Tour,* was published by Comma in 2011. She has an MA in Creative Writing at UEA and a PhD from Manchester Metropolitan University. She is currently a lecturer in English Literature and Creative Writing at the University of Lancaster.

Anna Lewis has won the Orange/*Harper's Bazaar* short story prize, been twice shortlisted for the Willesden Herald International short story competition, and been highly commended in the Commonwealth Foundation short story prize. She is a Hay Festival Scritture Giovani fellow. Her new poetry collection, *In Passing,* is due from Pindrop Press in 2019.

Irfan Master is the award-winning author of two novels for young adults, *A Beautiful Lie,* which was shortlisted for the Waterstone's Children's Book Prize and the Branford Boase Award for debut authors, and *Out of Heart*, which was longlisted for the CILIP Carnegie Medal for children. He also writes plays, poetry and has contributed short stories to numerous anthologies.

Editor, translator, commentator and critic, **Donny O'Rourke** has published several volumes of poetry and albums of song lyrics. A graduate of the universities of Glasgow and Cambridge, he has had overlapping careers as a journalist, broadcaster, television producer, film-maker and academic. The holder of many international fellowships, visiting professorships, bursaries and residencies, Donny teaches Film and Creative Writing at Glasgow University. This is his first short story.

Kamila Shamsie is the author of seven novels, which have been translated into over 20 languages. Her most recent novel, *Home Fire*, won the Women's Prize for Fiction, was shortlisted for the Costa Novel Award and longlisted for the Man Booker Prize. A Fellow of the Royal Society of Literature, and one of Granta's 'Best of Young British Novelists', she grew up in Karachi, and now lives in London.

Born to Jamaican parents who arrived in Britain in the 1960s, **Karline Smith** was one of the first black female crime writers to deal with the subject of drug gangs in inner-city Britain. She is the author of three novels, *Moss Side Massive*, which was dramatised by Liverpool's Unity Theatre, *Full Crew*, and *Goosebumps and Butterflies are Fairy Tales* (published by

Black Sapphire Press). She is also the author of several short stories, variously published in *The City Life Book of Manchester Short Stories* (Penguin), and *M.O.: Crimes of Practice* (Comma). She is currently working on her fourth novel.

Kim Squirrell is a writer and artist. She has published poetry and short fiction and collaborated with actors, dancers and musicians in environmental theatre productions and site-specific performance. She was included in the *Out of Bounds* anthology (Bloodaxe, 2012) and more recently took part in the Out of Bounds Poetry Project. Kim is currently in her final year of a Creative Writing MA at the University of Exeter and was shortlisted for the 2018 Dinesh Allirajah Prize for Short Fiction.

Lucas Stewart is a writer from Birkenhead and has spent 20 years living in Asia and Africa. A Fellow of the Royal Asiatic Society and former literature advisor to the British Council, his political travelogue, *The People Elsewhere: Unbound Journeys with the Storytellers of Myanmar* (Penguin/Viking, 2016) was shortlisted for the 2018 Saroyan International Prize for Writing. He co-edited *Hidden Words, Hidden Worlds,* the first anthology of short stories from Myanmar published in the UK. His own short fiction has been published in Asia and the UK winning the 2018 Dinesh Allirajah Prize for Short Fiction.

Eley Williams is a writer and lecturer based in Ealing. Her collection of short stories *Attrib. And Other Stories* (Influx Press) was chosen by Ali Smith as one of the best debut works of fiction published in 2017 and has since won The James Tait Black Prize 2018 and The Republic of Consciousness Prize 2018. Eley teaches both creative writing and children's literature at Royal Holloway, University of London, where she was recently awarded her doctorate. Twice shortlisted for *The White Review* Short Story Prize, her works have appeared in the *London Review of Books*, the *White Review, Ambit* and the *Cambridge Literary Review.* She has published one pamphlet of poetry, *Frit* (Sad Press).

About the Consultants

Richard C. Allen is a Visiting Fellow at Newcastle University and is a former Fulbright-Robertson Professor. He has research interests in the social, cultural and religious history of Wales, Britain and America, particularly dissenters and emigration to Pennsylvania. He has published widely on Quakerism, migration, and identity.

Dr Roger Ball has researched urban riots for over ten years, first as part of his PhD studies and more recently working with social psychologists on the Beyond Contagion project analysing the August 2011 disorders. He is currently a Research Fellow at Sussex University working on British colonial policy and the death penalty. Roger has published on a range of subjects including riots, labour history and workhouses and is currently co-authoring a book on slavery and abolition in Bristol.

Jo Blackman has spent much of her life involved in campaigns for human rights and sustainability, as well as grassroots campaigns for tenants' rights and democratic accountability. Currently, Jo is involved with Extinction Rebellion, demanding action on the climate and ecological emergency. She regularly delivers training in the theory and practice of civil disobedience and nonviolent direct action. She has also worked as a community project manager, an elected independent councillor, and an adult education tutor.

Mike Carden worked for the old Mersey docks and harbour board from 1970 until he was sacked in 1995. Four generations of his family had worked on the docks before him, starting when Thomas Carden, Mike's great-great-grandfather left Ballina in County Mayo for Liverpool in 1820; Mike's grandfather John, born in 1889, who was killed on the docks, and his father Joe, as well as his brother, and many uncles, all worked there for most of their lives.

Malcolm Chase is a Professor Emeritus at the University of Leeds, where he held the Chair of Social History from 2009 to 2019. His books include *Chartism: A New History* (Manchester University Press, 2007), *'The People's Farm': English Radical Agrarianism, 1775-1840* (2nd edition with new preface, Breviary, 2010; first published 1988), *Early trade unionism: fraternity, skill and the politics of labour* (2nd edition, Breviary, 2012, first published 2000), *1820: Disorder and Stability in the United Kingdom* (Manchester University Press, 2013), and *The Chartists: Perspectives and Legacies* (Merlin Press, 2015). He has also published in the journals *English Historical Review, Labour History Review, Parliamentary History, Past and Present* and in the *Oxford Dictionary of National Biography.*

Dr Chris Cocking is a Principal Lecturer at the University of Brighton, with a research interest in the psychology of crowd behaviour (particularly during mass emergencies). This interest stems from his early experiences of being involved in the anti-roads' movement of the 1990s and his PhD study of the protests against the Newbury bypass. Since then he has spent most of his academic career arguing that outdated irrationalist views of crowds can lead to crowd management approaches that increase risks to public safety, and so is a passionate advocate for an increased understanding of crowds.

Dr Ben Griffin is University Lecturer in Modern British History at the University of Cambridge and a Fellow of Girton College. His book *The Politics of Gender in Victorian Britain: Masculinity, Political Culture and the Struggle for Women's Rights* (Cambridge University Press, 2012) won the Royal Historical Society's Whitfield Prize for the best first book on British history. He is currently writing a book entitled *The Gender Order and the Judicial Imagination: Masculinity, Liberalism and Governmentality in Modern Britain.*

ABOUT THE CONSULTANTS

Richard Hingley is Professor of Roman Archaeology at Durham University. He focuses upon Roman imperialism and native reactions and has written a number of books on Roman topics, including a volume which he produced with his partner, Christina Unwin (in 2005). The September/October edition of the *National Geographic History* magazine has an article by Richard on Boudica's rebellion, retelling her tale and including some newly discovered information.

Rhian E. Jones writes on history, politics, popular culture and the places where they intersect. She is co-editor of the website *New Socialist* and writes for *Tribune* magazine. Her books include *Clampdown: Pop-Cultural Wars on Class and Gender* (Zero Books, 2013); *Petticoat Heroes: Gender, Culture and Popular Protest* (University of Wales Press, 2015); *Triptych: Three Studies of Manic Street Preachers'* The Holy Bible (Repeater, 2017) and the anthology of women's music writing *Under My Thumb: Songs That Hate Women and the Women Who Love Them* (Repeater, 2017).

Dr Billy Kenefick (additional consultant on 'Bright Red') was a Senior Lecturer in Modern History at the University of Dundee until he retired early in 2016. He has published widely on Scottish maritime and labour history, the impact of the Great War and the Russian Revolution on the Scottish working class, and Irish and Jewish relations in Scotland from c1870 to present. His publications include *Red Scotland! The Rise and Fall of the Radical Left c.1872-1932* (Edinburgh University Press, 2007).

Kenny Monrose is an affiliated researcher at the University of Cambridge in the department of Sociology, and a visiting college research associate at Wolfson College. He completed a PhD in Sociology at the University of Essex in 2013. His doctoral thesis was a qualitative study centred in East London, examining the life course of maturing black men, with a focus on criminal preclusion and non-criminal participation. He is the author of *Black Men in Britain: An Ethnographic Portrait of the Post-Windrush Generation* (Routledge, 2019).

Marcus Morris is Senior Lecturer in Modern European History at Manchester Metropolitan University. His research is centred on labour and socialist movements, including trade unions and political parties, in Britain and Europe during the nineteenth and twentieth century and has published on a wide variety of themes in relation to those movements.

Jonathan Moss is a lecturer in Politics at the University of Sussex, where he teaches modules on British Political History and Women's Political Activism. He is author of *Women, Workplace Protest and Political Identity in England, 1968-1985* (Manchester University Press, 2019).

Dr Mark O'Brien is a socialist researcher based in Liverpool. He writes about the social experience and historical struggles of workers. His previous publications include *Just Managing? What it Means for the Families of Austerity Britain* (Open Book Publishers 2017, co-author); and *When Adam Delved and Eve Span: A History of the Peasants' Revolt* (Bookmarks, 2016).

Jim Phillips is Senior Lecturer in Economic and Social History at the University of Glasgow and co-editor of *Scottish Labour History*. His latest book is *Scottish Coal Miners in the Twentieth Century* (Edinburgh University Press, 2019).

Robert Poole is the author of *Peterloo: the English Uprising* (2019) and co-author of the graphic novel, *Peterloo: Witnesses to a Massacre* (2019), www.peterloo.org. He is Professor of History at the University of Central Lancashire, and historical consultant to the Peterloo 2019 commemoration programme.

David Renton is a barrister, historian, author and longstanding anti-fascist activist. His books include *Never Again: Rock*

Against Racism and the Anti-Nazi League 1976-1982 (Routledge, 2018).

Daniel Renwick is a writer, videographer and youth worker. He has developed, produced, scripted and edited multiple productions around Grenfell, including *Failed by the State*, as well as authoring the essay 'Organising on Mute' in *After Grenfell* (Pluto, 2019).

David Rosenberg is an educator, writer and tour guide of London's radical history. He is the author of *Battle for the East End* (Five Leaves Publications, 2011), and *Rebel Footprints* (Pluto Press, 2nd edition, 2019). www.eastendwalks.com

Dave Steele is no stranger to protest, having been excluded from school aged 18 for campaigning against the military cadet force. He has campaigned against the Iraq War, GM crops, and nuclear weapons which fuelled his interest in crowds. He researches the dynamics of nineteenth century radical crowds for his PhD at Warwick University, early findings indicating smaller attendance than reported, leading him to question how political groups often punched above their weight.

Professor Emeritus of History at the University of Essex, **John Walter** researches the politics of early modern crowds. His publications include *Understanding Popular Violence in the English Revolution,* (Royal Historical Society Whitfield Prize, 1999) and *Crowds and Popular Politics in Early Modern England and Covenanting Citizens: The Protestation Oath and Popular Political Culture in the English Revolution* (Pepys Prize, 2017). His articles have inspired both an award–winning beer and the recent film, *Robinson in Ruins* (Patrick Keiller, 2010).

Special Thanks

The editor would like to thank Professor Stephen Constantine and Dr Katrina Navickas for their help in the development of the project, as well as Dr Billy Kenefick for acting as an additional consultant on Donny O'Rourke's story 'Bright Red', and Greg Dropkin who also helped the editor with research around the Liverpool Dockers' dispute. Comma would also like to thank Ross Bradshaw for his wealth of knowledge and suggestions. Anna Lewis, the author of 'Before Dawn', would like to thank Eluned Gramich for her help with the Welsh dialogue in her story, although she would like to point out any errors remaining are entirely her own.